The

STRAN

DIARIES

ELLY

GRIFFITHS

Author of the RUTH GALLOWAY MYSTERIES

"Reading *The Stranger Diaries* on the heels of Ruth Ware's *The Death of Mrs. Westaway* has made me a lover of a skilled gothic mystery! With just the right mix of atmosphere, murder, and sleuthing, *The Stranger Diaries* is a thoroughly enjoyable and engaging page-turner. I loved all three of the smart protagonists, each of whom added intrigue and nuance to this finely layered story."

— Zoje Stage, author of *Baby Teeth*

"A perfectly paced and compellingly page-turning mystery. Griffiths's use of shifting viewpoints and her pitch-perfect recreation of a Victorian gothic short story woven through the narrative serve to heighten the tension in this thrilling, and often spooky, tale. *The Stranger Diaries* will keeping you reading late into the night. You won't want to put it down . . . or turn out the light!"

— Charlie Lovett, *New York Times* best-selling author of
The Bookman's Tale and *The Lost Book of the Grail*

"Elly Griffiths's haunting tribute to gothic literature is a riveting, humane whodunnit that explores the impact of even our smallest deeds. Urgently paced and sprinkled with literary gems, *The Stranger Diaries* will have you turning pages until well past the witching hour!"

— Matthew Sullivan, author of
Midnight at the Bright Ideas Bookstore

"An English teacher with an expansive knowledge of gothic literature finds herself tangled in a web of murder and mystery that begins more and more to be a kind of twisted work of gothic storytelling in this impressive new mystery. Griffiths writes at the perfect intersection of procedural and psychological thriller, with her latest adding a strong dose of dark atmospherics to spin a truly unnerving story."

— *CrimeReads*

"This meticulously structured novel features some indelible characters, a vividly depicted setting, and a strong fair-play mystery . . . a delightful reading experience and one that many readers will cherish for years to come."

— *BOLO Books Review*

"It is clear from the start of Elly Griffiths's *The Stranger Diaries* that we are in for a treat . . . Griffiths has a lot of fun setting up the scares . . . Armed with an enjoyably sharp detective . . . Griffiths overlaps perspectives, timelines, and narrators, producing a darkly funny, enjoyable mystery."

— *Observer*

"Spooky . . . This is written with Griffiths's usual warmth and lightness of touch but has a genuine creepiness that gets under your skin."

— *Sunday Express*

"Griffiths has gifted readers with a gripping homage to the gothic novel . . . An entrancing literary tour de force in which Shakespeare's line, 'Hell is empty,' from *The Tempest,* cleverly connects past and present. Georgette Heyer fans will relish this, as will readers who enjoyed Diane Setterfield's *The Thirteenth Tale* and Anthony Horowitz's *Magpie Murders.*"

— *Booklist,* starred review

"A modern gothic that updates and plays with genre conventions to great effect. Highly recommended for fans of British mysteries and classic whodunit."

— *Library Journal,* starred review

"Gripping . . . eerie atmosphere . . . Aficionados of such gothic classics as Wilkie Collins's *The Woman in White,* which the killer may have read, will find this a satisfying novel for a rainy night."

— *Publishers Weekly*

"Griffiths hits a sweet spot for readers who love British mysteries and who are looking for something to satisfy an itch once *Broadchurch* has been binged and Wilkie Collins reread . . . in her first standalone novel, with immensely pleasurable results."

— *Kirkus Reviews*

THE STRANGER DIARIES

Also by Elly Griffiths

The
STRANGER
DIARIES

Elly Griffiths

Mariner Books

Houghton Mifflin Harcourt

Boston   New York

First Mariner Books edition 2019

hmhbooks.com

First published in Great Britain in 2018 by Quercus

Library of Congress Cataloging-in-Publication Data
Names: Griffiths, Elly, author.
Title: The stranger diaries / Elly Griffiths.
Description: First U.S. edition. | Boston ; New York : Houghton Mifflin
Harcourt, 2019. Identifiers: LCCN 2018035768|
ISBN 9781328577856 (hardcover) | ISBN 9781328576088 (ebook) |
ISBN 9780358117865 (pbk.)
Subjects: | BISAC: FICTION / Mystery & Detective / Women Sleuths. |
FICTION / Mystery & Detective / Police Procedural. | FICTION /
Romance / Gothic. | GSAFD: Mystery fiction. | Gothic fiction.
Classification: LCC PR6107.R534 S77 2019 | DDC 823/.92—dc23
LC record available at https://lccn.loc.gov/2018035768

Book design by Greta D. Sibley

Printed in the United States of America
DOC 10 9 8 7 6 5 4 3 2 1

For Alex and Juliet.
And for Gus, my companion animal.

PART THE FIRST

Clare

CHAPTER 1

'If you'll permit me,' said the Stranger, 'I'd like to tell you a story. After all, it's a long journey and, by the look of those skies, we're not going to be leaving this carriage for some time. So, why not pass the hours with some story-telling? The perfect thing for a late October evening.

'Are you quite comfortable there? Don't worry about Herbert. He won't hurt you. It's just this weather that makes him nervous. Now, where was I? What about some brandy to keep the chill out? You don't mind a hip flask, do you?

'Well, this is a story that actually happened. Those are the best kind, don't you think? Better still, it happened to me when I was a young man. About your age.

'I was a student at Cambridge. Studying Divinity, of course. There's no other subject, in my opinion, except possibly English Literature. We are such stuff as dreams are made on. I'd been there for almost a term. I was a shy boy from the country and I suppose I was lonely. I wasn't one of the swells, those young men in white bow ties who sauntered across the court as if they had letters patent from God. I kept myself to myself, went to lectures, wrote my essays and started up a friendship with another scholarship boy in my year, a timid soul called Gudgeon, of all things. I wrote home to my mother every week. I went to chapel. Yes, I believed in those days. I was even rather pious — "pi," we used to say. That was why I was surprised to be invited to join the Hell Club. Surprised and pleased. I'd heard about it, of course. Stories of midnight orgies, of bedders coming in to clean rooms and fainting dead away at what they discovered there, *of arcane chants from the* Book of the Dead, *of buried bones and gaping graves. But there were other stories too. Many successful men had their start at the Hell Club: politicians — even a cabinet member or two — writers, lawyers, scientists, business tycoons. You always knew them because of the badge, a discreet skull worn on the left lapel. Yes, like this one here.*

'So I was happy to be invited to the initiation ceremony. It was held on October 31st. Halloween, of course. All Hallows' Eve. Yes, of course. It's Halloween today. If one believed in coincidence one might think that was slightly sinister.

'To return to my story. The ceremony was simple and took place at midnight. Naturally. The three initiates were required to go to a ruined house just outside the college grounds. In turn, we would be blindfolded and given a candle. We had to walk to the house, climb the stairs and light our candle in the window on the first floor landing. Then we had to shout, as loudly as we could, "Hell is empty!" After all three had completed the task, we could take off our blindfolds and re-join our fellows. Feasting and revelry would follow. Gudgeon . . . did I tell you that poor Gudgeon was one of the three? Gudgeon was worried because, without his glasses, he was almost blind. But, as I told him, we were all blindfolded anyway. A man may see how the world goes with no eyes.'

'So,' I say, 'what's happening here?'

'Something bad,' says Peter.

'You're quite right,' I say, counting to ten silently. 'What makes you think that?'

'Well,' says Una, 'the setting, for one thing. Midnight on Halloween.'

'That's a bit of a cliché,' says Ted.

'It's a cliché because it works,' says Una. 'It's really spooky, with the weather and everything. What's the betting they get snowed in on the train?'

'That's a rip-off of *Murder on the Orient Express*,' says Peter.

'*The Stranger* pre-dates Agatha Christie,' I say. 'What else tells you what sort of story this is?'

'The narrator is so creepy,' says Sharon, 'all that "have a drink from my hip flask and don't mind Herbert". Who is Herbert anyway?'

'A good question,' I say. 'What does everyone think?'

'A deaf mute.'

'His servant.'

'His son. Has to be restrained because he's a dangerous lunatic.'

'His dog.'

Laughter.

'Actually,' I say, 'Ted is right, Herbert is a dog. The companion animal is an important trope in the ghost story genre because an animal can sense things that are beyond human comprehension. What can be scarier than a dog staring at something that isn't there? Cats are famously spooky, of course. Think of Edgar Allan Poe. And animals were often thought to be witches' familiars, helping them perform black magic. But Animal characters can be useful for another reason. Can anyone guess what it is?'

No one can. It's mid-afternoon, nearly break time, and they are thinking of coffee and biscuits rather than fictional archetypes. I look out of the window. The trees by the graveyard are dark even though it's only four o'clock. I should have saved the short story for the twilight session really, but it's so difficult to cover everything on a short course. Time to wrap things up.

'Animals are expendable,' I say. 'Authors often kill them to create tension. It's not as significant as killing a human but it can be surprisingly upsetting.'

The members of the creative writing group go clattering down the stairs in search of caffeine but I stay in the classroom for a bit. It's very strange being in this part of the school. Only adult education classes get taught here; the rooms are too small and too odd for lessons. This one has a fireplace and a rather disturbing oil painting of a child holding what looks like a dead ferret. I can just imagine the Year 7s trying to disappear up the fireplace like twenty-first-century chimney sweeps. Most school life at Talgarth High happens in the New Building, a 1970s monstrosity of plate glass and coloured bricks. This building, the Old Building, which was once called Holland House, is really just an annex. It has the dining hall, the kitchens and the chapel, as well as the head teacher's office. The first floor has rooms which are sometimes used for music practice or drama. The old library is there too, now only frequented by teachers because the students have a modern version in the New Building, with computers and armchairs and paperbacks in carousels. The top floor, which is out-of-bounds to students, is where R.M. Holland's study is, preserved just as he left it. The creative writing students are always excited to learn that the author of *The Stranger* actually lived in this house. In fact, he hardly ever left it. He was a recluse, the old-fashioned sort with a house-keeper and a full staff. I'm not sure I would leave the house myself if I had someone to cook and clean for me, to iron the *Times* and place it on a tray with my morning infusion. But I have a daughter, so I would have to rouse myself eventually. Georgie would probably never get out of bed without me to shout the time up the stairs, a problem R.M. Holland certainly never had, although he may, in fact, have had a daughter. Opinion is divided on this point.

It's October half-term and, with no pupils around, and spending all my time in the Old Building, it's easy to imagine that I'm teaching at a university, somewhere ancient and hallowed. There are parts of Holland House that look almost like an Oxford college, if you ignore the New Building and the smell of the gymnasium. I like having this time to myself. Georgie is with Simon and Herbert is in kennels. There's nothing for me to worry about and, when I get home, there's nothing to stop me writing all night. I'm working on a biography of R.M. Holland. He's always interested me, ever since I read *The Stranger* in a ghost story anthology as a teenager. I didn't know about his connection to the school when I first applied here. It wasn't mentioned in the advertisement and the interview was in the New Building. When I found out, it seemed like a sign. I would teach English by day and, in the eve-nings, inspired by my surroundings, I would write about Holland; about his strange, reclusive life, the mysterious death of his wife, his missing daugh-ter. I made a good start; I was even interviewed for a news item on local TV, walking awkwardly through the Old Building and talking about its pre-vious occupant. But, recently — I don't know why — the words have dried up. Write every day, that's what I tell my students. Don't wait for inspira-tion, that might not come until the end. The muse always finds you working. Look into your heart and write. But, like most teachers, I'm not brilliant at taking my own advice. I write in my diary every day, but that doesn't count because no one else is ever going to read it.

I suppose I should go downstairs and get a coffee while I still can. As I get up I look out of the window. It's getting dark and the trees are blowing in a sudden squall of wind. Leaves gust across the car park and, following their progress, I see what I should have noticed earlier: a strange car with two people sitting inside it. There's nothing particularly odd about this. This is a school, after all, despite it being half-term. Visitors are not entirely unexpected. They could even be staff members, coming in to prepare their classrooms and complete their planning for next week. But there's something about the car, and the people inside it, that makes me feel uneasy. It's an unremarkable grey vehicle — I'm useless at cars but Simon would know the make — something solid and workmanlike, the sort of thing a mini-cab driver would use. But why are its occupants just sitting there? I can't see their faces but they are both dressed in dark clothes and look, like the car itself, somehow both prosaic and menacing.

It's almost as if I am expecting a summons of some kind, so I'm not really surprised when my phone buzzes. I see it's Rick Lewis, my head of department.

'Clare,' he says, 'I've got some terrible news.'

Clare's Diary

Ella is dead. I didn't believe it when Rick told me. And, as the words began to sink in, I thought: a car crash, an accident, even an overdose of some kind. But when Rick said 'murdered', it was as if he was talking a different language.

'Murdered?' I repeated the word stupidly.

'The police said that someone broke into her house last night,' said Rick. 'They turned up on my doorstep this morning. Daisy thought I was about to be arrested.'

I still couldn't put the pieces together. Ella. My friend. My colleague. My ally in the English department. Murdered. Rick said that Tony already knew. He was going to write to all the parents tonight.

'It'll be in the papers,' said Rick. 'Thank God it's half-term.'

I'd thought the same thing. Thank God it's half-term, thank God Georgie's with Simon. But then I felt guilty. Rick must have realised that he'd got the tone wrong because he said, 'I'm sorry, Clare', as if he meant it.

He's sorry. Jesus.

And then I had to go back to my class and teach them about ghost stories. It wasn't one of my best teaching sessions. But *The Stranger* always does its bit, especially as it was dark by the time I'd finished. Una actually screamed at the end. I set them a writing task for the last hour: 'write about receiving bad news'. I looked at their bent heads as they scribbled their masterpieces ('The telegram arrived at half-past two . . .') and thought: if only they knew.

As soon as I got home, I rang Debra. She'd been out with the family and hadn't heard. She cried, said she didn't believe it, etc., etc. To think that the three of us had only been together on Friday night. Rick said that Ella was killed some time on Sunday. I remember I'd texted her about the *Strictly* results and hadn't had an answer. Was she already dead by then?

It wasn't so bad when I was teaching or talking to Debra, but now I'm alone, I feel such a sense of . . . well, *dread* . . . that I'm almost rigid with fear.

I'm sitting here with my diary on the bed and I don't want to turn the light off. Where is Ella? Have they taken her body away? Have her parents had to identify her? Rick didn't give me any of these details and, right now, they seem incredibly important.

I just can't believe that I'll never see her again.

CHAPTER 2

I'm at school early. I didn't really sleep. Horrible dreams, not actually about Ella, but searching for Georgie in war-ravaged cities, Herbert going missing, my dead grandfather calling from a room just out of sight. Herbert was at Doggy Day Care for the night — which was probably part of the reason for the anxiety dreams — but I didn't need him to wake me up demanding food, walkies and dancing girls. I was up at six and at Talgarth by eight. There were already a few people here, drinking coffee in the dining hall and attempting to start conversations. They always run a few courses here at half-term and I like to try to identify the participants: women with unusual jewellery tend to be doing tapestry or pottery, men with sandals and long fingernails are usually making stringed musical instruments. My students are always the hardest to spot. That's one of the nice things about teaching creative writing — you get retired teachers and solicitors, women who have brought up their families and now fancy doing something for themselves, twenty-somethings convinced that they are the next J.K. Rowling. My favourites are often the people who have done all the other courses and just take mine because it's next on the list after Candle Making. Those students always surprise you — and themselves.

I get a black coffee from the machine and take it to the very end of one of the tables. It feels strange to be eating and drinking, going through the usual routine, thinking about the day's teaching. I still can't get used to the thought that I'm living in a world without Ella. Although I'd probably describe Jen and Cathy from university as my best friends, there's no doubt that I saw Ella more than I saw either of them — I saw her every day during term time. We shared our frustrations about Rick and Tony, the students, our occasional triumphs, juicy gossip about the pastoral leader and one of the lab technicians. Even now, ridiculously, I want to text her. 'You'll never believe what's happened.'

'Can I sit here?'

It's Ted, from my creative writing class.

'Of course.' I arrange my face into a welcoming shape.

Ted's a good example of creative writing students being hard to classify. He's shaven-headed and tattooed and looks more like a potential 'Woodcarving: An Introduction' or even an 'Exploring Japanese Pottery'. But he had a few good insights yesterday and, thank God, doesn't seem to want to talk about his work in progress.

'I enjoyed yesterday,' he says, unwrapping a packet of biscuits, the sort they have in hotel bedrooms.

'Good,' I say.

'That ghost story. I kept thinking about it all night.'

'It's quite effective, isn't it? R.M. Holland wasn't the greatest writer but he certainly knew how to scare people.'

'And is it true that he actually lived here? In this house?'

'Yes. He lived here until 1902. The bedrooms were on the floor where we were yesterday. His study is in the attic.'

'This is a school now, isn't it?'

'Yes, a secondary school, Talgarth High. When Holland died, the building became a boarding school, then a grammar. It went comprehensive in the 1970s.'

'And this is where you teach?'

'Yes.'

'Do you tell your students that story? *The Stranger*?'

'No. Holland isn't on the curriculum. It's still all *Of Mice and Men* and *Remains of the Day*. I used to run a creative writing group for the GCSE students and sometimes I read them *The Stranger*.'

'Must have given them nightmares.'

'No, they loved it. Teenagers always love ghost stories.'

'I do too.' He grins at me, showing two gold teeth. 'There's a funny feeling about this place. I bet it's haunted.'

'There are a few stories. A woman was meant to have fallen from the top floor. Some people say it was Holland's wife. Or his daughter. I've had students say that they've seen a woman in a white nightdress floating down the stairs. Or sometimes you can see a falling figure out of the corner of your eye. Apparently the bloodstain is still visible; it's outside the head teacher's study.'

'Very appropriate.'

'Oh, he's the young and trendy type. Not Dickensian at all.'

'That's a shame.'

Ted dunks his biscuit but it's the wrong sort and half of it falls into his tea. 'What's the topic this morning?' he says. 'I left my timetable in the room yesterday.'

'Creating memorable characters,' I say. 'Time and place in the afternoon. Then home. Excuse me, I'd better go and prepare.'

I go up to the classroom to make sure everything is in place for the day but, when I get there, I just sit at the desk with my head in my hands. How the hell am I going to get through this day?

I first met Ella when we interviewed for jobs at Talgarth High five years ago. We were greeted by Rick, who was trying to pretend that a third of the English department hadn't resigned at the end of the Easter term, leaving him with a few short months to find two experienced English teachers. A little while ago I looked in my diary to find my first impressions of Rick but they were disappointingly banal. *Tall, thin, rumpled-looking.* Rick is the sort of person whose charms — such as they are — dawn on you gradually.

'It's a really vibrant department,' he told us as he gave us the tour. 'And the school's great, very diverse, lots of energy.'

By then we had worked out that there were two posts available and that we weren't in competition. We exchanged a look. We both knew what 'vibrant' meant. The school was on the edge of anarchy. It had just received a 'Requires Improvement' rating from its latest inspection. The old head,

Megan Williams, was still clinging on, but she was ousted two years later by Tony Sweetman, who had been helicoptered in from another school with only ten years' teaching experience. The school is rated Good now.

Afterwards Ella and I compared notes in the staffroom, a cheerless place in the New Building with passive-aggressive Post-its on the appliances — 'Please help empty the dishwasher. It can't always be my turn!!' We'd been left alone with coffee and a plate of biscuits while 'the panel' made their decision. We both knew that we'd be offered jobs. The prospect was made a lot less bleak by the woman sitting opposite me: long blonde hair, bony nose, not beautiful but extremely attractive. I learned later that Ella, a Jane Austen enthusiast, identified with Elizabeth Bennet. But, to me, she was always Emma.

'Why do you want to come here?' Ella had asked, stirring her tea with a pen.

'I've just got divorced,' I said. 'I want to move out of London. I've got a ten-year-old daughter. I thought it might be nice for her to live in the countryside. And be near the sea.'

The school was in West Sussex. Shoreham-by-Sea was only fifteen minutes away, Chichester half an hour on a good day. Both Rick and Tony had made a lot of this. I was trying to focus on the drive through the lush countryside and not the art rooms with the broken windows and the cheerless quad where the plants had all been killed by the salt winds.

'I'm escaping too,' Ella had said. 'I was teaching in Wales but I had an affair with my head of department. Not a good idea.'

I remember being touched, and slightly shocked, that she had confided in me so early in our acquaintance.

'I can't imagine having an affair with that Rick,' I said. 'He looks like a scarecrow.'

'If I only had a brain,' Ella sang in a surprisingly good imitation of the Scarecrow from *The Wizard of Oz.*

But she had a brain, and a good one, which is why she should have known about Rick. She should have listened to me.

Too late for that now.

· · ·

In the morning, I talk to the students about *The Stranger*.

'You often get archetypal characters in ghost stories,' I say. 'The innocent young man, the helper, the hinderer, the loathly lady.'

'I know a few of those,' says Ted with a slightly uncouth guffaw.

'I don't know what that means,' says Una. 'What is a loathly lady?' I recognise her as the type who makes heavy work of these things.

'She's a common character in gothic ghost stories,' I say. 'Think of *The Woman in Black* or Mrs Rochester in *Jane Eyre*. She descends from legends like the one in *The Wife of Bath's Tale*, where a beautiful woman becomes a hideous hag, or vice versa.'

'I've definitely met her,' says Ted.

I'm not going to be diverted. We have had enough about Ted's love life over the last two days. 'Of course,' I say, 'you have legends like the one in Keats' *Lamia* where a snake actually turns into a woman.'

'But there's no snake woman in *The Stranger*,' says Una.

'No,' I say. 'R.M. Holland tends to avoid women in his fiction altogether.'

'But you said that his wife haunts this house,' says Ted and I curse myself for our jolly chat over the biscuits.

'Tell us,' say several people. The more sensitive types shiver pleasurably but, with the autumn sun streaming in through the windows, it's hard to believe in ghosts.

'R.M. Holland married a woman called Alice Avery,' I say. 'They lived here, in this house, and Alice died, possibly from a fall down the stairs. Her ghost is meant to walk the place. You see her gliding along the corridors on the first floor or even floating down the stairs. Some people say that if you see her, it's a sign that a death is imminent.'

'Have you ever seen her?' asks someone.

'No,' I say, turning to the whiteboard. 'Now let's do an exercise on creating characters. Imagine that you're at a train station . . .'

I glance surreptitiously at my watch. Only six hours to go.

The day seems to go on for ever, for centuries, for millennia. But, at last, I'm saying goodbye to the students and promising to look out for their books in the *Sunday Times* culture section. I collect my papers and lock the classroom. Then I'm almost sprinting across the gravel towards my car. It's five o'clock but it feels like midnight. There are only a few lights left on in the school and the wind is blowing through the trees. I can't wait to get home, to have a glass of wine, to think about Ella and, most of all, to see Herbert.

If you would have told me five years ago that I would become this dependent on a dog, I would have laughed. I was never one of those children who adored animals. I was brought up in North London, my parents were both academics and the only animal we owned was a cat called Medusa who was rudely uninterested in anyone but my mother. But, when I got divorced and moved to Sussex, I decided that Georgie needed a dog. A dog would be motivation to get out into the countryside, to go for walks and cut down on the hours spent staring at her phone. She could pour out her teenage angst into its uncomplaining canine ear. I'd benefit too, I thought vaguely; a dog would keep me fit and allow me to meet other dog-walkers. Much better than a book club where there was always the danger that someone would suggest *The Girl on the Train*.

So we went to a rescue place and we chose Herbert. Or he chose us, because that's how it works, isn't it? I wanted a dog that was small enough to pick up in emergencies but not so small that it somehow ceased to be a dog. Herbert's origins are murky but the rescue place thought that he might be a cross between a cairn terrier and a poodle. He looked, in fact, just like an illustration in a child's picture book. A white *Hairy Maclary from Donaldson's Dairy,* a creature made by blobbing white paint on the page and adding legs.

And, of course, it was me that fell in love with Herbert. Oh, Georgie loves him. She takes him for walks and endows him with all sorts of anthropomorphic emotions. 'Herbert feels shy around other dogs. It's because he's an only child.' But I'm the one who dotes on him, who tells him my troubles and lets him sleep on — and often in — my bed. I love him so much that sometimes, when I look at him, I'm quite surprised to see that he's covered in hair.

Andy, the owner of Doggy Day Care (I know, don't judge me), is pleased to see me. He's a genial man who loves a chat. But, at the first sight of Herbert, with his cheerful, understanding woolly face, I find myself wanting to cry. I gather him into my arms, pay Andy and almost run back to the car. I just want to get home with my animal familiar. I stop off at the shops to buy wine and chocolate biscuits, Herbert panting in my ear.

I live in a town house, a terraced two up, two down with a black front door and wrought iron railings. It's just that this row of town houses is in the middle of the countryside, sheltered by a chalk cliff at the back. They were built to house workers at a cement factory but that's now derelict (sightless windows, rusting machinery, wind howling through the iron rooftops at night). The houses stay on though, pretty and gentrified, facing a meadow with grazing cows and resolutely ignoring the nightmare edifice behind them. We're used to the house now; it's quite convenient for school and not far from Steyning, where there are some nice cafes and a great bookshop. But once in a while I catch sight of the factory and all those gaping windows and think: why would anyone choose to live here?

The slip-road leads only to the houses so it's a surprise to see a car parked outside mine. Or is it? A feeling of foreboding has been following me all day. In fact, it's with a dull sense of inevitability that I recognise the car. As I park and unload an excited Herbert, a woman gets out of the vehicle.

'Hallo,' she says, 'are you Clare Cassidy? I'm DS Kaur. Can I come in for a moment?'

CHAPTER 3

DS Kaur is small with dark hair pulled back into a ponytail. She's probably ten years younger than me, around mid-thirties. She's a slight, almost girlish, figure but somehow she exudes authority, the way some teachers do. Behind DS Kaur is a man, older than her, greying and loosely put together. He introduces himself as DS Neil Winston. A pair of them, just like on TV.

Herbert tries to jump up on Kaur but I pull him away. After countless training sessions, he's still determined to embarrass me.

'It's OK,' she says. 'I like dogs.'

She brushes herself down all the same. Actually Herbert's part poodle so he doesn't shed much but DS Kaur is not to know this. She's wearing black trousers with a white shirt and a dark jacket. Plain clothes but anonymous enough to be a uniform. I'm certain that she and Winston are the two people I saw in the car park yesterday.

'Come in,' I say. We walk up the path and in through the shiny, urban front door. I pick up the post with one hand and direct my visitors towards the sitting room. Off the lead, Herbert rushes into the kitchen and starts barking at nothing.

'Can I get you a cup of tea?' I say to Kaur and Winston.

'No, thank you,' says Kaur just as Winston says, 'White, two sugars.'

The bottle in my carrier bag clanks incriminatingly when I put it down in the kitchen. I hope Kaur hasn't heard. Already I know she's the one to be reckoned with. I make the tea and put some biscuits on a plate. Then I head back to the sitting room with Herbert frisking at my heels.

'We're investigating the murder of Ella Elphick,' says Kaur as I sit down. 'I understand that you've been informed about this?'

'Yes. Rick Lewis, my head of department, phoned me yesterday.'

'I'm sorry,' says Kaur. 'I know it must be an awful shock for you, but we want to talk to all of Ella's friends and colleagues as soon as possible. We want to try to get a picture of her life so that we can work out who would have done this awful thing.'

'I thought . . .' I stop.

'What did you think?' says Kaur.

'I thought — I assumed . . . that she was killed by a stranger. A random attack. A robbery gone wrong.'

'Most murder victims are killed by people they know,' says Kaur, 'and we have reason to believe that this is the case here.'

'Rick said Ella was stabbed . . .'

'She was,' says Kaur. 'Multiple times.'

'Oh my God.'

There's a silence. Winston drinks his tea and Herbert whines softly.

'So,' Kaur gets out a notebook. 'You taught with Ella at Talgarth High. Is that correct?'

'Yes. We both teach English. Taught. Oh God.'

Kaur waits while I pull myself together.

'I'm head of Key Stage 3. Ella's head of Key Stage 4.'

'Key Stage 3 is . . . ?'

'Years 7 to 9. Eleven- to fourteen-year-olds. Key Stage 4 is Years 10 and 11. The GCSE exam years. Roughly fourteen- to sixteen-year-olds.'

'So you must have worked pretty closely together?'

'Yes, it's a small department, only six people. We have weekly meetings and Ella and I worked together on schemes of work, tracking progress, targets, that sort of thing.'

'Did you get on well?' asks Kaur. She has no problem with the past tense but then she never knew Ella when she was in the present tense.

'Very well.'

'Did you socialise outside work?'

Socialise. It's an odd word and seems too organised for the kind of relationship we had: walks with Herbert, meals where we ate and drank slightly too much, long chats on Facebook Messenger about *Strictly Come Dancing*.

'Yes,' I say.

'When did you last see Ella?'

'On Friday night. We went to the cinema then out for a meal.'

'Just the two of you?'

'With Debra Green. She teaches history at Talgarth High.'

'What film did you see?'

'The new *Blade Runner*,' I say.

'I want to see that,' says DS Winston, speaking for almost the first time. 'Was it any good?'

'A bit long,' I say, 'not as good as the first film.' I'd slept for most of the second half, could only remember Ryan Gosling walking very slowly through the snow, a single tear trickling down his face. I can hardly believe that we're sitting here discussing a film while Ella is lying dead somewhere.

'Did you hear from Ella on Sunday?' asks Kaur.

'No. I texted her before the *Strictly* results but didn't get an answer.'

'What time was that?'

'Seven-ish.'

'Is that what you were doing all evening? Watching television?'

'Some of the time. And I did some preparation for Monday. For the creative writing course.'

'Were you on your own all evening?'

'No, my daughter Georgia was with me.'

'All evening?'

'Yes. She was in her room for most of the time but she was in the house.'

'And on Monday you were teaching a creative writing course? That's at Talgarth High too, isn't it?'

'Yes. They run adult education courses during half-term.'

'Where is your daughter now?'

'She's gone to visit her dad. I took her to the station on Monday morning. She'll be back tomorrow.' Simon's driving her down, which is good. Except that I'll have to see him. Which is bad.

Kaur and Winston exchange glances. This must indicate a change in tone because Kaur leans back in my sagging armchair and says, 'What sort of a woman was Ella?'

It seems very important that I answer this question in the right way. Ella is the victim here, I don't want her to end up being blamed for her own murder, in the way that women often are. DS Kaur might seem like the sort of person who would wear a 'This is what a feminist looks like' T-shirt but I don't trust her. The question is inviting me to say that Ella had a sex life and so must, therefore, bear some responsibility for the fact that she has ended up dead. Stabbed. Multiple times. So I scroll through my memories of Ella; copying, replaying, deleting.

'She was a lovely person,' I say. 'Very intelligent, a lot of fun. Everyone liked her.'

Except someone obviously didn't. I plough on, 'Ella was a great teacher. The kids loved her. They'll be devastated when they find out . . .'

Kaur seems not to register this. 'Did Ella have a boyfriend?' she asks.

I knew it. 'Not that I know of,' I say.

'Any exes?'

'In the past,' I say carefully. 'Nobody recent.'

'Did she talk about anyone in particular?'

'She mentioned someone from her old school in Wales. Bradley something.'

Kaur makes a note. 'And she never mentioned anyone bothering her? Stalking her on Facebook? That sort of thing?'

Later I'm going to have to force myself to look at Ella's Facebook page. But not until I've had at least two glasses of wine.

'No,' I say.

I think they are going to ask more, so am surprised when they start up, as synchronised as if responding to a secret signal.

'Thank you,' says Kaur. 'You've been very helpful.'

'I'm sorry for your loss,' says Winston, on his way out. It sounds like a line from an American cop programme. Kaur, who stops to pat Herbert in a firm way that keeps him away from her trousers, says nothing.

When they've gone I go into the kitchen and pour myself a glass of wine. As I do so, I notice the post that I scooped up earlier. There are a few official-looking letters in brown envelopes, which I ignore, and one that looks very different, with thick, creamy paper and an embossed stamp from St Jude's College, Cambridge.

I know it's ridiculous but my first thought was Georgie. She's only fifteen, she hasn't taken any exams yet, why would a Cambridge college be writing to me about her? And, while Georgie is undoubtedly clever, it's clear that her intention is to glide through her school years on the minimum of work. I've already revised my expectations down from Oxbridge, through the Russell Group, to any good university with en-suite halls of residence. But I could read the words as if I'd already opened the envelope. 'Come to our attention . . . supremely gifted student . . . open scholarship.'

But the letter isn't offering Georgie an unconditional place at Girton. All the same, it is interesting.

> Dear Ms Cassidy,
>   I understand that you are in the process of writing a book about the life and works of R.M. Holland. I have recently come into possession of some letters which I think might interest you. I would be happy to show them to you if you care to visit me. I have some free time in the week beginning 23rd October.
>   Yours sincerely,
>   Henry H. Hamilton
>   Senior Lecturer in English

I look at this missive for a long time. It's as if I've received a letter from the nineteenth century, almost from Holland himself. There's a Victorian feel to that prim middle initial. Where did this Henry Hamilton even find my postal address? My email address is easy enough, it's on the school website and is, anyway, not hard to work out. Is that how this august-sounding personage found me? Please God, don't let him have watched the TV programme. Has HHH been watching me on YouTube? And what could these letters be, too precious to post or even scan?

My phone buzzes. I hope that it's Georgie but it's Debra.

'Are you home?' she says.

'Yes, got in about an hour ago.'

'I've just rung Ella's parents.'

I should do this too, but I'm dreading it. I met Nigel and Sarah Elphick once and they seemed a sweet, gentle couple. Ella was their only child.

'It was awful,' says Debra. 'What can you say? There's nothing you can say. Losing a child is the worst thing that can happen to someone.'

'Yes, it is,' I say.

'I started to cry and her mum ended up consoling me. I felt terrible.'

'It was still nice of you to phone.'

'I don't know,' says Debra and I can hear her drawing on a cigarette. That must mean that she's standing in the garden. Leo won't let her smoke indoors. 'But what can you do? Have you seen her Facebook page?'

'No.'

'It's full of people posting stuff like "rest in paradise" and "another angel in heaven". Most of them didn't even know her. Jesus.'

I think of DS Kaur asking if any ex-boyfriends were stalking Ella on Facebook.

'The police were here just now,' I say.

'The police? Why?'

'They're talking to all Ella's friends apparently. You'll probably be next.'

'God. The boys will love that. Two policemen turning up at the door.'

'One's a woman. She's the scary one too.'

'Do they have any idea who could have done it?'

'They were asking about ex-boyfriends.'

'What did you say?'

'I said there was no one recent.'

'You didn't mention Rick?'

'No.'

Another deep intake of breath. I steel myself for the next question but Debra only says, 'I still can't believe it. Ella dead. Murdered. It's like a nightmare.'

'Or a book,' I say. 'I keep thinking I'm in a book.'

'You always think that,' says Debra. 'Do you want to come over?'

'No. It's OK. I've got a bottle of wine. And Herbert.'

'Sounds perfect. I've got to collect the boys from Cubs in a minute, then make supper. Leo's out playing five-a-side.'

'Domesticity, eh?'

'Yeah. It's a trap all right. Maybe see you tomorrow?'

'Georgie's back tomorrow.'

'Give me a ring. Maybe we can meet up for coffee.'

'OK,' I say. 'Bye. Take care. Drive carefully.'

I drink my glass of wine standing up and then pour another. Then I click on Ella's Facebook page.

CHAPTER 4

Simon turns up the next day at four, about three hours after he was expected. Georgie texted me en-route so I wasn't waiting by the window but it is, nevertheless, annoying. I saw Debra this morning and went to the shops, but there were lots of things I could have done in the afternoon if Simon didn't have this curious belief that the drive from London to West Sussex takes twenty minutes.

'I was expecting you at one.' These are my first words to my ex-husband.

'Georgie texted you,' is his response.

'Hi, darling.' I hug my daughter. 'Did you have a good time?'

She hugs me back but lets go to give Herbert a much more enthusiastic reception.

'How's my puppy? How is he? Oh, bless him. Look at his little face.'

She scoops him up and covers him with kisses. Simon and I watch them. It's one of those moments where I know we're thinking the same thing (why isn't she that affectionate to *us*?) but I don't want to acknowledge it.

'Lucky Herbert,' says Simon at last, getting Georgie's bag out of the boot.

'Do you want to come in for a cup of tea?' I say.

He hesitates. He doesn't really want to be trapped in the house with me but he probably needs the loo (he's just the right age for prostate trouble).

'Just a quick one,' he says. 'Thank you.'

How long does he think it will take? I'm hardly planning a Japanese tea-drinking ceremony. I follow him into the house, aware that my teeth are gritted.

He goes to the loo immediately but emerges to chat to me while I go about the laborious and time-consuming task of putting tea-bags in water. Georgie has disappeared upstairs with Herbert.

'Kitchen looks nice,' Simon says. I had a new kitchen put in when I moved here and it *is* nice — shiny doors, granite tops, skylight and a view into the garden. But Simon always mentions it partly, I'm sure, because he resents the fact that I have the kitchen I've always wanted. We sold the London house when we divorced but, because Simon married a relatively wealthy woman, he was able to buy another place in the city. I was exiled to the countryside so, in my opinion, granite worktops are the least I deserve.

'How's Fleur?' I counter. I've nothing against Simon's wife. In fact I often sympathise with her, married, as she is, to man who colour-codes his socks. She's a lawyer, like Simon, but she's currently at home with a three-year-old and a twenty-month-old. Can't be much fun, especially since it would never occur to Simon — who thinks of himself as a new man — to take paternity leave.

'She's OK,' he says. 'A bit tired. Ocean still isn't sleeping through the night.' I don't blame her. She's probably traumatised by her ridiculous name.

'That's tough.' I bet Simon has decamped to the spare room. He looks pretty well-rested to me.

Simon is fiddling with his keys, a sure sign that he's nervous. 'I'm sorry about your friend,' he says at last. 'Georgie showed me something about it online.'

Ella's death is everywhere. In newspapers, on TV, online, floating through the ether. Apparently you can get your Facebook page 'memorialised' (Debra says we should suggest this to Ella's parents) so the deceased can exist in cyberspace for ever.

'It was a shock,' I say.

'Georgie says that she taught her, this Ellie.'

'Ella. Yes, she taught her English in Year 10.'

'It's a shock for her too. She kept talking about it.'

'It's her first brush with death, I suppose.' Simon looks hurt. 'Apart from your dad,' I say quickly. 'I wasn't forgetting that. But Georgie was only three when Derek died. Now she's a hormonal teenager.'

'Talking of hormones,' says Simon. 'She's still in touch with that Ty.'

'I know,' I say.

There's another of those serendipity moments, then Simon says, 'I suppose we can't stop her seeing him.'

'I think that would do more harm than good,' I say.

'It's been quite a long time, hasn't it?'

'Since the summer. That's eons in teenage time.'

'And you've met him, have you?'

I've told him this before but I say, as patiently as I can, 'Yes. He was perfectly pleasant. Very polite and so on. It's just that he's twenty-one.'

'Why can't she go out with somebody at school? Somebody her age. That's what's meant to happen.'

'I suppose Ty seems cool,' I say. 'He lives on his own, he's got a car. Those things matter at fifteen.' And he's good-looking, in a muscle-bound, straining-out-of-his-shirt kind of way. But I don't say this to Simon.

'Well, try to keep them apart if you can.'

I resent Simon telling me this, as if it's easy to keep apart two people who can communicate electronically every second of the day. But I think that I have the perfect retort.

'I'm taking her to Cambridge on Friday,' I say. 'I've got a meeting about my book and I thought it would be a nice day out.'

Simon and I met at university. It wasn't until a few months into our relationship that we shyly shared the fact that we were among the large group of students at Bristol known as 'Oxbridge rejects'. I had been interviewed but didn't get an offer, even though I did, in fact, achieve the required grades. Simon had an offer but didn't get the grades. It's hard to tell which is worse. I didn't really mind, at first. I loved Bristol and parts of the university, especially the Wills Memorial Building, look quite Oxbridgey in the right light. It's only recently, while I've been working on the book, that I've noticed how many people — writers, actors, academics — just happen to mention that they were at Oxford or Cambridge. R.M. Holland does it in the very first page of *The Stranger*. The rule is: if you went to Oxbridge, you have to say, otherwise it's just 'when I was at university'.

Simon was studying law so I ignored him for most of the first year. The lawyers went round in a pack, as did the medics. I was reading English and was caught up in the drama society, the debating club and an excitingly dysfunctional relationship with a philosophy student called Sebastian. I met Simon in the Christmas term of the second year. I was sharing a flat with Jen and Cathy. They were lovely people who became good friends but, in those days, they were what we would have called Sloanes, posh girls who wore their collars turned up and had pictures of their Labradors by their beds. My flatmates' idea of fun was having dinner parties; Delia's Spanish pork with olives, candles in Chianti bottles, spliffs circulating left to right. They were also very keen on having even numbers so I invited Sebastian even though our affair had cooled. Simon came with a girl from Modern Languages. He took one look at the elaborate place settings on our formica kitchen table and started to laugh. I caught his eye and that was it. During the port/spliff/truth-or-dare phase we sneaked out and ran through Bristol in the early hours of the morning, stopping to kiss by the Bordeaux Quay while the boats jangled in the harbour. We went back to Simon's flat in Clifton and made love on his bed which had black sheets and a poster of Che Guevara over the headboard. We were inseparable for the rest of our time at university. We got married when we were twenty-three, after Simon had done his solicitor's exams and I'd finished my teacher training. We were the first of our friends to get married and if you told me then that one day I would not be able to watch him drinking tea without becoming rigid with irritation, I would have laughed in your face.

The Cambridge thing intrigues him, as I had known it would.

'Oh, are you still working on the book?' is the best he can muster.

'Yes,' I say. 'It's going really well.'

'That's the one about the ghost story writer.'

'R.M. Holland. Yes.'

'The chap who murdered his wife?' says Simon, clearly thinking that this is quite a wheeze.

'No one knows if he murdered her,' I say. 'That might be one mystery I solve in the book. There's the query about his daughter too.'

'I didn't know he had a daughter.'

'No one knows for sure. There are mentions of an M in his diaries and I think she might be his illegitimate daughter. Yet she dies too, because there's a poem, "For M. RIP".'

Simon shivers in a theatrical way that I find irritating. 'Bloody hell. He was a charmer, all right. I can't believe all his stuff is still there in the school. In the attics. No wonder it's such a weird place.'

When I first moved to Sussex and got the job at Talgarth High, Simon insisted that Georgie go to the private school nearby. Despite some ideological objections (which, by the way, Simon used to share), I agreed. I'd accepted the job at Talgarth but I knew that it was a school in crisis. Georgie had had a lot of upheaval that year, what with her parents divorcing and the move from London, so we'd thought that maybe St Faith's, a small, select girls' school, was the answer. Georgie hated it. She hated the girls — most of whom had been to the adjoining prep school — the uniform, the petty rules, everything. In just one term she became depressed and withdrawn and worryingly thin (competitive dieting was the one sport St Faith's excelled in). I moved her to Talgarth in Year 8 and, by and large, she has thrived. She has lots of friends and does pretty well academically. Simon still secretly wishes that she wore a blazer and carried a flute case. Well, he's welcome to go down that route with Tiger and Ocean (his tolerance of exotic names has also changed over the years, I imagine this is Fleur's influence). But Simon can't deny that Georgie is happy at school, so he confines himself to describing Talgarth as a 'sink comprehensive' and making remarks about its apparently unwholesome atmosphere.

'The students aren't allowed on the top floor,' I say, 'and the GCSE results were good this year. One of the best in the county.'

'Georgia needs to work hard for her GCSEs,' says Simon, 'and stop spending her time going out with twenty-one-year-old layabouts.'

Although I agree with the sentiment, I find the fact that he has to say it annoying. Also, *layabouts*? Has Simon become a seventies sitcom character? I snatch away his cup and start washing it up.

'Isn't it time you were heading back?' I say.

• • •

Later, when Georgie and I are watching a DVD of *Grey's Anatomy* (our most intimate moments these days come to the accompaniment of cranial surgery and heart bypasses), I say, 'Do you fancy going to Cambridge on Friday?'

Georgie doesn't take her eyes from the screen where Meredith and Derek are emoting over a teenage leukaemia sufferer.

'Why?'

'I've got to see someone about my book, but we could have lunch and look around the town. It's a beautiful place.'

'Who do you have to see?'

'Someone who has some letters from R.M. Holland.' Georgie knows about Holland, all the students do, but she's never shown the slightest interest in him.

She stares at the screen for another minute before saying, 'You won't go on at me about applying to Oxbridge?'

'Have I ever done that?'

'Subtly,' says Georgie, typing into her phone without looking at it. 'All about how so-and-so's daughter went there and what a good time they're having. May Balls and all that crap.'

I didn't realise I did this although all my London friends do seem to have children at Oxford or Cambridge. Sometimes I wonder if the move to Sussex blighted both our futures.

'I won't mention it once,' I say.

'OK then. Can Ty come?'

'No,' I say. 'This is mother and daughter time.'

'Yuck,' says Georgie but she doesn't say no.

Clare's Diary

Wednesday 25th October 2017

I plucked up my courage to ring Ella's parents this morning. I didn't think I'd get through. Was rehearsing in my head, 'Well, I tried. They're probably not taking calls at the moment. Bit intrusive to ring, really. I think I'll just send a card.' But the phone was answered on the second ring. Ella's mother, Sarah. As soon as I introduced myself, 'Clare from school', she started to cry. 'Oh, Clare. How could this happen?' It was awful. I tried to say the right thing, but what is the right thing in these circumstances? There's no right thing. Ella is dead and her parents are left childless. Any hopes they might have had — of grandchildren, of growing old as a family — have been shattered. I just said how sorry I was and asked about the funeral. Sarah said she wanted to have it in the chapel at Talgarth, which threw me a bit. Of course I said I'd be there and asked if there was anything I could do, etc. But there's nothing I can do. That's the thing.

Had coffee in the village with Debra earlier. She's very upset about Ella but also strangely fascinated, asking me about the autopsy and the criminal investigation, as if the whole thing is a TV series. I keep thinking about the two detectives who came here, Kaur and Winston. They weren't hostile exactly, but they weren't friendly either. 'Most murder victims are killed by people they know,' said Kaur, 'and we have reason to believe that this is the case here.'

Who do they suspect?

'Nothing in the world is hidden forever' — Wilkie Collins, *No Name*.

CHAPTER 5

We drop Herbert at Doggy Day Care and set off early for the drive to Cambridge. It's a beautiful day, crisp and sunny, the fields outlined by fiery autumnal trees. Even the M25 isn't too bad. Georgie is plugged into her headphones, I listen to Radio 4. There's a feature about sexual harassment. I try to remember how many times I've had inappropriate comments made to me, at school, university and work. I give up when I get to double figures. Georgie unplugs herself and asks if we're there yet.

'Soonish,' I say, squinting at the satnav with its ever-hopeful estimated time of arrival. 'About an hour.'

Georgie slumps. We stop at a service station for drinks, sweets and the loo, then set off again. We take the M11, then the wonderfully named Fen Causeway. The land falls away from us; there is only sky and the road ahead. I remember something I once heard from an American writer: 'In Kansas you can see someone running away for days.' It might not be days here but it would be several hours before the running figure disappeared over the horizon. My grandmother lives in the highlands of Scotland but her house is in a fishing village, with shops and a proper community. My dad got away as quickly as he could, escaping to Edinburgh for university and then to London for work. Yet I love Scotland; some of my happiest memories are of being in the Ullapool house. This is something else. A strange, sullen landscape, even on a day like this. A place that rightly belongs at the bottom of the sea.

My problems start in Cambridge itself. I can't find St Jude's and the sat-nav gives up, muttering 'turn around where possible' to itself. Eventually I have to stop and ask the way, causing Georgie to slump even lower in her seat. Once more round the one-way system, passing ancient portals and gateways, glimpses of another world.

St Jude's appears with supernatural suddenness. I brake, the cars behind me hoot and I nearly hit a cyclist as I swerve through the low archway. An alarmingly large figure emerges from the porter's lodge but it appears that I'm on a list somewhere so I'm allowed to drive on, past an emerald green quad and into a small car park.

'Professor Hamilton will meet you by the library staircase,' I'm told, so I park nearby, next to the recycling bins, and we get out of the car.

Georgie looks around. There are low Tudor buildings on three sides of us, leaded light windows twinkling in the October sun.

'It's creepy,' says Georgie.

'In a good way,' I say. That's as far as I'm prepared to go.

The library is on the opposite side of the quad. We circle the grass, and arrive at another low door. I have to duck slightly. Perhaps it's just as well that I didn't come here. I'd have permanent concussion. A stone staircase is in front of us, dark and curiously forbidding, but on the left there's a sign saying 'library' in a comfortingly twenty-first-century typeface. I'm just about to push open the door when a voice says, 'Ms Cassidy?'

I turn round. If I had to duck, this man must have had to bend almost double to get under the door. I'm five-ten but I have to squint to look up at him, his head almost lost in the gloom of the hallway.

'Henry Hamilton.' A hand is extended.

'Clare Cassidy.' I adjust my eyes and see that Henry Hamilton has dark hair, worn slightly long, which gives him the look of a composer or a poet. He's probably in his forties and his face, what I can see of it in the semi-darkness, is thin and sensitive-looking. He's also about six-foot-four.

'This is my daughter Georgia.'

Georgie manages to shake hands and mumble something.

'How do you do,' says Henry. 'Is this your first trip to Cambridge?'

'Yes,' says Georgie.

'I hope you'll get to see something of the other colleges. St Jude's is a minnow compared to King's or Trinity.'

'It's a very pretty minnow,' I say.

'I like it,' says Hamilton. 'Would you like to step up to my office? I've made coffee. Georgia, would you like me to get one of the undergraduates to show you round?'

Georgie glares at me but doesn't say anything. Hamilton takes her silence for assent.

We all ascend the staircase and enter a door marked 'Professor H.H. Hamilton'. Do his friends call him HH, I wonder? It's a tiny room but it has a view out over the quad with golden buildings all around. Otherwise the office is disappointingly mundane: metal bookcases, a computer, a desk that looks like it came from IKEA. There is, however, a cafetière and a plate of biscuits on a tray.

Hamilton plunges the coffee and excuses himself for a minute. He comes back with a gangling ginger-haired youth, his acne gleaming gently. 'This is Edmund. He'll be happy to show Georgia around the college while I show you the papers.' As Georgie leaves the room, I have to swallow a ridiculous urge to tell her to be careful. Will she be safe in this creepy, gothic world? I'm also rather disappointed that Edmund doesn't exactly look the type to fill Georgie with enthusiasm for life at Cambridge.

'I hope that was all right,' says Henry Hamilton. 'I just thought she might be bored.'

'It's fine,' I say. 'I want her to see what a university is like. She's only in Year 11 but it's never too early.'

'Does she want to come to Cambridge?'

'I don't think she's thought about it.'

Hamilton smiles. 'I didn't think about universities until I'd left school and was working in a chip shop. No one from my family had ever been to university. I read about Cambridge in a newspaper that was going to go round some cod and chips. It was an article about getting working-class kids to apply. I thought, "It can't be worse than this".' He has a slight Northern accent that I hadn't registered before. Not Newcastle, like Simon, but something softer.

'My parents are both academics,' I say. 'They kept going on about university. You can't get it right really.'

There's a slight pause and Hamilton says, 'So how did you become interested in R.M. Holland?'

'He lived at the school where I teach,' I say. 'I'd read *The Stranger* before, of course, but there was something about being in his actual house. I've become quite obsessed. He's an interesting character and there's never been a biography.'

'*The Stranger* is a great little story.'

'Yes, it works well with students.'

'I bet. I didn't know much about Holland myself but, when these letters turned up, I did some research. I found a news clip where you were talking about him.'

I grimace. 'I hate seeing myself on screen. Not that I've been on TV before.'

'I was on *University Challenge*,' says Hamilton. 'We lost and my mum told me off for not wearing a tie.'

'How come the letters turned up here?' I say. 'I know Holland went to Peterhouse.'

'They're addressed to William Petherick. You know he was the model for Gudgeon in *The Stranger*?'

'Poor old Gudgeon.'

'Yes. But, unlike Gudgeon, Petherick did not come to an untimely end. He came here to St Jude's to teach theology. The college has always been popular with people wanting to take Holy Orders. Petherick wrote music too, and some of our choral scholars were going through his scores recently and they found these.' He pushes a transparent envelope across the table. I recognise Holland's cramped handwriting immediately. My own hands are shaking as I take out the papers.

'We didn't know at first who Roland was,' says Hamilton, 'but then I remembered the R.M. Holland connection.'

'Roland Montgomery Holland,' I say. I'm itching to read the letters. Hamilton must understand this because he says, 'Take your time. I've got a couple of emails to answer.' He turns to his computer.

November 1848

My dear Petherick,

Thank you for yours of the third. Friendship is indeed a
slow ripening fruit and ours is surely now full on the bough.
I was very low after the death of Alice but, as you say, Mariana is a constant solace. Even so, I do worry about her. It's
no life, really, being marooned in a large, empty house in the
middle of nowhere, her only companion a crusty old gentle-
man. Poor Mariana. Pray God her name does not prove an
ill-omen. But M is indeed an angel, sweet-natured and kind.
Yet still I fear she has inherited her mother's taint. I will not
keep her with me, though, like a selfish old tyrant. I will send
her to my sister and her family in Shropshire. Ah, but not yet.
I need her with me for a little longer.

Thank you for your sympathy, old friend. How I long for
the stones of Cambridge.

Yours,

Roland

The next sheet is obviously a page from a longer letter.

. . . imbeciles in the publishing world. *The Ravening Beast* is
strong meat, certainly, but not devoid of literary and artis-
tic merit. They only desire more short stories in the mould
of *The Stranger* and you know how much I regret that *jeu
d'esprit*. Mariana thinks *Beast* is the best thing I have ever
written, not that she's exactly a literary critic. But she is such
a comfort to me.

I was interested to hear of your new arrangement of the
Kyrie. How I would like to come to Cambridge and hear it
sung. But, as you know, I travel little these days. If only I . . .

There's no more. I read the pages again and look up to find Hamilton's
eyes — very deep-set and dark — on me.

'These are . . . interesting,' I say.

'I hoped you'd think so,' he says.

'The mention of Mariana,' I say, 'and the implication that she's Alice's daughter . . .'

'Tell me about Mariana,' says Hamilton. I half expect him to steeple his fingers in tutorial mode.

'Holland married a woman called Alice Avery,' I say. 'She was an actress. We don't know how they met because Holland hardly ever left Sussex and, after Alice died, he rarely left the house. He writes about Alice in his diary. He was dazzled at first but it soon starts to go wrong. Alice seems to have had some sort of mental instability. Holland called it "hysteria". A very common diagnosis in Victorian times, as I'm sure you know, and always used of women. They were only married four years when Alice died. He describes her taking a "dying fall" and I've always imagined that she fell down the stairs at Holland House, where the old part of the school is. Holland's marriage and Alice's death are noted in the family Bible but there's no mention of a Mariana. However, in another letter, he says, "my sweet child Mariana". Then there's a poem, "For M. RIP", about his grief at Mariana's death. She can only have been about thirteen. But there are no other mentions of her and she's not buried in the graveyard at Talgarth.'

'There's a graveyard at your school?'

'Yes. It's out-of-bounds but as you can imagine, it's a popular destination.'

'The perfect place for an illicit cigarette.'

'And the rest of it. But in this letter, Holland writes about Mariana inheriting "her mother's taint". That seems to imply that she was Alice's daughter.'

'Maybe he did send her to his sister in Shropshire?'

'It's possible. Holland's sister, Thomasina, was married to a clergyman and she wasn't one for letters or diaries. But they had a family Bible, too, and it lists all of Thomasina's children, including the two that died in infancy, but there's no mention of Mariana.'

'It's a little creepy,' says Hamilton, 'all that stuff about him needing Mariana with him.'

I'm struck by his use of the word 'creepy'. Not only is it distinctly unacademic but it's the word Georgie used to describe the college earlier.

'It's very odd,' I say, 'but then Holland *was* odd. And he took a hell of a lot of opium towards the end.'

'They all did,' says Hamilton. 'Wilkie Collins took so much that when his valet celebrated his bequest from Collins's will with a small dose of laudanum, an eighth of his master's daily intake, it killed him.'

'And there's Miss Gwilt in *Armadale*: "Who was the man who invented laudanum? I thank him with all my heart".'

'I've never read *Armadale*.'

This makes me feel slightly smug although he says it a bit like he's read every other book in the world. 'You should,' I say. 'It's got a great villainess in it. I've heard the valet story before. I wonder if it's true. It sounds almost too Wilkie Collins somehow.'

Hamilton laughs. 'Fair point. What was *The Ravening Beast*? An unpublished book?'

'Yes. There are some notes about it in his diaries. It's about a beast that lives in the wood and sometimes descends on a lonely village and drags off young women to kill and eat them. But there's some ambiguity as to whether it's an animal or a crazed madman, maybe even the narrator himself. Holland says it's a cross between *The Hound of the Baskervilles* and *The Strange Case of Dr Jekyll and Mr Hyde*.'

'Does the manuscript still survive?'

'It's not with his papers at Holland House but Holland quotes from it in his diaries. He's a great quoter. And there are several rejection letters from publishers in his files.'

'That's what he was talking about in the second letter?'

'Yes. The book certainly sounds as if it was "strong meat". There are several quite explicit passages. The parts I've seen read a bit like one long opium-induced nightmare. But, as Holland says, publishers only wanted more short stories like *The Stranger*.'

'And he says he regrets writing that.'

'Yes. He wrote it when he was still a young man. He'd just left Cambridge and was living in digs in London. He hadn't inherited Holland House then. *The Stranger* was published in a weekly magazine and later it was part of a collection of ghost stories. Holland grew to resent its success. Maybe he also felt sorry about killing Gudgeon, especially as he seems to have stayed friends with Petherick.'

'*Friendship is a slow ripening fruit,*' says Hamilton. 'That's Aristotle, by the way. I looked it up.'

'It's a rather unpleasant image. Fruit either withers or goes bad in the end.'

Hamilton looks slightly surprised, as if he didn't expect literary critique from a humble Bristol graduate. But then the door opens and Edmund ushers Georgie back in. He mutters an inarticulate goodbye and departs. Georgie looks after him thoughtfully.

'Thank you very much for your time,' I say, standing up. 'Could I take copies of the letters?'

'Of course,' says Hamilton. 'I've very much enjoyed our chat. Will you let me know if you find the truth about Mariana?'

'I'll send you a copy of the finished book,' I say, slightly tongue-in-cheek.

'I'd like that very much.'

We have lunch at a nice vegan cafe and wander round the public bits of some of the colleges. Georgie tells me that quads are called courts in Cambridge, which seems to be the only piece of information that she has picked up from Edmund. 'Is that really a college chapel?' says Georgie, staring at the soaring gothic windows of King's. 'It looks like a cathedral.'

'It's a bit bigger than the chapel at Talgarth High,' I say and, as I do so, I remember that Ella's parents want to hold her funeral there. Talgarth is non-denominational but the chapel is still in use, mostly as a wedding destination. Despite the horror of the modern buildings, some people actually choose to get married at the school and it's a much-needed source of revenue. I just can't imagine a funeral being held there, the coffin being carried up the main steps, the mourners walking along the corridors with the GCSE art on the walls. I can't think about it. I won't.

On the way home, Georgie surprises me by asking what was in the letters. She's never shown any interest in Holland before.

'They were interesting,' I say, 'and there was a mention of the mysterious daughter, Mariana. Something about worrying that she has inherited her mother's taint.'

'What was that, do you think?'

'Madness, I suppose.'

'Was his wife mad then?'

'Probably not. Women could be put into mental institutions in those days if they were suffering from post-natal depression or if they disobeyed their husbands. There are even cases of women being locked up for "excessive novel reading".'

'That's you done for then.'

I laugh. 'Women were often diagnosed with "hysteria". It's from the Latin word for womb . . .'

But Georgie is looking at her phone and I sense that I've lost my audience. As we join the M25, I say casually, 'What did you think of St Jude's?'

'It was OK,' says Georgie. 'That Edmund was a bit of a freak. He's studying Classics and he rows. You know, like in the boat race that they have on TV.'

'I know.'

Georgie giggles suddenly. 'I liked Professor Henry though. And he liked you.'

I am manoeuvring my way through three lanes of traffic but, when I can, I say, 'What do you mean?'

'All that "I'd like that very much",' she adopts a deep, patrician voice. Incidentally nothing like Henry Hamilton's. 'He wants to see you again.'

'Nonsense.' But I can't help being slightly pleased. I think about Henry's assumption that my book will be published one day. I suppose that's the world he lives in. You write a book and it gets published. It's not like that in the real world. I wrote to a few agents when I got the idea of writing about R.M. Holland and one was fairly interested. But I haven't got a contract and sometimes I don't think the book will ever be finished. I've written about sixty thousand words and on low days I think fifty thousand of them are utter shite.

A few miles later, Georgie says, 'Can Ty come round tonight?'

I try to keep my voice light. 'I thought we'd just have a quiet evening. We could get pizzas in.'

'Ty likes pizza.'

I say nothing.

'We can't see each other tomorrow because he's working.' Ty works at a pub in the village. I suppose I should be pleased that he does something (that he's not a 'layabout') but somehow it's only a reminder that he's not only old enough to drink legally, he can actually work in a bar.

'Please, Mum.'

'Oh, OK,' I say.

There's no point in ruining the day, after all.

Ty comes round promptly at seven. He looms in the doorway in his leather jacket and I can see exactly why Georgie likes him. He's good-looking in a very grown-up way; dark hair, hint of stubble, muscles very much in evidence. I watch Georgie surreptitiously as she takes his coat and asks him about pizza choices. She doesn't seem infatuated but I hope she's too cool to show it even if she is. She mocks him for wanting pineapple on his pizza (too right!) but he just grins at her in a lazy way and refuses to rise. I like that and I like the way he refuses a glass of wine, opting instead for water. While we're waiting for the pizzas I ask him about his family. He's from Kent and was brought up by his grandparents after his parents died in a car crash (I think Georgie had already told me this sad fact).

'My grandma's very cool though,' says Ty. 'She's got the internet and everything. She's a silver surfer. She goes to classes at the library.'

'How old is she?' asks Georgie.

'Not that old. Seventy-five.' Point to Ty.

'That's ancient.' Point deducted from Georgie.

'I mean it in a good way,' she says, when I protest. 'Old people are, like, well wise.'

'Gran always says I should listen to her because she's wise,' says Ty, 'but, then again, she follows Kim Kardashian on Snapchat.'

I'm quite impressed. I've only got the vaguest idea what Snapchat is.

The pizzas come and we eat them in front of the TV. It's the usual Friday night topical quiz show stuff and, while Ty has never heard of Michael Gove (lucky him), he's quite funny about Ian Hislop and *Private Eye*. He's clearly not stupid. Ty and Georgie sit on the sofa and I share my chair with Herbert.

He's always wary of male visitors and watches Ty underneath his fringe. Ty, for his part, seems quite nervous of Herbert.

'I couldn't have a dog when I was growing up because of my allergies,' he says, sneezing as if to prove a point.

'Poodles are good for allergic people because of their fur,' says Georgie. 'It's more like wool.'

'Herbert's only part poodle,' I say. But, by the end of *Have I Got News for You,* Herbert consents to let Ty pat him.

Georgie wants to watch Graham Norton because some brainless celebrity is on it. I'm torn. I'm tired after the drive and want to write my diary and think about the day, about the letters from R.M. Holland and the meeting with Henry. But should I leave Ty and Georgie downstairs unchaperoned? Simon would say definitely not. He'd want me to stay here glaring at them, possibly wearing a lace cap. This decides me. I'm not going to do Simon's dirty work. I say goodnight and go upstairs. Funnily enough, for once Herbert doesn't follow me. He stays in the sitting room, perhaps because the fire is still burning. Anyway, it's good because he'll definitely bark if Ty lunges at Georgie. I don't want to think of lunging, or of any of the other components of teenage snogging. It makes me feel old and sad and slightly pathetic. I don't want to be a repressive parent or — worse — a jealous one. But I haven't kissed a man since Simon left me. That's been my choice, I know, but, right at this minute, that doesn't seem much of a comfort. I remember DS Kaur asking me whether Ella had a boyfriend. Should I have answered differently? Told her the truth about Rick?

At any rate, Herbert's presence does the trick. Ty has gone before the end of Graham Norton. I hear a brief goodbye in the hall and Georgie takes Herbert out for his last wee. Then both my babies come upstairs to bed.

I think I'll go to sleep quickly but the day's events keep rearranging themselves in my head: the drive, the ancient buildings grouped around the quad, the office with H.H. Hamilton on the door, the letters, Mariana, the ravening beast. After a while I give up and put the light on. I look in my bookcase for something reassuring to read — P.G. Wodehouse or Georgette Heyer —

and see my battered copy of Tennyson. Holland said he prays that Mariana's name wouldn't prove to be a bad omen. I flick through the thin pages to find the poem.

> Upon the middle of the night,
> Waking she heard the night-fowl crow:
> The cock sung out an hour ere light:
> From the dark fen the oxen's low
> Came to her: without hope of change,
> In sleep she seem'd to walk forlorn,
> Till cold winds woke the gray-eyed morn
> About the lonely moated grange.
> She only said, 'The day is dreary,
> He cometh not,' she said;
> She said, 'I am aweary, aweary,
> I would that I were dead!'

The 'dark fen' reminds me of Cambridge and the drive over the causeway, the road the highest point in the landscape, the flat fields stretching away on either side. It's a spooky passage: the night fowl, the darkness, the cold winds and the gray-eyed morn. Did Holland's Mariana feel like this? Did she too wish that she was dead? I must find out more about her. This could be my breakthrough, my reason for getting the book published. But, more than that, I feel a strange fellow-feeling for her, this girl who seems to exist only in words. Holland obviously loved her but he was also very patronising, 'not that she's exactly a literary critic'. But maybe Mariana was clever as well as being 'sweet-natured and kind', maybe she too was a thwarted writer . . .

My curtains are slightly open and I can see the moon high over the old factory, illuminating the broken windows and ghostly tower. I get up to close them and, just for a second, the light reflects on glass as if a candle is flickering, high up in the ramparts. Then all is dark again. Another Tennyson line comes back to me, 'Four grey walls and four grey towers'. I have the ridiculous feeling that someone is watching me. I pull the curtains tightly and turn back to the bookcase. Herbert, who is sitting on my bed, growls softly. 'Don't you start,' I tell him.

I select *Jeeves in the Springtime* and get back into bed. Herbert continues to gaze at the window, doing that whole annoying 'psychic animal' thing. Sometimes I regret naming him after the dog in Holland's story. I remember what I said to my students on Monday, 'Animals are expendable.' Why would I say such a thing?

'It's all right, Herbert,' I say. 'There's no one there.' I stroke my beloved companion animal and let Jeeves and Wooster lull me to sleep with Homburg hats, lunch at the Ritz and a scheme to prevent Bingo Little from being disinherited for wanting to marry a waitress.

Clare's Diary

I'm dreading school tomorrow. All the students will be hysterical about Ella — half genuinely upset, half enjoying the drama of it all. These last few days — Cambridge, Saturday with G — I've managed to put Ella to the back of my mind but now she's here again. I don't dream about her but the bad dreams are back. Last night I had lost Georgia in a forest and had to make a path for her by pulling out my own hair. I don't need Freud to tell me that there's some deep mother anxiety going on there. Is it pelicans who feed their offspring by tearing the flesh from their own breasts? I would do that for Georgie, but I doubt she'd be delighted to be offered chunks of human flesh on toast. She's always threatening to go vegetarian.

I rang Mum and Dad for our traditional Sunday phone call. I didn't want to tell them about Ella but I thought they might read about it in the papers (despite only reading the arts pages of the *Guardian*). Mum seemed to have trouble understanding the word 'murder'. 'Is she dead?' she kept asking. 'Yes, Mum. She's dead.' 'But she was such a lovely girl,' said Mum, not seeming to realise that lovely girls often do get murdered. Neither of them seemed to think about how it would affect me, one of my best friends and closest work colleagues killed. Dad said it was 'shocking' but in a way that seemed to close down the conversation. Mum said how sad but immediately started talking about arrangements for Christmas. I told her we'll just stay for one night. That's about as much as I can take and G is sure to want to see her friends on Boxing Day. Martin isn't even staying for that long. He thinks he'll be 'on call'. I swear he makes it up. He's been on call for the last five Christmases, by my reckoning.

I put the phone down feeling obscurely resentful, as I always do. But I've had a good few days, despite everything. Last night G's friend Tash came round and we all watched the Halloween *Strictly*. I did think about Ella then because I often used to text her during the show. But it was so nice, just the three of us and Herbert on the sofa, yelling insults at Craig and cheering on

Jonnie and Susan. The girls are merciless — 'they need more swivel in the cha-cha' — but I just love the whole thing, the glitz and the glitter, the big band renditions of pop songs. I did briefly wonder what Henry Hamilton would make of it. Probably far too low-brow for him although he wasn't the grey-bearded academic that I had imagined. Georgie said that he 'liked' me. Did I like him? I suppose I did a bit. He was attractive in an Abe Lincoln kind of way and it was nice to meet someone who had actually heard of Holland and seemed interested in him.

Georgie is out with Ty tonight. Nebulous plans, 'going to see some friends in Brighton'. No point in saying she can't go, though I did mutter about homework and made her promise to be back by ten because it's school tomorrow. It's ten o'clock now and I wish she would come in. At least Ty has a car and she's not shivering at a bus stop. But, on the other hand, a car brings all sorts of new worries. Ty could be drunk or on drugs for all I know. High on something, the modern equivalent of opium, like Wilkie Collins. Why am I still suspicious of Ty? OK, he's too old for Georgie but he seems sensible — he didn't drink on Friday night — and he's cleverer than I first thought. It's just, there's something *opaque* about him; I felt as if I wasn't seeing the real person behind the good-looking agreeable mask. But he's not the sort to drive under the influence of drugs. His parents died in a car crash, so he's probably a super cautious driver. Nevertheless, I can picture him swerving all over the coast road, music playing, Georgie laughing, neither of them looking where they're going. Shall I turn on the local radio or Google 'car crash West Sussex'? No. Thank God. There's her key in the door.

CHAPTER 6

I can sense the atmosphere as soon as I drive in through the school gates. There's still quite an impressive entrance left over from the Holland House days, with wrought-iron gates and stone lions on either side, but today the driveway is full of teenagers in blue sweatshirts, the girls with kilts rolled over at the waist to form strangely unflattering minis, the boys wearing black jeans in defiance of school rules. They move to let my car past but it seems to me that they stare more than usual, nudge each other and point. I can imagine them saying, 'There's Miss Cassidy. She was best friends with Miss Elphick.'

Georgie is almost horizontal in the front seat.

'Let me out here,' she says.

I stop and she leaps out of the car. Within seconds she is lost in the blue crowd. I drive on to the car park in front of the Old Building. Rick has called a department meeting before school today. He has to do this, I know, but I am dreading it. I collect my bag, crammed full of half-term marking, and walk quickly in through the main doors, not looking left or right.

The English staffroom is on the first floor of the Old Building, next to the library. It's hot in the summer and freezing in the winter but at least it has high ceilings and sash windows, unlike the science block which is in the basement and never sees natural light. But, today, when I push open the door, there's a pall of sadness and shock over the place. Vera and Alan are sitting on the sofa in silence, Anoushka is in tears and Rick stands hopelessly in the middle of the room as if he's just finished speaking. There's a stranger sitting in the blue armchair. I can't see his face but assume that this is the supply teacher brought in to cover Ella's classes.

When she sees me, Vera comes over and gives me a hug. It feels odd because she's so small, her head under my chin, the hair from her bun tickling my nose. Besides, we're not really a staff that does physical contact. We get on well and we go out for end-of-term meals but we don't do hugs, team bonding, talking about emotions. So it seems strange, standing there by the department noticeboard, with tiny Vera hugging me and Anoushka, who's only twenty-five, sobbing in the background. Eventually Vera lets go and we sit on the sofa beside Alan. He's not crying but his hands, holding an 'Old Teachers Never Die' mug, are shaking visibly.

'What's Tony going to do?' he says to Rick. 'Have a group therapy session?' Alan is old school and doesn't get on with Tony. His tone suggests that, whatever Tony does, it will be wrong.

'He's going to talk to the kids at assembly today,' says Rick. 'Counselling will be offered.'

'Counselling!' Alan snorts. But he liked Ella, I know. They shared lots of in-jokes and they also shared an open contempt for Tony and his new-age growth mindset culture.

'I think it's a good idea,' says Anoushka. 'The kids will be heartbroken. They loved Ella.'

'We're all heartbroken,' says Rick. 'But we've got to get through it somehow. Now, I'd like to introduce you to Don, who'll be covering Ella's classes this week. Don's got a lot of experience and we're lucky to have him.'

Don certainly looks as if he's had a lot of experience and not all of it good. He's probably in his fifties, with suspiciously dark, thinning hair and pouchy skin.

'I'm sorry to be here in such sad circumstances,' he says. He has a voice that the students will immediately classify as 'posh' and, most likely, 'gay' (however much I tell them that this is a sexuality and not an insult).

'Clare,' Rick turns to me. 'I'm making you head of Key Stage 4 with immediate effect. We'll meet later in the week to discuss GCSE predictions.'

Rick has already warned me about this so I don't have to do more than nod. It's a promotion really, but I certainly can't feel pleased about it.

'Vera will take over Key Stage 3,' says Rick. 'I know we'll all pull together at this difficult time.'

'Can we . . . you know . . . do something for Ella?' asks Anoushka. 'Plant a tree or establish a prize in her honour? Something to remember her by.'

'Tony's opening a book of condolence,' says Rick. 'Her parents want to hold her funeral here, in the chapel, so we can celebrate her life then. But it would be good to do something as a department. Let's think about it.'

'What about the play?' says Vera.

Ella was always in charge of the Christmas production. This year it's *Little Shop of Horrors*. Rick looks more wretched than ever.

'I did think about cancelling it but Tony thinks we need something to raise morale. Clare, do you think you and Anoushka could take it over?'

Anoushka perks up slightly. 'We'll make it a wonderful show in Ella's memory,' she says. 'Won't we, Clare?'

Suddenly, as clear as day, I see Ella standing in front of me, hands on hips, hair over her face. 'You've got my job,' she says, 'and you've got my play. Are you taking over my life?' The vision is so clear that I have to rub my eyes to get rid of it.

'Clare?' Rick is looking at me.

'Sorry,' I say. 'Yes, we'll put on the show in Ella's memory.'

'We'll never forget her,' says Vera. 'She'll always be with us.'

I'm starting to believe that this really might be true.

On the way out, Rick stops me. He looks terrible, I think: pale, red-eyed, a rash creeping up from his neck.

'How are you doing?' he asks.

'Oh . . . you know . . .' I'm always telling my Year 7s not to use 'you know' as punctuation but it comes in useful sometimes.

'Have you spoken to the police?'

'Yes, on Tuesday. They came to my house.'

'Did they . . .' Rick looks around the room as if he has been asked to mime the word 'furtive'. 'Did they mention Hythe?'

I stare at him. I can't believe he's asking this. 'No,' I say.

Rick runs his hand through his hair which is now standing up like a crest. 'If they do, please don't tell them about Ella and me. I know she confided in you. There were no secrets between you two, were there?'

Oh, there were plenty of secrets, I want to tell him. But, of course, I did know about the affair with Ella. If it can be described as such.

'What happened between you and Ella is your business,' I say. 'I've never told anyone.'

'Thank you,' he says. And I'm embarrassed to see the relief in his face. 'It's just . . . Daisy's very vulnerable at the moment.'

This strikes me as low, even for Rick.

'It was over,' he says. 'It was over between me and Ella back in the summer.'

Back in the summer is not that long ago and, before that, Rick was telling me that he'd kill himself if I didn't sleep with him. I'm surprised at the anger that suddenly surges through me.

'If you say so,' I say. 'I have to get to assembly now.'

'Clare . . .' Rick stretches out a hand but I evade it. As I leave the room I can hear his ragged intake of breath. It sounds as if he is crying.

There's nowhere in the school big enough for everyone to gather together so Tony speaks to the students in two separate assemblies. I go to the one for the Upper School, five hundred teenagers crammed together in the gymnasium with a basketball hoop hovering over Tony's head like a halo.

He does it well. He says that we'll never forget Ella and that our lives are better for having known her. He says that the way she died was tragic but we must remember the way she had lived and how she had brought light and laughter to the school. 'As you start out on your journey through life,' he says, 'remember Miss Elphick and the values she represented.' Next to me, Alan rolls his eyes at the word 'values' but a lot of the students are in tears and my own eyes are wet. As Years 9 to 11 file out, Alan says, 'I'm so sick of everyone being on a fucking journey. Why does no one ever arrive these days?'

'I thought it was OK,' I say. 'It's a hard thing to do.'

Tony steps down from the hastily erected podium and comes towards us. He's in his forties with a figure kept in check by constant exercise and dieting. Judging by the graffiti around the school, some of the students think he's 'hot'. There are also lots of plays on his surname 'Sweetman'. But, for me, his eyes are too close together and he smiles too much. However, he's not smiling now.

'Well done,' I say. 'That must have been tough.'

Tony rubs his eyes. 'It's a nightmare. I haven't slept for days. The police are coming in today. They want to talk to Ella's tutor group. I've had to get the parents' permission and a lot of them haven't given it.'

'Why not?' I say.

'You know what the parents round here are like. Some of them have first-hand experience with the police.'

He's right. This is a middle-class area but most of the well-off families send their children to private schools like St Faith's. Many of our students have what we call 'complex issues'.

'A lot of them have probably been victimised by the police,' says Alan, rising to the bait. 'Who can blame them for not wanting their children to be interviewed?'

'It's a murder investigation,' says Tony. 'You'd think they'd want to help.'

'Why?' says Alan. 'Why should they want to prop up the system?'

'Because their teacher has been killed.' Tony's voice rises and he looks round guiltily. 'Spare me the student Marxism, Alan.'

'It's quite traumatic being interviewed,' I say. 'I was surprised how upsetting I found it.'

'We've got counsellors standing by,' says Tony.

'For staff as well?'

Tony gives me a 'don't crack up now' look. 'Are you all right, Clare?'

'I'm fine,' I say. And I will be. I will have to be. 'I'd better get to my lesson now.'

My first class is with a group of Year 10s in their first year of GCSE work. We should be discussing *Of Mice and Men* but, inevitably, we end up talking about Ella. It's not fulfilling my lesson plan or learning objectives but it's surely what the students want and need.

'Miss Elphick was so nice to me when I first started at Talgarth.'

'Do you remember when she dressed up as Wonder Woman for the staff v students netball match?'

'Or when she sang "Somewhere Over the Rainbow" at the talent competition?'

'She was so pretty.'

'So kind.'

'Her hair . . .'

'Her voice . . .'

'She was the best teacher in this school.'

Did you tell her that when she was alive, I wonder. But I know that, in their earnest teenage way, they are genuine. At this moment, they do love Ella, do miss her, do think of her with sadness. But, as Tony said, they are at the very start of their lives. This will pass, as it should do. The present is what's important to this group of young men and women, red-eyed and sentimental as they are now. In a few years, maybe even a few months, they'll have trouble remembering Ella's name.

Eventually we get back to talking about Curley's wife. She was murdered too, I think, and Steinbeck doesn't even tell us her name.

'What's the significance of her red dress?' I ask them.

'Red for danger,' says someone.

'It's the colour of passion,' says someone else, earning them a few catcalls.

'She's all dressed up,' says Josh Brown, an earnest boy with glasses. 'Especially for someone who lives on a ranch. Maybe we're meant to think she leads men on.'

'What do you mean by "leads men on", Josh?' I say. I think of DS Kaur asking about Ella's boyfriends. This is what happens; a woman is murdered and people imply that, by having a sex life or being in possession of a dangerous pair of breasts, she contributed in some way to her own death. I'm sure that Ella had plenty of red dresses in her wardrobe but this does not mean that she deserved to die. I prepare myself for a discussion about responsibility and consent but am almost relieved when the door opens and a Year 7 girl appears. She's today's 'runner', a scheme designed to help the new pupils get used to the layout of the school.

The runner is small and scared-looking, with her hair in plaits. 'Isn't she sweet?' says one of the Year 10 girls, only three years older.

Plaits hands me a note.

'Police want a word,' it says. 'Can you come to my office at break? T.'

I hand it back. 'Tell Mr Sweetman I'll be there.'

DS Kaur and DS Winston are waiting in Tony's office, which they have clearly made their own. They have Styrofoam cups of coffee in front of them and there's a box of doughnuts on the desk, just like in the films. Tony has obviously been banished to his secretary's office. The connecting door is firmly shut.

'Hallo, Clare,' says Kaur. 'Thank you for coming.'

'As we're on first name terms,' I say, 'what's yours?'

She gives me a look. 'Harbinder.'

'Well, Harbinder, I haven't got much time. I have a class in fifteen minutes.'

You can tell it's break because the students are thundering up and down the corridors. They're meant to be outside unless it's raining, but discipline is obviously slack today.

'We'll be quick,' says Harbinder. She pushes a plastic envelope towards me. 'We've been looking at Ella's social media profile,' she says, 'and there are a few questions I'd like to ask you.'

Whatever I was expecting, it isn't this. What does she mean by 'social media profile'? I'm on Facebook, but that's it. I mainly use it for group chats—we even have an English department one. Georgie uses Snapchat and Instagram but I'd feel stupid sending pictures of my face (or my supper) out into the ether. I don't use Twitter, either, because I'm not famous or mad.

'In July, you and Ella went to a teacher training course in Hythe,' says Harbinder. 'Something happened there. We know that from her Facebook messages. What was it?'

So this is what Rick was talking about. The police know that something happened in Hythe. They might even know that Ella slept with someone but they don't have a name. I think about Curley's wife and the red dress.

I'm not going to help them. This isn't about Rick; it's about Ella. 'What do you mean?'

'We know something happened in Hythe that disturbed Ella,' says Harbinder. 'You were there, you were her friend. I thought you might know what it was.'

'No,' I say. 'It was just the usual training course stuff. You know.'

'No, I don't,' says Harbinder, straight-faced. 'Sussex police don't run to residential courses. What happened at Hythe?'

I know that I can't blink or look away. 'Nothing,' I say. 'It was the usual thing. Lots of talks, group activities, drinks in the evening.'

'Drinks?'

'Yes.' I keep my voice steady. 'There's a social side. People go out for drinks and meals.'

'Who did you go for drinks with?'

'Lots of different people.'

'Ella?'

'Yes.'

'And Rick? Your head of department?'

'Yes, once or twice.'

'Anyone else there from Talgarth High?'

'Anoushka. She was an NQT then.'

'NQT?'

'Newly Qualified Teacher.'

'In here,' Harbinder taps the pages, 'Ella mentions wanting to forget Hythe. What do you think she meant?'

I try to keep my face blank.

'I've no idea,' I say.

'She talks about Doctor Jekyll and Mr Hythe,' says Harbinder, still giving me the hard stare. 'What do you think that means?'

'A misspelling?' I suggest. I'm willing to bet that neither Harbinder nor DS Winston has read the book.

Harbinder ignores this. 'She says, "C knows". Is C you?'

'I don't know.' I have to look away now. I'm sweating and I hope they don't notice. Harbinder would probably just assume that I'm menopausal anyway.

Neil Winston speaks and it's almost a shock to hear his voice. He's got a flat estuary accent that sucks the drama out of his words.

'There was a note found by Ella's body,' he says.

I'm not expecting this. 'What did it say?'

Neil reads from his phone. '"Hell is empty". Does that mean anything to you?'

'It's a quote,' I say. 'From *The Tempest.*'

'What's the next line?' says Harbinder though I'm sure she's looked it up.

'Hell is empty,' I say, 'and all the devils are here.'

CHAPTER 7

It's a frantic day so I can't check Facebook until I'm home. I don't want to, anyway. I wouldn't have been able to concentrate with my colleagues around me, students knocking on the staffroom door, Vera asking earnest questions about coursework. But, as soon as I get in, I sit at the breakfast bar and open my laptop. Georgie is at Tash's, supposedly doing homework, and Herbert is still at Doggy Day Care (it's as expensive as childcare) and I don't have to collect him until six. My designer kitchen hums silently in the background as I find the little blue Facebook app.

I haven't looked at Ella's page since that first time. Maybe it won't be open anymore. Maybe there will just be a black square, RIP, nothingness. Maybe her parents will have done what Debra was suggesting and 'memorialised' it, so that her cyberself can live on although her corporeal body is dead. But, when I click on Ella's name, she's still there. Her profile picture was taken at last year's English department Christmas meal. Her hair is loose and she's wearing a paper hat that looks, in the light of Marini's Italian restaurant, like a Tudor headdress, studded with jewels. She is smiling and looking directly at the camera, slightly challenging, eyes wide. Who took the picture? I can't remember. In her 'photos' file, there's one of me on the same occasion. I'm not smiling and look rather angry, as I often do in repose. I've got a small head and paper hats never stay on so I look like the spectre at the feast. *Lay not that flattering unction to your soul, That not your trespass but my madness speaks.*

There are no photos of Hythe and I don't know how to scroll back as far as July on her timeline. Where did Harbinder find the comments she was mentioning? In Ella's supposedly secure Messenger app? In private messages to other people? I go onto my own page. I haven't posted since 2015 ('Lovely day for Georgie's 13th birthday. Suddenly I'm the mother of a teenager!') but I regularly send private messages and contribute to chats. My last message to 'When shall we three . . . ?', my chat group with Ella and Debra, was on the Sunday that she died. It says, 'Only four for that paso. Are they blind???' I've no idea who was dancing the *paso doble* but a bitchy comment about low-brow TV is hardly going to impress DS Kaur. Three question marks, too. I won't have written about Hythe on social media but I will have recorded it in my diary. I write almost every day and my journals fill a small, locked cupboard in my bedroom. I sometimes take the current book into work with me but the old volumes — the archives, I call them in my head — are locked away.

It's only five o'clock. I don't have to collect Herbert yet and Georgie won't be back for hours. I go into my room and the cupboard. The books are all there, different sizes and colours, but neatly stacked according to date. I started the current one in August so Hythe will be in the one before. It's a pale blue Moleskine, 'Jan to August 2017'.

I flick through the pages. 20th July 2017. Term had ended the day before, on the Thursday. There had been an end-of-term feeling in the air, I remembered. It was a beautiful day, the sea striped blue and green and dotted with sailing boats. I had driven to Hythe with Ella, windows open, singing along to the radio. Georgie was with Simon — they were going on what he insisted on calling a 'family holiday' to Cornwall the next day. But even that couldn't dent my spirits. Term was over and I had a weekend with my best friend and my favourite colleagues. The course interested me too, for all that it had a typical education-speak name that managed to mean nothing: Journaling for Writing. But I was enthusiastic. Next year the English department at Talgarth High would be a model of best practice.

At least that's how I think I felt.

21st July 2017

I've got a good room this year. King-sized bed, view of the sea, even a sofa that makes it a sort of suite. Ella has just texted to say that she's only got an ordinary double. 'So the orgy had better be at your place.' 'Ha ha,' I text back. Not much chance of an orgy but there's a drinks reception at six before the first twilight session. I wonder whether Paul from Stockport will be here this year. Ella will say I fancy him (that was what she was like in the car — wide-eyed teenager crossed with woman of the world) but it's just nice to have one male teacher who's not married or gay. Anyway, I've got a few hours in my room first. I love being in hotels on my own. I can watch *Antiques Roadshow,* drink speciality tea and eat biscuits. Think this weekend is going to be a good one.

Later

Ella really got on my nerves this evening. The sixth-form high jinks mood turned into manic flirtation accompanied by barbs aimed in my direction. 'Oh, Clare thinks we're making too much noise.' 'Clare doesn't approve of people having fun.' She annexed Paul from Stockport early on, sat next to him at dinner. I could hear their laughter floating down to my duller end of the table. I sat next to Rick, who seemed sunk in gloom.

The twilight session was OK. It was called 'Dear Diary' and it was about how writing every day improves your literacy, even if what you write is complete rubbish. 'Clare keeps a diary,' piped up Ella. 'Do you?' said Paul. 'I didn't think anyone did that except in Victorian novels.' Bloody cheek. I just smiled and said, 'Oh, I'm full of surprises', but inwardly I was seething.

Afterwards we walked along the promenade. Ella walked with Rick and I actually saw her take his arm at one point. I stopped to look at the sea and, by the time I turned round, they were almost back at the hotel. They hadn't even noticed that I wasn't there.

22nd July 2017

It's nearly midnight. Ella has just left my room. I can't quite believe what has just happened. She was manic again today but nicer to me this time. Too nice, in fact. Grabbing my arm, calling me her 'best mate', telling stories where we featured as the wild children of the English department. I was glad not to be in her working party when we split into small groups for the afternoon. Paul was in my group, as was Anoushka, and Louise and Beth, two nice teachers from Northern Ireland. We actually had a lot of fun and I was starting to enjoy myself again. Our group sat together at dinner and I saw Ella with Rick, a few tables away, talking very intently. Then they disappeared. I had a couple of drinks in the bar and went to bed. Ella tapped on my door a few minutes ago. Her hair was dishevelled and her eyes were twice their normal size. I wondered if she'd taken something.

Ella flung herself on my king-sized bed. 'I think I'm going to sleep with Rick,' she said. I just stared at her. Ella started going on about how they'd snogged on the beach 'like teenagers' and how it would be 'away-day sex', something that didn't count in the real world. 'But he's married,' I said. Ella said that Rick was mad about her, 'completely obsessed'. 'He says he's ill with me.'

It was him using the exact same words that did it for me. He'd said that to ME, only a few months earlier. 'I'm mad about you, Clare. I think about you all the time. I'm ill with you.' I remember thinking at the time what an ill-omened phrase that was. *Ill* with me. 'If you're ill, you need help,' that's what I told him. 'You're married,' I said, 'and I'm not going to sleep with a married man.' But I had been tempted. God knows why, but I was seriously tempted. Maybe that's why I got so angry with Ella. I shouted at her. Told her I thought she was behaving childishly and stupidly. She flung back that I was incapable of enjoying myself. 'Why don't you shag Paul? Or that barman who's been giving you the glad eye all weekend? Because you've always got to be better than everyone else. But you're not better. You're just boring.'

I was shaking when she left. I don't think I'll ever forgive her.

Or Rick.

I'm shaking again when I stop reading. I remember Ella's fling with Rick, of course I do. It only lasted for that weekend. Ella was bored with him by the end of it. I remember the long drive home through the rain, Ella laughing about Rick's earnestness, his lack of humour, his penchant for the missionary position. It seemed to rain for the whole of August, although the pictures of Cornwall on Georgie's Facebook page showed golden summer days, merry-go-rounds and kayaks, barbeques on the beach, and Georgie posing in a bikini with her half-brother Tiger in a fetching Boden beach robe.

Rick became a bit obsessed with Ella. Apparently he kept ringing her up, begging to see her, saying he'd leave his wife, the works. I despised Rick for that, remembering how only a few months earlier, he had been sitting outside my house, begging *me* to sleep with him. But what I didn't remember was that in Hythe, I had been so angry, so uptight, so *jealous*. I had thought it was stupid of Ella to have an affair with her head of department. After all, wasn't that what went wrong in her previous school? And I didn't set much store by Rick's declarations of undying love. But it was her business. Why the hell should I say that I'd never forgive her?

I look back at my diary entry, almost willing it to be different this time, and, as I do so, I notice something written at the very bottom of the page. Tiny letters, all in capitals.

HALLO, CLARE. YOU DON'T KNOW ME.

CHAPTER 8

Hallo, Clare. You don't know me. The words echo in my head all evening, as I chat to Georgie about Tash's new hairstyle and remind her that her history homework is due the next day. I offer Georgie some supper but she says she has eaten with Tash. Whenever Georgie refuses food, an alarm bell goes off in my head — 'anorexia alert!' — but although she's very thin (like me), she doesn't look unhealthy. Anyhow, I can't face food either. I take Herbert for a last walk along the road. There are only a few street lights for our fake street of town houses, otherwise the darkness of the countryside is all around. Cars are rare at this time of night so Herbert and I walk in the road, him teasing me by pretending to lift his leg on bushes and then thinking better of it.

Hallo, Clare. You don't know me.

Someone has written in my diary. I didn't recognise the handwriting. It was thin and spiky, written with what we used to call an italic pen. I keep thinking of that bit in *I, Claudius* where Caligula drives his father to madness and death by, amongst other things, writing his name on the wall in tiny letters. One letter less each day until, by the time that he got to the G in Germanicus, his father was dead. Who is my Caligula?

This isn't getting me anywhere. I have to think about who might have had access to the diary. It was with me in Hythe and I might have taken it into work a couple of times. But I'm always very careful not to write when anyone's watching. Even Georgie has never seen me writing in it. There's something rather strange and obsessive about keeping a diary. It's not exactly a secret but it's not something I would ever discuss, either. But Ella had known.

It's all there in the diary entry. 'Clare keeps a diary.' 'I didn't think anyone did that except in Victorian novels.' Could Ella have written it? On the one hand, it would be the sort of thing she would have thought funny (the past tense is becoming easier) but, on the other, it doesn't look like her handwriting, which was large, loose and flowing.

I also can't stop thinking about 'Hell is empty'. *The Tempest* is a set text for GCSE. I'm pretty sure Harbinder Kaur will have checked this and know that everyone in the English department is familiar with this line; it's what we call a 'key quotation'. But does Kaur know that it also comes into R.M. Holland's short story? If so, she must think that the note points to me. Can she seriously think that I was involved in Ella's murder? I remember her asking what I was doing on that Sunday night, whether anyone was with me. Did she, even then, have her suspicions about me? And they'd asked for a sample of my handwriting. Were they doing that with everyone? I'm becoming so paranoid that I actually start to wonder if my handwriting *was* on the original note.

Herbert finally has a wee and we go back into the house. Georgie is in her room, I can hear the *Friends* theme tune coming from her laptop. Simon and I were always determined not to let her have a TV in her room, but in her MacBook, she has a portable TV/cinema/CD player/camera/video recorder that she takes everywhere with her. I turn off the lights downstairs and double lock the front door. Herbert watches me, head on one side, as if wondering why I'm being so security conscious. Then I check the back door again and take my phone and handbag upstairs with me. Just in case.

In bed I look carefully through the pale blue diary but the mysterious handwriting doesn't strike again. I can't face looking in any other diaries. At 1997 ('Reader, I married him'), or 2002 ('Georgia May Newton was born today') or 2013 ('My divorce became final today. Dark, dark, dark'). Instead I get out my current diary and begin to write.

· · ·

The next day is Halloween and I have to hold my first after-school rehearsal of *Little Shop of Horrors*. I'm not keen on Georgie coming home to an empty house but don't want to spook her by saying so.

'I'll be late tonight,' I say, as we join the traffic at the roundabout. 'I've got a rehearsal.'

'Are you really doing the play?' Georgie looks up from her phone.

'Yes. With Miss Palmer. I'm dreading it.'

'I'm not surprised with Peppa Pig in it.'

Peppa Pig is what Georgie and her cronies call Pippa Parsons, the girl who has the main part of Audrey. Pippa is in Year 11, a tall blonde with an impressive singing voice and, yes, a rather porcine nose. She's always wheeled out to sing at prize-giving and carol services. Maybe this is why Georgie dislikes her.

'I don't know who you mean,' I say.

'Yeah, you do.'

'Anyway, you can go to Tash's if you like.'

'Tash is in it. She's in the chorus.'

'Stay and watch the rehearsal then.'

'No, you're all right. I'll collect Herbert and go home.'

'I don't want you walking back from Andy's in the dark.'

'Doggy Day Care, you mean,' Georgie always says this in a sing-song American accent. 'It's only ten minutes away. Along the main road.'

'Fine. Keep to the main road and don't put your headphones in. You need to hear if cars are coming.'

'OK, OK. Chill out, Mum.'

'You can have someone round if you want.'

'Mum, are you feeling OK? You never want me to have anyone round "on a school night".' She puts the phrase in ironical aural quotation marks.

'I just thought you might want some company. You might get trick-or-treaters round.'

'I'll tell them "trick". That'll fix them.'

'There are some sweets in the tin with the London bus on it.'

'That's OK, Mum. I can cope with a few kids dressed up as witches. I'll have Herbert to keep me company. And you won't be late, will you?'

'No, I won't be late,' I say.

We drive in silence the rest of the way.

You don't know me. I think about those words intermittently all day long. Luckily it's another manic one. Ella's classes are playing up for poor old Don and twice I have to 'pop in' to glare at people and restore order. I'm also grappling with the masses of GCSE data. I had always felt a bit miffed that Ella got Key Stage 4 while I was stuck with Key Stage 3 but, honestly, the amount of data checking that's required is driving me mad. It doesn't help that the government seems to change the GCSE specifications every few seconds. Their latest wheeze is to mark English and maths 1 to 9 instead of A* to E. 'This means I'll never get an A in English, Mum,' said Georgie, with mock sadness when she found out. I didn't let on that I'd shed actual tears over this fact.

The rehearsal starts at five, to give students the chance to go home if they want to. It also gives me an opportunity to do something I've wanted to do since the trip to Cambridge.

R.M. Holland's attic study has been left virtually unchanged since the day he died. It's kept locked but, as a senior teacher and the resident Holland expert, I have the key. I want to go up there after school finishes and have a look around. I've been there before, of course. We even give tours sometimes. But this time I want to have a proper look at the photographs. There are loads of them framed on the wall or mounted in silver on the desk. What if Mariana is in one of them? I'll take pictures on my phone and examine them when I get home. In my head, I imagine ringing Henry Hamilton, 'I've made a rather interesting discovery.'

After my last class, I walk quickly along the ground floor of the Old Building. It's usually quiet here after school, as most of the students stick to the New Building, where all the form rooms are. But today there are a few teenage witches and vampires hanging about, hoping to give some poor teacher a fright. In the light of Ella's death, Tony has banned any official Halloween activity (in previous years we've had non-uniform days or even, once, a ball) but the students are still over-excited and liable to be even sillier than normal.

'What are you lot doing here?' I say to the witches and vampires. 'Have you got after-school clubs?'

'No, miss,' says a giggling witch in a Harry Potter cape. Ashley Something. I taught her in Year 7.

'Well, go home then. Go and do some trick-or-treating.'

'Trick-or-treating's for kids,' says a deep-voiced vampire. Patrick O'Leary: Year 11, rugby player, trouble.

'Go and do your homework then. Try reading some set texts, Patrick. That might help in the mocks, you know.'

He laughs and ambles off, the others following him. I watch them until they go out through the front door and then I take the stairs to the first floor.

This floor is out-of-bounds after school but it's not unheard of for students to sneak up here. Today, though, it's quiet. In fact, it seems as if all the door-crashing, floorboard-thumping, football-pitch-shouting noises of the school have vanished altogether. There's a preternatural silence as I walk along. There's carpet here, unlike the parquet on the ground floor and the ghastly lino in the New Building. It's green, like moss, and it seems to cushion my footsteps. The doors are all shut and, like an exercise in perspective, the lines all point to the end of the corridor where the spiral staircase leads to R.M. Holland's study. And here is one of the oddities of the house: apparently Holland's wife Alice often used to go up to his office barefoot (naked, in some versions of the story) and, after she died, Holland had a special carpet made with the imprint of her feet on it. It's almost impossible to climb the stairs without putting your feet in those ghostly imprints. I've noticed before that they are just my size.

I pause at the foot of the stairs. Silence, somehow more oppressive than ever, swells around me. I reach for my phone, hoping for some comfortingly twenty-first-century chirrups, but I've left it in my office. Don't be ridiculous, I tell myself, you're in the school, you're a teacher, what could happen to you? I start to climb the stairs, placing my booted feet where Alice Avery once walked.

The door opens easily. In front of me is Holland's desk, his books on the shelves, his photographs on the walls. And, behind the desk, Roland Montgomery Holland himself, his arms outstretched in welcome.

Are you cold? The wind is getting up, isn't it? See how the snow hammers a fusillade against the windows. Ah, the train has stopped again. I very much doubt if we'll get farther tonight.

Some brandy? Do share my travelling rug. I always prepare myself for the worst on these journeys. A good maxim for life, young man. Always prepare yourself for the worst.

So, where was I? Ah yes. So Gudgeon and I, together with a third fellow — let's call him Wilberforce — approached the house. Three established members of the Hell Club provided us with blindfolds. They were masked, of course, but we knew some of them by their voices. There was Lord Bastian and his henchman, Collins. The third had a foreign accent, possibly Arabian.

Wilberforce was the first to don his blindfold. He set off, holding his candle and a box of matches, stumbling like a blind man towards the ruined house. We waited and we waited. The winter wind roared around us. Like this one, yes. We waited and, after what seemed a lifetime, we saw a candle flickering in the window embrasure. Very faintly, on the night air, we heard, 'Hell is empty!'

We cheered and our voices echoed against stone and silence. Bastian handed a candle to Gudgeon, together with a box of matches. Slowly Gudgeon removed his glasses and pulled the blindfold over his eyes.

'Good luck,' I said.

He smiled. Funny, I remember it now. He smiled and made a strange gesture with his hands, splaying them out like a shopkeeper advertising his wares. I can see it as clearly as if he were standing in front of me. Lord Bastian gave him a push and Gudgeon too staggered off over the frosty grass.

We waited and we waited and we waited. A night bird called. I heard somebody cough and someone else smother a laugh. I was breathing hard though I scarcely knew why.

We waited and, eventually, a candle shone in the window. 'Hell is empty!' Our answering cheers rang out.

Now it was my turn. I was handed the candle and matches. Then I pulled on the blindfold. Immediately the night seemed not just darker, but colder, more hostile. I didn't need Bastian's push to start me on my journey. I was anxious for it to be over. Yet, how long that walk seemed when you couldn't see. I became convinced that I was heading in the wrong direction, that I had missed the ruined house altogether, but then I heard Bastian's voice behind me, 'Straight ahead, you fool!' Stretching my hands out in front of me, I stumbled forwards.

My hands hit stone. I was at the house. Feeling my way along the façade I eventually reached a void. The doorway. I tripped over the doorstep, landing heavily on flagstones, but at least I was in the building. Inside, the wind was less, but the cold, if anything, more. And the silence! It echoed and re-echoed around me, seeming to weigh down on me, to press me close to the earth. I knew that I was bending almost double, like a beggar under his sack. I could hear my breathing, jagged and stertorous. It was my only companion as I inched towards the staircase.

How many steps? I had been told it was twenty but lost count after fifteen. Only when I stepped on a phantom stair did I realise that I was on the landing. I had thought that Gudgeon or Wilberforce might whisper a greeting but they were silent. Waiting. I edged forwards. I had to find the window and bring this pantomime to an end. My hands swept the plaster of the wall in front of me until . . . there! I found the wooden sill. I pulled off my blindfold and my cold fingers fumbled with a match to light the candle. Then I dripped some wax onto the sill and stood it upright.

'Hell is empty!' My voice sounded puny in my own ears. It was only then that I turned around and saw the dead bodies at my feet.

PART THE SECOND

Harbinder

CHAPTER 9

I disliked Clare Cassidy from the outset. She was too tall, for a start. Short dark hair, big eyes, long neck, legs that go on forever. The sort of woman who floats about in a dress that would be a tent on me. Even Neil was smitten. 'She looks like a model,' he said. 'In a really shit magazine,' he added, when he saw my face. He's not a bad sort, Neil.

That first day, when we drove into the school grounds, I knew that something was going on at Talgarth High. Didn't surprise me for a minute, knowing that place.

We sat in the car park in front of the Old Building. 'I just want to see it again,' I'd said to Neil. It was half-term so I thought it would be empty but I'd forgotten they do adult education classes there now. I saw people going in through the main doors carrying folders and art equipment. You wouldn't catch me doing schoolwork in my time off but there's no accounting for tastes.

'I still can't believe you came here,' said Neil.

'Well, I did,' I said. 'There's even a Harbinder Kaur wing.'

'Really?'

It's too easy with Neil. It really is.

'No, of course not. I barely got a handshake when I left. Here are your GCSE certificates. Now piss off.'

'But you went to uni.' Neil seemed pathetically anxious to prove that I wasn't an academic failure.

'Chichester. That hardly counts. I lived at home too.' That was my parents' proviso. I could go to university as long as I stayed at home and didn't do any of the things that students are meant to do: drink, do drugs, have sex. Didn't stop me doing them, of course, but it did mostly stop me enjoying them.

I stared up at the steps, the double doors, the rows of windows. There was more ivy than I remembered, red and green like a Christmas card. My mum used to say how beautiful this part of the school was ('like a private school, like Roedean') but there were still too many memories for me to see it clearly.

'What are we doing here?' said Neil, after a few minutes. 'We should be back at the station talking to Ella's parents.'

'I just want to imagine Ella here,' I said. 'Just for a minute. Indulge me.' I looked up at the windows one more time and saw someone looking down at me. White face, dark eyes.

Clare Cassidy.

I got the call at ten o'clock on Sunday night. Neighbours had heard sounds of an altercation at Ella Elphick's house in Shoreham. Uniform attended and found a woman, aged about forty, dead in the kitchen. She appeared to have multiple stab wounds.

CSI were already there when I arrived. Blue lights flashing in the dark street, an awning erected over the front door. Ella Elphick lived in one of those cute cottages behind the church. I could just imagine what the neighbours were making of it all. I put on a paper suit and tucked my hair into a cap. I wanted to see the body before the place became too full of white suits, taking photographs, kneeling on the floor to take samples of dust, calculating the arc of blood stains. I wanted a chance to see the scene as it was.

The small kitchen was already pretty full. One of the uniforms was there, pressed up against the back door, looking queasy, while a team of CSI crouched over the body. Ella was lying full length. It was one of those galley-type kitchens (quite nice; shiny white units, dark blue tiles) and she took up almost all of the floor space. Her hands were at her sides as if she'd been posed that way and there were cut marks on them, deep gashes on each palm.

There was blood everywhere — on her chest, in her hair, on the shiny kitchen units. I couldn't see her neck because of a CSI officer that was bent over her, but, from the colour of the blood, it looked like she had been stabbed in the throat. I looked at her feet. I once heard an actress say that when she was creating a character, she started with the feet. I would never say anything so wanky but I do always notice shoes. Ella was wearing pink Converse.

'DS Kaur.' I waved my ID over the hunched figures of the CSI team.

'PC Patel,' said the uniform by the door.

'Are you on your own?'

'My partner's outside.' He gestured, rather helplessly.

Being sick, I supposed. PCs are not used to this sort of stuff.

'Do you have an identity for the deceased?'

'Ella Elphick. She's a teacher at Talgarth High. Her lanyard's in her handbag.'

Even then, I thought this was a pretty bad sign. I don't go around telling people I was at Talgarth. There's something a bit embarrassing about staying in the area where you went to school. And it's even worse if you're still living at home at thirty-five, although only Donna and Neil know that. Three people at the station are old Talgarthians, as we would say if we were the sort of school that had an alumni association. But I'm the only one on the murder squad.

'Have you contacted next-of-kin?'

'No.'

So that would be a job for me.

'Meet me in the sitting room,' I said. 'Go out the back way, don't step over the body.'

The body. That's what she had become, with her blonde hair and pink trainers. I left the CSI people bending over her and went into the next room, which was just what I would have expected: bookcases, sofa with lots of cushions, candles and potpourri on every surface.

Neil arrived just as PC Patel appeared at the door. Neil looked bigger than ever in his white suit, like a polar bear, which — as we all know — are not as cute as they look.

'Murder?' he said.

'Unless she cut her own throat,' I said.

Patel looked pale despite being, like me, what the HR people would call a 'person of colour'.

'Looks like she was stabbed in the throat and chest with a kitchen knife,' he said. 'We found the weapon by the front door.'

'They left the weapon?' said Neil. 'That was stupid.'

'Or clever,' I said. 'Must mean there are no marks on it.'

'It looks like she tried to fight her attacker off,' said Patel. 'There are wounds on her hands.'

'We should check those carefully,' I said. 'They looked significant. The same wound on each hand. I think the cuts were made after death.'

'The stigmata,' said Neil. 'Like Jesus,' he added, for my benefit.

'Thank you, Neil,' I said. 'I may be a Sikh but I have heard of Jesus. Jewish carpenter, wasn't he?'

'OK, OK.' Neil turned to Patel. 'Anything else we should know?'

'There was a note,' said Patel. 'A Post-it, really. Left on the floor by her body.'

The murderer really is being kind to us, I thought. So many places where we can lift DNA — and handwriting to analyse, too.

'What did it say?' I asked.

'Hell is empty,' said Patel.

'What the hell does that mean?' said Neil, not seeming to notice the echo.

'Sounds like a quote,' I said. 'We can look it up. Have you got the Post-it in an evidence bag?'

Patel nodded.

'Any blood on it?'

'I don't think so.'

'That means the murderer must have written it before and had it ready,' I said. 'Otherwise there certainly would be. The kitchen is awash.'

At this unfortunate moment, Patel's queasy partner, a young female officer, made her appearance. She too was pale but she seemed in control. I told her to go through Ella's bag and find her next-of-kin.

'If her phone isn't locked, that's easiest,' I said. 'Look for "Mum" in "Contacts".'

'Jesus,' said Neil, who is softer than me. It comes of having children. 'The poor sods.'

I looked around the room. Most of the books seemed like classics — you could tell by the spines — but the TV was flat-screen and there was a pile of glossy magazines on the coffee table. So Ella didn't live her life on an entirely elevated plane. I wondered what she taught at Talgarth. English or art were my guesses. There were a couple of those geometric prints on the walls and no one buys those because they really like the look of them. I thought there had been a Tate Modern calendar in the kitchen too. A cup on the table by the magazines looked as if it had herbal tea in it.

'We need to seize that,' I said to Patel. I wondered what had happened. Had Ella been sitting here, sipping her tea and watching TV, when the killer rang the doorbell?

'Was the TV on when you got here?' I asked.

'No.'

And her phone had been in her bag. The female officer was going through it now. So Ella hadn't been scrolling through Facebook or playing Panda Pop (two of my favourite evening activities). There were no open books or magazines either.

'Do we know time of death?'

'We got here at nine,' said Patel. 'She was already dead but she was . . . you know . . . warm.'

'Have you spoken to the neighbours?'

'Not yet.'

'Go and do that now. Have you got the number for me?' I turned to the second officer. She nodded and handed me the phone. 'Thanks. What's your name?'

'Olivia. Olivia Grant.'

'OK, Olivia. You go with Patel and interview the neighbours. Find out exactly when they first heard noises coming from this house. Neil, you and I need to talk to Ella's friends and family.'

Neil didn't move from the sofa. 'Who put you in charge?'

'Let's assume I am,' I said. 'It'll make things easier.'

CHAPTER 10

Clare Cassidy's name came up quite early on. After I had spoken to Ella's mother — just telling her that there had been 'an accident' and getting the address so local police could go round and break the news — Neil and I went back to the station. DI Malone was the Senior Investigating Officer and she made me her deputy, as I had known she would. Donna can seem a bit flaky but she's decisive when she needs to be and she knows how to organise an investigation. She made this one a priority and we were given a fairly generous manpower and intel allocation. We also worked out a plan of action. We would tell Tony Sweetman, the head teacher at Talgarth, in the morning. We wanted to catch him unawares, to see his reaction. We'd also talk to Ella's key friends and colleagues. We had Ella's phone and applied to the service provider for a production order which would mean that we could search all her encrypted messages. I got home about midnight. Mum didn't wait up for me but it was a near thing. I just saw a swish of sari disappearing up the stairs as I unlocked the front door.

We were at Tony Sweetman's house at eight a.m. Neil had wanted to go earlier but I reckoned that eight would cause maximum disruption. It was half-term and I knew that he had young children. Sweetman lived in a very nice house on the outskirts of Steyning. I'd been trying to work out his salary. Talgarth has one thousand two hundred pupils so, after a quick shufti at TES ads, I thought he must be on a hundred thousand plus. Was that enough to buy The Old Rectory: honey-coloured stone, double garage, large garden? I didn't know but I intended to find out.

Sweetman himself answered the door. I'd looked at his picture online but, even so, I was surprised how young he was. Mrs Williams was the head in my day. She looked about a hundred then and she only retired three years ago, by which time she must have been on her last legs. Tony Sweetman was dark and fit-looking, wearing jeans and a rugby shirt. Not my type — even when I was still sleeping with men — but definitely good-looking for a teacher (not as damning as 'good-looking for a politician', but almost). He was also very suntanned for England in October. Skiing or was it too early in the year? Sunbed then. Either way it prejudiced me against him.

'Mr Sweetman? I'm DS Kaur from the Sussex police and this is DS Winston. Can we have a word?'

'What's this about?' Sweetman looked behind him rather distractedly. We could hear mingled sounds of dogs and children, counterpointed by the *SpongeBob* theme tune.

'It's urgent, I'm afraid,' I said. 'Is there anywhere we could talk privately?'

'It's a bit difficult . . .' He ran his hands through his hair, which was worn slightly too long for a white man, in my opinion. He was obviously proud of it though, he carried his head very high, as if balancing a football on top.

'It's important,' I said. 'We're from the murder squad.'

He gave me a horrified look and quickly ushered us into a small room that I took to be the study. There were educational textbooks on the shelves, as well as photographs of Tony in various rugby teams. What did his wife do, I wondered. Although the children were in evidence (music stands, a television with PlayStation remotes attached) there was nothing that indicated another adult's interests. Neil and I sat side-by-side on a futon/sofa thing. I was tempted to take the desk chair but thought that might look provocative so early on in an investigation.

Tony was having a whispered offstage conversation with someone. His wife? The nanny? An au pair? He appeared again in the doorway, looking more distracted than ever.

'Sorry,' he said. 'My wife's at work and it's half-term.'

'That's OK,' I said. 'We understand. I'm afraid we've got some bad news for you.'

He sat at the desk and swivelled himself to face us.

'I understand Ella Elphick works at your school.'

Tony's mouth fell open slightly. 'Yes,' he said.

'I'm sorry to tell you that Ella was found dead last night. We're treating her death as suspicious.'

I watched Tony closely. He did look genuinely shocked. The suntan seemed to fade and the hair was ruffled again.

'Ella? I can't . . . I can't believe it . . .'

'We want to talk to Ella's friends and colleagues as soon as possible,' I said. 'The first hours in a murder investigation are crucial.'

'Murder?' said Tony. 'Are you sure?'

'We're still at an early stage in our enquiry,' said Neil, in his best wooden manner, 'but, as DS Kaur said, we are treating Ms Elphick's death as suspicious.'

I got out my notebook. We'd do a recorded interview at the station later but I wanted Tony to know that I was taking notes.

'So,' I said, 'Ella taught English at Talgarth High.'

'Yes.' Tony seemed to be trying to pull himself together. 'She's been at Talgarth for about five years. She's an excellent teacher.'

'How long have you been head teacher?'

'Three years. I brought the school out of special measures.'

'Congratulations,' I said, to let him know I thought this was a touch inappropriate.

'I didn't mean . . .'

'Was Ella popular with her colleagues?' asked Neil.

Tony looked appalled. 'Everyone loved her. You can't think . . .'

Don't tell us what to think, I told him silently. Aloud I said, 'Can we have a list of everyone in the English department and anyone who was a particular friend of Ella's?'

'Of course,' said Tony. 'I'll do it for you now. She had lots of friends on the staff.'

'Who were her closest?'

Tony looked up to the left, the way you do when you are meant to be remembering. Or he may have been looking at a helium balloon with an eight on it, which was stuck to the ceiling.

'Clare Cassidy,' he said at last. 'She teaches English too. They started at the same time. And Debra Green in the history department. The three musketeers, I called them.' He smiled sadly at this remembered witticism.

'Can we have their contact details?' I said, scribbling in the book.

'I'll get them for you. They're all on file.'

'Did Ella have a boyfriend?' said Neil.

'Not that I know of. Rick Lewis is head of English. He'll be devastated.'

'Have you got an address for Mr Lewis?'

'I'll get it.' Tony opened the laptop in front of him and started scrolling through it. He used his thumb only, like a teenager. I bet Mrs Williams had never even *seen* a laptop.

'How did Ella seem when you last saw her?' I asked. 'Any worries or concerns?'

Tony kept his face turned to the screen. 'She seemed fine. Looking forward to half-term. You know how tired teachers get.'

You may get tired, I thought, but you also finish at three and have long holidays. Police officers work long hours, for not much pay, and you don't see many of us with an October suntan. But I made sympathetic noises, 'Must be a tough job.'

'Getting tougher all the time,' said Tony, taking the bait obediently. 'We have so many targets to achieve. We also have to be on top of safeguarding, pupil premium, exam predictions. It's right that we're accountable but it's a terrible strain sometimes.'

'Did Ella find it a strain?'

Tony immediately started to backtrack. 'Oh, Ella was always completely on top of things. The English GCSE specs changed last year and that led to a lot of extra work. But Ella had it all under control and we had our best ever results in the summer. She was head of Key Stage 4. That's GCSE,' he explained. I was more interested by how easily he had slipped into using the past tense. I may only have achieved a B in GCSE English but I notice tenses.

• • •

I parked in the lane, out of sight of the house, and Neil and I had a brief discussion.

'What did you think of him?' I asked.

'A bit smooth. And how can he afford a house like that?'

'His wife's a lawyer.' Tony had vouchsafed this piece of information on the way out. 'They both earn well.'

'And leave a foreign au pair to look after their kids,' said Neil, with all the disapproval of a man with an eighteen-month-old baby and a wife at home.

'I'll have an au pair if I ever have kids,' I said. '*And* a nanny and a wet-nurse.' Neil laughed, though whether at the idea of me having kids or me with the money to pay for childcare, I didn't know.

'What now?' said Neil. 'We should ask the FLO if we can see the parents.'

A Family Liaison Officer had accompanied the Elphicks to the morgue last night, where they had identified Ella's body. They were now staying in police accommodation nearby. Neil was right, we should do a formal interview with them.

'Let's see Rick Lewis first,' I said. 'He's only about a mile away.'

'Why?' said Neil, putting on his stubborn face.

'Because of what Tony said about boyfriends.'

'He said Ella didn't have one.'

'Yes,' I said, 'and he mentioned Rick Lewis immediately afterwards.'

Rick Lewis' house was an end of terrace in Shoreham. Definitely a step down from the Sweetman mansion but a pleasant family house all the same. Rick, a tall man in a polo-neck jumper, opened the door.

I showed him my warrant card and asked if we could have a word. A woman joined him on the doorstep. She was fortyish, plump but pretty in one of those dress/trouser combinations that plus-size women favour.

'What's going on, Rick?'

She sounded panicky. Interesting.

'We've got bad news about a member of your department,' I said. 'Is there somewhere we could talk?'

'Oh God,' said Rick Lewis. 'Is it Clare?'

Very interesting.

We told them together. It wasn't worth insisting on a private chat at this stage and besides, Daisy, the wife, interested me. Why was she so upset? When I told Rick about Ella she let out a little scream and covered her face with her hands.

'I can't believe it,' said Rick. 'I only saw her on Friday. God, her parents will be devastated.'

I asked Rick about Ella's state of mind but got the same answers: fine, a bit tired, looking forward to half-term. I also asked Rick what he had been doing on Sunday night. A quick glance at Daisy and he said, 'We were in, watching TV. A take-away, a bottle of wine, *Strictly Come Dancing*. That's our Sunday night ritual.'

'Very nice,' I said. Tony's alibi had been the same, albeit with a whole-some family meal rather than a take-away. But it appeared that, despite a house that screamed 2.4 children, the Lewises were childless. Was this by choice, I wondered. Maybe it explained the couple's closeness. They were practically sitting on the same chair.

On the way out, while Neil was talking to Daisy about Southern Rail, I asked Rick how he had got on with Ella.

'Very well,' he said. 'She was a beautiful person.'

He meant her character, I know, but I'd seen pictures and knew that Ella *was* rather beautiful, if you like tall, slim women with long blonde hair, which sadly quite a lot of people do. Either way, it was an interesting choice of adjective. *You see,* I told Miss Cathcart, my old English teacher, in my head. *I can do grammar too.*

It was as we were driving away that I told Neil I'd gone to Talgarth High. He was flatteringly surprised.

'I wouldn't have guessed.'

'Why not? It's the local comp.'

'Still, it's a bit of a shit-hole, isn't it? I'd want better for Lily.'

Jesus, the child wasn't even two yet but they were already planning schools.

'My parents didn't know any better,' I said. 'We all went to Talgarth and we've all done OK.'

Kush works at the shop and Abid is an electrician. My brothers have five children between them and both still wear their turbans. As far as my parents are concerned, this is an outstanding success. The less said about me, thirty-five and unmarried, doing what Mum calls a 'man's job', the better. If they knew I was gay, that would finish them off altogether.

'Let's go to Talgarth now,' I said. 'On our way back. Just to have a look at the place.'

CHAPTER 11

We didn't get to see Clare Cassidy until the second day. I toyed with the idea of turning up at her classroom just as she finished teaching, but then I decided that I'd like to see her in her home environment. However, I was surprised when we pulled up outside the house. I'd always wondered who would live in this row of houses, so close to the old cement works. Now I had my answer.

'Bloody hell,' said Neil. 'I wouldn't live here for a million pounds. You know what they say about this place?'

'I've heard a few versions,' I said.

'It's haunted. Did you hear about the child who fell in the cement? Apparently you can still hear her crying at night. And —'

'Yes, all right,' I said. 'It was similar at school. Everyone told the same ghost story, about a woman who fell down the stairs in the Old Building. A woman in white, floating along the corridors. She was meant to appear when someone died.'

'Wonder if she appeared on Sunday night then.'

'We can ask Clare,' I said. 'Here she is now.'

I watched her approach. Black Renault Clio, very much what I'd expect her to drive. She parked behind us at the kerb and got out of the car. Just the sight of her annoyed me. She was wearing black jeans and a grey knitted top. Sounds basic but the trousers were tight and tucked into knee-high boots and the top was cashmere, the sort of drapey affair with an attached scarf that would look ludicrous on me but, I'm sorry to say, looked very good on Clare. She had a carrier bag in one hand and got a holdall (Cath Kidston, I recognised it from the catalogue) out of the boot. Then she opened the passenger door. A small white dog jumped out, barking wildly.

I've got nothing against dogs but I like them to look like dogs. My parents have a German Shepherd called Sultan. He's meant to guard the shop but, in reality, he sleeps on their bed and gets treated like a son (and rather better than their daughter). It annoys me sometimes but at least Sultan is a beautiful creature, a prince among animals. This barking white furball was just an irrelevance.

As I approached, the dog made a beeline for my black trousers. Clare pulled him away rather ineffectually. I introduced myself and asked if I could have a word. Clare gave me a sharp look before apologising for the still-salivating animal, which was apparently called Herbert.

'It's OK,' I said, brushing my trousers down. 'I like dogs.'

The house was quite nice inside, the sitting room painted that fashionable colour between grey and blue, white bookshelves, wooden floors. I could see that Neil was impressed. Clare offered us tea. She had a low voice — not posh exactly, but very much what you'd hear on Radio 4 announcing some financial disaster. I could see that Neil was impressed with her too. He asked for tea with two sugars and Clare smiled patronisingly. Then she drifted away, but not before I'd heard her carrier bag clanking. Someone was planning to drink alone that evening.

I could hear the dog barking from the kitchen. That's the worst of small dogs, the constant background noise. When Sultan barks, you know it's important. I looked at the photographs on the mantelpiece. Clare with a teenage girl, tall and thin like her but with long, dark hair. The teenager with Herbert. Herbert on his own. A flyer for a baroque music concert. A card from someone signing themselves R.

'She's coming back,' said Neil.

Clare put the tea and biscuits on a low wooden table. It reminded me of Ella's house, of her single cup of herbal tea.

'We're investigating the murder of Ella Elphick,' I said. 'I understand that you've been informed about this?'

She nodded, blinking slightly. She had huge eyes and used them to great effect. Perhaps I'm being unfair. Presumably she *was* upset. 'Yes,' she said. 'Rick, my head of department, phoned me yesterday.'

'I'm sorry. I know it must be an awful shock for you, but we want to talk to all of Ella's friends and colleagues as soon as possible. We want to try to get a picture of her life so that we can work out who would have done this awful thing.'

Clare's eyelashes fluttered; she looked at Neil and then at me. 'I thought…'

'What did you think?' I said, unhelpfully.

'I thought — I assumed … that she was killed by a stranger. A random attack. A robbery gone wrong.'

'Most murder victims are killed by people they know,' I said, deliberately keeping my voice as matter-of-fact as possible, 'and we have reason to believe that this is the case here.'

I stopped to let this sink in. I wasn't going to tell her about 'Hell is empty' yet, but I'd looked it up and knew it was from *The Tempest,* which was a GCSE text that year. Ella, Clare and Rick all taught GCSE English.

Pulling out my notebook, I asked her if she taught with Ella.

'Yes. We both teach English. Taught. Oh God.'

She, at least, noticed the change in tense. She took a deep breath, calming herself. Herbert put a paw on her leg. It was quite sweet really.

She explained that she was head of Key Stage 3 and Ella was head of Key Stage 4; there were six people in the English department and they all worked closely together. I asked her if she got on well with Ella. She said that she did and that they socialised outside work. She'd last seen Ella on Friday night when they went to the cinema and a meal with Debra Green, who taught history at Talgarth. I remembered Tony's remark about the three musketeers. Clare seemed nervous, even answering these routine questions, so I let Neil butt in with some film chat to try to set up a rapport. After all, he was the one who had asked for a cup of tea. This, according to the psychologists, meant that they already had some sort of relationship.

I asked if she'd heard from Ella on Sunday and she said that she'd texted about the *Strictly* results but didn't get an answer. I loathe *Strictly Come Dancing,* all those intelligent, successful women putting on sequins and embracing their 'girly side'. It makes me feel sick. I was willing to bet that Clare Cassidy had done ballet as a child. She looked just the type. She probably gave up when she got too tall.

Clare claimed to be in all evening, watching television and preparing for her creative writing course. Her daughter, Georgia, was in the house but — in true teenage style — shut away in her room most of the time. Georgia was with her dad for a half-term visit, due back tomorrow. So Clare was divorced. I could have guessed as much from looking at the room. No man would put up with all those scented candles.

She seemed much more relaxed now, leaning back in her chair, legs crossed at the ankle. I looked at Neil and tried for a conversational tone. 'What sort of woman was Ella?'

Clare seemed to pause for a long time before answering. She looked up and to the left. She uncrossed her legs and crossed them again, shifting slightly away from us. Herbert whined softly. A mobile phone buzzed somewhere in the background.

'She was a lovely person,' said Clare at last. 'Very intelligent, a lot of fun. Everyone liked her. Ella was a great teacher. The kids loved her. They'll be devastated when they find out . . .'

'Did Ella have a boyfriend?' I asked, before she had time to consider her answer.

'Not that I know of.'

An odd answer and, incidentally, the same reply given by Tony Sweetman. 'Any exes?' I said, once again trying for the chummy tone.

'In the past. Nobody recent.'

'Did she talk about anyone in particular?'

'She mentioned someone from her old school in Wales. Bradley Something.'

I made a note. 'And she never mentioned anyone bothering her? Stalking her on Facebook? That sort of thing?'

'No,' said Clare, looking at us rather defiantly.

There was more that I wanted to ask Ms Cassidy, but first I wanted to look at Ella's social media records. There was something there, I thought: Ella, Clare, Rick, Tony. Something was going on in my old school. *Hell is empty and all the devils are here.*

'Thank you,' I said. 'You've been very helpful.'

It was on the way back to the station that Neil made the remark about Clare looking like a model. He backtracked immediately but, as we drove through the endless series of roundabouts on the approach to Chichester, I reflected that he had a point. Surely it was unusual to have two such gorgeous women on the staff of a secondary school? Thinking back to my own days at Talgarth High, all the teachers had seemed ancient and dowdy in the extreme. Miss Cathcart had an incipient moustache and smelled of mingled sweat and talcum powder. Clare Cassidy had worn Jo Malone English Pear and Freesia — I'm very good at perfume.

Could Clare Cassidy and Ella Elphick have incited the male staff to passion, or even to murder? I mentioned this thought to Neil.

'Tony Sweetman and Rick Lewis are both married,' he said, wincing as I overtook on the inside. We take turns with the driving and he's much more cautious than me.

'What's that got to do with anything?'

'Do you really think one of her colleagues could have killed her? That was a brutal murder.'

'Stabbing is passionate,' I said. 'Someone got up close to kill her. That argues strength of feeling. Not to mention they already had that neat little Shakespeare quote to hand.'

'I never understood Shakespeare.'

'That's why you're a copper,' I said, though, to be honest, I had quite enjoyed some of the plays, even when taught by Miss Cathcart. *Macbeth*. Now there's a good murder story.

'And don't forget,' I said. 'Ella had a relationship with a colleague before. Clare mentioned him just now.' Her parents had told us about Bradley Jones yesterday. He was Ella's head of department when she was teaching in Wales. Ella and Bradley had an affair which had, in Ella's mother's words, 'ended badly'. We were going to see Jones tomorrow.

'So Ella had an affair with Tony or Rick, Clare got jealous and stabbed her,' said Neil. 'Doesn't stack up to me.'

'Remember what Rick said? "Is it Clare?" Something is going on there.'

'You just don't like her,' said Neil.

'I don't like or dislike her,' I said. 'I just think she's hiding something.'

CHAPTER 12

We learned a lot more about Ella Elphick over the next few days. She was born in Surrey in 1977, educated at a girls' grammar school, read English at Exeter, then travelled in the Far East and worked in Japan for a while. After five years abroad, she came home and did a teacher training course. She received glowing reports from her tutors and from her first work placement. Ella worked at a secondary school in Plymouth before moving to Cardiff as head of Key Stage 4 ('a mistake', said her mother). We didn't have the CSI reports from the scene yet and the neighbours hadn't been particularly helpful. They had heard raised voices on Sunday night ('a man's voice', someone said, but they didn't seem too sure) and no one had spotted a visitor approaching Ella's cottage. There were CCTV cameras outside the church but between the hours of six and ten the footage was spectacularly dull: the vicar, a man walking his dog, two teenagers immersed in their phones.

The post-mortem showed that Ella had died from stab wounds to the neck and chest. As I'd thought, the wounds on her hands had been inflicted after death.

'The stigmata,' said Donna. 'Maybe our killer was a religious maniac. The note mentioned hell too.'

'It was a quote,' I said. 'I think that's the significance. A quote from a play that Ella taught at school.'

'Do you really think that the killer could be linked to Talgarth?' said Donna, with a sly glance at me. 'Your alma mater?'

'I don't think a crap comprehensive can be an alma mater,' I said. 'It was just my old school. But . . . I don't know, there's something there. The head teacher, the head of department, even Clare Cassidy. They all seemed nervous, as if they were hiding something.'

'Ella's killer got up close,' said Donna. 'That implies that passion was involved.'

That was true. The police sometimes talk about 'distantiation', the theory that it's easier to shoot than stab because you can be distanced from your victim. Think of drone attacks. I'm sure the operators don't feel like killers and yet they are. Ella's killer had got near enough to stab her where it would do the most damage, which argued that they were cold and fearless. Or that Ella knew them well.

On Wednesday we drove to Cardiff to see Bradley Jones, a good-looking but oddly ineffectual man who spent most of the interview telling us that Ella 'came on to him' and that she 'made all of the running'. Not one expression of condolence or regret. Sadly Jones had an alibi for Sunday night. He had been watching his daughter, Sadie, in a ballet show. What is it with bloody dance? On Sunday night it seemed that everyone in the country was either dancing or watching other people dance. Regardless, it would have been impossible for Jones to have watched his daughter perform in Wales at eight o'clock and then travelled to Sussex to kill Ella before ten. Sadie had only been a baby when Jones had slept with Ella but this too was somehow her fault. 'I was so tired from all those sleepless nights,' he tried a man-to-man smile with Neil, 'I just couldn't resist.' I'm pleased to say that Neil just stared at him stonily.

'Scumbag,' he said on the way home. 'He didn't even say that he was sorry that she was dead.'

'Ella had bad taste in men,' I said. 'That may be significant.'

Ella had left Cardiff for Talgarth High, where she was head of Key Stage 4 again. A sideways move but she had seemed happy there, according to her parents. Was Key Stage 4 better than Key Stage 3, I wondered. Was Clare Cassidy jealous that Ella had the better job? Maybe, but it was hard to imagine Clare stabbing her colleague to death over a few points on the pay scale. They were both well-liked, well-respected teachers, we knew that.

At the end of the week we received Ella's social media records. She was on Facebook as Ella Louise (presumably to stop students finding her profile page) and also on Twitter as @lizziebennet77. I had to explain that one to Neil. 'She's a character from *Pride and Prejudice*.' He said that Kelly had seen the film. It was interesting that Ella saw herself as Elizabeth Bennet, feisty and attractive, refusing to marry the boring clergyman, holding out for Mr Darcy. For all that, her Twitter feed wasn't very interesting — she mostly retweeted left-wing stuff and pictures of cats. Her Facebook records were more illuminating. They showed that she kept in touch with her old school friends Megan and Anna, that she messaged her mum every day and that she liked the Labour Party, John Lewis and videos of small animals behaving cutely. There was also a flurry of WhatsApp messages to Megan over the summer mentioning 'what happened at Hythe' and, once, 'Doctor Jekyll and Mr Hythe'. It seemed that Ella had done something she regretted whilst on a training course at Hythe ('I wish it had never happened') but that she hoped to keep it quiet ('Thank God it's the holidays now. C knows but she won't tell').

'Clare Cassidy?' said Neil, who was reading over my shoulder.

'Maybe. Wonder who Doctor Jeykll was?'

'Must have been someone at the school if they were on the same course. Rick Lewis?'

We contacted Megan (a chiropodist living in Leeds) and she admitted that Ella had told her that she had slept with 'someone from work' and regretted it immediately afterwards. Frustratingly, Megan couldn't come up with a name. A phone call to Tony Sweetman confirmed that four members of the English department had attended a course on 'Journaling for Writing' in Hythe at the end of the summer term. They were Rick Lewis, Ella Elphick, Clare Cassidy and Anoushka Palmer.

We were going into the school on Monday to talk to staff and students but we decided to call Rick into the station on Saturday. He seemed the most likely candidate to have had an affair with Ella, although — as Neil kept reminding me (with a hopeful leer) — 'we shouldn't ignore the gay angle'. The Gay Angle sounded like a pub in Brighton and, while I was the last person to assume people were straight, Ella and Clare had been resolutely heterosexual up till now. It wasn't impossible that they'd had a one-night stand in Hythe but I thought it was unlikely.

We ushered Rick into Interview Room 1. Donna was watching through the two-way mirror. If Rick had looked nervous at his house, he looked really anxious now. He wasn't bad-looking, though, tall and thin with horn-rimmed glasses that probably made him seem cleverer than he was. It wasn't out of the question that Ella could have had an affair with him.

At first Rick tried to impose his authority on the proceedings, rather as if we were an unruly Year 8 English class.

'What's all this about?' he kept saying. 'I'm a busy man.'

'Just a few questions,' said Neil soothingly. I was keeping quiet. I knew that Rick Lewis was wary of me and wanted to keep him on his toes.

After we'd gone through the formalities, I said, 'Tell us about Hythe, Rick.'

He stared at me over his glasses. I could see one leg jiggling under the table. 'What?'

Don't say 'what', say 'pardon', my mum would say, although somehow 'pardon' turns out to be unforgivably common.

'We know something happened between you and Ella in Hythe,' I said. 'Why don't you tell us about it in your own words, so we can get the record straight.'

I pictured Donna on the other side of the window. Accuse, sympathise, offer alternatives. That's what they tell you at police training school. I was probably doing it in the wrong order.

'Nothing happened,' said Rick. Jiggle, jiggle.

We both waited.

'It was a course at the end of term,' said Rick. 'Everyone let their hair down.'

'Ella slept with someone at Hythe,' I said, 'and we think it was you.'

'It wasn't,' said Rick, clearly trying to keep his temper. 'I'm a married man.'

'What about Clare Cassidy?' I say.

He stopped fidgeting and went suddenly completely still. 'What about Clare?'

'What's your relationship with Clare?'

'We're colleagues, friends. That's all.'

'She's a good-looking woman,' said Neil, all laddish chumminess.

'Is she? Yes. I suppose she is.'

'Ella Elphick too.'

'Yes.'

'What will Clare say if we ask her about your relationship with Ella?' I said.

Rick seemed to control his voice with an effort. 'She'll say we were friends because that's the truth.'

He wouldn't budge after that. It was frustrating but it's a long game. We told him he was free to go.

On Monday we went into Talgarth High. It was the first time I'd been inside since the day I collected my GCSE certificates. The smell was exactly the same: floor polish mixed with feet. We signed in at reception (a new innovation since my day, they didn't worry as much about safeguarding in the nineties) and a pigtailed girl with a badge saying 'Runner' led us along the corridor to the head teacher's office. This part of the school hadn't changed at all; it seemed as if the same pieces of art were on the walls, the same laminated signs asking people to sign up for the Christmas play (*Little Shop of Horrors* — ha!) and not to run on the stairs. The photos of pupils opening their exam results — Talgarth's Best Ever GCSE Results! — were new though. My GCSEs had been quite good, better than either of my brothers', but no one made a song and dance of it. Certainly I was never photographed with a beaming head teacher, holding that dreaded typewritten slip up to the camera. I was quite academic when I was at Talgarth. Things went downhill for me at the sixth-form college, although I managed to scrape together enough UCAS points to get to Chichester. There are no photos of me on A-Level results day either.

But, walking along that corridor with its parquet floor, panelled walls, and high ceilings, it seemed almost impossible that, turning the corner, I wouldn't run into my twelve-year-old self, my hair in long plaits, wearing a navy-blue blazer, my tie ragged where I had chewed the end. The uniform *has* changed since my time; it's sweatshirts now, no blazer, no tie. Practical but not very smart. Mind you, my brother Kush always wore a leather jacket instead of the blazer and I don't remember anyone telling him off. Kush was always cool, which was handy for me, because I wasn't.

We passed the double doors to the chapel, now firmly closed. Mrs Elphick had told us that she wanted to have Ella's funeral there. I hadn't been inside since I snogged my first boyfriend, Gary Carter, behind the choir stalls. Past the main stairs, where, on certain nights, you can see the woman in white floating through the air like thistledown. I saw her myself once, though she was less ethereal and more like an avenging angel. But I wasn't about to tell Neil this.

'This is quite smart,' said Neil, craning his head to look up the winding staircase.

'You should see the modern building,' I said. 'It was falling down, even in my day. We had to put buckets along the art corridor when it rained.'

'We still do,' piped up our guide unexpectedly. 'And there's mould growing in the science labs. Actual mushrooms.'

'Handy for home economics,' I said, before realising that they probably didn't do HE anymore. The girl looked confused and didn't speak again. She left us at a door saying 'Mr Sweetman, Head Teacher' and clattered away in her heavy school shoes, as fast as she could go without running.

We had planned to see Ella's form group that morning. At Talgarth High, teachers stayed with the same class throughout their entire school career, which meant that, although they only saw their students at the beginning and the end of the day, by Year 11 they knew them pretty well. Ella's form was 11EL which meant that Ella had had them for five years, since they joined the school in Year 7. The students might well be useful witnesses but we had to go very gently. We'd had to get permission from all the parents and Mrs Francis, the deputy head, was going to sit in on the interviews, acting as 'appropriate adult'.

'They're not children though,' Neil had said on the drive in, 'they're sixteen and some of the boys are as big as me. They could easily overpower a slim woman like Ella.'

'As far as we're concerned today, they are children,' I said but I knew that Neil had a point. It wasn't impossible that one of her students could have had a crush on Ella and reacted violently when rejected. It wasn't a theory I was going to express openly though.

Tony and Mrs Francis (Liz) met us in his office. We'd asked to do the interviews there, partly because it was separate from the main part of the school and partly because the room itself had gravitas. It was the head teacher's office and I hoped that, even in these lax sweatshirt-wearing times, it still had a certain power.

We'd brought coffee from McDonald's and I saw Tony looking at the Styrofoam cups with disapproval.

'I've asked my secretary to make us some proper coffee,' he said.

'Have a Dunkin' Donut.' Neil proffered the box.

Tony shuddered. 'No thank you.'

I liked Liz Francis. She was older than Tony, no-nonsense in a navy-blue suit and flat shoes, she had a humorous face, as if she'd seen it all before and didn't take any of it too seriously. She took a doughnut, remarking that, as it contained jam, it counted as one of her five a day.

'Remember our Healthy Eating Charter, Liz,' said Tony, only half-joking.

Tony explained that he was talking to all the students at assembly that morning. 'They will probably all know about Ella,' he said, 'you know how news travels these days. But I think it's best that they hear it from me.' He sounded sincere but also rather self-important.

'We'll start seeing the students afterwards then,' I said. Liz had copies of the students' timetables (as they were in Year 11 they were all doing different subjects) and had prepared a schedule for us. But, as soon as the teachers had left, I turned to Neil. 'Let's see Clare again. Ask her about Hythe.'

'She'll be teaching.'

'Let's see her in break then. That'll rattle her.'

Neil sighed. 'I don't know why you've got it in for her.'

'I haven't,' I said.

We saw the students from 11EL one at a time, with Mrs Francis present. We asked them all the same questions.

1. How did you get on with Miss Elphick?
2. Do you know of anyone who didn't get on with Miss Elphick?
3. Is there anything else you'd like to tell us?

The students all said that they liked Ella. Their tributes ranged from 'she was all right', with a shrug, to 'I loved her', eyes brimming with tears. I didn't take too much notice of the brimming. Liz Francis had told us that the students were over-excited today. 'It's the first day back after half-term. Their teacher has just been killed. They're genuinely upset but also some of them will be enjoying the drama of it.' She smiled. 'And it's Halloween tomorrow which always gets them worked up.' I loathe Halloween. Mum always has loads of sweets by the door in case kids come trick-or-treating but they mostly ignore our house because one, we've got a big dog and two, we're foreign and 'dress funny'.

Ella's pupils didn't seem exactly over-excited. Some of them were emotional, some were nervous and some acted as if being interviewed by the police was all part of a day in the life of a bored teen. No one could think of a person who didn't get on with Ella and no one had anything significant to tell us. We'd sent the runner with a message for Clare and, at break time, she appeared, looking haughty and disdainful.

'Hallo, Clare,' I said. 'Thank you for coming.'

She sat down. She was wearing a black skirt and a dark grey jumper. Very understated but also mysteriously elegant. The knee-high boots again, a glimpse of black tights.

'As we're on first name terms,' she said coolly, 'what's yours?'

I thought this was rather a cheek but kept my voice pleasant. 'Harbinder.'

'Well, Harbinder, I haven't got much time. I have a class in fifteen minutes.'

Charming. 'We'll be quick,' I said. 'We've been looking at Ella's social media profile and there are a few questions I'd like to ask you. In July, you and Ella went to a teacher training course in Hythe. Something happened there. We know that from her Facebook messages. What was it?'

I watched her closely. She looked quickly at Neil, then back to me. 'What do you mean?'

Playing for time. 'We know something happened in Hythe that disturbed Ella,' I said. 'You were there, you were her friend. I thought you might know what it was.'

'No. It was just the usual training course stuff. You know.' She tried for a matey 'professional women together' tone.

'No, I don't,' I said. 'Sussex police don't run to residential courses. What happened at Hythe?'

'Nothing,' said Clare, doing her wide-eyed look. 'It was the usual thing. Lots of talks, group activities, drinks in the evening.'

I wasn't buying this. Something happened on this training course and it wasn't just someone not buying their round. I asked who she had drinks with and she said Ella and, when prompted, Rick Lewis. She also mentioned another member of the department, Anoushka Palmer.

I pointed to the file in front of me, hoping to convey that I already knew the answers to the questions I was putting to her. 'In here, Ella mentions wanting to forget Hythe. What do you think she meant?'

Clare crossed and recrossed her legs, one of her signs of tension. 'I've no idea.'

'She talks about Doctor Jekyll and Mr Hythe. What do you think that means?'

'A misspelling?'

I gave her a look. She probably thinks we've never read the book. Well, she's basically right, as it happens, but I wanted to wipe the superior look off her face.

'She says, "C knows". Is C you?'

'I don't know,' said Clare and now she did look rattled. Beads of sweat appeared on her forehead. A hot flush? Perhaps. She's forty-five, after all. But maybe something else. Now it was time for Neil to mention the note and he did it well, voice flat and unemotional.

'What did it say?' Clare almost whispered it. Neil told her and Clare said the quote was from *The Tempest*. She probably thinks we haven't read that either.

'What's the next line?' I said, although I already knew.

'Hell is empty,' said Clare, 'and all the devils are here.'

Something about the note really bothered her. We could both see it. She put her hand up to wipe her forehead and then probably realised how this would look. She settled for pushing her hair back. It's cut very short but with a longer bit at the front, dark brown with gold highlights. Classy looking.

I asked for a sample of her handwriting. She must have realised why I was asking but she responded calmly enough. She wrote out the words using Tony's smart Montblanc pen.

'Hell is empty and all the devils are here.'

It wasn't the same writing.

Only one of Ella's students said anything at all interesting. It was nearly lunchtime by the time we got round to a boy called Tom Creeve, a gangling youth with spots and hair shaved at the sides. They seem to be much more relaxed about hair these days at Talgarth. When I was here it was short back and sides for the boys and hair tied back for the girls. I know that my dad had to come into the school to explain that Sikh children couldn't cut their hair and, yes, the turban was mandatory for boys. But today I'd seen beehives, dreadlocks, skinheads and all manner of bad dye jobs. Tom couldn't quite carry off the look. He sat slumped in front of us, picking at a hole in his sweatshirt. But at the question, 'Do you know of anyone who didn't get on with Miss Elphick?' he answered, 'Well there was the thing with Patrick O'Leary.'

Neil and I looked at each other. 'What thing?'

'Patrick sent her a valentine's card. We all knew about it. Miss Elphick told Mr Lewis and Patrick had to move forms.'

'How did Patrick feel about that?' I asked.

'I don't know.' Tom started to look panicky. 'I'm not his friend.' He ran his fingers through his remaining hair. 'He won't know I told you, will he?'

'It's entirely confidential,' I assured him.

While we waited for the long-suffering runner to find Patrick, Liz tried to put things into perspective. 'It might not be such a big thing. Students often get crushes on teachers and the only answer is never to be alone with that pupil ever. Ella did the right thing in telling Rick because he was her line manager.'

'What sort of a boy is Patrick?' I asked.

'He's quite bright, very good at sport, plays rugby,' said Liz. 'But he's had his share of trouble while he's been here.'

'What kind of trouble?'

'Fighting, talking back to teachers. That sort of thing.'

'He sounds like me at school,' said Neil.

But Patrick O'Leary, when he appeared, was nothing like Neil. He was a dark, good-looking boy who carried himself with a swagger. He sat down opposite us and spread his legs wide. If he'd been next to me on a train, I would have kicked him.

I didn't waste much time. 'I understand that you once sent a valentine to Miss Elphick.'

Patrick didn't seem disconcerted. He even smiled slightly. 'Yeah. What about it?'

'Did Miss Elphick talk to you about it?' I said.

'Yeah.' He shrugged. 'She said I shouldn't of sent it but it was just a laugh.'

'And she told Mr Lewis, the head of department?'

'Yeah, and he went on about it being inappropriate. "We need to maintain the boundaries".' He assumed a high, pernickety voice that was obviously meant to be Rick.

'That's a bit harsh.' Neil was going into lad mode. 'You said it was just a laugh.'

Patrick looked at Neil under his brows. He could see what was going on. 'I wasn't bothered, to be honest.'

'Did you ever see Miss Elphick out of school?' I asked. 'Ever go to her house?'

'No.' Patrick sat up slightly straighter. 'If anyone tells you I did, they're lying.'

'Who would say something like that?'

Patrick didn't answer. Liz leaned forward. 'You're not in any trouble, Patrick, but you have to answer the questions.'

'I dunno,' he said at last.

'You were moved into another class, weren't you?' I said.

'Yeah. 11GN.'

'That must have been tough,' said Neil.

'It's OK. I don't see them much. Just for registration and that. I've still got my mates.'

'How do you feel about Miss Elphick now?' I asked.

He looked me straight in the eye. 'I'm sorry she's dead,' he said. 'But that's it. I don't think about her. I've got a girlfriend. It was all just a laugh.'

Tony said that we could have lunch in school but I wasn't keen. The dining room is in the old part of the building and I could smell the food from the office. Tony said that there was a canteen in the New Building now — 'it sells pizza slices and everything' — but I said we'd go out for a breath of fresh air. We still had to see a few remaining students as well as the rest of the English department. I thought a Nandos in Chichester might help maintain our concentration.

We walked across the quad to the car. Blue sweatshirts were everywhere, making the kind of subdued roar that you hear from a distant football crowd. A group of boys loitered by the car park. I could tell that they were about to light up. They had that kind of furtive but defiant look. A teacher approached them. 'What are you doing here? The car park's out-of-bounds. Aren't you going into lunch?'

'I'm watching my figure, Mr Carter,' said one of the boys.

We were passing at that moment and I stopped to look at the teacher. Tweed jacket, green tie, thinning hair, slightly hopeless look.

Gary Carter hadn't changed at all.

CHAPTER 13

'I saw Gary Carter today,' I told Mum.

'I liked Gary,' she said, pausing from her chopping. 'Didn't I?'

'You like everyone.'

'That's not true. I didn't like that little boy in primary school. The one who pushed you off the slide. And I wasn't keen on Margaret Thatcher.'

'You didn't like that UKIP man on the TV the other night.'

'I'd be friendly to him if he came into the shop,' she said, pushing her hair back with one hand, 'but I'm not that keen on the mindless racism.'

This is typical of my mum. She always takes hypothetical situations very seriously. 'If I had the Queen for lunch, I'd be very careful what I gave her to eat because Prince Philip has trouble with his digestion.' 'If I was a racing driver' — she can't drive — 'I'd ask for Prosecco instead of Champagne at the end of the race. You still get a nice fizz and it's much cheaper.' The understatement is typical too. Mum 'isn't keen' on racism, genocide makes her 'quite angry' and war 'really isn't such a good idea when you think about it'.

'Gary's a teacher at Talgarth now,' I said. 'I talked to him today. He teaches geography.'

'Oh, you were always good at geography. You drew lovely maps.'

'I gave it up in Year 8, Mum.' But I was good at maps, she was right. I loved edging the continents with blue and drawing in the mountains, each with a little white ice cap.

'Is Gary married?' She's so obvious sometimes. She wasn't even looking at me, she was putting onions and garlic into a pan and watching them sizzle.

'I didn't ask.' Though I did and he wasn't. We'd also arranged to meet for a drink tomorrow night. It was only so that I could get some gossip about the staff at Talgarth but I still didn't tell Mum. I didn't want her to get the wrong idea. And, besides, too much excitement is bad for her.

'He's done well if he's a teacher,' she said, in a faux casual voice, adding spices.

'It's no cleverer than being in the police,' I said, no doubt a bit defensively.

'I think being in the police is very clever,' she protested, turning to look at me. 'I'm always showing off about you.'

I doubted this. I was sure that my parents tried to change the subject whenever my name came up at the gurdwara. 'What's Harbinder doing?' 'Is she married yet?' 'Children?'

Sultan started barking which meant that Dad was coming in. I looked at the clock, which is a weird copper thing in the shape of India. The little hand on Mysuru. Seven o'clock. The shop shuts at nine so Kush must be taking over.

My parents run a small convenience store in Shoreham. They used to sell DVDs but Netflix has done for these. Now they make most of their money from alcohol sales, even though neither of them drinks, not even my Prosecco-spraying mother. When I was young, we all used to help in the shop and I'd have to yell for my parents if anyone wanted to buy beer or wine. I never thought of questioning anyone's right to buy the stuff. Nowadays it's just Kush and Dad and sometimes Kush's son, Hakim, serving. They spend a lot of time asking to see IDs.

'Look, Bibi,' Dad said when he saw me. 'Our little girl is home.' He does this because he knows it gets on my nerves. He stooped to kiss me and I smelled his aftershave. My father never looks tired or untidy or anything less than immaculate. His kurti is always snowy white and his turban dark blue. He always smells of aftershave and soap, even after serving in the shop all day.

'How's the case?' he said, getting a spoon to taste the curry, a habit that drives my mother mad.

'It's so sad,' said Mum. 'That woman, that teacher, was so beautiful. I saw her picture in the paper.'

'Would it be less sad if she was ugly?' I said.

'Be careful, Bibi,' said Dad.

'Of course not,' said my mother, with dignity. 'I'm just making an observation.'

'The case is a pain,' I said. 'We're pretty sure she knew her killer, which *should* narrow it down, but it hasn't.'

'We'd better lock the doors at night,' said Mum.

'We always do,' said Dad. 'And we've got a guard dog.'

They both looked dotingly at Sultan, who was lying in the middle of the floor as if determined to be as big a nuisance as possible.

'He wouldn't protect us,' I said. 'He's too soft.'

'He's a trained killer,' said Dad.

'Trained by who?'

'By me. Sultan!' He addressed the dog. 'Play dead.' The dog's muscular tail pounded the floor.

'He's already playing dead,' I said. 'How long will supper be? Have I got time to have a shower first?'

I had never meant to live at home as an adult. I joined the police straight from university and, at first, I shared a flat with three other cadets. But, I don't know, they just got on my nerves after a while. They were so untidy and they never cooked proper meals. They'd come in at two a.m. with kebabs and, in the morning, I'd find beer cans and shredded lettuce all over the kitchen. They drank my special milk and they wanted to watch *I'm a Celebrity*. After a year, I moved back in with Mum and Dad. It was meant to be a temporary measure. 'Just until she gets married,' I heard Mum say to Auntie Dipa. Well, that will be a long wait. Same-sex marriage doesn't qualify for the Blissful Union (which always sounds a bit like an ocean-going liner but is the literal translation of the Sikh wedding ceremony). My parents don't know that I'm gay and, in my current, more-celibate-than-the-Pope stage, I don't really feel it's worth telling them. Maybe I'll just wait until they've given up all hope of me finding Mr Right. I think my mum might be all right about it, actually. She's very friendly with Steve and Duncan, who run the pet-grooming place opposite the shop, and she adores Graham Norton. But I'm pretty sure that, like Queen Victoria, she's never really entertained the idea of women having sex with each other. Far better not to tell her for now. Like I said, too much excitement is dangerous at her age.

All in all, it's not so bad living with the old dears. I have an en-suite shower room and an endless supply of wonderful food. My parents don't ask when I'm coming home in the evenings, although I know my mum won't go to sleep until she hears my key in the lock. They don't nag me too much about boyfriends and Mum has finally stopped putting me in touch with distant cousins in the Punjab. They're good company, most of the time. I love watching old films with them on a Sunday, listening to Mum's delusional belief that she looks like 'an Indian Ingrid Bergman' and Dad's wry commentary. 'Oh, here he is, the comic foreigner, lobotomised to mispronounce his own name.' I like seeing my brothers at weekends and — especially — my nieces and nephews. It's fun to be the cool aunt with a police walkie-talkie and a siren on my car, even if my sisters-in-law do sometimes say, 'She's so good with children. It seems a pity . . .' But I don't particularly like kids. No, that seems insulting. I like a few, specific ones, just as I have a small but very select group of friends. 'You're too choosy,' Mum tells me. She married the first man her parents presented to her. She got lucky but that doesn't alter the fact that she wasn't choosy enough.

After my shower I went into my room to check my emails. My phone was buzzing. Donna. I put on some clothes because it seemed wrong to talk to my boss wrapped only in a towel.

'We've had the CSI results back,' she said. Her mouth was full and I was sure that she was still at the office, eating chips. Donna is married with two young children and she once told me that it was easier to wait at work until they had gone to bed.

'Anything interesting?' I said.

'No prints on the knife.'

'What about the note?'

'Nothing. Apparently there's a trace of plastic coating. It might mean that it was kept in one of those freezer bags.'

'Can we trace the make of bag?'

'No. They're all the same, I think. Ten a penny.'

'Anything else?'

'Our best bet is some thread caught on a bush in the garden. Looks like it might have come from some sort of outdoor clothing. A waxed hiking jacket or similar. I've got the lab looking into it now.'

I thought of Tony Sweetman's suntan. 'A skiing jacket?'

'Perhaps. How did it go at the school?'

'One interesting thing. A Year 11 boy had a crush on Ella. Sent her a valentine card.'

'How old's Year 11?'

'Fifteen to sixteen.'

Some thoughtful chomping. 'Old enough.'

'Yeah,' I said. 'Old enough. He was big too, strongly built, plays rugby. He didn't seem obsessed, though. Kept saying it was all just a laugh.'

'It's still a lead. We should check him out.'

'He doesn't have much of an alibi,' I said. 'He says he was at home playing war games on the computer.'

'Like all teenagers everywhere.'

'And there was no one else at home. I suppose we could do a location trace on the computer.'

'Interesting,' said Donna. 'Let's dig a bit deeper.'

'I met an old friend who's teaching at the school,' I said. 'I'm meeting him tomorrow. I'll see if I can get some inside stuff.'

'Good idea.'

'My mother's all excited. She thinks he might be The One.'

Donna laughed. 'What are you eating tonight? Tell me so that I can salivate.' Donna has only eaten at our house once but she still goes on about it.

'Lamb passenda, chapattis and rice.'

'Can I move in?'

'Go home, Donna,' I said. 'I'll bring some chapattis into work tomorrow.'

CHAPTER 14

I'd temporarily forgotten that it was Halloween. I'd arranged to meet Gary in The Compass, which is in the nearest village to Talgarth High. The streets seemed to throng with midget witches and devils as doting parents ushered their offspring on a middle-class begging spree. *Hell is empty and all the devils are here.* I hoped Mum would have some callers tonight. She would love the chance to coo over a bunch of mini-zombies. If it was me, I'd turn off the lights and pretend to be dead.

Even The Compass had got in on the act. I had to duck under spiders' webs to get to the bar and, when I spotted Gary, he was sitting at a corner table with a pumpkin-shaped candle in front of him.

Gary insisted on getting the first drinks. He had a pint but I stuck to orange juice. People often assume I don't drink because I'm a Sikh, but actually I'm quite partial to a glass of red wine or a gin and tonic. Mum and Dad are teetotal so there's never any alcohol in the house, although Mum once bought me a bottle of Baileys at Christmas 'because that's what young people drink'. It was unbelievably disgusting, liquid vomit flavoured with coffee powder. I really felt like a large Merlot but I was driving, and besides, I wasn't about to start drinking with Gary.

'Halloween was never such a big deal in our day,' I said, when he had fought his way back through Shelob's lair to our table.

'It's the influence of America,' said Gary, and I guessed this was something he'd said many times before. 'We see it all the time at school.'

'But in America, kids dress up as anything, don't they? Superheroes, princesses?' I said. I've never been to the States. 'Here it's all the black magic stuff. Oh, how cute. Dress your kid up as the undead.'

Gary laughed. 'Still the same old Harbs.'

I wasn't sure how to take this, and what did he mean anyway? Still funny? Still mean-spirited and a bit weird? And I hadn't heard Harbs for years.

'How long have you been teaching at Talgarth?' I asked.

'Ten years,' he said, with a slightly self-conscious laugh. 'It was my first job after my NQT year. Bit pathetic, isn't it? Still living and working in the same place where you were brought up.'

'At least you're not still living with your parents.'

'No,' he laughed heartily then got the point. 'Oh. Are you?'

'Yes. Still at home with Mum and Dad.'

'I liked your mum,' said Gary. 'I'll never forget those meals at your house. I've never eaten food that good ever. But I was always a bit scared of your dad and your brothers.'

'They're pussy cats,' I said. 'Mum has always ruled the roost.'

'I always thought you'd get married,' said Gary. 'Seems like everyone from school is married with kids now. Except me.'

'And me,' I said. 'I've never been married.'

'But you joined the police,' said Gary, obviously wanting to cheer me up. 'That's cool.'

'Is it?'

'Yes! Have you . . .'

'Don't ask me if I've got a gun.'

Gary laughs the embarrassed laugh again. 'Sorry.'

'British police officers don't routinely carry guns,' I said, relenting. 'But I have done a firearms course.'

'Well, that's still cooler than being a geography teacher.'

'What's it like teaching at Talgarth?' I asked.

'OK,' he took a gulp of beer and wiped the foam from his upper lip. 'Tony's a hard taskmaster. Always on about getting the data right, knows all the trendy buzzwords. But there's no doubt that he's improved the school. Discipline's much better now. You don't live in fear of being locked in the stationery cupboard.'

He laughed again but I wondered if this example was taken from personal experience.

'Must have been tough this week,' I said. 'The news about Ella.'

Gary's face crumpled slightly. He's in quite good shape for his age but, at certain moments, he looks like a much older man. 'It's been awful. People gossiping all over the place. People who didn't even really know Ella.'

This was interesting. 'Did you know Ella?'

He blushed. 'A little. We both did the staff talent show every year. She sang and I . . . you remember . . . I play the guitar.'

My God. Gary's guitar playing was one of the things I had managed to forget over the years, but he said it with a tender light in his eyes that showed he still thought of himself as the Jimi Hendrix of Shoreham. I went to the bar to get us another drink. I was tempted to have a glass of wine to get myself through the reminiscences that would surely follow but I needed to keep my wits about me. This is work, I told myself.

Back at the table, Gary told me that Ella was a 'lovely person'.

'Really talented too,' he said. 'She could sing and dance. She could have made it as an actress.'

'Did she have a boyfriend?'

I said it a bit too bluntly and he looked taken aback.

'Are you . . . do you suspect . . . ?'

'I just want to get a sense of her as a person,' I said soothingly.

'I don't think she had a boyfriend,' said Gary. 'She mentioned someone at her old school once or twice. I think she'd been badly hurt. She didn't want to get involved again.'

'Involved?'

'Well, most of the staff are married or in relationships,' he said, a shade defensively. You're not, I thought.

'So she wouldn't get involved with a married man?'

'No, I'm sure she wouldn't.'

'You mentioned gossip. What are people gossiping about?'

Gary looked really uncomfortable now. 'Ella was so attractive,' he said, at last. 'People always gossip.'

'About Ella and Rick Lewis?'

Gary let out a sigh of relief. 'So you had heard that. I didn't like to say. People talked about Rick and Ella but I don't think there was anything between them. For a start, Rick had a thing for Clare.'

'Clare Cassidy?'

'Yes. Have you met her? She's another English teacher. Good-looking but a bit stuck-up, in my opinion. Clare and Ella were great friends though.'

'I've met her,' I said. 'So Rick fancied Clare?'

'Yes. We all knew about it. He had a real thing for her a while back. I heard that he used to sit outside her house for hours. He's married, too, but that didn't stop him.'

'What did Clare think about Rick?' I asked. I was thinking of the little house in the shadow of the old factory. Had Rick really been stalking Clare? If so, why didn't she tell Tony and get him sacked?

Gary laughed again but this time it had a harsh, cynical note. 'Clare wouldn't look twice at Rick Lewis. She's the sort of woman who only goes out with merchant bankers.'

This was obviously Gary's idea of unobtainable wealth.

'What about the students? Did any of them have a crush on Ella? It happens, I know.'

'I know,' Gary stared mistily into his beer. 'I remember fancying Miss Creed. You remember, the drama teacher? I was mad about her.'

'I don't remember her at all,' I said. 'I was never very keen on acting. So did anyone have an adolescent crush on Ella?'

'Not that I know of.' He suddenly seemed to remember that he was talking to a detective. 'You can't suspect one of the students?'

'I think Ella knew her murderer,' I said. 'That means you might know them too.'

That effectively killed the atmosphere.

I left when I'd finished my drink. I didn't think I could take another Britvic and Gary had started talking about 'the old days'. He might have happy memories of teenage parties and football games but I left all that behind the day I left Talgarth High. Never go back, that's my motto. Gary even suggested that we get together one day 'for a curry'. Is he joking? Why would I eat at an Indian restaurant when my mum cooks the best curries in England? I muttered something non-committal and escaped to my car. I offered Gary a lift but he said he'd walk home. He lives in the village apparently. Above the betting shop.

The High Street was deserted. All the mini-devils had gone home. There weren't any street lights and the Downs loomed above, dark and silent. It was a bit spooky sitting there in the car park. I suddenly wanted to be at home, listening to my parents argue about the ten o'clock news. Before I set off, I checked my work phone, just for form's sake, and saw that I had two missed calls from an unknown number. I pressed Voicemail.

'DS Kaur. This is Clare Cassidy. Can you give me a call back? There's something I have to tell you.'

CHAPTER 15

I always give my card to everyone I interview but it's rare for anyone to use it. I rang Clare back immediately.

'Something's happened,' she said. 'I think it might be important.'

'Are you at home?' I said.

'Yes.'

'I'll come over.'

The roads were dark but deserted. I kept my beam on and it illuminated hedgerows and farm gates, a spectral signpost in the middle of a crossroads, a dead badger on the grass verge, a fox trotting past on some nocturnal adventure of its own. Was it the thought of Rick Lewis sitting outside Clare's house that made me decide to prioritise her call? Maybe it was just the desire to do something useful after spending the last few hours wallowing in the past. At any rate, I was there in ten minutes.

There were lights on in the row of cottages, buttery and warm, but behind them the factory loomed like some monstrous, manmade cliff in front of the real, chalk cliff. It may have been a trick of the light, or a glimpse of the moon, but suddenly I seemed to see a glimmer in one of the broken windows. It was like candlelight, an almost subliminal flicker. Morse code. On off, on off. I watched for a full minute but I didn't see it again.

Clare opened the door to me. She was obviously still wearing her work clothes (white shirt, black trousers) but she had those fluffy slipper socks on her feet. It suddenly made me like her more.

'Thanks for coming,' she said, stepping aside to let me in.

'I was in the area,' I said.

The blue-grey sitting room was cosy. The wood-burning stove was lit and the only other light came from a fringed table lamp. The TV was off and I could see a book face down on the coffee table. *The Woman in White* by Wilkie Collins. I thought of Ella Elphick, sitting in the dark with her herbal tea. Someone really should teach these women about Netflix.

Clare offered tea or coffee and I said yes to tea, if only to get rid of the taste of orange juice. It gave the whole thing a spurious intimacy, to be sipping hot drinks by the fire, keeping our voices down because Clare's daughter, Georgia, was upstairs.

'It might be nothing,' said Clare.

'But it might be something,' I said, 'otherwise you wouldn't have called.'

'Yes,' said Clare. 'It might.' She stared into her mug (Harry Potter: Gryffindor) for a moment before saying, 'I keep a diary.'

I didn't know what response she expected. Surprise? Admiration? In fact, it was entirely in line with my image of Clare that she kept a diary, like the heroine of a nineteenth-century novel. I was pretty sure that Clare saw herself as the heroine of her own life.

But she was still talking. 'When you asked me about Hythe, it made me want to look back and see what had actually happened between Ella and Rick.'

I knew it. 'I thought you didn't know anything about that,' I said.

'You block things out,' she said, blushing slightly. 'Besides, it was their business.'

'And this is a murder enquiry,' I said. But I let it go. I wanted to know where this was leading.

'I looked back in my diary,' said Clare, 'to see what I'd thought at the time and, when I found the page, someone had written something on it.'

'What do you mean?'

'Someone else had written *in my diary*,' she said, sounding impatient. 'Someone had found my diary and written in it.'

I was still finding this hard to compute. 'What did it say?'

'Hallo, Clare. You don't know me.'

'Can I see?'

She looked reluctant but she must have been expecting this because there was a pale blue book on the table labelled 'Jan to August 2017'. She picked it up but before she handed it over she said, in a rush, 'There's something else too. I was working late tonight. I've got to take over the end-of-term play from Ella.'

'Little Shop of Horrors?'

She looked surprised. 'That's right. Well, I was waiting for the rehearsal to start and I decided to go up to the top floor. To R.M. Holland's study.'

'Is that still there?' I said.

'Yes,' she said, 'though it's out-of-bounds to students, of course.'

'I've never seen the room,' I said. 'But I read the story, *The Stranger*.'

'Have you?' she said, sounding surprised. 'Did you like it?'

I shrugged. 'Not much. It's a bit melodramatic. All that "we waited and we waited and we waited" stuff.'

'It's the gothic tradition,' said Clare. 'Things happen in threes.'

'What happened to you tonight?' I asked, hoping to end the book group stuff.

She looked away and then back at me, still doing the doe-eye thing despite there being no men present. 'I went up to Holland's study. I'm writing a book about him and I wanted to look at some of the photographs in the room. Anyway, when I got there — it's up that spiral staircase at the end of the corridor — there was someone sitting at the desk.'

'Bloody hell,' I said, despite myself. 'Who was it?'

'It was a shop-window dummy,' she said. 'It must have come from the textiles department. But it was all dressed up in Victorian clothes with its arms outstretched. I think it was meant to look like R.M. Holland.'

'That must have given you a fright.'

'I nearly died,' she said. 'I screamed but, of course, there was no one to hear me. Then I realised what it was. But the point is, someone must have put it there to scare me. I'm the only one who ever goes up to the attic.'

'Who else has the key?'

'The caretaker, I suppose. He's got duplicate keys to everything.'

'Is that still Pervy Pat?' I said without thinking.

'Mr Patterson left about ten years ago, I think. Before my time,' she added. 'How did you know about him?'

'I used to go to Talgarth High,' I said. She would probably find out sooner or later. 'I'm an old girl. Feeling older by the second.'

'Does Tony know?' she said. 'Be careful or he'll have you talking to the Year 10s on careers day.'

'I haven't told him,' I said. I didn't, strictly speaking, dislike the idea of talking to the students.

'Who do you think could have put the dummy there?' I asked.

'I don't know,' she said. 'I've been thinking and thinking about it.'

'Is there anyone with a grudge against you?'

'Not that I know of.'

'What about Rick Lewis?'

She sat up very straight and looked at me like I was a Year 7 who had asked what her first name was. 'Why do you ask that?'

'I understand that he once had a bit of a thing for you.'

'That was ages ago. It's all forgotten now.'

That was the problem. The evening with Gary had taught me that nothing was ever really forgotten.

'Tell me about it,' I said encouragingly.

She sighed. 'Rick had always been very friendly. He's a good head of department, really. Very approachable.'

'I bet.'

'Well, he didn't approach me. Not at first. It started with him sending me little notes, quotations from books that we both liked, that sort of thing. Ella and I used to laugh about it. Then, earlier this year, we'd been out for a staff meal and Rick and I ended up walking back to our cars together. Suddenly he just lunged at me and started kissing me.'

'Bloody hell,' I said again. She said it lightly but this was sexual assault.

'I pushed him away, of course. Told him to pull himself together.' She sounded just like a teacher then. 'I mean, I assumed he was drunk. But, the next day, he turned up outside my house. He said that he'd fallen in love with me. "I'm ill with you", that's what he said.'

'Charming phrase.'

'That's what I thought. I told him that I would never have an affair with a married man.'

'Were you tempted?' I said, idly. 'He's quite good-looking.'

'No,' she sat up very straight. 'I wasn't tempted for one second. I thought Rick seemed to accept it, but a few days later, I saw him sitting outside the house. It was weird. He was just sitting there. I thought he might be lost or on his way somewhere. But he was there the next day. And the next.'

'He was stalking you.'

'I didn't really see it like that. But I told him it had to stop. I mean, he was my head of department. He couldn't carry on like that. People would start talking.'

Everyone knows, I wanted to tell her. Because Gary is the sort of person who always hears gossip last.

'And did it stop?' I asked.

'More or less. He still sends me the odd card with bitter little tags from Shakespeare. *Farewell thou art too dear for my possessing.* But mostly, yes, we're just colleagues.'

I thought of the card I'd seen on the mantelpiece when I'd first sat in this room. The one signed 'R'. I couldn't remember what was in it or, sadly, what the handwriting was like. I looked at the fireplace but the card was no longer there.

'Would you recognise his handwriting?' I asked.

'I think so,' said Clare. 'He handwrites a lot of his notes to staff. He thinks it's less formal.'

'Can I see the writing in the diary?' I asked.

She handed over the blue book. I scanned through the entry — just taking in enough to register that Ella had slept with Rick and dumped him fairly quickly afterwards — and then focused on the tiny writing at the foot of the page.

'Is that Rick's writing?' I asked.

'I don't think so,' said Clare. 'Rick's is much bigger and loopier. This is al-most italic. And it's so small.'

It was small but it was big enough for one thing to be clear.

The writer was the same person who had written 'Hell is empty' and left it by Ella's body.

I heard a scream echoing through the corridors of the deserted house and I realised that it was mine. My friend, Gudgeon, lay dead at my feet. Wilberforce was a few yards away. I felt both their necks for a heartbeat but I knew that there was nothing to be done. Someone, or something, had fallen on these men like a beast from hell and slaughtered them. Gudgeon's chest was red with blood where he had been stabbed again and again. His arms were spread wide and I could see on his palms — oh horrible sacrilege! — gashes which resembled the stigmata of Our Blessed Lord. I thought at first that Wilberforce had been stabbed to death too, but, looking closer in the flickering light from my candle, I saw that he had been garrotted, a white cloth pulled tight around his neck, making his appearance ghastly in the extreme. However, the assassin's knife had not escaped him. The handle of a dagger was embedded in his chest.

I was shaking, my candle making wild shapes on the wall, and, for several minutes, was frozen with fear. Because the fiend that had killed my companions was surely close at hand. Would he now descend on me, knife and hands incarnadine?

But the ruined house was still. I could hear nothing except the rats scuttling on the floor above. Then, from outside, I heard a cry. 'What's happening in there?' Then Collins, Bastian and the third man came running up the stairs. I still held the candle and their first sight must have been my ashen face, illuminated by the spectral light, before the true horror of the scene unfolded itself.

I will draw a veil — no, not a veil, a heavy curtain — over what happened next. I wanted to inform the college authorities but Lord Bastian pointed out that we would get in trouble, perhaps even be sent down. Besides, he said, the Hell Club would not be happy if the news got out. This opinion seemed to carry great weight with the other two, and they were all senior men, you must remember. To cut a long story short, I was persuaded that the best course of action would be to leave the dread house and return to college as if nothing had happened. The bodies would be found, of course, and there would be an enquiry, but we would deny any knowledge of the events. We would never speak of this night again.

'We must swear,' said Bastian and, to my horror, he knelt down and, in a horrible echo of Doubting Thomas testing Our Lord, put his fingers into the wound on Gudgeon's hand.

'Swear,' he said. 'Swear on his blood.'

Can you imagine the scene? The candlelight, the wind outside now rising to a crescendo, Bastian standing there with Gudgeon's blood on his hands. We were all half-mad, that's the only way I can explain it. Bastian pressed his bloody thumbprint to our foreheads as if he were a priest administering the ashes. Remember, man, that thou art dust and to dust thou shalt return.

'I swear,' we said, one after another. 'I swear.'

What happened next? Ah, my dear young man, there's no need to look so alarmed. Time passed, as it must always do. The bodies were discovered. There was a police enquiry but no murderer was ever found. No one ever asked me about my movements that night. The Junior Dean made a point of consoling me over my friend's death and I said, truthfully, that I was devastated. He sympathised but quoted a chilling little epithet from Homer, doubtless intended to foster a stoical spirit. Be strong, saith my heart; I am a soldier; I have seen worse sights than this. *And it was over.* Consummatum est.

Or so I thought.

PART THE THIRD

Georgia

CHAPTER 16

It's almost dark when I collect Herbert from Doggy Day Care. We walk back along the main road, cars whirring past, their headlights illuminating the flying leaves. Herbert whimpers and shrinks as close to the hedge as he can. He's a wimp, that dog. Eventually I have to carry him. He's only little but he's surprisingly solid and heavy. I'm exhausted by the time I get home. Perhaps Mum is right and I should do more exercise. 'Exercise releases endorphins, prevents teenagers from becoming depressed or obese, encourages healthy routines, and allows you to join sports teams at university instead of getting off your head on drugs . . .' etc., etc., etc. This is one of Mum's favourite lectures, second only to: 'You'll regret it if you don't work hard for your exams. University is the best time of your life but only if you go to a Russell Group uni or, better still, Oxbridge. I didn't get into Oxford but I'm not bitter . . .'

Back in the house, I feed Herbert and light some of my favourite candles. I don't think I'll get any trick-or-treaters because our house is quite a long way from the village but I'd bought some Haribos just in case. Mum has a serious sweet tooth but she only eats dark chocolate made from cocoa beans hand-crafted by the Aztecs. I'm pretty sure that little kids prefer their sugar more mainstream. So I light the candles, recite the incantation that Miss Hughes taught us and open *The Stranger*.

For the past four years I've read *The Stranger* every Halloween. Mum doesn't know and I don't think she would approve, despite always using the story on that course of hers. She reads it aloud to them as well. She can't have candles because of Health and Safety but she puts an open fire app on her laptop and has that crackling away in the background. I'm sure it's spooky as hell. I used to love Mum reading to me when I was little. We progressed from picture books and Noel Streatfeild to Agatha Christie and Georgette Heyer. *Devil's Cub* is still my favourite book and Dominic is my perfect romantic hero. I told that to Ty and he was actually quite jealous. 'Read the book,' I told him, 'and you'll understand.' But I don't think Ty would ever read anything that has a crinoline on the cover. Why are Georgette Heyer's covers so naff? When you think of all the exciting things that happen — abductions, false identities, wild horseback chases — the front of the book nearly always shows a woman in a ballgown, simpering sweetly up at a man. Venetia loves GH too, after all, she was named after one of the books.

> *'If you'll permit me,' said the Stranger, 'I'd like to tell you a story. After all, it's a long journey and, by the look of those skies, we're not going to be leaving this carriage for some time. So, why not pass the hours with some story-telling? The perfect thing for a late October evening . . .'*

It's *such* a good beginning. My book has had three different beginnings. One from the protagonist's point of view, one from the antagonist, and one omniscient narrator that I was just trying on for size. In some ways, I think I'll only know how to begin it when I've finished the thing. Miss Hughes says that most writers could scrap their first chapters and their books would be better for it. But it's different with a short story like *The Stranger*. There, every word counts.

Mum doesn't know that I'm writing a book. She doesn't even know about the creative writing class. She thinks I'm just hanging around at Tash's, watching girlie movies and painting my nails. She likes this version, despite the nagging and the lectures, because it makes me seem like a 'normal teenager', whatever that is. Even Ty, the 'unsuitable boyfriend', fits into this narrative. She and Dad worry that I was traumatised by them getting divorced. That's why they made me go to that god-awful St Faith's when we first moved down here. 'A protective environment', Dad called it. Jesus, only in the sense that Strangeways is a protective environment. I couldn't bear it. All those prissy girls talking about their ponies and whether their bum looked big in their jodhpurs (short answer: yes). And they were *obsessed* with boys because they hardly ever saw a live one. When the window cleaner came round I was embarrassed for them, I really was.

When I moved to Talgarth everything changed. It was Ella — Miss El-phick — who started it off really. That's why I was so sad when she died. Was killed. I hate euphemisms. Miss Elphick liked my essays and she suggested that I join Miss Hughes' creative writing group. I met Tash there and Patrick and Venetia. My best friends in the world. Miss Hughes teaches at the sixth-form college so we go there on Mondays after school. Tash and Patrick are at Talgarth like me but Venetia is from St Faith's. Vee says that she used to not like me at St Faith's but that was probably because I was busy hiding my true aura. I don't really remember Vee at all, to be honest. She says that she has learned how to be almost invisible at school, which is surprising consider-ing she has about a metre of bright red hair. Natasha — Tash — is my 'official' best friend, recognised as such by all the family and approved of by Mum for the usual, subtly snobbish reasons. Tash's parents are professionals who went to university. T herself speaks nicely and has only the regular number of piercings. They live in a nice house and shop at Waitrose. We don't see much of Patrick at school because he plays rugby and hangs around with all the meatheads. Tash and I have discussed it and, although we both love Pat-rick, we would never date him because it would ruin the energy in the group. Besides, he has a girlfriend called Rosie. A nice little thing.

We didn't know that Miss Hughes was a white witch at first. I just knew that she was a brilliant teacher. She knows immediately when words are right and when they're wrong. But, when she suggests changes, she doesn't make you feel like a fool. She encourages you, inspires you to do your best work. She's not glamorous like Miss Elphick, or even like Mum, I suppose. She's quite dumpy and has long grey hair in a bun. She does have a wonderful voice, however, very deep with just a hint of Welsh. The first hint that Miss Hughes wasn't your usual atheist slash C of E was when she mentioned going to Glastonbury for a holiday. 'Is that where your family is from?' Tash asked.

We were mildly obsessed with her by then. 'My sisters are there,' she said, with a smile. Another time, Venetia was scared because she was going into hospital for an operation (she was born with a hole in her heart, not that serious but she makes a lot of it) and Miss Hughes gave her some oil to sprinkle on her pillow and a picture of a hare staring at the moon with 'May the Goddess Keep You' on the back. Vee said that the oil gave her wonderful dreams.

It was only at the end of Year 9, when we were talking about *Macbeth,* that she told us. Patrick had said that the play would only have really worked in the seventeenth century when people were afraid of witches. Miss Hughes did her inward smile again and said, 'People are still afraid of witches. We always fear what we don't understand. I only tell very special people that I'm a white witch. Ordinary souls just could not comprehend it.' Of course, we were thrilled that we were special and not ordinary. She hasn't told us much and she certainly hasn't tried to convert us, like those people Mum is always arguing with on the doorstep, the ones with the magazine that says we're all going to hell because we use smartphones. But Miss Hughes has taught us some meditation techniques and some simple chants. She has taught us how to create a circle of protection and how to rid ourselves of pestilential spirits. She's also given each of us a black obsidian stone that guards against evil spirits. That's why I'm not scared to be sitting alone on Halloween reading a ghost story. On the contrary, I want to be open to the souls that are walking abroad tonight, to help them if I can.

'Unquiet souls, be not afraid. Loose the bonds of earth and turn your faces to the light . . .'

Herbert starts to bark loudly. I can hear someone walking up the steps. I'm slightly irritated but I remember the Haribos and go to the door with a welcoming smile on my face.

'Hallo, beautiful.'

It's not trick-or-treaters. It's Ty.

He's on his way to do his shift at the pub but he says that he doesn't want me to be alone on Halloween. 'I'll just stay here till your mum gets in.'

I bite back my annoyance because he means well. Ty always means well. He's like an overgrown puppy. God knows why Mum and Dad think he's the Prince of Darkness. Ever since we met in that club last summer, when

I'd used my fake ID and got super drunk, he has tried to look after me. 'You don't know about the world,' he would say, from the height of his twenty-one years of experience, 'it's a scary place.' But, thanks to Miss Hughes and the creative writing group, I have travelled the length and breadth of this world and the next. I'm not scared of anything.

Ty comes and sits on the sofa, laughs at the candles and eats a handful of Haribos. Herbert growls at him from the other side of the room. I swear that animal is Mum's familiar. He makes Ty sneeze, even though poodle fur is usually non-allergic.

Ty picks up my ghost story anthology and starts to read it but I know the moment for R.M. Holland has passed. I turn on the TV and Ty slides his arm round me. Now we are into our regular snog/wrestle-athon. Don't get me wrong. I'd like to have sex with Ty. He's good-looking and he knows what he's doing, unlike the boys in our year. It's important to embrace sexuality, Miss Hughes says, it's a powerful force. But Ty is determined not to sleep with me until I'm sixteen in February. So we have these exhausting sessions where we do almost everything but. He keeps breaking off to groan and stare into space and even I feel like a spring that has been coiled so far that it would explode. Now he's kissing me and one hand is in my waistband and the other is undoing my bra. I stop thinking about anything much. My mind is red and black, full of buzzing insects. Then Herbert starts to bark.

Ty sits up straight. 'Is it your mum?' He's terrified of Mum. It's hilarious.

'It's far too early. She's got to take a rehearsal. Listening to Peppa Pig singing about man-eating plants.'

Ty looks blank. As well he might.

But Herbert is wagging his tail and squealing in the way that he only does for Mum. He jumps on the back of the sofa and starts yapping in my ear. Headlights shine into the sitting room. I blow out the candles and switch on the main light. Ty is tucking himself in. I do up my bra and switch the channel onto *Friends*. The sort of thing a normal teenager might watch.

The door opens but Mum doesn't come into the sitting room. She must have seen Ty's car and realised that he is here. It annoys me that she will think this is what I had planned. A clandestine evening with my boyfriend. When, in fact, my motives were much higher and purer.

Mum goes into the kitchen and I follow her. She is standing there in her swingy red coat, pouring wine into a glass.

'What happened?' I say. 'Was the rehearsal cancelled?'

She turns and I'm shocked. She looks terrible. Her face is usually pale but now it looks as if someone has thrown white paint at it. Her mascara is smudged as if she's been crying.

'Are you OK?' I say.

She takes a gulp of wine. 'I've just had a shock,' she says and tries to smile. 'Is Ty here?'

'He's just going,' I say.

'He doesn't have to go immediately,' she says, 'but someone might be popping round later. It's probably better if he isn't here then.'

'He has to leave by six,' I say. 'He's working in the pub tonight.'

Mum looks relieved. She clearly wants me out of the way, too, so I take pity on her.

'I've got lots of homework to do when he's gone,' I say.

CHAPTER 17

Mum's visitor arrives at about ten. I look out of my window and see a grey car, quite cool, and a woman getting out. I can't see her face but I'm pretty sure that it's the policewoman who was in school yesterday. Patrick had to see her because he was in Miss Elphick's class and he said that she was really scary, the sort who looks like she knows exactly what you're thinking and isn't impressed by it. The dead souls in the old factory are doing their thing tonight, lights flickering, strange sounds, electrical energy so strong that I'm surprised not to see forked lightning cutting through the sky. The police-woman senses something; she stops and looks up. But she obviously decides not to listen to her inner voice because she shakes her head and continues on her way towards our front door.

Mum thanks her for coming and the policewoman says, 'I was in the area' as if brushing off any suggestion that she was being kind. Then they go into the sitting room and I can't hear any more. After a bit, Herbert comes up-stairs and sits on my bed. He must be bored with all the murder talk. I'm not. I long to know what they're saying. No one has talked to me about Ella, in spite of the fact that I knew her quite well. She was always coming here. But I'm just a child. Worse, a moody teenager. No one wants to hear my opinion, which is their loss, really.

Stroking Herbert with one hand, I open my laptop. I do have home-work to do, history and Spanish, but right now I have to do something more important — complete today's diary entry. It can be quite a chore, keeping a diary, but that's the point, you have to do it whether you feel like it or not. It's great training for becoming a writer, Miss Hughes says. Tash, Venetia, Patrick and I are all on MySecretDiary.com. It's actually only as secret as you want it to be; a lot of people make their entries public (well, within the website, that is; only members can view posts, not the entire internet). I share mine sometimes, but only when I think my writing is especially good, which does defeat the object of a diary — it's meant to be a workaday document, not a finished piece of prose. But I do polish and hone my entries. I think this is because I'm doing it on the laptop where it's easy to edit yourself. I can't imagine how it must feel to write your diary by hand, knowing that you only have one chance to express yourself, that the ink is on the paper for ever. I bet no one keeps that kind of diary nowadays.

I log in. Herbert17 is my password, which is dangerous because I use it for everything. Herbert himself is pretending to be asleep but I know he's watching me. I scroll down the entries from this evening. Venetia has posted, so has Patrick. There are also entries from LittleBear, whom I find annoying, and CyberWolf, whom I sort of fancy.

Patrick's off on one of his fantasy trips again, where you don't know if it's him or his alter-ego Puma who's writing. That doesn't interest me very much. I think real life is always darker and more complicated than fantasy. Venetia has too much real life in hers. It's all 'my mum doesn't understand me', 'this boy didn't notice me', 'nobody liked my Instagram picture'. The point is, *none* of our mothers understand us, they are congenitally and sociologically incapable of understanding us. Venetia is like all St Faith's girls, obsessed with boys but also rather afraid of them. She's always lusting after someone she's seen on the bus or who she only knows on Facebook. She would say (I can hear her voice so clearly that I wonder if she's done an audible projection spell), 'It's OK for you, Georgie, you've got a boyfriend'. And I suppose there's some truth in that. But all that Instagram/Snapchat stuff is so boring. Mum and Dad love to pretend that I'm addicted to social media. I hear them talking to their friends, that light-hearted voice that conceals real emotion, 'Georgie's always on her phone, texting, WhatsApping, whatever it's called. It can't be healthy. At her age I was out playing hockey/doing a paper round/meeting my friends. Teenagers today . . .' And so on *ad infinitum*. I let them think this because it's easier (also interesting how they think: reading a book — good, reading on screen — bad) but actually I never post on social media. I use chat groups, of course — even some of our teachers have study groups on Facebook — but the only site I ever visit is MySecretDiary.

I start typing: 'Halloween was cancelled this year because of Miss El-phick's death. It's as if the Grim Reaper can't intrude into the kitsch glitter-fest that All Hallows' Eve has become. Some people at school wore witch hats or vampire teeth but the teachers, many of them still red-eyed over Miss E, told them off. In Geography, Mr Carter almost cried when someone asked him about the funeral. It's to be in the school chapel, apparently. That's the last place I'd want for my last rites. But then I don't want a church funeral. I want to be scattered to the four elements. Earth my body, water my blood, air my breath, fire my spirit.'

I pause. Thinking. If I'm going to publish this, I should stop here. It's quite good, especially the line about the Grim Reaper. But if I go on, to men-tion Ty and my mum and the fact that a police officer is here now, in this house, then it should stay private. I've written about Miss Elphick's death on here but I don't want people to think that Mum could be involved in any way. I want to publish, to show Patrick and Venetia that I'm writing, but you never know who else has an account on here. Parents think that we don't un-derstand this but we do. I switch the setting to 'Private'.

'Something happened at school today. Mum came home looking as if she'd seen a ghost. Maybe she had? The spirit of R.M. Holland's wife is meant to haunt the school. I've never seen her but I've certainly felt a chill atmosphere on the first floor of the Old Building. Everyone hates going there for lessons. It's not so much that it's spooky, it's more that it's *sad*. You can feel the sadness of Alice Holland, her despair as she took that fateful plunge from the top floor landing. I know that Mariana is there too; sometimes I've felt her very close to me. I *wish* Mum had let me stay in her meeting with Henry Hamilton. But no, I had to be parcelled off with spotty Edmund. "Young people together". Mum, of course, hoping that I'd fall for the Cam-bridge vibe and vow to dedicate myself to getting all A*s in my exams. I'm so much more interested in R.M. Holland than I am in university. Or boys, for that matter.

'Ty came over tonight. He thought he was being kind, or protective, or something. He didn't want me to be alone on Halloween when, of course, that was *all* I wanted. And, of course, he kissed me and the whole thing started again. I wish we could just have sex and be done with it. But he has his scruples. "You're under age," he keeps saying. But age is just a number. Besides, Miss Hughes thinks that I might have had a former life as an old wise woman (another word for witch, of course). Anyway, Mum came in before things could get too heated. Ty is ridiculously in awe of Mum so he disappeared after exchanging a few stuttered words with her. Then I cooked supper because Mum was still too distracted. She said she was expecting "a visitor" so I went upstairs to "do homework." The visitor turned out to be the policewoman investigating Miss Elphick's murder. Why did Mum ask her to come over? Does Mum have some evidence about Ella's death? They were good friends, I know. E often used to come here and they'd drink wine and watch *Strictly* (the opium of the middle-aged). Did something happen this evening? Just like in the books, when Poirot suddenly "knows" who the murderer is, but won't tell anyone because there are a hundred pages still to go. Well, Mum won't tell me and I can't even discuss this in the group because Patrick is still obviously hung up on Miss E. Age might be just a number but sixteen-year-olds aren't allowed to send valentines to their teachers. I told him so at the time. But people often don't listen to me.

'Their mistake.'

CHAPTER 18

Miss Elphick's funeral is on Saturday but Mum makes me wear my school uniform. 'Mr Sweetman wants students to wear uniform. That way you'll stand out; he thinks Ella's parents will like it.' Mr Sweetman — Tony to Mum, of course — is always thinking about how things will look. Still, he's not a bad head teacher. Some of the girls think he's hot, which is ridiculous. He looks like a Radio 2 DJ.

Mum looks really nice in her black dress and coat. I look like an idiot in my sweatshirt and kilt. It's a really cold morning so I also wear my parka and a black beanie. We must look like a supermodel and a tramp walking to the car. I don't complain because one, I'm training myself not to think about outward appearance and two, Mum seems really, really stressed. She was on the verge of tears when we were having breakfast but then, when Herbert jumped onto the table and started nosing at the Marmite, she started to laugh hysterically.

'Take a chill pill, Mum,' I said, lifting Herbert down. It's one of my stock 'normal teenager' phrases. Something to make the parents roll their eyes and talk about the influence of America on today's youth.

'I'm sorry,' Mum said, wiping her eyes. 'I'm so strung up. I'm just dreading today.'

'The only way to get through it is to get through it,' I said, paraphrasing one of Miss Hughes' sayings.

'You're a wise old thing sometimes,' said Mum, giving me a quick hug. 'You know that?'

In the car Mum brakes twice for imaginary foxes and once because a bird of prey flies right in front of us, very low, its wings almost scraping our windscreen. That's an omen, all right. I'm just not sure what it signifies.

There are lots of cars already in the car park when we arrive. It looks weird to see the caretakers in suits with black ties standing by the main steps. Mum stops to have a word with Dodgy Dave, the older of the two. He gives me a wink when we move on. I ignore him.

We only go into the chapel for special assemblies or music concerts. It's usually kept locked. I don't play an instrument and I left the choir in Year 9 so I haven't been inside for ages. Today I'm surprised how big it is, how many people it can hold. The main part of the church and the choir stalls are almost full. There are white flowers on the altar. Lilies, fleshy and somehow obscene, their scent filling the air. The front two rows are empty, presumably for Miss Elphick's family. Mum sits about two rows back. Mr Lewis is in front of us with a fat woman who I assume is his wife. There are lots of other teachers here. Mrs Francis, the deputy head. Miss Palmer, my English teacher. Mr Carter, who teaches Geography. No sign of Mr Sweetman but maybe he's waiting for the family. Eventually, after craning my head round, I see her, near the back, her hair in grey plaits wound round her head. Miss Hughes smiles at me and I smile back. Patrick and Venetia are sitting with her but I can't really leave Mum. After a bit, Tash and her mother come to sit with us so that's all right.

Then there's a movement at the back of the church and we know that the coffin has arrived. I've never been to a funeral before. I've only been to one wedding, when Dad married Fleur, but that was in a registry office. They didn't even have bridesmaids. Still, Fleur wanted me to have a role — which was quite sweet of her really — so I wore this Laura Ashley dress and carried a bunch of flowers. I was twelve and felt a real idiot. Mum wasn't there, for obvious reasons, so I sat with Granny — Dad's mum — who kept stroking my hair and sighing. She didn't approve of Fleur then, but she slightly changed her mind when Fleur pumped out two babies in quick succession, one of them a *boy*.

This is a bit like a wedding, in an awful way. The coffin comes up the aisle, carried by men in black, and people follow behind, like bridesmaids and pageboys. These must be Miss Elphick's family, a grey-haired man and woman, holding hands tightly, and an older couple. Are they Miss Elphick's grandparents? It seems so awful somehow to outlive your grandchildren. Another middle-aged couple follow and then Mr Sweetman brings up the rear, looking like he has practised his caring face in the mirror.

It feels so shocking somehow to think that Miss Elphick's body is inside that box. Actually, it's not a box, more like a wicker casket with flowers entwined, very pretty. When people go up to read or speak, they have to pass right by it, just a few metres away from a dead body, a corpse. All the words for death are horrible. But death isn't horrible, Miss Hughes says, it's just a transition from one state to another.

Mr Sweetman reads something from Scripture, trying a bit too hard to sound sincere. The words are beautiful though. *I am the resurrection and the life, saith the Lord.* One of the relatives is next with that poem, 'Do not stand at my grave and weep . . . I am not there, I did not die'. For me this is less successful. We should weep and she did die. All those weasel words: passed away, fell asleep, safe in the arms of Jesus. I always think this when I visit old graveyards (a favourite pastime of Mum's). 'Joe Bloggs. Fell Asleep 10th May 1884.' Well, why on earth did you bury him then?

There are a few hymns, sung rather raggedly by the choir with Miss Rossetti taking all the solos. The organ sounds tinny and faint. It's an electric one because no one plays the original organ anymore, with its painted sides and its pipes soaring up to the ceiling. This chapel was added after R.M. Holland's time, when this was a private school. It's vaguely Art Nouveau with stained glass windows depicting lilies and knights. It's not really old, it has no deep energy.

The vicar talks about Miss Elphick. 'A dedicated teacher who inspired so many young people.' It doesn't sound as if he knew her very well. Neither of her parents gets up to speak. Then another hymn and the men in black are lifting the wicker coffin onto their shoulders. Miss Elphick's family follow behind. 'They're having a private interment,' I hear Mum telling Tash's mother. Interment, that's another euphemism. They are going to bury her.

Tash and I look at each other and sneak out past our mothers, who are now talking to Mr Lewis and his wife. There are going to be refreshments in the old dining hall, which should give us a chance to catch up with Miss Hughes and the rest of the group.

As we walk back down the aisle, I see the policewoman standing at the back. She's with the man who was also here the other day, grey-haired, rather bovine-looking. To my surprise, as I pass, she says, 'You must be Georgia Cassidy.'

'Georgia Newton,' I say. I don't approve of patriarchal surnames but nevertheless it annoys me when people assume I share Mum's.

'I'm DS Kaur and this is DS Winston.'

'Hallo,' I say, rather awkwardly. I can see Miss Hughes' plaits disappearing into the crowd.

'I've heard a lot about you,' says DS Kaur. She's small with dark skin and dark shoulder-length hair. Not pretty, exactly, but kind of striking. Her eyes are deep-set and the skin around them is shadowed. She looks as if she wouldn't rest if she was on the trail of a murderer. Which she is, of course.

'Did Miss Elphick teach you?' DS Winston asks.

'In Year 10,' I say. 'Excuse me, I must catch up with my friends.' I don't want to lose my chance of talking to Miss Hughes.

We meet outside the dining hall. People are already queuing up for food and drink. It's only midday, obscene really. I can't see Mum anywhere.

'That was a farce,' says Patrick.

'Her body should have been released to the elements,' says Venetia.

'I thought some of the singing was nice,' says Miss Hughes kindly. 'Especially *Amazing Grace*.'

'That was Miss Rossetti,' I say. 'The choir were quite bad, I thought.'

'It's not what Miss Elphick would have wanted,' says Tash. 'She was a very spiritual person.'

'She was indeed,' says Miss Hughes. Of course she knew Miss Elphick well; they were friends. No wonder she is looking so sombre today.

'We should have our own ceremony for her,' I say. 'Maybe on the winter solstice.'

'A lovely idea, Georgia.' Miss Hughes puts her hand on mine and I feel energy rushing through my veins.

'That's what I said,' says Venetia, rather sulkily. She's jealous of my bond with Miss H.

Another teacher comes up to talk to Miss Hughes, and Tash and Venetia drift away towards the food. Patrick takes my arm. 'Georgie, can I talk to you? In private.'

'OK,' I say. 'Let's go upstairs.'

There are no notices up but we know the rest of the school is out-of-bounds today. The caretakers are still shepherding people into the hall so there's no one to see us running up the back staircase. We go up to the first floor. R.M. Holland's apartments. There's a different energy up here. You could be in a different world, a different time. It's not just because there are carpets and proper light shades. It's deeper than that. I can just imagine R.M. Holland, quill in hand, or Alice drifting along like Lady Macbeth, candle held aloft.

Patrick doesn't seem to notice the atmosphere. He strides along, trying door handles. He's not in school uniform. He's wearing a dark suit and, from the back, he looks like a stranger.

'They're all locked,' I say. I'm not actually sure if that's true. I think I once heard Mum say that most of the keys are lost.

We reach the spiral staircase that leads to Holland's study. I've been here once before with Mum and I remember what she told me about the footprints in the carpet. Suddenly I feel as if Alice's spirit is very near.

'Let's go up,' says Patrick.

'It's locked,' I say.

'No, it's not. Dodgy Dave always forgets.'

I don't want to go into the study with Patrick. We're like brother and sister but for some reason I don't want to be alone with him. He looks so grown-up today, handsome but also slightly intimidating. Also, the petty law-abiding side of me does not want to be discovered in the attic room with Patrick O'Leary. I can just imagine what my mother would say. She'd probably make me take the morning-after pill.

But Patrick is climbing the stairs. I follow, putting my feet carefully in the embossed footprints. When I get to the top of the stairs and step into the study, my heart stops. There's a man sitting in Holland's chair, his arms stretched out like a zombie. For a moment I think: it's him, he's come for me. Like the man in *The Stranger*. I start to move backwards but Patrick's laugh stops me.

'Do you like my dummy?'

'What?' The spell is broken. 'Did you put that there? Why?'

Patrick shrugs. He's in darkness so I can't see his face but his voice sounds hard and abrasive, the sort of voice he uses with his rugby mates.

'Just for a laugh. A few of us came up here on Halloween. It's from the textiles department.'

'Where did you get the clothes?'

'Left over from *Oliver*.' The show Miss Elphick put on last year. 'That's probably Mr Pickwick or someone.' I don't correct him. I'm thinking: this is what Mum must have seen on the night of Halloween. That's why she came home early and in such a state. For a moment I almost hate Patrick.

'Georgie,' he says, in an entirely different voice. 'I need to talk to you.' He sits on the little velvet chaise longue in the corner and pats the seat next to him. After a moment's hesitation, I sit down next to him.

'What do you want to talk to me about?' I say. I try to stop myself looking at the photographs on the walls and on the desk. It's ages since I've been up here and I wish I had time to appreciate it. But Patrick says, plunging me back into reality, 'The police are here.'

'I know,' I say. 'The policewoman, DS Kaur, talked to me just now.'

'What did she say?'

'Nothing much. The other one, the man, asked if Miss Elphick had taught me.'

Patrick runs a hand through his hair.

'Georgie, I think they suspect me.'

I stare at him. 'Why would they suspect you?'

'They've found out about the valentine card. They're asking what I was doing on the night that she was killed.'

'What were you doing?'

He doesn't answer for a second and then he says, head in hands, 'I went round to her house.'

'*What?*' I very much hope that I've misunderstood.

He looks up and now he looks young, much younger than sixteen. He looks almost like my little brother Tiger, who is not three yet.

'I went to Miss Elphick's house. I just wanted to see her. I was upset. She shouldn't have told Mr Lewis about the card. Then everyone in the form knew. I had to switch classes. I pretended I didn't mind but I was . . . upset.'

I can understand this. Patrick made light of it at the time but it must have been embarrassing for him — one of the coolest boys in school — to be known to have a crush on a teacher.

'Why now?' I say. 'Valentine's was ages ago.' I had two cards: one from a boy in my Spanish class and one of unknown origin. I didn't know Ty then or I'm sure he would have come up with something red and sparkly, involving animals wearing clothes.

'Miss Hughes told me to,' says Patrick. 'She said that the unresolved feelings were blocking my spiritual progress. She said I had to make amends.'

Immediately I am jealous. Patrick has been having private meetings with Miss Hughes. I try hard to squash these feelings. Jealousy is a purely negative emotion.

'Did you see Miss Elphick?' I ask.

'No,' he says. 'I knocked on the door but there was no answer. I just hung around waiting. I was in the shadows by the church so no one saw me. But I saw him. I saw him leaving her house.'

'Who?'

'Mr Lewis.'

CHAPTER 19

Patrick asks me not to tell anyone. He's only confiding in me now because he's worried he hasn't got a proper alibi for the night that Miss Elphick was killed. He told them that he was playing Call of Duty on his computer (classic 'normal teenager' behaviour) but he was actually writing on MySecretDiary. He was alone in the house because his parents were at a party (they're very sociable, Patrick's parents, I can tell Mum slightly disapproves) and his older brother was out with his girlfriend.

'It looks bad,' he keeps saying. 'What if someone saw me at the house?'

'But we ought to tell the police about Mr Lewis. I mean, he could be the murderer.'

It sounds absurd even as I say it. Mr Lewis is a *teacher;* reliable, boring sometimes, given to saying things like 'here's a fun factoid about John Steinbeck'. He can't be a murderer, a person who goes around in a mask carrying a dagger dripping with blood. *Incarnadine,* as *Macbeth* and R.M. Holland would say. Mr Lewis was sitting in front of us in the chapel just now, his arm around his wife, wiping his eyes occasionally. He seemed upset but he didn't seem wracked with guilt. Surely, if he'd killed Miss Elphick, there would be some wracking going on?

'No!' says Patrick. And he grabs my arm, looking grown-up again. He's very strong, I think. He works out every day and he plays rugby. He could overpower me in an instant. But then reality reasserts itself. This is *Patrick,* my friend, my almost brother, one of The Group. He wouldn't hurt me. He's upset and he needs my help.

'You can't tell anyone,' he says. 'They'd find out I was there and they would think I killed her. You can see the headlines, can't you? *Disturbed Teen Kills Teacher After Rejection.* "Friends say Patrick O'Leary was a loner who liked playing war games on his computer".'

I laugh, despite myself. '*Blonde* teacher,' I say. 'They'd be sure to mention her hair, if not her bra size.'

Patrick doesn't laugh and he doesn't let go of my arm.

'Promise you won't tell anyone.'

'I promise.'

He lets go.

'Swear by the circle.'

To swear by the circle is to invoke the power of our group — our coven, if you like. If I break the oath, we'll all suffer.

'I swear by the circle,' I sigh.

Patrick stands up and tries to smile, as if this has all been a bit of a joke, a bit of rugby players' banter.

'We'd better go down,' he says. 'They'll think we're up to no good.'

Up to no good. It's a strange phrase. Old-fashioned but also somehow sinister.

'You go first,' I say, trying to keep my voice light too. 'We'd better not be seen together.'

I listen to Patrick's heavy steps descending the spiral staircase. I'm alone in Holland's study, as I've always wanted to be. I look round the room. There are two windows, one an odd shape like a shamrock with a stained glass flower — a poppy, I think — in the middle, the other a normal, sloping attic sort. Holland's desk is under this window, with a carved chair, currently occupied by the dummy. The walls are papered in red, slightly faded with a watery stripe, but you can hardly see the colour because two of the walls have bookshelves up to the ceiling and the other two are covered with framed photographs. There's also the chaise longue, where Patrick and I have been sitting, and a small fireplace with an iron grate. It's the centre of the house, I think. A glowing red heart under the eaves.

I should go back downstairs, eat sausage rolls and speak about Miss Elphick in hushed tones. But I want to spend a few more minutes in here first. It's almost as if R.M. Holland is protecting me against what lies below: secrets and threats and death itself. I get up and look at the photographs on the walls. They are all black and white, mostly showing men with beards and women with hooped dresses. There are a couple of university pictures: a large one entitled 'Peterhouse 1832' showing a crowd of students in gowns outside a college that looks just like St Jude's, and another of four young men holding guns. 'Peterhouse small bore club' runs the handwritten message underneath. I wonder if people made jokes about the name even then.

There are only two pictures of him alone. One shows him in this room, sitting in the chair now occupied by the scary dummy, and pretending to write. Who took it, I wonder? Alice, in a rare moment of domestic bliss? The other shows him in a deckchair on the lawn, where the netball court is now. He looks relaxed, legs stretched out in front of him, wearing a panama hat and raising a hand to the invisible photographer. I look at the caption underneath. 'With Mariana,' it says.

But there's no one else in the picture.

I manage to slide into the dining room without being noticed. Mum is talking to her friend Debra; they are both alternately wiping their eyes and laughing so I presume they are talking about Miss Elphick. Tash and Vee are talking with some girls in my year. There aren't that many students here and, with the exception of Vee, who goes to a different school and isn't wearing uniform anyway, we all look rather self-conscious in our blue sweatshirts. I can't see Patrick anywhere. I go over to the group. One girl, Isla Bates, is crying in that really fake way, wafting her hand over her eyes to dry the non-existent tears.

'It's just, like, so sad,' she is saying. 'I loved Miss Elphick.'

'It is sad,' says Tash, patting Isla on the back and crossing her eyes at me.

'They're saying the killer is still out there somewhere,' says Isla's friend, Paige.

Of course the killer is still out there, I want to say. You don't need to be a criminal mastermind to work that one out. Instead I say, 'The detectives were at the funeral. The ones investigating the case.'

Isla gives a little scream. 'Where?'

'They're undercover,' I say, straight-faced, 'so you can't spot them.'

'They could be in this room,' says Vee. 'In fact, the killer could be here too.'

'Oh my God,' Isla clutches her. 'Seriously. Don't.'

I can't stop myself looking over to where Mr Lewis is standing with Mr Sweetman. They are talking very intently, heads together. Mr Lewis looks the same as ever — tall, a bit untidy, rather beaten down by life. He can't be the murderer. Can he?

'Did you see the Sweetman's wife?' says Paige. 'Over there, in the black trouser suit. Talking to Miss Palmer.'

I look over and see a slim blonde woman in sharply-cut trousers. She's exactly the wife I would have picked out for our head teacher: attractive but hard. Her aura is bright but insubstantial, sunlight reflecting on shallow water. Miss Palmer, who is really sweet, looks as if she is finding her hard-going.

'She's really pretty,' says Isla. 'What a shame.' Isla is one of the girls who makes a big thing about fancying Mr Sweetman.

'She's a lawyer,' I say. I think I've heard this from Mum.

'They've got two really cute kids,' says Paige. 'My friend babysits sometimes.'

'No *way*,' says Isla, as if this is the most amazing news ever.

Tash catches my eye. 'Must go and see someone,' she says, grabbing my arm. Vee follows us as we make our way through the crowd (there are still loads of people here, though I can't see Miss Elphick's family anywhere) towards Miss Hughes. She is standing on her own by the drinks table. But she doesn't look awkward or lonely; she is smiling gently as if thinking benevolent thoughts.

'Hallo, girls,' she says. 'Enjoying the funeral meats?'

Miss Hughes is a vegan.

'Isn't that from *Hamlet*?' I say. 'Something about funeral baked meats?'

'Clever girl,' says Miss Hughes. ' "*The funeral baked meats did coldly furnish forth the marriage tables*". It's about Gertrude marrying again so soon after her husband's death.'

I can tell Vee is impatient with this. She hates it when I get a quote right. 'Miss Hughes,' she says, 'who do you think killed Miss Elphick?'

Miss Hughes looks at her steadily, her eyes very blue. 'That's not the question we should be asking,' she says.

'What is the question?' says Tash.

'Whether Ella's spirit is still with us,' says Miss Hughes. 'Or whether we need to help her towards the light.'

'Were you talking to that odd woman from the sixth-form college?' says Mum, as we drive home. 'What's her name, Bryony something? Bryony Hughes, that's it. How do you know her?'

'She used to teach Venetia,' I say.

'She's a bit of an oddball,' says Mum. 'Ella used to say that she was a witch.'

We are both silent for a few minutes. Mum is obviously thinking about Ella and I'm wondering how much Miss Elphick knew about Miss Hughes' powers. Probably it was just a joke to her, as it clearly is for Mum. She's been in an odd mood ever since we left the school, almost manic. Laughing about the terrible singing one minute, wiping away tears the next, the car wandering over to the other side of the road. I can't wait until I'm seventeen and can do the driving.

'I saw you talking to Patrick O'Leary,' she says.

I decide that silence is best. I watch the grey winter fields slide past; they look soft, like fur.

'Is he a friend of yours?' asks Mum, after a long pause.

I shrug (as teens are meant to do).

'I can see that he's quite dishy,' she says, in a truly gruesome attempt to seem relatable.

I say nothing.

'Bad boys are always attractive.'

Dear God. Make it stop. To put us both out of our misery, I say, 'I don't know him very well. He seems a bit boring. You know, rugby player and all that.'

Mum relaxes visibly. Her shoulders lowering, her hands unclenching on the steering wheel.

'Do you prefer Ty to Patrick?' I can't help teasing her a little.

'I don't dislike Ty,' she says. 'He's a nice boy. A nice man. I just think he's a little old for you.'

'Would you rather I went out with Patrick?'

She gives me a quick look. 'Has he asked you out?'

'No,' I say. 'Chill out, Mum.' That piece of teen speak obviously reassures her. We drive home in what passes for a companionable silence.

Listen to the wind howling. It seems to rock the train, does it not? We're quite safe here, though. After all, there's no connecting door between the carriages. No one can come in or out. More brandy?

What happened next? Well, the prosaic truth is: nothing much to speak of. Gudgeon's parents took his body away and he was buried at his home in Gloucestershire. I didn't attend. I don't know what happened to Wilberforce. And as I said before, the police never found their killer. A year later, the ruined house was demolished. I continued my studies. I think I became quite solitary and strange. Other students would look at me oddly as I crossed the quad or sat in the dining hall. 'That's him,' I heard someone whisper once. 'The other one.' I suppose I became 'the other one' to most men in Peterhouse, possibly even to myself.

I didn't see much of Bastian or Collins. I was now officially a member of the Hell Club but I didn't attend their meetings or the infamous Blood Ball, which was held every year. I spent most of my time in my rooms or in the library. My only contact with my fellow students was with members of the shooting club. With them, at least, I managed some uncomplicated, comradely hours.

I graduated with a first, which was gratifying. I had heard that Lord Bastian had been sent down and that Collins did not complete his degree. But they were at different colleges and our paths had long since diverged. I began to read for a doctorate, continuing with the solitary, bachelor existence that I had established in my undergraduate days.

Then, in my first term as a postgraduate student, I received some rather strange correspondence. It was November, a bitterly cold day, and I remember the frost crunching under my feet as I walked to the porters' lodge to collect my post. Not that I ever received many letters. My mother wrote occasionally and I subscribed to a couple of scholarly theological journals. That was it. But on this day there was something else. A letter with a foreign postmark, inscribed in a strange, slanting hand. I opened it with some curiosity. Inside was a cutting from a Persian newspaper. I did not, of course, understand the Perso-Arabic script but there was a translation, written with the same italic pen. It said that a man called Amir Ebrahimi had been killed in a freak accident involving a hot air balloon. The ascent had gone perfectly but, at some point during the flight, Ebrahimi had fallen from the basket underneath the balloon and had plummeted to his death. I turned the letter over in my hands, wondering why someone would have thought that I would be interested in this gruesome event. It was then that I saw the words written on the reverse of the paper. Hell is empty. *And I remembered that Ebrahimi had been the name of the third man, the companion of Bastian and Collins.*

The other one.

Clare

I feel a little uneasy about leaving Georgie at home on the evening of Ella's funeral. But Debra begs me. 'I'll go mad if I'm home with Leo and the kids tonight. I need to be with someone who loved Ella. We can go to the pub in the village. Have a curry, share a bottle of wine. It doesn't have to be a late one.' So I ask Georgie and she seems fine with it. She says she'll have Tash and Venetia round to watch *Strictly*. I don't ask if Ty is coming but I presume it'll just be the girls. I wasn't too pleased to see Georgie chatting to Patrick O'Leary after the funeral. I taught him in Year 9 and he's the sort of boy who is acquiring a power over women and the ruthlessness to use it. I know his parents slightly. They're hard-drinking, hard-partying Irish people. Nice enough but not the sort to talk to their son about his misogynistic attitudes. But, when I brought the subject up, Georgie said airily that Patrick was rather boring. I found this reassuring and probably true. I don't suppose that there's much in Patrick O'Leary's head besides rugby.

I was also rather disturbed to see Georgie in a group that included Miss Hughes, an English teacher at the sixth-form college. Bryony Hughes is a bit of an old hippy, hair in Brunhilda plaits, dripping with crystals and silver jewellery. Apparently she gets great exam results but she's one of those teachers who relies on charisma — a sort of Welsh Miss Jean Brodie — and I always find that rather suspect. Ella was a bit that way inclined, which is maybe why she was friends with her. Mind you, I think they had a falling out not too long ago. Ella used to say that Bryony was a white witch who got her kicks from dancing around graveyards at midnight. I don't suppose that's true but maybe Ella started to find the whole Weird Sister act a little creepy. Anyway, I didn't want Georgie falling under her spell. She'll probably go to the sixth-form college after Talgarth and I'd like to make sure that she isn't in Miss Hughes' class. Mind you, I don't expect that Georgie will take English. She's never been that interested in books.

Natasha and Venetia arrive just as I'm leaving, dropped off by Venetia's older brother in a rather flashy sports car. They're nice girls. Tash is full of enthusiasm, like a setter puppy. I find her a bit flaky sometimes but I can see that she would be good fun to have as a friend. She's bright, too, and doesn't seem too boy-obsessed. Her mother is a music teacher and her father is a doctor so my middle-class anxieties are soothed. Venetia is a redhead, very thin and slightly nervous-looking. Her parents are rather upper-class, which I find as off-putting as the O'Learys and their Derby Day drinking sessions. Really, it's very difficult to get the class thing right for me. Simon would say I'm only happy with *Guardian* readers who own their own homes and he's probably right. I suppose Georgie met Venetia during her time at St Faith's so it's nice — if slightly surprising — that they've stayed friends.

I'd told Georgie she could order pizza on my account and Tash thanks me profusely.

'You're the best, Clare.' All Georgie's friends call me Clare at home and Miss Cassidy at school. They seem to manage the switch quite easily. I'm the one who can't forget that I once gave Tash a detention for forgetting her homework or that, in Year 8, Georgie's friend Paige wrote an essay about her mum's boyfriend and his drug habit.

Debra and I meet at The Royal Oak, one of the many inns where Charles II is meant to have sheltered whilst on the run from the Roundheads. These days it's a gastro pub, rather prone to balancing food in little towers but they do a good curry and it's not too noisy, even on a Saturday night. I usually try not to drink at all if I'm driving but I have a small glass of red wine. Debra has a large gin and tonic.

'I need it,' she says, clinking glasses. 'God, I hate funerals.'

'I don't suppose anyone enjoys them,' I say.

'I don't know,' she says, knocking back half the drink although she, too, has a car outside. 'Some of my older relatives seem to love them. But it's different when it's someone old, who's lived a good life, all their children and grandchildren there. Remembering them. But with Ella. Jesus. She had so much living left to do.'

'I know,' I say. 'Her poor parents. Did you talk to them?'

Ella's parents returned from the crematorium just before I left the wake. I'd only managed a few quick words, an awkward embrace, a nebulous promise to keep in touch.

'Just briefly,' says Debra. 'They're being so brave but her mum looked devastated. "I've lost my best friend", she said to me.'

Would Georgie describe me as her best friend? Almost certainly not, which is probably as it should be, but, just for a moment, I feel a pang of something that is close to envy. I'm not exactly friends with my mum, though I love her, I suppose. I feel closer to my grandmother in Scotland, although I don't get to see her often enough. She writes me letters but I never seem to have time to answer them. I'd like to set her up with Skype but she says the Wi-Fi connection is too weak in Ullapool. I must go see her soon.

I take a sip of wine, trying to drink slowly. I'm thinking about mothers and daughters and almost miss Debra saying, 'How's Rick bearing up?'

'OK,' I say. 'He sat in front of me at the funeral.'

'With his wife?'

'Yes.'

'His wife never knew about Ella, did she?'

'I'm pretty sure she didn't.'

Debra leans forward, in spite of the fact we're in one of the booths and there's nobody within earshot.

'The police asked me about Rick.'

'Did they?'

'Yes, they asked me what happened in Hythe. I said I didn't know because I wasn't there.' Debra does know about Ella's one-night stand with Rick, however. Ella told her, dwelling on Rick's pathetic lovelorn behaviour. It's only now that I'm wondering if his behaviour was more sinister than pathetic.

'They asked me about Rick too,' I say.

'Did you tell them that he had a thing for you too?'

'She seemed to know already. DS Kaur, I mean.'

'She's a toughie, isn't she? Did you know that she used to go to Talgarth?'

'Yes, she told me.'

'Dorothy Lodden in textiles remembers teaching her.'

'Really?' I'm interested in this. 'What was she like as a schoolgirl?'

'Bright, apparently. But she didn't like textiles — or needlework as it was called then — much. Used to sit at the back and read James Herbert books.'

I can just imagine the young Harbinder being a fan of the horror genre.

'Do you really think they suspect someone at the school?' I say.

'Well, it's usually someone close to the victim, isn't it?' says Debra. 'That's what they say in the books.' Then suddenly her face crumples and tears start to pour down her cheeks. She dabs at them with her red napkin. 'Jesus,' she says. 'Listen to me! The victim. I sound like someone in a TV drama, the sort Leo likes to watch on a Saturday night. But Ella was our friend.'

I remember how interested Debra was in the police and their investigation. Maybe that's what we all do: construct a story to avoid facing the reality.

'The whole thing is like being in a play,' I say. 'Or a nightmare. I keep thinking that she'll come back.'

'As a ghost, you mean?' says Debra.

That wasn't what I meant but, now she says it, I imagine Ella gliding towards me, her long blonde hair streaming out behind her. Like Lady Macbeth. Like Alice Holland. The ghost Ella doesn't speak but I know that she is angry with me.

Debra puts her hand on mine. 'She won't come back,' she says gently. 'She's dead, Clare.'

'I know,' I say. At that moment I feel utterly despairing.

I drive home very slowly. A mist has blown in from the sea — a sea fret they call it round here — and visibility is down to a few metres. Putting on the beam doesn't help; it just lights up the fog, making it look theatrically spooky, like dry ice. When I get back, Georgie is in bed. Three burnt-out candles are on the coffee table, reminding me suddenly of *The Stranger*. There are some dried leaves on the table too and I sniff them suspiciously. I don't think Georgie smokes weed but you never know. This smells like potpourri. I always get masses of the stuff as end-of-year presents, along with chocolates, candles, the occasional bottle of wine or fridge magnets that say, 'My best teacher'. Herbert is frisking around, trying to get in the way. He also sniffs at the leaves curiously, one ear up, one ear down.

'Come on, sniffer dog,' I say. 'Time for your night-time wee.'

I take him across the road. There's a full moon but it's hazy in the mist, shining a faint diffused light over the factory ramparts. I think of the lights that I saw there the other night. Is it possible that someone is sleeping rough in the building? Should I tell someone? The police? A homeless charity? Maybe Harbinder Kaur could help? I saw her at the funeral but she didn't speak to me. I suppose she and Neil were just there out of respect. I didn't see them at the wake.

Herbert lifts his leg at last so I hurry back inside. I put the security chain on and check the back door. Then I go upstairs. Georgie's light is on so I knock.

'Come in.'

She's sitting up in bed reading Harry Potter. Her cuddly Meerkat (a present from Simon) is propped up next to her. She looks about seven.

I sit on the bed. 'Did you have a nice evening?'

'Yes,' she says. '*Strictly* was boring so we played Cards Against Humanity.'

'Did Venetia's brother pick her up?'

'Tash's mum. She said she'd ring you.'

I smooth down Georgie's Hogwarts duvet. Her room is a mixture of child and teenager. She still has her Sylvanian dolls' house but there is a plethora of electronic gadgets too, the charging leads snaking across the room. The polaroids pinned up above her bed show Georgie and her girlfriends smiling into the camera selfie-style, lips pouting, hair cascading.

'Did you have a good time with Debra?' she asks politely.

'Yes,' I say. 'A bit sad. We kept talking about Ella.'

'It's not wrong to be sad. She was one of your best friends.'

'You're right,' I say, kissing her on the head. 'Goodnight, darling. Don't read too late.'

I have a quick shower, put on my warmest pyjamas and get into bed. Herbert is already snoring. I open my diary, prepared to relive the day. I haven't written for the last few days — too strung up probably — but I feel that the funeral deserves a record.

My last entry was on Monday 30th October. It ends, 'Halloween tomorrow. God help us.' My writing ends there but on the page opposite there is a new note. Handwriting that is at once alien and horribly familiar. It begins: 'Greetings from a sincere friend.'

CHAPTER 21

'It's from *The Woman in White*,' I say.

'What is?' says Neil.

I rang Harbinder first thing this morning but I didn't expect her to be at work on a Sunday. However, she asked me to meet her at the police station and, when I get there, the place is full of people staring at their screens. I guess crime never sleeps, even in West Sussex. I've never been inside a police station before and I'm surprised at how office-like it is. There are computers and coffee machines and notices about yoga in the lunch break. There are also more women than men.

Harbinder ushers us into a tiny meeting room. There are armchairs and even a vase with artificial flowers in it, but the space still feels faintly sinister. There's a darkened window opposite and I wonder if people are watching from the other side.

Last night Harbinder told me to put my diary in a plastic bag without touching it any more. Now she turns the pages, wearing thin plastic gloves.

'In *The Woman in White*,' I say, 'Count Fosco, the villain, starts writing in Marian Halcombe's diary. He takes over the narrative for a few pages. His section is called "Postscript by a sincere friend".'

Harbinder says, 'You were reading *The Woman in White* when I came round the other evening.'

I'm surprised she has remembered. 'Yes,' I say, 'it's one of my favourite books.'

Harbinder flicks back the pages and begins to read, in her flat, emotionless voice.

> *Greetings from a sincere friend. I refer to the perusal (which I have just completed) of this interesting Diary. There are many hundred pages here. I can lay my hand on my heart, and declare that every page has charmed, refreshed, delighted me.*
>
> *Admirable woman!*
>
> *But, Clare, not everyone appreciates you as I do. It breaks my heart to say so but there are people who are working against you. I have already disposed of one of these creatures. I will fall on the others like a ravening beast.*

'The first bit is directly from the book,' I say. 'Up until *Admirable woman.*' I've brought my copy with me, an old Dover edition with a cover showing a woman in a sumptuous white satin dress that Anne Catherick could never have afforded. I've marked the place and pass the book over to the two detectives.

Neil reads with his mouth slightly open. Harbinder has scanned the page in seconds.

'Well, our man has definitely read *The Woman in White*,' she says. 'If it is a man.'

'It goes on a bit, doesn't it?' says Neil, weighing the book in his hand as if it's a piece of meat.

'Do you teach *The Woman in White* in school?' asks Harbinder.

'No. It's not on the syllabus.'

'What about with your adult students? Your creative writing classes?'

'Sometimes. I use it as an example of the use of multiple narrators.'

'Do you recognise anything else here?'

'Yes,' I say. '*The Ravening Beast* is the name of an unpublished book by R.M. Holland.'

'Who's he?' says Neil.

Harbinder answers him. 'He's the writer who used to live at the school.

About a hundred years ago. His study's on the top floor of the Old Building. He wrote that ghost story, *The Stranger*. It was on TV a few years back.'

'So everyone would know about this . . . this Ravening Beast?'

'No,' I say. 'We don't teach R.M. Holland and he's not on the syllabus, either. But even people who have heard of Holland won't know of *The Ravening Beast*. It was never published and the manuscript has vanished. There are extracts in his diaries, that's all.'

'Bloody hell,' says Neil. 'I thought only Adrian Mole wrote a diary but everyone's at it.'

Harbinder gives him a look. 'Let's concentrate on *your* diary, Clare. Who would have had access to it?'

'Access?' It seems such a stiff, legalistic word.

Harbinder sighs patiently. 'Who would have been able to write in your diary? Do you always keep it at home?'

'No. I often take the current book to school. I write in my breaks sometimes.'

'Did you take it with you this week?'

'Yes.' I'd been intending to write on Halloween, whilst waiting for the rehearsal to begin, but then I went up to Holland's study and saw that figure in his chair. I went home immediately, leaving Anoushka to cope with *Little Shop of Horrors*.

'Where do you keep it when you're at school?'

'In my bag or in my locker.'

'Where's the locker?'

'In the English common room.'

'Is it locked?'

'No.' The keys vanished long before I arrived at the school.

'It's not much of a locker, then, is it?' says Neil, with an abrupt laugh.

Harbinder ignores him. 'We'll need to take fingerprints of everyone in the English department,' she says. 'Handwriting samples too, to eliminate them. We already have yours but we'll also need your daughter's.'

'Georgie's?'

'Yes. She's the one at home with you. We need to eliminate her too.'

That's another chilling word. *Eliminate*. I think of the diary entry. *I have already disposed of one of these creatures.*

I say, 'Do you think the person who wrote this is the person who killed Ella?'

Harbinder and Neil look at each other, as if deciding how much to tell me. Eventually Harbinder says, 'There was a handwriting match between the first entry you showed me and the note found at the scene. There just weren't enough words for it to be conclusive.'

For a moment I'm genuinely afraid that I'm going to vomit or faint. It's one thing to fear a thing for yourself, another to hear it confirmed in a matter-of-fact way by a Detective Sergeant. It's as if the angel of death has flown over the room, flapping his grisly wings.

Hell is empty.

'But that doesn't mean that this person,' Harbinder taps my diary with her gloved hand, 'is the perpetrator. It's always a mistake to believe letters purporting to be from killers. That's what held up the Yorkshire Ripper case, back in the seventies. They believed that "I'm Jack" tape and had voice experts analysing the accent, wasting hours of manpower, and it was just some nutter who wanted attention. That might be the case here too.'

'But the note at the scene . . .' I say.

'Yes,' says Harbinder, 'that makes it a little more significant.'

'Whoever wrote that had read *The Stranger*,' I say. '*Hell is empty* is a key line in the story. It's what they have to shout when they get to the ruined house.'

'I remember,' says Harbinder. 'And a load of crap it was too. So the quote could be from *The Stranger*. But it seems more likely it's from *The Tempest* — that's a GCSE text, isn't it?'

'Yes,' I say.

'So anyone in the English department would be familiar with it?'

'I suppose so. But you can't think . . .'

'We have to follow every line of investigation,' says Neil. 'We'll need all your diaries too.'

'All of them?'

'How many are there?' said Neil.

'About thirty,' I say. 'I've been keeping a diary since I was eleven. On and off.' That was the year I started secondary school. I was obsessed with a boy I used to see at the bus stop and almost every entry ends: *Saw PB* or *Did Not See PB.* I stopped keeping a diary when I was at university but started again when things started to sour with Simon. First entry of my new single state: *Ten weeks since Simon left but I'll never measure my life in terms of him again.*

'Why do you need them all?' I ask.

'We know someone wrote in at least one of your previous diaries,' says Harbinder. 'We need to check the rest out. Even if they didn't write in them, they may've read them, left fingerprints.'

I don't want to give them my diaries. I imagine Harbinder reading them with that contemptuous smile lifting the corner of her mouth. Or regaling her colleagues with the choicest incidents. 'Now she thinks she's pregnant after a one-night stand with a taxi driver!'

Neil obviously takes my silence for terror. And he's not far wrong.

'We'll issue you some police protection,' he says. 'A patrol car will watch your house and we'll give you a special number that you can ring if you're worried.'

'Do you really think I might be in danger?'

'I don't think so,' says Harbinder. 'This person' — she taps the book again — 'seems keen to protect you, if anything.' After a pause she says, 'Still, it might be just as well not to go out after dark.'

I drive home in a state of shock. Has a murderer been reading my diary? Has he (I think of him as a he, while I noticed that Harbinder did not commit herself) been following my innermost thoughts, the feelings that I would be too embarrassed to express out loud? All the times I've resented Simon and Fleur, my petty jealousies at work, my ridiculous belief that I'm going to write a book? Did he read that awful entry about Ella? Was that why she was killed? *I have already disposed of one of these creatures.* It doesn't bear thinking about. And someone had not only read my diary but *written in it.* The tiny, sinister script that apparently matched the note found by Ella's body. Had the writer been close to me at work or at home? Was he, as the police seemed to think, someone I actually know?

When I get home I have a raging headache and just want to go to bed with a hot water bottle and some aspirin. But I'm greeted by the pungent smell of frying mince and onions and, in the kitchen, Georgie and Ty are cooking.

'We thought we'd cook you a proper Sunday lunch, Mum,' says Georgie, tipping in a tin of tomatoes. 'It was Ty's idea.'

Suddenly I think of my grandparents in Scotland, the table loaded with roast meat and potatoes. Everything golden and glistening, tasting strongly of itself. The blue and white gravy boat steaming in the centre. Today's lunch seems to be spaghetti bolognaise, heavy on garlic and oregano. I'm still feeling slightly sick and my stomach churns at the thought of the meal to come but there's no denying that it's a very sweet gesture. Ty is chopping up a green pepper, taking a lot of care to keep the pieces the same size. Georgie has laid the table and made a rather lovely arrangement of holly and ivy. Herbert is watching her as she stirs the sauce. I don't want him to get fat so never feed him scraps. Georgie does though and he's expectant. He loves human food.

'I brought some wine,' says Ty. He wraps a napkin round the bottle like a proper barman and pours me a glass.

'Thank you, Ty.' I try not to take too big a gulp. Ty pours Georgie a glass too but I decide not to say anything.

I need some ibuprofen but don't want to take them with the wine so I force myself to sit at the table and chat. I try to find out whether Ty has ambitions beyond working in a pub and I'm pleased to find out that he is thinking of applying to university next year.

'I've got A-Levels,' he says. 'English, IT and art. Not great grades but maybe I could get in to do English somewhere. I liked English at school. I had a really good teacher.'

People often remember their English teacher fondly. It's never maths or ICT. This is something that sustains me on the days when my Year 8, Group C, are being particularly devilish, the idea that one day a Booker Prize winner will mention me in their acceptance speech.

'You need good grades for English,' says Georgie, rather tactlessly.

Ty blushes. 'Media Studies then. Or Creative Writing.'

'Mum teaches creative writing,' says Georgie. 'Why don't you go to her class?'

Ty mutters something incomprehensible. I take pity on him and say, 'Good luck. Let me know if I can help with your personal statement or anything.'

'I might not go to university,' says Georgie. 'I might just travel or something like that.'

Immediately my headache ratchets up several notches.

'It's too early to decide yet,' I say. 'You could travel *and* go to university. Take a gap year.'

'Fleur went to Thailand on her gap year.'

I bet she did. 'There are lots of options,' I say, keeping an encouraging smile firmly fixed on.

'Anyway,' says Georgie, 'writers are born, not made.'

'Who told you that?'

'I read it somewhere,' says Georgie. 'How can you tell if pasta is done? Do you have to throw it at the wall?'

I manage to eat a good helping of the pasta. Ty has thirds and seems delighted with their culinary prowess. 'It's just like the sauce at Pizza Express,' he keeps saying. Georgie scowls, perhaps realising that this is not the compliment he imagines it to be. There's cheesecake to follow and Georgie even makes coffee in the machine, the way I like it. They won't let me clear away either, so I go into the sitting room and toy with the Sunday paper. The magazine has gold and red stars on the cover and a model wearing a dress that seems to be made from bottle tops, the sort I used to collect for Blue Peter. 'Five Fashion Fireworks'. Oh God, it's November the fifth. Guy Fawkes Night. I'll have Herbert shivering and whimpering all night as idiots set off bangers. We're quite isolated here but you can hear the fireworks for miles. I often wonder if this was what it was like in Sussex in the war, hearing the guns from France.

Ty leaves at five, just as the first rockets go off. Herbert jumps on the sofa and jams his head under my arm.

'Poor baby,' Georgie strokes him. 'It's just people commemorating some-one being tortured to death, Herbie. Nothing to worry about.' She says this every year.

'Georgie,' I say. 'I've got something to tell you.'

Instantly she looks wary, the good mood engendered by the meal fizzling away.

'I went to see the police this morning,' I say. 'I don't want to scare you, but they think there's a chance that . . . a chance that Ella's killer might be . . . well, interested in me.'

'Interested in you?' Georgie's face is pale and her dark eyes (like mine, people say) are huge.

'He wrote something,' I say. 'Something that was left at the scene of the crime.' I don't want to tell her about the diary; she might panic, imagine some-one creeping into the house, pen in hand. Is that, in fact, what happened?

'There's going to be a police car outside the house,' I say, 'protecting us. And I've got a number to ring if I'm worried about anything. I'll give it to you too. These are just precautions, however. I'm sure there's nothing to worry about. The police are pretty close to finding the person who did it.' I try to voice this outright lie with conviction.

'Are they really?'

'Yes. The police are very efficient these days, you know. It's all forensics and stuff.'

She still looks pale so I take her hand. 'It's all right, darling. We'll be fine. But we must be sensible. I don't want you coming home alone. I want you to wait for me at school.'

Now she just looks mutinous. 'What if you've got a rehearsal?'

'You can work in the library.'

'Great. Thanks very much.'

'It's not for long. Just until the police have made an arrest.' Herbert whim-pers behind the cushions as if he realises how unlikely this is.

'Can I go to Tash's?'

'If you stay together. I'll speak to her mum. Explain the situation.'

'What about Ty? Can I still see him?'

'I suppose so. As long as he picks you up and drops you off.' For the first time I'm glad that Ty is a fully grown man with a car. 'Just be careful. Promise me that you will.'

'I will,' she says, pulling Herbert out from behind the cushions and putting him on her lap. 'But I'm sure it will all be OK.'

This is meant to be my line, I think.

'I'm sure you're right,' I say.

A crash outside makes all three of us jump and the sky explodes into multicoloured stars.

CHAPTER 22

I drop my diaries at the police station on my way to school. Last night, when I couldn't sleep, I found myself reading the old volumes. A snapshot of the years.

'Good day. Had swimming. Saw PB.'

'I am more unhappy than I have ever been in my life. Karen told Alison who told ME that Peter is going out with Sue Frost, from Alleyns.'

'Tomorrow I go to Bristol to start university. My whole life lies before me like a tapestry . . .'

'I refuse to hate Simon because that way he wins but secretly I do hate him, with a passion beyond anything I felt when I loved him.'

'Spoke to Rick today. Forced myself to say it plainly: there can never be anything between us. He asked if it was because he is married. I wanted to say no, it's because you are you.'

I leave the diaries in reception, which is like a grim version of Argos, full of desperate-looking people sitting in nailed-down chairs waiting to be called to talk to officials behind glass partitions. I don't bother with taking a ticket and waiting my turn, I just leave my package, addressed to DS Kaur, on the front desk. I'm sure it'll get to her.

Georgie is waiting in the car. Our new regime starts today — I will take her to school and collect her. If I had my way, she would never be out of my sight. I rang Simon last night and told him a highly edited version: my name was found in a note possibly written by the killer and they are giving Georgie and me extra protection, but they don't think we're in any danger. Simon — predictably — started demanding that Georgie go and stay with him.

'She can't miss school,' I said. 'This is a vital year for her.'

'I can homeschool her.'

'You're at work all day.'

'Fleur can then.'

'With two young children? She'd love that.'

So Simon reluctantly gave way. Georgie's going to him this weekend anyway. I have to admit that I'm quite relieved about this. I could laugh — or cry — when I think that I believed, in coming to Sussex, I was bringing Georgie up in a safe, rural community. Suddenly London seems far safer.

As usual Georgie disappears as soon as we get through the gates of Talgarth. At least she'll be safe here, I think. Year 11s aren't allowed off-site anymore after a few shoplifting incidents in the village. I park in my usual space, by the gate. Ella used to park next to me and I still can't get used to not seeing her sporty black Golf with its 'Stronger in Europe' sticker. Now her space is taken by Rick's blue Volvo. I recognise the car instantly. I used to see it outside my house all the time. And, what's worse, Rick is sitting in the driving seat. Waiting for me.

I try to pretend that I haven't seen him, taking my time getting my briefcase and coat out of the boot. When I straighten up, he's there, standing behind me.

'We need to talk,' he says.

'I'm running late,' I say. The detour to the police station, while brief, had cost me fifteen minutes. It's eight forty-five and the Monday briefing, run by Rick, is at ten to nine.

He accompanies me as we walk towards the school.

'The police want to see me again,' he says. 'They know about Hythe.'

I don't stop, skirting a group of students loafing by the double doors of the Old Building and heading for the stairs. 'They read about it in my diary,' I say, on the first step.

'What?'

'The police wanted my diaries,' I say. 'I'd written about you and Ella in Hythe.'

'Why would you do that?'

We're climbing the stairs and I try not to look at him. I think of Alice Holland taking her 'dying fall' from the top landing, the shattered bannister, the sickening sound as the body hit the ground.

'That's what you do in a diary,' I say. 'You write about what happened. Your private thoughts. Remember, "Journaling for Writing". That's what the course in Hythe was all about.'

'Why did you show it to the police?'

We've reached the first floor so I stop and look at Rick. He's never very tidy but today he looks wilder than ever, hair on end, jumper apparently on inside-out. I can't believe that I ever thought he was attractive, that I ever considered sleeping with him. That's something I didn't tell Harbinder, though she'll know when she's read my diaries.

'Someone wrote in my diary,' I say. 'The police think it was the killer.'

The silence lasts until the staffroom. Vera and Anoushka are sitting on the sofa, talking about the play.

'Hallo, you two,' Anoushka looks up. 'You've got your top on inside-out, Rick. That's meant to be lucky.'

I'm teaching all morning so Rick doesn't get another chance to corner me. It's a busy day; I have a rehearsal at lunchtime and a planning meeting with Vera in the afternoon. It's not until the end of the day that I see I have an answerphone message. So much has happened over the last two weeks that, for a moment, the name Henry Hamilton doesn't register.

'Hi, Clare. It's Henry, from St Jude's. I'm visiting some friends in Brighton at the weekend and I wondered if you'd like to go out for a meal. Gosh, it's nerve-wracking doing it like this. If you don't want to, just say, or ignore this message. But I hope you do. I'm rambling now. But text me if you'd like to. I do hope you will.'

I sit in the library, where I'm waiting for Georgie, staring at my phone as if it's going to tell me what to do. Then, before I have a chance to regret it, I type the words, 'I'd like to. Where and when? C.'

The door opens and Georgie comes in, accompanied, I'm not thrilled to see, by Patrick O'Leary.

'Hi, Mum,' she says, 'am I late?'

'Hallo, Miss Cassidy.' Patrick smirks at me.

'Hallo, Patrick,' I say coldly. 'Hi, Georgie. No, you're OK. I was just checking my messages.'

'Ah, young people and their phones,' says Patrick.

I ignore him. 'Are you ready, Georgie?'

Patrick follows us all the way to the car park and stands there while I put my bag in the boot.

'Do you want a lift?' Georgie asks him. Why is she suddenly displaying such consideration and good manners? I don't like it at all. I pray that he'll refuse.

'Nah, you're all right. I've got my bike.'

But, as I drive away, he's still standing there in the car park. Watching us.

CHAPTER 23

I keep Georgie close all week. On Wednesday morning we go into the police station so that they can take her fingerprints and handwriting samples. We are talked through the process by a uniformed female police officer who has all the social skills lacking in Harbinder and Neil. In fact, she is so sympathetic — talking about school and dogs and whether we'll have a white Christmas — that I almost want to sit there, in the little cubicle off the room with all the computers, and tell her everything: about Rick and Henry Hamilton, about the Count Fosco impersonator writing in my diary, about my fears that Simon will use the situation to take Georgie away from me for ever. But I don't. I chat pleasantly to PC Olivia Grant, sipping a cup of disgusting coffee and watching Georgie write 'Hell is empty' on a lined refill pad from Ryman.

At the end of the week Simon drives down from London to collect Georgie from school. I'm irritated by him, by the way that he comes into reception and waits there, jingling his keys, by the way that he greets me with a world-weary sigh, mentioning that he has taken the afternoon off work, which is 'mad' at the moment (this to someone about to spend two unpaid hours watching teenagers singing about a carnivorous plant). But there's no doubt that when Georgie accompanies Simon out of the main doors, rolling her eyes at me behind her father's back, I can feel my headache lifting for the first time in a week. Now I only have to worry about keeping myself safe.

The police car is outside my house when I get home. I never know whether I'm meant to acknowledge them or not so I compromise with a furtive wave. Herbert shows no such restraint, rushing up to the unmarked car and barking shrilly. I drag him inside. Then I put on the double lock, pull the curtains, and pour myself a glass of wine. Three glasses later I realise that I've forgotten to eat and make myself some toast. I'm worried that I won't sleep. On Thursday I cracked and bought myself a new diary, a utilitarian notebook with 'Reporter's Pad' written on it. I imagine myself sitting up until dawn, writing and writing. But the alcohol does its work and, when I get into bed, I fall asleep immediately. I wake up at three to find Herbert staring at the window and growling softly. It's a long time before I sleep again.

Saturday is a long day. I'm meeting Henry in Chichester at eight-thirty but I'm trying on clothes at midday, wondering what to wear. I don't want to look too keen or too casual. My black skirt is too teachery, my grey cardigan too much like a mum. In the end, I compromise with black trousers and a slightly sheer shirt. I take Herbert out for his last walk, tentative in my suede boots, which have a slight heel (one benefit of going out with someone so tall). The police car is still there and I imagine its occupants eating hamburgers and flirting half-heartedly.

'Give us a chip.'

'What'll you give me back?'

'Shut up and pass the ketchup.'

But when I walk past them, I see that they are both middle-aged men, sitting in stony silence.

I'm meeting Henry at an Italian restaurant near the Buttercross, an elaborate stone structure in the centre of the town which was apparently once a covered market. As I approach, I can see Henry in the window, wearing glasses as he reads the menu with an expression of faint surprise. He's thinner than I remember and slightly cadaverous-looking in the light of the candle in front of him. Just for a minute, I want to turn and run away, back to Herbert and home and safety. Instead I run my hands through my hair, rearrange my scarf and push open the door.

'Clare!' His head brushes the light fitting as he stands up.

'Hi.'

There's an awkward moment when we don't know whether to kiss but in the end we shake hands, almost knocking over the candle. The waiter takes my coat and Henry asks me if I'd like a drink.

'I'm driving,' I say.

He doesn't urge me to have 'just one' but I do anyway. Henry is drinking water.

'It's very good of you to meet me,' he says.

'It's nice to get out,' I say, hoping that I don't sound like a pathetic loner with no social life.

The waiter arrives and Henry orders heartily, starter and main course. I'm not very hungry and had been hoping to get away with just a salad. I dither in a way that would have annoyed Simon intensely. In the end I order *prosciutto melone* and pasta *puttanesca*.

'I love Italian food,' says Henry. 'I'm not sure about this place though. The waiter's from Russia and apparently the chef's from Albania.'

I laugh. 'How do you know?'

'I asked,' he says, looking surprised. I hope that he's not going to turn out to be one of those foodie people who asks how they make their *ragu*. Simon has become a real food bore since marrying Fleur. Georgie told me they gave each other porcini mushrooms for Valentine's Day.

'How's Georgia?' he says, when the menus have been cleared away.

'She's with her dad this weekend. We're divorced.' I realise that Henry has never asked about my marital status. Is this because his intentions are strictly honourable? Did he really just want to meet for a cosy chat about R.M. Holland?

'How long have you been divorced?'

'Five years,' I say. I leave a gap for him to fill and thankfully he does so.

'I've been divorced for ten,' he says. 'Seems like longer.'

'You must have married young,' I say.

'We met at university,' he says. 'But I suppose it was down to upbringing as well. Both my brothers married in their early twenties. I felt that I was quite slow leaving it until twenty-five. Sandra felt the same. She was from a working class family too. Her mother was already hinting that she'd missed the boat. It's incredible really. It was only the nineties but it feels like the eighteen nineties.'

'I met Simon at university too,' I say. 'We were the first of our friends to get married. I don't know what we were thinking.'

'I know,' he says. 'My son has a steady girlfriend and I want to say "for God's sake, don't get married yet". I don't, of course.'

'How many children do you have?'

'Two boys, Freddy and Luke. Freddy's studying maths at Durham, Luke's in sixth-form. He's the one with the girlfriend.'

'Georgie's got a boyfriend,' I say. 'He's six years older than her. I don't want her to have a relationship at her age but, like you say, you can't give them advice. You have to let them work it out for themselves.'

Our starters arrive. Henry forks up salami without really noticing what he's eating, which is better than going on about how it's made in Calabria from contented pigs.

'So,' he says, 'have you got any further with the mystery of R.M. Holland?'

'Which one?' I say. There are so many mysteries in my life at the moment that I genuinely can't remember what had so interested me in the letters Henry had found. Was it whether RMH had killed his wife or what he had done with his daughter?

'Mariana,' says Henry. 'The letters mentioned the mysterious daughter. The one who seemed to die but didn't have a grave.'

'Oh yes,' I say. 'No. I haven't been able to find out more. The thing is . . .'

I hesitate. Now is the time when I should tell him about Ella's murder, explain that I've been rather distracted recently. But I don't want to. It's so nice to be with someone who isn't talking about 'what could have happened' or 'what the police are doing.' But, if he finds out and I haven't mentioned it, I'll look cold-hearted at best, suspicious at worst.

'The thing is,' I say, 'things are difficult at work at the moment. We're all very upset — a colleague, a friend of mine, died a few weeks ago.'

'I'm so sorry,' says Henry. 'How did your friend die?'

'She was killed,' I say. I'm horrified to find my eyes filling with tears.

But Henry is looking at me with calm kindness. 'What an awful thing to happen. Do you want to talk about it or would you rather have a night off?'

I'm so relieved that I almost laugh aloud. I wipe my eyes, hoping that my mascara hasn't run. 'A night off,' I say.

So we talk about books and music and whether TV adaptations are ever as good as the original. He says that he loved the BBC version of *War and Peace*. I say I thought there was too much peace.

'Most people skip the war bits,' he says.

'They're the best bits,' I say. 'I really didn't care about Natasha and Pierre.'

'You're a hard woman,' he says.

'I suppose I must be.'

My prosciutto is chewy and my pasta is too salty but I don't care. It's so nice to be in a restaurant talking about Tolstoy with a good-looking man. And Henry is good-looking, I realise, somewhere around the pasta stage. I don't know why it took me so long to notice.

Over coffee, he asks me about the school.

'I'm fascinated by the thought of the R.M. Holland rooms.'

'There's not that much to see,' I say. 'We use the old part of the school for some lessons but it's not very convenient for large classes. The teacher's library is there, though, and the dining hall and chapel. The chapel's newish, nineteen-twenties, very Art Nouveau and kitsch. The only untouched room is Holland's study. It's up a spiral staircase and all his old books and pictures are there. We take groups of adult learners up there sometimes. It's out-of-bounds to students, of course.'

'I'd love to see it,' he says.

'I'll show you one day,' I say. 'I've got the key.' I've got a key to the study, of course, but actually I have the school keys too because I locked up after the rehearsal yesterday.

'What about now?' says Henry. 'When we leave here?'

I don't know if he's joking or not. The thought of going into the empty school with Henry fills me with such contradictory emotions that I genuinely don't know what I feel. Would it be romantic? Creepy? Weird? Or just an adventure? Then I remember, as if I had ever really forgotten, that a stranger who is probably also a killer has been writing in my private diaries. I should go home, bolt the doors, and spend the night cuddling my dog.

'Are you serious?' I say.

'I thought it would be fun,' he says. 'And I'd like to be alone with you.'

We look at each other. His eyes are very dark, almost black.

'I have to get back for my dog,' I say.

'Of course,' he says. 'I understand.'

It's him giving in so quickly that makes me change my mind. Why not? I think. It *will* be an adventure. And maybe it'll be romantic too, who knows? I have a sudden vision of us having sex on the chaise longue in Holland's study. I surprise myself at the readiness with which this X-rated fantasy appears. Even when I had — briefly — contemplated going to bed with Rick, the actual act had remained veiled in my mind. PG, at the very most.

Henry insists on paying and I don't demur too much. We go out into the frosty night and walk to the car park. I'm relieved that we'll be travelling in two cars. At least I'll be able to escape if I have to. Then I think: why am I planning my escape?

'I'll follow you,' he says.

'The roads are twisty,' I warn. 'Use your satnav as well.'

The roads are winding and very dark. There's a sliver of moon but it's shifting through the clouds, at one moment appearing like a ghostly smile, at other times hidden completely. My headlights hardly seem to penetrate the blackness as I take the country route, past frozen fields and spectral trees. Not a car or another human to be seen. The driveway to Holland House is the darkest of all; overhanging branches scrape against my roof and the gates appear almost out of nowhere, stark and black, with the stone lions on either side. They are padlocked but I have the key. As I get out of the car, I see that Henry, in a black jeep-like vehicle, is right behind me.

We park in front of the main entrance, in a way that is forbidden when students are around. The doors open easily and I disable the alarm. I hope the caretaker won't take it into his head to do one of his night rounds but, if all the rumours about his drinking are true, he'll be spark out in front of the TV by now.

We climb the stairs, our feet suddenly very loud on the wooden steps. *Hear not my steps, which way they walk.* I don't want to switch on the overhead lights, so I use the torch app on my phone. It illuminates the occasional school notice or age-old portrait. Long-dead Hollands in their gilt frames. I think of Alice and her dying fall. Now would be the perfect time to see her ghost. But the house is silent.

We walk along the first floor corridor, past the locked doors, the empty windows. At the spiral staircase I stop to get out the second set of keys.

Henry says, 'Clare.' I turn. He pulls me towards him and kisses me.

It's one of the best kisses of my life, long and passionate, his hands in my hair, his body pressed against me. Is it going to happen, I wonder. Are we going to have sex? Surely two adults can't kiss like that without having sex?

After what seems like hours I pull away. 'The study,' I say, slightly breathless.

'The study,' he says. And I see the gleam of his teeth as he smiles.

We climb the stairs. I have the keys in my hand but see that the door is very slightly ajar. I push it open.

I'm prepared for the dummy in the chair. I have warned Henry and remind myself not to be shocked. But I'm not prepared for the figure lolling behind the desk, his features illuminated by a sudden shaft of moonlight.

It's Rick. Rick with a knife in his heart.

Of course Ebrahimi's death was a terrible shock. I remember standing there with the newspaper cutting in my hand, then going back to my rooms, lying down on my bed and shaking. Who had sent me the fateful papers? Who had written the translation with that slender, slanting pen? And who had written the words 'Hell is empty' on the reverse? Could it be Bastian? Or Collins? It seemed impossible but who else could possibly have known about the Hell Club and that terrible night?

I pondered these questions over the next few days. Indeed, I thought of little else. But in the end, I pushed my fears away and carried on with my life. After all, what else could I do? And I was young, I had my health and my strength. You understand, my dear young friend? Yes, I see that you do. Youth is arrogant, which is as it should be. I was sorry that Ebrahimi was dead — and I sincerely mourned my friend Gudgeon — but there was nothing that I could do to bring them back to life. So I continued with my studies and even began to court a young lady, the daughter of my tutor. Life was sweet that spring, perhaps all the sweeter for the thought that I had escaped from the pall of death. For, at that time, I believed that I had escaped.

How the wind howls.

Harbinder

I was in bed when I got the call. I wasn't asleep, just flicking through my phone, making a move in Scrabble, popping a few balloons in Panda Pop, reading about people's stupid lives on Facebook. Then Control rang to say that a body had been found at Talgarth High. I was on my feet immediately, texting Neil to meet me at the school.

I was halfway downstairs when Mum appeared on the landing, Dad's dressing gown over her nightdress.

'Where are you going, Heena?'

She must have seen that I was wearing my reflective police jacket. I was hardly going out to a rave.

'Work,' I said. 'There's been a development on the case.'

'Be careful,' she said.

'I always am.' I was out of the door before she could suggest making me a flask of haldi doodh.

Once I got out of Seaford, the roads were icy. I drove as quickly as I dared. It was nearly midnight. My car dial changed to the slightly sinister 00.00 as I turned into the gates of Talgarth High. A uniform was standing by the stone pedestal with a lion on it (Kush and his friends once painted its balls bright blue).

'Get in the car,' I said. He looked frozen. In fact, he might have been suffering from the same fate as the lion.

'Thank you, ma'am.' Nice to see some respect from the younger generation.

I drove slowly up to the main entrance. The uniform told me that the call had come in at eleven-thirty. 'A woman, sounding hysterical.' She said that a man had been killed at the school. Uniform had attended and contacted CID. He didn't know much more. His Sarge had told him to wait at the gates until I arrived.

The doors were open. I didn't need the uniform to tell me that the body was upstairs. Of course it was. I told the PC to wait for Neil in the hall and took the stairs two at a time.

I went straight for Holland's study and wasn't even that surprised to see Clare Cassidy at the foot of the spiral staircase, sitting on a chair obviously brought from a classroom. A woman police officer was hovering round her, and a Sergeant that I vaguely recognised was talking to another, very tall man that I didn't.

They all turned when I approached. The Sergeant, Derek Something, said, 'DS Kaur. You were quick.'

'I live nearby,' I said. 'Clare. Fancy meeting you here.'

Clare looked up at me. She was very pale but her eyes were dark with mascara and smoky eye-liner, slightly streaked. Who had she been making up for? Was it Mr Tall?

'Ms Cassidy phoned 999,' said Sergeant Derek. 'A deceased male was found in the room at the top of that staircase. He appears to have been stabbed.'

'Have you secured the scene? Called CSI?'

'Yes. They're on their way.'

'I'll have a look.'

I climbed the stairs with the odd footprints on the carpet. It was funny. I'd heard so much about this room but had never been up here before. The door was open and I saw a man sitting at a desk. For a moment I thought it was the dummy Clare had mentioned before, but then I saw that it was, in fact, Rick Lewis. A knife was protruding from his chest and rigor mortis had set in. I didn't go further into the room as I didn't want to contaminate the scene.

When I got back downstairs, Neil had arrived. I heard him asking Clare if she wanted a drink of water. That's right, Neil. Suck up to Clare as usual.

I spoke to the Sergeant. 'The dead man is Rick Lewis. He's a teacher here. His details are on file at the station. Next of kin will need to be informed.'

'I'll get on to it,' he said, 'unless you need me here.'

'No. That's OK. I'll wait for CSI. I just want to talk to the witness first. Are any of these rooms open?'

'There's a classroom three doors down,' said the female officer. 'It's where I got these chairs.'

'OK,' I said. 'Neil and I will have a word with Miss Cassidy. Can you . . .'

'PC Jill Monroe.'

'PC Monroe. Can you stay with . . . ?' I looked at the tall man who said, 'Henry Hamilton.' His voice wasn't what I expected. It was northern. Cumbria, I thought. He was wearing expensive shoes, oxblood leather.

Neil and I ushered Clare into the empty classroom.

'Is this going to take long?' she said. 'I need to get home for Herbert.'

'What about your daughter?'

'She's with her father.'

So you had a clear weekend to see your boyfriend, I thought.

'We'll be as quick as we can,' I said, 'but we'll need to ask some questions back at the station.'

She looked from me to Neil. 'Can I have a glass of water?'

I sighed. God knows where we'd find water or a glass in this place. The dining room was sure to be locked. But Neil went out and came back with a plastic bottle. I think it was PC Monroe's. Clare looked at it with distaste and took a tiny sip.

'So,' I said. 'You just happened to be in an empty school at midnight?'

She flashed me an unfriendly look but answered in a calm, flat voice. 'I wanted to show Henry R.M. Holland's study.'

'Of course you did.'

'We'd been out for a meal in Chichester. We got talking about Holland.'

Yeah right, I thought. Clare had not got all dressed up like this for a cosy booksy chat. She was wearing a red coat but underneath I could see a flimsy blouse and lots of jewellery. High heels, too. It did change my perception of her that she had broken into the school for a shag. Especially considering she had an empty house with a perfectly serviceable bed. Maybe she wasn't such a cold fish after all.

'How do you know Mr Hamilton?' I was betting it would be online but she said that she'd met him at Cambridge. He'd come across some letters from R.M. Holland that he thought might interest her. Didn't change the fact that she'd been planning to bonk him in an empty school though.

'Did you see anyone at the school when you arrived?' I asked. 'The caretaker?'

'No,' she said. 'I had the keys. I didn't want to wake Dave.'

'Well, we'd better wake him now,' I said, making a mental note to tell the uniform downstairs. I was surprised that Dave hadn't seen the flashing lights.

'What did you do when you got here?' I asked.

'We came straight up here,' she said. 'Henry wanted to see the study. We went in and we saw . . .' She took another sip of water, hands shaking.

'Did you recognise Mr Lewis straight away?'

'Yes.' In a whisper.

'Have you any idea who could have done this?'

She looked at me, mascaraed eyes huge. 'It was him. The person who's writing in my diaries.'

I didn't ask any more questions as I wanted to do a proper interview back at the station. I sent Clare home with PC Monroe to walk and feed the poor dog. Neil and I talked to Henry Hamilton. He seemed rather embarrassed about the whole thing: about meeting Clare in the first place, about sneaking into the school at night, about finding a dead body. I took his address and asked where he was staying tonight.

'At The Royal Albion in Brighton.'

Another perfectly good bed going begging.

'You can go back there now,' I said. 'But we'll need to talk to you first thing in the morning.'

'It's morning now,' he said.

I looked at my watch. It was almost one.

'Can you come into the station at nine?' I said. 'DS Winston will give you the address.'

'Of course,' he said. Henry stood up. He really was stupidly tall. He seemed to want to say something, looking from me to Neil and rocking slightly from oxblood foot to foot.

'Clare . . .' he said at last.

'What about her?' I stood up too. Not that it made much difference.

'You seemed to . . . You can't . . . You don't *suspect* her of anything, do you?'

'Ms Cassidy is an important witness,' I said, 'as are you.'

'Do *you* suspect her?' asked Neil. A very good question.

He laughed unconvincingly. 'God, no. I don't know her well but she's so . . .'

Isn't she just, I thought.

'You can go back to your hotel now,' I said. 'Try to get some rest. We'll see you in a few hours.'

The uniform, who was called PC Lee Parsons, fetched the caretaker. Dave Bannerman was a dishevelled-looking man of about fifty who had obviously been in a deep (possibly alcohol-induced) sleep. I asked Dave if he'd seen or heard anything at the school tonight.

'No,' he said. 'I did my last round at nine. Everything seemed in order.'

I knew that the caretaker lived in a cottage in the grounds. In my day, there were rumours that Pervy Pete used to lure girls there with sweets. We thought that sort of thing was funny back then.

'What did you do after nine?'

'Watched TV. Had a beer.'

Or three, I thought.

'What did you watch?' asked Neil.

'Something on Netflix. I can't remember.'

That's the trouble with TV now. You used to be able to place someone's movements based on whether they'd seen the end of *Match of the Day* or not. Netflix and box sets have ruined everything.

'Did you know that Clare Cassidy had the keys?' I asked.

He nodded. 'Yes, she locked up after the rehearsal on Friday.'

'Shouldn't she have returned the keys to you?'

He shrugged. 'Strictly speaking, yes, but people often wait until Monday.'

Safeguarding here was definitely slack. I would have a word with Tony Sweetman about that.

'When did you last see Rick Lewis, head of English?' asked Neil.

Dave blinked at us. 'Why? Is he . . . ?'

'Just answer the question, please.'

'I suppose it was on Friday. I think I saw him leaving at the end of the day. Yes, that's right, he was one of the last. There was only Ms Cassidy and Ms Palmer left after him. They were taking the rehearsal. They're doing *Little Shop of Horrors* this year.'

'What about Mr Sweetman?' Surely the head teacher should leave last, like captains and sinking ships?

A slight sneer. 'He left early. Apparently he was going away for the weekend.'

'Thank you, Mr Bannerman,' I said. 'We'll need a proper statement tomorrow but that's all for now.'

PC Parsons ushered the caretaker out. Neil and I sat in the empty classroom and looked at each other.

'What do you think?' said Neil. 'Is it the same person? Was there another note?'

'I couldn't see,' I said. 'CSI will find it if there is. But I think it's the same person. Another stabbing. And the diary writer said that there might be more.'

'You think it's the person who wrote in Clare's diary?'

'Unless it was Clare herself.'

'The writing is different. That's what the handwriting expert said.'

'She couldn't be certain,' I said. 'They're never certain. It wouldn't stand up in court.'

'You think Clare stabbed Rick and then came back here with her fancy man?'

'Fancy man,' I said. 'What century are you living in?'

'He was fancy,' said Neil. 'I didn't trust him.'

'She could have orchestrated the whole thing,' I said. 'Made us think she was just coming back here for a shag to divert attention.'

'But why?' said Neil. 'Why not just let the caretaker — poor sod — discover the body on Monday morning?'

'If he ever comes up here,' I said. 'I bet Rick could have stayed in that chair for a long time.'

Neil gave a theatrical shudder. 'But why would Clare kill Rick?'

'We know that he had a thing about her, that he stalked her. Maybe she wanted to teach him a lesson.'

'Why would she want to do that?'

'Well, she is a teacher,' I said. 'Come on, let's get back to the station and interview her.'

We walked down the main staircase just as the CSI team, monstrous and bloated in their white coveralls, were climbing upwards.

CHAPTER 25

Neil and I interviewed Clare Cassidy with Donna watching behind the two-way mirror. Clare had changed into jeans and a thick navy-blue jumper. She'd wiped the war-paint off but I wondered if she'd put a little grey shadow on her eyelids, just to give her that wan, vulnerable look. But perhaps I was being unfair.

We interviewed her under caution. I'd asked if she wanted a solicitor present and she said no. She seemed quite calm, taking her seat and moving her chair a centimetre or two away from us, just to establish some control over the space. We had offered a hot drink but she'd brought a water bottle with her, the reusable, ecologically sound kind. She held it tightly in one hand.

I introduced myself and Neil for the tape, then I asked Clare to go through her movements last night. She described getting ready for the date, taking the dog out, meeting Henry Hamilton at the restaurant. She remembered what they had both eaten and that he'd paid the bill.

'Whose idea was it to go to Talgarth?' I asked.

'His,' said Clare. 'We were talking about R.M. Holland's study and he said that he'd love to see it. I thought he was joking at first.'

'But you did go to see it,' I said. 'You let yourself into the school in the middle of the night, probably breaking all the health and safety guidelines. Why?'

She shrugged slightly. 'I don't know. Perhaps I thought it would be romantic. An adventure.'

'Romantic?' I said. 'What do you mean?'

She fixed me with her big-eyed stare. 'Sometimes breaking rules is exciting.'

'Were you planning to have sex with Henry?' If she said yes, it would look damning in court. Juries hate women to have a sex life.

'I wasn't planning anything,' she said. 'I just thought it might be fun.'

'Fun?'

'Well,' she said, 'I clearly got that one wrong.'

I looked at Neil and he obediently changed tack. 'When did you last see Rick Lewis?'

'At school on Friday. I went to hand Georgie over to her dad. We're being extra careful, as you told us. When I was going back upstairs, Rick was coming down. He asked if I had a rehearsal that night. I said yes. He said that he was going home and I wished him a good weekend.'

Except he hadn't gone straight home, I thought. Dave Bannerman had said that he was one of the last to leave.

'How did he seem? In himself?'

'OK. The same as ever. Of course everyone is still upset about Ella's death.'

She stopped, perhaps remembering that they would soon have another death to be upset about. The ever-decreasing English department.

'When you found Rick's body,' I said, 'what did you do?'

'I screamed, I think. Henry was behind me. He didn't realise what had happened at first. I'd told him about the dummy. I think he thought that's what it . . . he . . . was.'

'Did you go into the room? Touch anything? This is important for our forensic work.'

'I think I went in. Yes, I touched Rick's hand. He was cold. That's how I knew he was dead.'

'What about Henry?'

'I think he came in. I don't remember.'

'What did you do next?'

'I had my phone in my hand. I was using the torch app. I phoned 999. I didn't have your card so I couldn't call you directly.'

'That's OK,' I said. 'What did you do while you were waiting for the police to come?'

'Henry said we should go to the main doors to wait for them. We'd left the gates open. I was only too glad to get away from that room.'

'How long did the police take to respond?'

'They were there almost as soon as we got downstairs. We went back up to show them. I felt faint and the woman police officer got me a chair. Then you arrived.'

The interview room has no windows but I looked away, as if I was admiring the view. 'Did you kill Rick Lewis?' I asked.

'No!' It was almost a shout but it was also a teacher's voice, shocked that I would dare to ask such a question.

'Was he still bothering you?' asked Neil, sounding sympathetic. 'Hanging round outside your house? Pestering you?'

'No. That was all over ages ago. Before the summer.'

'In your diary you said that you were jealous of Ella and Rick,' I said. 'Did you still feel like that?'

'I never really felt like that,' she said. 'I'd forgotten I'd written that. It was just momentary. That's what a diary is, a snapshot of how you're feeling at that moment. It didn't last. Rick was a colleague. Nothing else.'

'Did you like him?'

She hesitated. 'Yes. He was a good boss and a good teacher. He cared about the kids.' Her voice quivered for the first time.

'Have you any idea who could have killed him?' asked Neil.

'I told you, it's the person who wrote in my diary. He said, *I have already disposed of one of these creatures. I will fall on the others like a ravening beast.*'

'You remember it word for word,' I said.

'I'm good at remembering quotes. Besides, it's not the sort of thing you would forget.'

'So who do you think wrote that?'

'I've no idea,' she said, rather wearily.

'Interview suspended,' I said, into the microphone.

'Is there something suspicious about them being in the school last night?' said Donna. 'Could she have killed Rick?'

We were having a hasty debrief with Donna while Clare took a comfort break.

'We've got Hamilton as a witness that they just found him dead in the chair,' I said. 'Of course, she could have killed him earlier. It depends what the post-mortem says about time of death.'

'Do you really think she could have killed Rick?' says Neil. 'Why?'

'She sounded pretty annoyed with him in the diaries,' I said.

'You're often annoyed with me,' said Neil, 'but you don't try to kill me.'

Ah, motive and opportunity, what fickle bedfellows you are. But Neil was right, really. It was hard to imagine Clare killing Rick because of a crush he'd had months ago or because he'd made her do more than her fair share of the marking.

'She's a cold fish though,' said Donna. 'Was she really planning to have sex with her boyfriend in the school? After everything that's happened?'

Clare had come back into the interview room and we all watched her through the window. She sat in the chair with her hands on the arms. She wasn't fidgeting or looking at her phone, as most people would be. She was simply staring straight in front of her, her face inscrutable.

'Maybe it was the danger that made it exciting,' I said, thinking of the only time I'd planned to have sex in an empty classroom. 'I don't think Clare killed Rick but she's the key to the case all the same. After all, it's her diaries that have the writing in them.'

'Unless she wrote them herself,' said Donna.

'The handwriting expert thought that it was a different person,' I said. 'Probably a man.'

'There's definitely something not quite right about her,' said Donna.

We interviewed Henry Hamilton at nine. He didn't have much to add, but he did admit, in answer to Neil's question, that he had been hoping to sleep with Clare. There was nothing else to link him to the case. He had never met Rick, or been to Talgarth High before that night.

We contacted Tony Sweetman, who was away skiing for the weekend, if you please. Apparently they had 'a part share of a chalet near Annecy' and there was 'early snow this year'. I told him to come back to Sussex immediately and that the school would have to close tomorrow, possibly for the week.

'I'll need to contact the governors.'

'Then contact them.'

He gave a kind of groan. 'This'll be the end of us, after all my improvements.'

The man really was an arse. I was sorry, in a way, that he had a cast-iron alibi for Rick's murder.

Rick's wife had identified his body. The Family Liaison Officer was still with her but Neil and I were hoping to interview Daisy Lewis in the afternoon. By midday we were flagging slightly. Neil went out for burgers and chips and we ate them in Donna's office.

'We'll need to do a statement for the press,' said Donna. 'I've already had the *Herald* on the phone. People saw the flashing lights last night.'

'It's on Twitter,' said Neil, scrolling through his phone. '*Wtf happnin @ Talgarth. My old schl wot a dump.*'

'Who wrote that?' I said, looking over Neil's shoulder.

'Someone called FoxyLadee.'

'That narrows it down a bit.'

'We'll just say that a man was found dead,' said Donna. 'Police investigating. No link to Ella's death.'

'Nevertheless, people will make the link,' I said.

'Here's a good one,' said Neil, still looking at his Twitter feed. '*It could of bin the Talgarth ghost #whitelady*. That one's from Big Mac.' He laughed and took a bite of his burger.

I wiped my fingers on my jeans and took his phone. 'Someone's answered. *The white lady has had her revenge.*'

'Who's that from?' said Neil.

'MrCarter.'

Gary Carter hadn't even had the sense to change his name.

CHAPTER 26

We went to see Daisy Lewis at three. The roads were quiet, as if everyone was indoors enjoying a Sunday lunch with all the trimmings.

'Roast beef,' said Neil.

'Chicken tikka masala,' I said, just to wind him up. 'That's the nation's favourite dish now.'

'My mum's Yorkshire puddings are to die for.' Neil was off down Nostalgia Lane. 'Kelly's aren't nearly as good.'

'Why don't you make them yourself?' I said. 'Hasn't Kelly got enough to do, what with looking after Lily and all that?'

'I cook,' said Neil, sounding offended. 'More than you do, I bet.'

'You're right,' I said, nosing through another Shoreham backstreet trying to find a parking space. 'But then I've got the sense to live with my mum.'

I eventually found a space outside the library. It was near the maze of small roads where Ella had lived. It struck me that the two victims' homes were very close to each other.

The door was opened by the FLO, a pleasant woman called Maggie O'Hara. We would debrief her later; the FLO always has valuable insights because they see the victim's family at their lowest. Maggie led us into a large kitchen with an old-fashioned range oven and a scrubbed wooden table. A family kitchen, I thought, before remembering again that the Lewises didn't have children. Daisy was sitting at the table with another woman who could have been her identical twin.

'This is my sister, Lauren,' she said. 'Can she stay?'

'Of course,' I said. 'I'm sorry for your loss, Mrs Lewis.'

She acknowledged this with a gulp, rubbing her eyes with an already sodden tissue.

'Maggie thought you might be up to answering a few questions,' I said.

'Maggie's been so kind,' said Daisy, looking round vaguely.

'That's good,' I said. 'I know it's hard, Daisy, but we want to catch the person who did this terrible thing and that means we have to act quickly. So anything that you could remember would be very valuable.'

It's my standard speech but it seemed to work. Daisy sat up straighter and tucked her tissue into her sleeve. Lauren offered us tea or coffee and Neil and I both asked for coffee. I don't know about Neil but I was so tired that my eyelids seemed to be turning themselves inside-out.

'When did you last see Rick?' I asked, when we all had our drinks and were sitting round the table like some parody of a tea party.

'Yesterday,' said Daisy. 'We'd just watched *Strictly*' — of course they had — 'and we were going to watch a Swedish film on BBC4 when Rick got a call on his mobile and said he had to go into the school.'

'On a Saturday night?' I said. 'Was that usual?'

'No,' said Daisy. 'I mean, he's gone in at the weekend before. When they were preparing for an inspection, or something like that. But this was out of the blue. He just got the call and said he had to go in.'

'Do you know who the call was from?'

'I assumed it was Tony. The head.'

But Tony was off disporting himself on the ski-slopes. 'Was it a man's voice?' I asked.

'I couldn't hear,' she said. 'But I assumed so. I think Rick may have said "he".'

But, given Rick's track record, I didn't think this was anything to go by.

'What happened then?'

'He just kissed me goodbye. Picked up the car keys and left. He said I might be in bed when he got in. And I was . . .' Her face crumpled. 'I was asleep when I got the call . . .'

Lauren patted her shoulder. 'It's OK, Dais. It's OK.'

Rick Lewis' car had been found in the car park at Talgarth so he *had* gone to the school. Who had called him? *Strictly* ends at about eight and Clare and Henry had arrived at eleven. That left three hours for someone to murder Rick and prop his body up in R.M. Holland's study. There had been no blood in the room that I could see so I assumed that he had been killed elsewhere. Rick Lewis had been a tall man, quite thin but still a dead weight to lug up that spiral staircase. Could a woman have managed it? Could Clare have managed it? Her Italian meal was booked for eight-thirty and I suppose she could just have got to Talgarth, killed Rick, and sprinted to Chichester, but that would be cutting it very fine. Not to mention the lack of bloodstains on her fancy clothes.

'How did Rick seem when he got the call?' asked Neil.

'OK. A bit irritated maybe. I mean, it was the weekend, after all. But he was OK. He kissed me goodbye,' she repeated, as if this proved something. Well, perhaps it did.

'Daisy,' I said, leaning forward across the table. 'We're working on a theory that Rick's death was linked to that of Ella Elphick. Did Rick say anything about Ella's death that seemed strange to you? Did he mention anyone getting in touch with him about it?'

'Getting in touch with him?'

'A letter or a phone call? A text message?'

'No,' she shook her head. 'He was sad about Ella, of course. She was one of his best teachers. But he didn't know anything about her death.'

This was interesting because it wasn't what I had asked.

'Did Rick get on well with Ella?' I asked.

'They didn't have an affair,' said Daisy, 'if that's what you mean. If you ask me, it's all that bitch's fault.'

'Ella?'

'No. The other one. Clare Cassidy. She's always had it in for Rick.'

I was tantalisingly close to home but I had to drive Neil back to the station. While I was there I thought I might as well pick up Clare's diaries. Forensics had finished with them and, if Clare was indeed the key to the case, what could be better than spending the evening reading through her innermost thoughts? I was struck by the way that Daisy Lewis had blamed Clare, not Ella, for Rick's death. She'd called her a 'bitch' which was strong language coming from a woman like Daisy. Clare was obviously the sort of woman who aroused strong emotions.

I drove home slowly, aware that I was so tired I almost felt drunk. When I got in, Mum was in the kitchen, cooking as usual, accompanied by Kiaan and Alisha. On one hand I was irritated that Abid and Cara had dumped their kids on Mum again, on the other it was always nice to see my nephews and nieces, especially the young impressionable ones.

'Auntie Harbinder! Have you been arresting people?'

'Have you killed anyone?'

'Sadly no.' I sat down at the table and started to eat. There's always a running buffet at Mum's while we are waiting for the main event: samosas, bhajias, roti and my favourite, crunchy peanut vadas.

'Where's your mum and dad?' I asked Alisha, through the crunching. She had come to sit on my lap. She's five, still young enough to do stuff like that. Kiaan is seven and starting to keep his distance, although he was demonstrating tai chi moves to keep my attention.

'Gone to the cinema,' said Kiaan, mid-lunge. 'It's their date night.'

'It's good to keep the romance alive,' said Mum, whilst kneading, chopping and frying, seemingly all at once. 'Have some time together without the kids.'

'They've gone to see *Murder on the Oreo Express,*' Alisha told me. 'It's not suitable for children.'

'It doesn't sound it,' I say, pushing her off and standing up. 'Now I've got to go and do some work.'

'You've been up all night,' said Mum. 'Relax. Play some computer games with the children.'

'Yes!' shouted Kiaan. 'Grand Theft Auto!'

'That's not suitable for children either,' I said. 'Come on, let's go and watch a film in the den.'

I slept solidly through *Harry Potter and the Chamber of Secrets,* only waking up when someone was stabbing a diary with a giant incisor. The blood/ink flowed over the pages in a way that disturbed me but seemed to have no effect on Alisha and Kiaan, partly because Dad had come in and was doing his famous Tickling Monster That Overturns the Furniture act. I left them to it and sneaked upstairs to my room.

I put my work bag on my bed but sat in the desk chair. It would be fatal to go to sleep again. Before I started the secret diaries of Clare Cassidy, aged 45, I had a call to make.

'Hallo?' Gary answered warily, in spite of the fact that my name must have come up on his phone.

'Hi, Gary. How are you?'

'I'm all right. What's going on at the school? Is that why you're ringing?'

'In a way,' I said. 'I saw what you wrote on Twitter, about the white lady.'

There was a pause, then Gary said, 'I didn't know you were on Twitter', which so much wasn't the point that I almost laughed.

'I'm not,' I said. 'My partner is though. My work partner,' I added quickly. 'You should know that the police check stuff like this.'

'But I didn't say anything wrong.'

'No, but what did you mean about the white lady having her revenge?'

Another pause, a longer one with heavy breathing in it. 'I just meant . . . if someone has died . . .'

'Who says someone has died?'

'It's what people are saying,' said Gary, sounding panicky now. 'That someone's been killed at the school.'

'Who's saying that?'

A silence.

'Come on, Gary. You have to tell me.'

'My mate Alan in PE,' said Gary at last. 'He heard it from Dave, the caretaker. They play Sunday football together.'

I was surprised that Dave was fit enough for football but then I remembered the bloated, track-suited figures that I sometimes saw stumbling round the park. I almost called the paramedics to resuscitate one of them once.

'He shouldn't be talking about it,' I said.

'I haven't got him into trouble, have I?'

'No,' I said. 'It's bound to get out soon.'

'Is it true then?' Gary's voice dropped to a whisper even though I was pretty sure that he was alone. 'That Rick Lewis has been killed?'

'I can't give you that information,' I said. Thus, of course, giving it to him.

'Bloody hell.' The penny dropped slowly and rattled to the bottom of the box.

'What did you mean?' I asked again. 'The white lady has had her revenge?'

'Well, it's the legend, isn't it? That the white lady appears when someone dies. You must remember. That time we saw her . . .'

'Bye Gary,' I said. 'Be careful what you say on social media.'

CHAPTER 27

We were fifteen when we saw the ghost. We were in school late because Gary had a rehearsal with his band, a group of almost talent-free Year 11s with their own guitars and a passion for Tolkien. They were called Boromir's Brother. I wasn't the sort of girl who sat around watching her boyfriend's band rehearse so I was working in the library, which was in the Old Building then. The librarian — what was her name? Miss McKenzie, that was it — was a funny old thing but she liked me. I think it was because I was almost the only person who read the old books, the leather-bound volumes with the gilt lettering crumbling to dust: Dickens, Collins, Mrs Gaskell, Trollope. I was also obsessed with James Herbert, but I didn't tell Miss McKenzie that.

So I sat in the library doing my history homework. It was easier to work there than at home. In those days I had a tiny bedroom; Kush and Abid shared the big room that I have now. And there were always so many people at home, eating Mum's cooking, talking Punjabi, crying about leaving the old homeland. Plus, Dad might make me do a shift in the shop.

It was great in the old library, the shelves reaching up to the ceiling, the big windows looking out onto the field. There were window seats, too, and I spent many an afternoon there, immersed in a pleasant horror fantasy while the first eleven lost to some posher school down below. The library they have now is horrible; all plastic sofas and carousels and paperbacks in protective covers. The old library had history, you could feel it seeping through the walls and rising up from the floorboards, which were knotted and wide, like the gangplanks of a ship.

The library shut at six. It was the Christmas term and dark outside. At about five to, Miss McKenzie gathered up her knitting (it was endless and always in virulent blues and pinks — who can it have been for?) and started to check that no one was hiding behind the curtains.

'Time to go, Harbinder,' she said. 'Is Gary still making that awful noise in the basement?'

She always knew who was going out with whom.

'I expect so,' I said.

But at that moment Gary appeared in the doorway, carrying his guitar case. I said goodbye to Miss McKenzie.

'Bye, Harbinder. Bye, Gary. Go straight home now.'

But instead, we sneaked along the first floor corridor, looking for a room to snog in. We were quite passionate in those days. It's hard to imagine it now. I think, even then, I had my doubts about men but I was determined to give it my best shot. Gary was just desperate to lose his virginity.

Eventually we found an empty classroom, one of the odd rooms that might have been a bedroom in its original incarnation. It had a little, wrought-iron fireplace, with a rather elaborate design of poppies and leaves. Was it near the room where Rick Lewis was murdered? I can't think. Possibly.

We were getting quite intense. My bra was off and he had his hand down my trousers. My generation fought to wear trousers at school but all the Talgarth girls wear skirts now; that's gratitude for you. Then something happened. The room suddenly became very cold. But it was much more than that. It was desolate, like the wind blowing across the estuary at night. I felt as if I'd never be happy again. We drew apart. I did up my bra and Gary zipped up his fly. We didn't speak. We grabbed our stuff and left the room.

We walked back along the corridor. I remember Gary's guitar case banging against my legs, the lights turning off one by one as Pervy Pete did his final rounds. And then — something flew past us. It's hard to describe. Afterwards I remembered a woman in a long, white dress but Gary said that it was more like a whirlwind, something black and featureless. All I know is that all the cold, and all the horror, seemed to be coming from this creature, this *thing*. We heard a crack as the shape hit the balustrade on the staircase and then a terrible, terrible scream. I've never heard anything like it and I hope I never will again.

Gary and I ran. We were mindless with fear. I think either of us would have abandoned the other to be murdered by the phantom. Our only thought was to get out of that place. We flew down the stairs and out through the main door. We ran all the way to the front gate where Pete was locking up.

'Haven't you kids got homes to go to?'

His familiar, irritable voice brought us back to reality. We muttered a goodnight and walked to the bus stop. There was no one there but we still talked in whispers.

'It was her,' I said. 'R.M. Holland's wife. The woman in white. The one who threw herself down the staircase.'

'It wasn't a woman,' said Gary. 'I don't know what the hell it was.'

'That scream,' I said. 'Do you think anyone else heard it?'

'I don't know,' said Gary, huddled and miserable in his anorak.

'Seeing the white lady,' I said. 'It's meant to mean someone's about to die.'

'Don't,' said Gary.

We stood there in silence. My bus came and I got on. We didn't even kiss goodbye. We knew that our brief romance was over. Two days later we heard that Sue Black, a girl in the third year who had been ill for a while, had died from leukaemia. The school was febrile with sadness and curiosity and several people raised the legend of the white lady, but Gary and I never mentioned what we had seen.

We never spoke about the ghost again. Until today.

CHAPTER 28

I opened one of Clare's diaries at random.

> It's not that I don't love Simon. I do. It's more that I want more. I love my job and I think I'm good at it. God knows I love Georgie (so sweet and loving right now). But while I love Simon, I notice that he now automatically comes second on the list. Is married love always a casualty of maternal love? But it's not about me and Simon. It's just that I thought I was going to do something with my life. Be someone...

Jesus. I didn't think I could stand much more of this. I looked at the date at the top of the page. 3/3/10. By my calculations Clare and Simon divorced two years later and Georgia — so sweet and loving — would have been eight. I decided to try something more recent.

> Monday 11th September 2017
>
> Rick is really getting on my nerves. It's the second week of term and he still hasn't properly sorted the timetables. Ella's planning for the GCSEs is all over the place but he won't say anything to her. Does he still have a crush on her? Probably. He keeps sighing and looking more rumpled and disconsolate than ever. His crush on me disappeared quickly enough. But

then I told it to him straight, which Ella won't. I wasn't prepared to sleep with a married man. But that didn't bother her.

I'm sick of covering up for her at work. I should have had
Ella's job and Rick knows it.

I got out my notebook and started making a timeline. In July Ella and
Rick had slept together, by September Rick was obviously still mooning over
her and Clare was resentful. I turned a couple of pages.

Friday 15th September 2017
So happy to see the end of the week. Ella still hasn't com-
pleted her GCSE predictions. I asked her when she was going
to do it and she just laughed and said 'You worry too much'.
Then she said that she was going out with Bryony Hughes on
Saturday. 'Is it a coven meeting?' I said, sounding pretty sour,
I'm sure. 'Yes,' she said, 'we're summoning the dead at Il Pap-
pagallo in Chichester.' 'Hope it keeps fine for you,' I said.

Il Pappagallo was where Clare had met Henry Hamilton on Saturday night. I made a note of that too. I also started a list of names. Bryony
Hughes??

Why do people do this? Why do they pour out their hopes and fears,
night after night, to an audience of no one? Clare had this habit of pep-
pering her diary entries with what were clearly quotations. Why did she do
that? Did she imagine that her diaries would be read out on Radio 4 one
day? Sometimes she even takes the time to attribute the quotes, as if she
were writing a sixth-form English essay. *'Nothing in the world is hidden forever'* — Wilkie Collins, *No Name.* And why, when she was supposedly writing for herself, did she take so much care to craft her sentences? *Is married
love always a casualty of maternal love?* Who the hell is she asking? And all
that dialogue, in careful quotation marks. *'Hope it keeps fine for you.'* It reads
like a chick-lit novel, the sort you buy at the airport and regret before the
cabin staff have finished their safety demonstration.

I turned to the days before Ella Elphick's murder.

Friday 20th October 2017

Busy day at school, finishing up before half-term. I wished I hadn't agreed to go out with Ella and Debra tonight but, in the end, I was glad I did. We saw *Blade Runner 2049.* I remember liking the first film but this was unbelievably boring. Mind you, my tolerance for films is limited these days. I slept through approximately two-thirds of it, waking to find Ryan Gosling walking very slowly through an aircraft hangar in the snow. Afterwards we went for a meal at The Royal Oak. At first Ella annoyed me by going on about *The Rick Thing.* Debra just encourages her — 'He's obsessed with you', etc., etc. I was starting to get really pissed off but, luckily, Ella seemed to sense this and steered the conversation onto safer topics — *Strictly,* school and whether Debra looks better with long or short hair. A good evening, all in all.

Georgie was still out when I got in. She came in at about 11. Ty saw her to the door. He's very polite, almost chivalrous, I'll give him that. It's just that he's a man and she's still a child, however glamorous she looks these days. Am I jealous of Georgie? Am I jealous of Ella? God, time to stop.

There's no entry for Saturday 21st or for Sunday 22nd, the day Ella was killed. But there are several pages for Monday 23rd, the handwriting scrawling and unsteady-looking.

Monday 23rd October 2017

Ella is dead. I didn't believe it when Rick told me ...

Clare sounded genuinely shocked but, further down the page, when Rick says he's sorry, she writes: *'He's sorry. Jesus.'* What did she mean? That Rick was to blame for Ella's death? But if she'd suspected him surely she'd write in here, in her private journal? Clare also wrote that Rick had told her that

Daisy had thought he was about to be arrested. Interesting. She must have picked up our suspicions.

I kept going. I wanted to see what Clare had said about me.

> When I got back from work the police were waiting outside my house. I recognised their car. It was the one I'd seen in the car park at Talgarth yesterday. This made me nervous. There were two detectives, a man and a woman, just like in the films. The woman, DS Kaur, was Indian, short and not unattractive, but with a deliberately charmless manner, as if she were trying to trip me up.

Ha ha. Deliberately charmless, I must tell Donna. And is it borderline racist that her first adjective (get me, Miss Cathcart) is 'Indian'? 'Not unattractive'. I'm furious to find myself not displeased with that, especially coming from someone as glamorous as Clare. But who the hell is she calling short? I'm not short; she's too tall. But she had noticed our car, that day at Talgarth. And why was she nervous?

Later on, she wrote:

> I keep thinking about the two detectives who came here, Kaur and Winston. They weren't hostile exactly, but they weren't friendly either. 'Most murder victims are killed by people they know,' said Kaur, 'and we have reason to believe that this is the case here.'
>
> Who do they suspect?

Who indeed?

I skimmed through all the volumes, reading an extract here and there, but the mysterious handwriting appeared only twice. Once after Hythe. That was just one line: *Hallo, Clare. You don't know me.* Then there was the longer note, written after Clare's entry on 30th October.

Greetings from a sincere friend. I refer to the perusal (which I
have just completed) of this interesting Diary.

I looked at the writing. It was thin and slanting, almost as if it was in
italics. Slanting forwards, what was that supposed to mean? Bella, the handwriting expert, had said that it was 'probably' a man but I didn't see how she
could tell. It did look strangely old-fashioned, but maybe that was just the effect of the words.

There are many hundred pages here. I can lay my hand on my
heart and declare that every page has charmed, refreshed, delighted me.
Admirable woman!

Clare had said that this was where Wilkie Collins ended and the stranger
began.

But, Clare, not everyone appreciates you as I do. It breaks my
heart to say so but there are people who are working against
you. I have already disposed of one of these creatures. I will fall
on the others like a ravening beast.

Who were these people who were working against Clare? I read back
through her entry for 30th October. My head was pounding now and Clare's
handwriting, far rounder and looser than that of the intruder, was beginning
to swirl in an unpleasant way.

Monday 30th October 2017
Truly terrible day. Briefing in the morning and Rick tells
me that I'm now head of KS4. What's more, I have to produce
the play. I loathe musicals and it felt wrong somehow, like tres-
passing on Ella's territory. Climbing into her grave, that's what
they say, isn't it? Rick has no idea. He's just thinking about his

precious department. I honestly think that I hate Rick at the moment. Ella has just died and he's forcing me to take on all her work, without thinking of how it will affect me, her best friend. To think that he once professed to be in love with me. It makes me feel sick to think about it.

Then, to add insult to injury, R asked me to stay behind and begged me not to tell the police about him and Ella. He said that Daisy was 'very vulnerable at the moment'. The nerve of him. To blame it on his wife. I said I wouldn't say anything. Not for Rick's sake, or for Daisy's, but for Ella's. I know what the police are thinking. I knew from the moment Kaur asked whether Ella had a boyfriend. If they found out about Rick, he'd be suspect number one and she'd be the scarlet woman. Curley's wife in her red dress. Ella is dead. Let what happened in Hythe die with her.

Tony did assembly well. It was very moving, actually. The kids really did love Ella and she was a great teacher. Must remember that. But then, in first lesson, I was summoned to see the police officers who had taken up residence in T's office. It was horrible. Much worse than before. They were asking questions about Hythe, about Ella and Rick. I didn't give anything away but then they told me something absolutely horrible. A note had been found by Ella's body. A note saying 'Hell is empty'.

The worst thing happened when I got home. I looked back through my old diaries to see what I'd written about Hythe. I honestly couldn't remember what I'd said at the time and it was *awful*. So judgemental and mean. And then I saw, right at the bottom of the page, someone had written, 'Hallo, Clare. You don't know me.'

Now I am really freaked out. Who the hell could have written in my diary? The note was right. Hell is empty and all the devils are here.

Halloween tomorrow. God help us.

I read this entry several times. The detail about Rick and his 'vulnerable' wife was interesting. Daisy Lewis had both a motive to dislike Ella and a grievance against Rick. We should really take her seriously as a suspect. Clare certainly takes the moral high ground where Ella is concerned but I didn't really buy the feminist stuff about saving Ella's reputation from the brutal sexist police officers. We had to ask about lovers because — as an intelligent woman like Clare should know — they were the people who were most likely to have committed the murder. I wonder whether Clare just didn't want to talk about Hythe because she had been briefly tempted by Rick. I knew this from earlier diary entries. When Rick first made his pass, Clare wrote about the 'primal need' to have someone's arms around her but now it made her feel sick to think of him.

I still couldn't quite get my head around the whole business of diary writing. Given that the worst thing had happened at the end of the day, why did Clare still recount events in chronological order? We had the briefing, assembly, her interview with us and *then* the mysterious writing. Surely that should have come first? One thing did strike me: if the new writer really was intending to purge the world of people who didn't appreciate Clare, then Rick was the obvious next target.

Who else had Clare slagged off in her diaries?

CHAPTER 29

I was back at Talgarth High in the morning. Tony Sweetman must have spoken to the governors because the school was closed with a notice on the gates. Dave Bannerman, caretaker and Sunday footballer, let me in.

'They're on the first floor,' he said, meaning the CSI team. 'Making a hell of a mess.'

'Were all the classrooms on the first floor locked on Saturday night?' I said.

'No,' he said. 'We don't have keys to most of them. I just shut them so it looks secure.'

When I got up to the first floor, CSI had found the room. It was next door to the one where we had interviewed Clare.

'Not much blood,' I said, looking round the room which, like most on this floor, was closer to an old-fashioned bedroom than a classroom. It had skirting boards and cornices, an elaborate ceiling rose and a small, cast-iron fireplace. Was it the room Gary and I had snogged in that night? If it wasn't, it was very similar.

'That's because he wasn't stabbed to death,' said Colin Harris, the chief investigator. He loves a chance to put CID right but he's not a bad bloke on the whole.

'Really?' I said. 'I seem to remember a bloody great knife in his chest.'

'That was just window dressing,' said Colin. 'The deceased was garrot-ted, strangled from behind, probably with a thin piece of wire. We think it happened here because there are some blood spatters, likely from when the knife was inserted soon after death. Not that many though. I think the killer must have laid down some plastic or a tarpaulin.'

'They came prepared then. Anything else?'

'We think he was sitting down when he was killed, but there's no trace of the chair, which would have had blood on it. There are several splinters though. It looks as if the killer broke up the chair and took the pieces away with him.'

I noticed he said 'him' and I must admit, the physical evidence — chair chopping, body carrying — did seem to point to a man.

'Why would he do that?' I said.

'Search me,' said Colin. 'The mind of a murderer is a murky place.'

That remark sounded as if he'd said it many times before.

'Then what happened? He was taken up to the attic?'

'Yes, traces of hair were found on the door frame, consistent with a body being carried. You'll have my report later today.' Colin was a man who liked to do things the right way.

'Anything you can tell me now?' Whereas I was someone who wanted to get on as quickly as possible.

Colin sighed and pushed his glasses back with a gloved hand. 'Looks as if the deceased was carried into the room and placed in the desk chair. The perpetrator wore gloves but we have some good blood-stained footprints. And,' he knew this was what I wanted, 'a note.'

'What did it say?'

'*Hell is empty.* Same as before. Note was inside a freezer bag. Placed on the desk. No prints, no blood.'

I felt a surge of something that I called adrenalin but was really excitement. Here was possible evidence that the two murders had been committed by the same person.

'Anything else significant?' I asked.

'Three candles on the desk and some plant material.'

'Plant material?'

'We've sent them to be analysed but they looked like herbs, leaves and dried petals, the sort of thing you'd find in a potpourri. Plus a black stone, like a shiny pebble. That was next to the candles.'

A faint bell rang somewhere in my brain but I couldn't waste time trying to locate the sound. I had to get back to the station and tell Donna and Neil the latest.

I ran down the main staircase and saw a man by the double doors, staring moodily into the distance. It was Tony Sweetman, wearing jeans, jumper and trainers. The trainers were expensive-looking, far too clean and white.

'Hallo,' I said.

He jumped slightly. Under the newly replenished tan, Tony looked dreadful, hollow-eyed and almost tearful. Despite myself, I felt slightly sorry for him.

'DS Kaur. I gather your experts are still at work.'

'Yes,' I said. 'Crime scene investigation takes a long time. They're very thorough.'

He shuddered. 'I can't bear to think of my school as a crime scene.'

My school. But I could see why he was upset. Now, when someone Googled Talgarth High, they wouldn't see 'best ever GCSE results', they'd see 'man found murdered'.

'I've just spoken to Daisy Lewis,' he said. 'She's devastated. They're childless, you know. All they had was each other.'

He said it in the way that parents often describe the child-free, pity matched with slight disapproval.

'Have you any idea who could have done this?' I asked.

'No,' he said, opening his eyes wide in a way that reminded me of Clare. 'Rick was popular with everyone.'

'Really?'

'Yes.' He bridled slightly at my tone. 'He was an excellent teacher and department head.'

'I've heard rumours of affairs with both Ella Elphick and Clare Cassidy,' I said.

Tony's face went blank, as if a cloth had erased the previous day's teaching on a whiteboard. 'I never listen to those sort of rumours.'

But he didn't deny it. I was about to ask more when my phone buzzed. Neil.

'Come back to the station. I've found something on the CCTV.'

Neil was full of excitement. He loves being the one to make a breakthrough. To be fair, it doesn't happen often.

'I was looking through the CCTV from the church outside Ella's house,' he said. 'Just to see if we missed anything the first time.' What did he want? A bloody medal? A prefect's badge?

Neil was almost dragging me towards his computer. 'Remember there were a couple of teenagers on their phones?'

'Yes.'

'Well, look again. I've enlarged the image.'

I looked. There on the screen, in grainy pixels, was a hooded youth, phone in hand. The camera had caught a moment when he'd looked up, face illuminated by a blue security light.

It was Patrick O'Leary.

CHAPTER 30

We drove straight to Patrick's house. He lived in Shoreham, over the ferry bridge, by the towpath where the houseboats clanked gently in the water. I used to love the houseboats when I was a child. The neat ones, with window boxes and names like 'Youanme', the dilapidated ones, low in the water, with rotting timbers and dirty net curtains at the windows, the hippyish ones, with stars and wind-chimes where, even in my pre-police days, I could smell marijuana. The O'Learys had a small, modern house on one of the roads between the sea and the estuary. There was something insubstantial about it, as if it hadn't been built to last, with yellow plastic facings and a tiny balcony, too small for a person to stand on. There was rubbish in the front garden as if someone had wanted to light a bonfire and then lost interest. The whole place looked sad and unloved.

Patrick opened the door himself, looking as if he had just got out of bed.

'Hallo, Patrick,' I said. 'Are your mum and dad in?'

He stared, holding the door half shut. 'No, they're at work.'

'Can you call them? We need to talk to you and we need an adult present.'

'I'm an adult,' said a voice behind Patrick. Another youth came to slouch beside him. They were clearly brothers, both heavily built with black hair and surly expressions. Right now, though, Patrick looked more frightened than surly.

'It's the police, Declan. They want to talk to me.'

'Have you got a warrant?' said Declan, stepping in front of his younger brother.

I sighed. Another one who watched too much TV. 'We don't need a warrant. We're not arresting Patrick or searching your house. We just need to talk to him and we need an appropriate adult present.'

'I'm an appropriate adult,' said Declan.

'No,' said Patrick, rather to my relief. 'I'm calling Mum.'

We waited in the car until Maureen O'Leary arrived, still wearing her nurse's uniform. Patrick met her at the door and they both turned as Neil and I approached.

'Thanks so much for coming, Mrs O'Leary,' I said. 'I'm DS Kaur and this is DS Winston. We need to talk to Patrick in connection with the murder of Ella Elphick.'

'Murder?' said Mrs O'Leary. 'What are you talking about?' She was a small woman — the boys must get their height from their dad — but she was pretty formidable all the same, the sort of nurse who plunges in the needle before you've even rolled up your sleeve.

'The murder of Ella Elphick,' I repeated.

'Ella? Oh, the teacher. Is that why the school's shut again today? It's a disgrace. Patrick's got his GCSEs this year.'

'Can we go inside?' I said. 'Then I can explain.'

We sat in a tiny room dominated by a huge television and a fluorescent fish tank. Declan stayed beside his brother and I didn't think it was worth asking him to leave. I was pretty sure that anything we said would be heard throughout the flimsy house. Even so, it was a tight squeeze. Declan, Maureen and Patrick jammed together on the sofa. Neil and I sat on chairs facing them.

I showed Patrick the enlarged photograph.

'Is this you?'

'I don't know,' he said. 'Why?'

'It was taken outside Ella Elphick's house on the night that she was murdered.'

A silence. Maureen said, but without much conviction, 'That's not Patrick.'

'Is it you, Patrick?'

A silence, then Patrick said, almost in a whisper, 'Yes.'

'Can you tell us what you were doing there that night?'

'I wanted to see her. Miss Elphick,' he said. 'To explain about the card.'

'What card? The valentine you sent her?' I could tell that it was news to Maureen O'Leary, but probably not to Declan.

'Yes,' said Patrick, looking down at his hands. He had a complicated-looking watch on one wrist, a tangle of friendship bracelets on the other. He was wearing trainers. Nike Air, just like Mr Sweetman. They looked better on Patrick.

'What made you think about the card?' said Neil. 'Valentine's Day was nine months ago.'

'I had to make amends,' said Patrick. 'That's what Miss Hughes said. So I went to Miss Elphick's house that evening. Just to explain why I'd sent the card. Mr Lewis made out like I was *stalking* her or something when he kicked me out of her form. But it wasn't like that. I just liked her. I wanted to tell her that. No one knew I went there. Mum, Dad and Declan were all out. I walked over and I knocked on the door but there was no answer.'

'What did you do then?' I asked.

'I waited. I thought she was in because I saw her car in the street. I waited over the road by the church.'

'How long did you wait?'

'I don't know. Maybe ten, fifteen minutes?'

He'd only been caught on the CCTV once but it really just captured the church porch. Thinking of this, I asked, on the off-chance, 'While you were outside, did you see anyone going into Miss Elphick's house or leaving it?'

I hadn't expected an answer but Patrick looked straight at me for the first time. 'Yes,' he said, 'I saw Mr Lewis leaving the house.'

'Mr Lewis? Are you sure?'

'Yeah.' A short laugh. 'I'd recognise that wanker anywhere.'

Maureen aimed a slap at him. 'Patrick O'Leary!'

'What were you doing on Saturday night, Patrick?' I asked.

'Why are you asking him that?' This was Declan, who seemed determined to be his brother's spokesperson. He was the type who would go on to become a lawyer. Or a criminal.

'It's a simple question,' I said.

Patrick looked down at his trainers. 'I was at home.'

'Alone?'

Maureen said, sounding defensive, 'Pat and I were at the pub with friends. Declan was out with his girlfriend.'

'So, you were alone, Patrick?'

He raised his head. 'Yes. I was alone.'

'When did you get back, Mrs O'Leary?'

'About midnight. Why are you asking him these questions?'

But Patrick knew. 'Is it true then, that Mr Lewis has been murdered?'

'So Rick had been at Ella's house that night,' said Neil. We were driving along the beach road. The sea was still and grey, blending with the grey stony beach and grey sky.

'Yes,' I said. 'Pity we can't ask him about it.'

'It looks like the same MO for Ella and Rick,' said Neil.

'Except that Rick was strangled — garrotted — not stabbed.'

'Yeah, but the note and everything. It's definitely the same person. Do you think it could be Patrick?'

'It's possible,' I said. 'He's big and strong enough. He had a crush on Ella and clearly resented Rick. Did you hear him say that Rick made out he was stalking Ella? There was real anger there. And he doesn't have an alibi for Saturday.'

'I thought he was lying about being home alone,' said Neil.

'So did I,' I said, 'but it could just have been something he didn't want his mum to know about. We'll have to interview him again. Maybe with his dad this time.'

'So you like him for it?'

'I don't know,' I said. 'These murders are well-thought-out, planned carefully in advance. The note in the plastic bag, the tarpaulin on the floor. I don't see Patrick as a planner somehow.'

'What did his teachers say about him?' Neil took the turning back inland. Mirror, signal, manoeuvre. It was like watching someone take their driving test.

I looked back through my notes. 'Clever enough, good at sport, sometimes in trouble for fighting. Like I said, a bit of a hothead. There was one thing, though — did you hear the teacher he mentioned? The one who told him to make amends?'

'No. Who was it?'

'Miss Hughes. I don't think she teaches at Talgarth. The funny thing is, Clare mentions a Bryony Hughes in her diaries. Says she's a witch.'

'Jesus,' said Neil. 'That's all we need.'

My phone buzzed. Clare Cassidy. I pressed 'speakerphone'.

'DS Kaur. Please come quickly.' Clare's voice filled the car, sobbing, frantic. 'I think someone's taken Herbert.'

CHAPTER 31

'Who the hell's Herbert?' said Neil.

'Her dog,' I said. 'Let's go straight to her place.'

'For a missing dog? Why doesn't she call the RSPCA? And there's a squad car outside her house. Can't they help?'

'You heard her voice,' I said. 'Clare's letting her guard down for the first time. If I can go over there, be all sympathetic, I might just find something out.'

'Like what?'

'Like what she really felt about Ella and Rick.'

'I thought you'd read her diaries.'

'Diaries don't tell you what people think. Just what they think they think. You don't have to stay. Just drop me off.'

'It's a waste of your time,' said Neil but he took the turning under the fly-over towards Steyning. I was always amazed by the way the horses grazed in the fields below, seemingly unconcerned by the cars roaring over their heads.

'Maybe,' I said. 'But you're forgetting one thing: maybe someone *has* taken Herbert. Maybe the person who wrote in her diary *is* stalking Clare. They might go for the dog today and the daughter tomorrow.'

'Bloody hell, Kaur. Are you always this cheerful?'

'You know I'm right,' I said.

. . .

Neil dropped me off outside the row of town houses in the middle of nowhere. Clare opened the door before I'd knocked.

'Georgie took him over the field,' she said. 'She stopped to look at her phone and, when she looked up, he'd gone.'

'It wasn't my fault,' Georgie appeared in the background, her face tearstained. 'I only looked at my phone for, like, a minute.'

'Of course it's not your fault, darling.' Clare put her arm round her daughter and, for the very first time, I almost liked her. Even so, what were these two thinking? They were still under police protection and Georgia should not have been out on her own. Had Clare forgotten that she'd almost witnessed a murder the day before yesterday?

'He's probably still in the field,' I said, insinuating myself into the house. 'Rabbiting or something.'

'We've been round the field,' said Clare. 'And in the lanes. Barry and Steve are driving round the streets now, looking for him.'

'Who?'

'The policemen outside our house.' Clare looked surprised. 'Don't you know their names?'

'Not offhand,' I said. 'Now the most important thing to do is keep calm. The first hours are vital in a misper.'

'A what?'

'Missing person case,' supplied Georgia. So Georgia was a fan of cop dramas, was she?

'First thing,' I shepherded them into the kitchen. I hadn't been there before and I must say I was impressed. They'd extended into the garden and there was a skylight, a breakfast bar and a separate dining area. Cooking utensils and dried herbs hung from the ceiling but the surfaces were clear and shiny, like a CSI lab.

'The first thing,' I said, 'is tea. Georgia, can you put the kettle on? Second thing, plan of attack.' I got out my notebook. 'When did you last see Herbert?'

'Eleven twenty-four,' said Georgia immediately. 'It was when I looked at my phone.'

I looked at the oversized clock over the dining table. There were no numbers but the hands were forming a right angle.

'We're still in the golden hour,' I said. 'So you've searched the field and the surrounding area. What about closer to home? Missing persons often gravitate back home. I was called out for a missing teenager once and she was asleep in her bed.'

Clare actually laughed at this one. She seemed to be calming down slightly. Georgia placed a mug of tea in front of her.

'I've looked in the garden,' said Georgia, 'and shaken his dog biscuits.'

'Look again,' I said. 'Have you got a shed?'

'Yes,' said Clare. She and Georgia went into the garden and I watched them poking around the corners of the tiny space as if the dog could possibly be there. I took a thoughtful swig of tea. If I could find Herbert, Clare and Georgia would definitely be my friends for life.

I put my mug down and joined them in the garden. They were looking in the shed, which, like sheds everywhere, smelled of turpentine and housed old flower pots and a lawnmower. But no white, fluffy dog.

Clare actually clutched my arm.

'What if he's been taken? What if someone's taken him?'

'He'll come back, Mum,' said Georgia. It was probably the least convincing thing I'd heard since Neil said that I wasn't bossy.

'But what if it's *him*?' Clare was still holding on to me. 'You know, the one who wrote to me . . .'

'Shh,' I said. Not just to shut her up and stop her terrifying her daughter — I'd heard something.

'What is it?' said Clare.

'I thought I heard . . .' I stopped. There it was again. A very faint bark.

This time Clare and Georgia heard it too.

'It's him!' said Clare. They both started calling, 'Herbert! Herbert!'

'Shh,' I said again. 'Let's work out where it's coming from.'

Of course, the barking had stopped now. But I thought it had come from quite a way away, in a north-easterly direction. I looked beyond Clare's garden and the three neat gardens next to it, towards the monster that no one in this smart terrace seemed to want to acknowledge. The factory.

'Come on,' I said. 'Let's go and look. Have you got a special whistle or anything?'

I'd meant something like a policeman's whistle but Clare pursed her lips and two notes came floating out.

'That's his special sign,' said Georgia proudly. 'We can both do it.'

'Terrific,' I said. 'Get ready to whistle.' I felt like someone in one of Mum and Dad's favourite black-and-white films. *You know how to whistle, don't you? You just put your lips together and blow.*

We went out the front door. It was a still day but cold and grey. The sun had never really come up and now, at just past midday, the shadows already seemed to be lengthening. I was wearing my jacket but neither Clare nor Georgia had a coat on. We walked to the end of the row of houses. Clare whistled. We waited.

And there it was again. A shrill, sharp bark. And this time there was no doubting the direction.

'He's in the old factory,' said Clare.

The factory was fenced off but you could see places where local youths had got through the wire. I found an opening and squeezed through. Clare followed, not seeming to care that she had snagged her pink cashmere jumper.

Surprisingly, Georgia held back. 'Are we allowed?' she said. 'There's CCTV.'

'Good,' I said. 'We'll get backup.' Privately, I thought it unlikely that the cameras still worked.

'It's against the law.'

'I am the law,' I said meaning to lighten the atmosphere but Georgie just stared at me.

'You can wait here if you want,' said Clare.

'No,' I said. 'I want us to stay together. Come on, Georgie.' I held the fence back for her and she edged through.

We crossed the forecourt. It was weird. The place seemed to be left exactly as it had been when it stopped manufacturing. There were still lorries parked outside, their tyres rotten and wheel rims rusted. A monstrous chute hovered overhead as if it were about to deposit a ton of liquid cement. The main doors were locked and bolted but I knew there had to be a way in.

We skirted the huge, square building. It was about seven stories high, with a tower at the back. Rows and rows of broken windows but none of them on the ground floor. Clare whistled again, and once more the answering bark came back.

We walked around the building. At the rear the chalk cliffs rose up, higher than the tower. Did the cliffs mean that the sea used to come this far inland? I'd have to ask someone who knew about geology. Gary maybe. There was a small yard at the back and a door, wedged open by what looked like a tin of paint. I switched on my phone torch, wishing I had my Maglite with me.

'Come on.'

We were in what looked like a packing area. There were a few pallets left, with empty sacks that looked (and smelled) as if foxes had been living in them. There was wood too, chopped up as if for firewood. I thought of the chair that Rick Lewis had sat on before he was killed. CSI thought that the killer had taken the pieces away with them. Could they be here?

There were three doors, like one of those computer games where you have to choose and risk being attacked by aliens or zombies. I chose the middle one and it led into a huge space, three stories high and completely empty. Light slanted in from windows at the top and I could hear birds — or bats — overhead. There was a kind of balcony around three sides at first floor level. Like a prison, I thought. Clare whistled and a bark came back, loud and clear, almost directly above us.

I pointed to an iron staircase, like a fire escape, at the back.

'You stay here,' I said. 'I'll go up.'

'No,' said Clare. 'Herbert doesn't know you. He'll want to see me.'

So we all climbed the staircase, our footsteps echoing horribly in the cavernous space. I thought of R.M. Holland's study at the school. The killer carrying Rick's body up the spiral staircase. Whoever it was must have been strong. I was out of breath just from this climb and I'm pretty fit.

The barking was loud and constant now. We all moved towards the sound, which was coming from a room at the far end of the landing. The metal door looked very shut but it opened easily when I turned the handle. And there he was.

'Herbert!' Clare was sobbing. 'My baby.'

She was on her knees cuddling him and Georgia was beside her. Herbert was wagging his tail and snuffling with joy but there was a bandage around his leg and he clearly couldn't put that foot down.

I looked around the tiny room, mentally committing its contents to memory.

Item 1: sleeping bag
Item 2: camping stove
Item 3: battery-operated lantern
Item 4: tarpaulin on the floor
Item 5: battered copy of *The Tempest*

CHAPTER 32

Clare and Georgia took Herbert to the vet. He'd cut his foot but someone had cleaned it and wrapped it in a bandage. I called the station and waited for backup and CSI. I wanted DNA and fingerprints from every item in the room. It was obvious to me that someone had been living in the old factory for a while. The room had a small window that looked directly onto the row of cottages, with Clare's at the end. I thought of the lights that I'd seen in the building that night. A candle had been lit on the window ledge, even though there was a flashlight. Was this where the killer had been sitting, watching Clare and lighting candles?

When I got back to the station, Donna was torn between bawling me out for going into the factory without backup and excitement at the thought of a lead.

'If the DNA matches any from the crime scenes, we've got a suspect. They might even be in the database. Good work, Harbinder. But never do anything like that again.'

'Why would they take the dog, though?' Neil didn't like it that I'd been right about Herbert.

'Maybe he was a sort of hostage,' said Donna. 'Poor little fellow.' She liked dogs and owned a large spaniel. Out of control, like her kids.

'If it's the diary writer,' I said, 'he clearly wants to help Clare. Maybe that's why he looked after Herbert. His paw was neatly bandaged.'

'Why not give him back to her then?' said Neil.

'Maybe he was waiting until dark.'

It was getting dark outside now, at only three o'clock. One of those winter days when it feels as if those old men with placards are right and the end of the world is on its way.

'We've got the other members of the English department coming in,' said Neil. 'Do you want to interview them with me?'

'We need to ask them about *The Stranger*,' I said.

'What? Oh, that book Clare's obsessed with.'

'I think someone else is obsessed with it too.'

'What do you mean?' said Donna.

'In the book, two men are killed in an old house. One is stabbed and he had marks on his hands, like the stigmata.'

'Like Ella,' said Neil.

'Exactly. And the second man was garrotted. Like Rick Lewis.'

'Are you really suggesting that the killer is re-enacting some obscure Victorian short story?' said Donna, searching in her desk drawer for something to eat.

'I'm not suggesting anything,' I said. 'But there was a quote from the book at both scenes. I think that's a pretty significant link.'

'I thought you said it was from Shakespeare,' said Neil, sounding aggrieved.

'It's from Shakespeare *and* from *The Stranger*. Don't you remember Clare telling us that?'

'She was talking about all sorts of books. What about the one where the bloke writes in the diary?'

'*The Woman in White*,' I said. 'Another starter for ten for the English teachers.'

The *University Challenge* reference was wasted on Neil.

We interviewed Vera Prentice, Alan Smith and Anoushka Palmer. All of them had alibis for Rick. Vera had been watching television at home with her mother. This amazed me because Vera seemed about a hundred years old — but she turned out to be 'only' sixty, and her mother was in her eighties. Alan had been at home with his wife and grown-up daughter, watching a French film on Netflix. No *Strictly* for them. Alan clearly saw himself as an intellectual as well as an old-school socialist. He said that Tony was 'trying to turn Talgarth into an academy.' 'What's wrong with that?' Neil asked me afterwards. 'Academy sounds posher than school.' 'Exactly,' I said.

Both Vera and Alan had read *The Stranger* 'years ago' but neither of them taught it. 'It's typical white, middle-class male stuff,' said Alan. 'The only women in it are servants.' I didn't remember the servants, which told me that Alan recalled the text better than he pretended.

Anoushka Palmer was last. I was interested in her particularly because she'd been on the training course at Hythe. She was young and pretty, mixed-race, with long hair in a complicated plait.

'Rick was so kind to me,' she kept saying. I bet he was.

Anoushka had been out with her boyfriend on Saturday night and had 'stayed over at his'. She gave us his address. His name was Sam Isaacs and he was a teacher at the sixth-form college.

'Do you teach *The Tempest*?' I asked.

'Yes.' She looked surprised. 'I have a couple of GCSE classes.'

'What about *The Stranger* by R.M. Holland?'

'No. I've never even read it. I know I should because of the school's connection but I'm not really a fan of Victorian fiction.'

I'm not a great reader but I found it quite shocking that an English teacher would say something like that.

Before she left, I asked Anoushka if the name Bryony Hughes meant anything to her.

'Yes,' she said. 'She teaches English at the sixth-form college. Sam knows her quite well.'

'She was a friend of Ella's too, wasn't she?'

'I'm not sure, but most of the English teachers round here know each other. We're always meeting at training courses and things like that.'

This rang a bell. 'Was Bryony Hughes on the Hythe course?'

'Yes,' said Anoushka. 'Yes, she was. And come to think of it, I did see her with Ella a few times.'

'But she doesn't teach any kids at your Talgarth? Patrick O'Leary, say?'

'No, unless she does some private tutoring. Lots of teachers do and you can't tutor kids in your own school. But I wouldn't think Patrick was the type for a private tutor.'

I didn't think so either.

'She runs a creative writing evening course,' said Anoushka. 'I've heard it's really good but, again, not quite Patrick's thing.'

So both Clare and Bryony Hughes taught creative writing. I always thought it seemed a weird thing to teach. Either you can write or you can't. But maybe there was a link there. I thanked Anoushka and she left in a flurry of scarves and bags, Neil holding the door open like a butler.

By the time I'd written up my notes, it was six o'clock and I decided to call it a day. With any luck we'd get the crime scene report tomorrow and the investigation could move forward. Talgarth High would open again but the Old Building would remain closed. I wondered how Tony felt about abandoning his grand head teacher's office. I suspected that he'd be happy never to see Holland House again; he was probably already filling out job applications for September.

On an impulse, on the way home, I called in on Clare. This time I got a very warm welcome. Herbert was ensconced on the sofa like a king, his foot professionally bandaged and tempting snacks within reach. Georgia was in her room.

'Would you like a cup of tea?' said Clare. 'Or a glass of wine? It's after six.'

'A glass of wine would be nice,' I said. 'As I'm off-duty.'

Clare poured us both a large glass of red wine and I sat on the sofa stroking Herbert.

'He doesn't seem too bad,' I said.

'No,' said Clare. 'The vet said he'd probably cut his foot on some glass but it's not too deep and it had been cleaned. I mean ... he ... someone had cleaned it. And put that bandage on it.'

We were hopeful that there would be prints on the bandage. I said, 'You've no idea who it could have been?'

Clare shook her head. She was still in the slightly torn pink cardigan and had her fluffy slippers on. Somehow, she still managed to look glamorous.

'I've seen lights in the factory sometimes,' she said. 'But I always thought

I was imagining it. I told myself I'd been reading *The Stranger* too much. You remember the bit where the candles shine in the window of the old house?'

'I remember,' I said. I didn't add that I had reread the short story that day.

'I cover it on my creative writing course,' Clare was saying, 'and one of the things I always teach is that, in the ghost story tradition, things happen in threes. Remember you mentioned the "we waited and we waited and we waited" bit in *The Stranger*? Well, I went to the attic study and I saw the dummy in the chair. That was the first time. Then I went there with Henry and I saw . . . we saw Rick. That was the second time. I keep thinking, what will happen the third time?'

'It doesn't work like that in real life,' I said. 'Things aren't that neat. You can drive yourself mad looking for patterns.'

'There are other things too,' she said. 'I talk about the totemic animal. How animals in books can be used to raise tension. Sometimes authors kill them because they want a death and can't face killing a human. They can play a vital role in the plot. Well, that was Herbert today.'

'But he's not dead. Thank God.' I was playing with Herbert's ears. Then I said, 'The dog in *The Stranger* . . .'

'Is called Herbert,' said Clare.

'Did you name your dog after him?'

'In a way,' said Clare, taking a swig of wine. 'But also it just seemed to suit him.'

I looked at the dog, who was now just a circle of white wool, nose hidden under tail. To me he looked more like a Ferdy or a Dougal. Herbert was too dignified for him.

'He's not just a dog,' I said. 'He's my animal familiar, my soul in dog form.'

Clare stared at me for a minute, mouth slightly open. 'Oh my God,' she said. 'You're quoting from my diary. That's *horrible*.'

'I'm sorry,' I said. And I did feel slightly guilty.

'You write that sort of thing,' she said, 'but you never expect anyone to read it.'

'Why do you keep a diary then?' I said. 'What's the point of it?'

Clare held her wine up to the light and squinted at it. There were thick white candles on the table and they smelled wonderful. Jo Malone, like Clare's scent.

'It's to make sense of things,' she said, at last. 'Nothing's as bad if you put it in writing. It helps you to take control, order things. Find a pattern, like you said. When I was at my happiest, or when I was having most fun, at university, I didn't write at all. I started again when my marriage began to go wrong. It's a form of therapy, I suppose. There's a strange comfort in looking back at your worst times and realising that you got through them.'

'But you never intended to show it to anyone else?'

She didn't answer straight away. She drained her glass, filled it up again and offered some to me. I had to say no because I was driving.

'When I was working in London,' she said, 'my head of department was a man called Lucca. He wasn't conventionally attractive but he was very clever and charming and a lot of women liked him. He kept a diary and he used to write it at work, I think to stop his wife finding it. Anyway, there was a woman there, a newly qualified teacher, who had a crush on Lucca and, one night, she broke into the school to read his diaries. She was desperate to see what he'd written about her.'

'What had he written about her?'

Clare laughed. 'That's the irony. Nothing. He hadn't mentioned her at all. Lucca told me that himself. The caretaker caught the woman breaking in and she had to leave the school. I mean, she was obviously unbalanced. But actually, that's not the real irony. Do you know what the real irony is?'

'No,' I said, feeling some response was required.

'The real irony was that after that, he *had* to write about her.'

I wondered why Clare had told me this story. There were obvious similarities to Clare's own behaviour. She wrote her diary at work, she'd broken into the school. Well, technically she had a key but it was still pretty unbalanced, if you ask me. Was Clare saying that the person who wrote in her diary was just hoping to find themselves mentioned in future entries? It all made my head swim. Though that could have been the wine. I remembered that there was something else I wanted to ask Clare.

'Tell me about Bryony Hughes,' I said.

'Bryony Hughes?' She had been sitting curled up in her chair with her legs tucked under her but now she sat up straighter and put her feet on the floor.

'You mention her in your diary. Ella was going out with her and you said it was a coven meeting.'

'You've got a good memory.'

'For some things. Yes.' I was good at remembering things people had said. That was useful for work. But I'm useless at other things: birthdays, appointments, my computer password.

'Why did you say that it was a coven meeting?'

Clare laughed but it didn't come out right. 'There have always been rumours about Bryony. That she's a white witch, stuff like that. She looks the part — long, grey hair, lots of silver jewellery. And she keeps making these gnomic statements. "You have a golden aura". You know the sort of thing.'

I had no idea what 'gnomic' meant and I wasn't going to ask.

'And Ella was friends with her?'

'Yes,' said Clare, but there was hesitation in her voice. She ran her finger around the rim of her wine glass.

'Were they close?'

'Yes.' Another pause. 'But I think they fell out shortly before Ella died.'

'Do you know why?'

'No. Ella could be like that with her friends. Bosom pals one minute and then, the next, something would happen and she would drop them.'

There was definitely some bitterness here. I remembered the diaries. I still wasn't sure whether Clare had been jealous of Ella for sleeping with Rick or Rick for taking Ella away from her.

'Why are you interested in Bryony?' said Clare.

'Her name's come up a couple of times,' I said. 'That's all. It's not important.' I looked at my watch. 'I should go.'

'I'm going to make some pasta for me and Georgie,' said Clare. 'Blot up the alcohol. Do you want to stay and have some?' Herbert sat up and wagged his tail. He obviously understood the word 'pasta'.

'Thanks very much,' I said. 'But I should be getting home. My mum always cooks a feast in the evenings.'

'Do you live at home?' said Clare.

'Yes.' In a funny way, I felt I owed her this much. After all, I'd read her diaries. 'I'm a thirty-five-year-old woman who lives at home with her parents. You can judge me now.'

'I'm not judging,' said Clare. 'I'm envious, if anything. I can't stand my parents for two days at Christmas, let alone every night.'

'It's OK,' I said. 'They're good company, on the whole. I think my mum still hopes I'll find a nice man though.'

'Well, that's easier said than done,' said Clare.

'I'm sure you're right,' I said. 'But I'm gay so it's not really an issue.'

I really don't know why I told her. I may have read her diaries, but that didn't mean I had to tell her my deepest secrets in return. Not that it's something I hide; I'm not ashamed of it or anything. I'm out at work and to my friends. Not to my parents, of course. It's just, I like to keep some things private and Clare was, after all, a person of interest in our enquiry. She's not a friend.

'Oh, are you?' she said. Not shocked, not embarrassed, not that interested. Just right, really.

'Yes,' I said. 'Well, I'd better go before my mother sends out a search party.' I got up, brushing my clothes down.

'He's part poodle,' said Clare. 'He doesn't shed.'

I was dubious, but to be fair, there weren't dog hairs all over the place.

'Are you OK?' I said. 'Scott and Bailey are still outside if you need them.'

She laughed. 'I think of them as Cagney and Lacey. Showing my age. No, I'm OK. Do you think he'll come back, whoever was living in the factory?'

'I don't think so,' I said, 'but we're keeping a watch on it, just in case. You should really think of moving to a safer place. I suppose there's no chance you could go and stay with a friend for a bit? Or with your parents?'

'Not really,' she said. 'Tony rang me today. It's going to be a nightmare at school. I'm acting head of department apparently. I need to stay until the end of term. Anyway, I wouldn't go to my parents. In an emergency I'd go to my grandmother. She lives in Scotland. Near Inverness.'

'Sounds nice and remote,' I said. 'Bye, Clare. Thanks for the wine. Keep your door locked.'

CHAPTER 33

In the morning I went to see Bryony Hughes. I hadn't been back to the sixth-form college since I left after my last exam. I didn't even attend my leaving prom. It's funny, I remember my Talgarth days with almost uncomfortable clarity, but I have almost no recollection of my A-Level years. I spent two years of my life in this place but it seems to have left no mark on me. Did I have teachers, friends, enemies? I honestly can't remember. It's as if it happened to someone else.

The buildings are the same: a series of concrete rectangles with absolutely no character at all. The opposite of Talgarth really. There was no heady school atmosphere here, no pictures of teams or flyers for plays, just corridors and classrooms, identifiable only by letters and numbers. As I signed at reception I watched a group of students slouch past. They looked so grown-up, as if far more than a few months separated them from the blue sweatshirts at Talgarth. Two of the boys had beards and the girls exuded the type of sophisticated glamour that I would have thought unobtainable at eighteen — or at any age, come to that. I wondered what they'd think of me in my non-uniform uniform of dark trousers and jacket and my name badge saying 'DS Kaur, Sussex Police', but I needn't have worried. Not one of them even registered my existence.

I was directed up to the English office. No student guide in this place, just a badly photocopied floor plan. Eventually I found the room on the second floor, knocked and was told to come in. Miss Hughes was on her own, sitting at a desk in a room whose walls were entirely papered in playbills and Shakespeare quotes. Immediately, as if it had been highlighted by an eager student, I saw the line from *The Tempest: Hell is empty and all the devils are here.*

Bryony Hughes was probably in her late-fifties — nearing retirement age, anyway — but she didn't have the harried look of most older teachers. She sat serenely in her chair waiting for me to explain why I was there. I remembered Clare's description — 'long, grey hair, lots of silver jewellery' — but that didn't really do Bryony justice. Her hair was silvery but it was contained in a neat bun and she didn't have any jewellery that I could see. She wore a cream polo-neck jumper and — a quick glance under the desk told me — black trousers with flat black shoes of the type favoured by nurses or nuns. She had pale blue eyes and she didn't blink enough.

Bryony didn't ask me to sit down but I did so anyway. I moved my chair back so that I didn't look like a pupil who had been called in to discuss missing coursework. 'I'm DS Harbinder Kaur,' I said. 'I'm investigating the deaths of Ella Elphick and Rick Lewis.'

She nodded as if acknowledging this.

'Did you know Ella and Rick?'

'Ella was a dear friend.' She had a low voice with a hint of a Welsh accent.

'And Rick Lewis?'

'I knew Richard a little.'

'He wasn't a dear friend then?'

'Richard was a dedicated teacher,' said Bryony, with dignity. 'He was a valued colleague.'

'When did you last see Ella?'

'A few weeks before she died. We went for a walk and some spiritual sustenance.' She was the sort of person who would never admit to going out for a meal.

'Spiritual sustenance?'

'We went for a walk by the sea. There is something so healing about being near water.'

'Why did Ella need healing?'

Was it my imagination or was the gentle voice becoming a little strained? 'Teaching can be exhausting work. You give all the time and sometimes you get little in return.'

'I heard that you had fallen out with Ella.'

'Who told you that?' Serenity definitely ruffled now.

'Is it true?'

'Good friends sometimes disagree.'

'What did you disagree about?'

She hesitated and rearranged the papers on the desk. They looked like essays. I've never understood how you can write so much about books.

'We disagreed on teaching methods,' she said at last.

'Was it a serious argument?'

'No, just a debate about pedagogy. We both cared so much about our students that sometimes emotions were heightened.'

'Do you teach a student called Patrick O'Leary?'

'He comes to my creative writing class.'

'The after-school group? He doesn't seem the type.'

'He's a talented writer,' said Bryony. 'I've learned not to judge by appearances.'

That was a definite dig at me. I smiled at her blandly. 'Who else comes to this class?'

'Just a few students. A small and select group.'

I didn't like the way she said this. 'Who's in this select group?' I asked.

'Patrick and three girls. Natasha White, Venetia Sherbourne and Georgia Newton.'

'Georgia? Clare's daughter?'

'Clare Cassidy? Yes, I believe so.'

'Do you know Clare?'

'I've met her at various teacher training days.'

'Were you on the course at Hythe in July?'

'Yes.' She fixed me with that blue stare again.

'Do you remember anything about Ella on that course? Anything between Ella and Rick?'

'I never listen to gossip.'

That seemed to answer the question. 'When did you last see Rick Lewis?' I asked.

'I really can't remember.' She looked at her watch. 'If you'll excuse me, I've got a class in a few minutes.'

I stood up but she remained seated. 'You've got an angry aura,' she told me.

'Thanks very much.'

'But then again,' her voice was very soft now, 'it must be hard coming back here.'

'What do you mean?'

'I remember you as a student,' she said.

'I didn't do English A-Level.'

'No, but I remember you all the same.'

'I don't remember you, I'm afraid.'

'Oh, I think you do,' said Bryony Hughes. 'I think you do.'

I thought about this gnomic remark (I'd looked the word up) all the way back to the station. I also thought about the objects on the bookshelf behind Miss Hughes: a KitKat mug full of pens, a Collins dictionary and thesaurus, and a black stone, very like the one found on R.M. Holland's desk, beside Rick Lewis' dead body.

'What happened next?' Ah, the perennial, unanswered question. That is the very essence of narrative, is it not? 'Please read another page', begs the child at bedtime. Anything to ward off the horrors of the dark. And you have not long left childhood behind yourself, my dear young friend. It is only natural that you should want to know what happens in the next chapter.

Another year passed. I became engaged to Ada, the daughter of my tutor. I started work on my thesis, which dealt with the Albigensian heresy. I also taught undergraduates, though, in truth, I was a solid and uninspiring lecturer. I heard them whispering about me sometimes, caught the words 'Hell Club' and 'murder'. But I chose to dwell in the light that year. And I acquired a companion. Yes, the very animal that you see before you in this train carriage. What a friend dear Herbert has been to me in my trials. Truer and more steadfast than any human acolyte.

Autumn passed and with it Halloween. I confess I breathed a sigh of relief when the dread day passed without incident. But then, several weeks later, I heard the bedders talking in the corridor and caught the name 'Collins' and the word 'killed'.

I burst out of my room and demanded, with a passion that surprised them, 'What are you talking about?'

'Mr Collins, from King's, as was, sir,' came the reply. 'We were talking about the way he died. So unnatural.'

'What happened?' I said, aware that a coldness had swept over me. Collins, the companion of Lord Bastian, had been a student at King's.

'He was killed, sir. He was driving his own carriage across the fens. He set off from Ely, as right as rain, heading for Cambridge. No one knows what happened but his horse was found a day later, running wild, still harnessed to the carriage. A search party was sent out and Mr Collins was found in a ditch. His throat had been cut, sir.'

'When was this?'

The older of the two bedders answered me. 'It was on Halloween night, sir. I remember because Bert, who was one of the searchers, said it fair chilled the blood to see the horse galloping on his own as if the hounds of hell were after him.'

It was another week before the newspaper cutting reached me. 'Cambridge man found murdered on the fens.' And scrawled across the headline the hand-written words, 'Hell is empty.'

Georgia

We invoked Miss Elphick's spirit on the night of her funeral. It felt right somehow. Mum was going out with Debra so Tash and Vee came round and made all the right 'Hi, Clare' noises as if we were preparing for a jolly girls' night in. I can tell Mum thinks that they are *suitable* friends despite Vee probably being too posh and Tash too flaky. Patrick cycled over and waited around the corner until Mum was out of sight.

I was a bit worried about seeing Patrick again in case it was awkward. I mean, after he'd told me about Mr Lewis and I'd sworn on the circle and everything. But it was fine. When we're all together, I kind of take the lead. It's funny because I'm not like this in any other aspect of my life. No teacher has ever singled me out for my leadership qualities and I've never even been on a team, let alone captained one. But in the circle, I seem to know what to do. Tash always backs me up. She's the supporter, Patrick the doubter, Vee the nervous one. That night was no exception.

I had prepared the room. I'd taken out anything with negative connotations: the newspaper (worldly concerns), the suede cushions (dead animals), the picture of my dead great-grandfather (the auras might get confused). The coffee table was clear except for three candles on a black saucer and a bowl of herbs. Miss Hughes said that it should be thyme but the best I could do was some mixed herbs and one of Mum's packets of potpourri (she always gets this sort of thing as an end-of-term present). I put a picture of

Miss Elphick next to the candles. I'd printed it out from her Facebook page and it showed her at some sort of Christmas party, wearing a paper hat. I'd chosen it because she looked happy and because she herself must have liked it if she'd chosen it as her profile picture.

Venetia immediately started making difficulties.

'What if her ghost appears?' she said. 'It'll be so scary.'

'There is no such thing as ghosts,' I reminded her. 'Simply the spirits of those who have gone before.'

'We're sending Miss Elphick towards the light,' said Tash, eating one of the crisps I'd put out. 'It's important to fulfil our physical needs, too.'

'Her spirit won't appear,' said Patrick, leaning over and grabbing a handful. 'We don't have that sort of power.'

'We do if we're together in the circle,' I said. 'You just have to believe.'

'What about Herbert?' said Tash. 'Poor little darling.' Tash loves Herbert and so does Vee, despite being allergic to dogs. Even Patrick thinks he's cute. Herbert was looking up meltingly. Tash thinks that he loves her back but really he just wanted a crisp.

'Can he stay with us?' said Tash.

'He'll make me sneeze,' said Venetia. Which isn't really true because even genuinely allergic people aren't allergic to poodles.

'I think we'd better lock him out,' I said. 'He'll be a distraction. He'll be quite happy in the kitchen if I feed him.'

I tempted Herbert into the kitchen with a Pringle, then I put some dog food in his bowl. Mum watches his weight even more carefully than she watches her own but I didn't think she'd notice if I gave him an extra meal. He always licks the plate clean.

Back in the sitting room I lit the candles, scattered some herbs on the table and turned out the lights. We held hands; Tash's was sweaty but Patrick's was dry and his grip was extremely strong.

I began the invocation taught to me by Miss Hughes.

'You who lived yesterday. I call you from my mind to yours. Come back from the shadows into the light and show yourself here.'

We waited. The candles flickered.

'I'm scared,' whispered Vee.

'Shh!'

At first I thought Patrick was right and it hadn't worked. But we didn't break the circle. We just stood there, holding hands, and I repeated the invocation. *Come back from the shadows into the light and show yourself here.* Then, suddenly, there was a cold chill. I could feel Tash shivering next to me. The room grew colder and colder. The door opened and shut. The candles blew out and we were in darkness.

'I don't like it,' said Vee. 'Make it stop.'

'Don't break the circle,' I said.

I waited for a full minute before saying the spell to free Miss Elphick's spirit.

Ella. You who lived yesterday. Thank you. Now fly away from this earth and join the world of spirits.

Immediately, the room felt warmer. I could hear us all breathing in the darkness, Herbert whining softly from the kitchen. I waited for a couple of beats and then let go of the hands to light the candles again.

We looked at each other. We were all somewhere between shock, tears and laughter.

'Wow,' said Tash. 'That was . . . intense.'

Patrick laughed out loud.

'I guess she's gone now. Ella, I mean.'

'I think so,' I said. I went to turn on the overhead lights and let Herbert in. He went straight up to the table and tried to eat the leaves. I picked him up and cuddled him. He felt warm and very alive.

Venetia was still shaking. 'Was that it? Was that her ghost?'

'Of course it bloody was,' said Patrick. 'Didn't you see the candles blow out?'

'It's all good, babe,' Tash put her arm round Vee. I felt a momentary twitch of jealousy, as I always do if those two get too close. 'We freed her spirit. She's at peace. We won't be troubled again.'

Patrick looked at me across the table.

'What do we do now, Georgie?'

I picked up the photo of Ella, folded it and put it in my pocket. 'Let's put the TV on,' I said. 'Watch something comforting like *Friends*. I'll order the pizzas.'

Patrick left after the pizzas. He had to cycle home and it was getting cold. Tash's mum came to collect the girls at ten thirty.

'Will you be all right on your own?' Tash whispered but, to tell you the truth, I was looking forward to it. As soon as they'd gone, I switched off the sitting room lights and went upstairs. Herbert stayed in the hall because he was waiting for Mum. I washed, did my teeth, got into my pyjamas and into bed. Then I got out my laptop and started to write on MySecretDiary.

> Tonight we summoned a spirit. It sounds almost mundane put like that. Part of a 'to do' list. Do homework, put recycling out, summon a spirit. But, in truth, it was the most extraordinary thing that has ever happened to me. Epic. Life-changing.
>
> I prepared meticulously. I cleansed the room, lit candles and strewed herbs. Then we formed a circle, held hands and spoke the invocation. At first I thought it hadn't worked but then I felt a supernatural chill filling the room. The door opened and shut. Heaven and hell were roaring in fiery splendour. The realm of the dead lay open and gaping. All the angels and devils were here, in the room with us. I knew that, if I let myself, I would become utterly consumed by the fire. I spoke the words of release and, as quickly as it came, the spirit left us. The atoms rearranged themselves and we were just four teenagers holding hands. But I know that I, for one, will never be the same again.

I read through this piece. I thought it was good. I liked the juxtaposition of the 'to do' list and the realm of the dead. Perhaps it was a bit melodramatic but what had happened *was* melodramatic. We had opened the portal to another world, after all. I pressed 'publish'.

Shortly afterwards I heard Mum come in and take Herbert out for his last walk. I shut my laptop and picked up the Harry Potter book that is always beside my bed. I was about a chapter in when Mum knocked on my door. I asked if she'd had a good time. She said that they'd talked about Ella. I wanted to tell her that Ella was at peace but that would involve too much explanation. I said something soothing and she kissed me goodnight.

I waited until the hall light was off and then I got out my laptop again.

CHAPTER 35

We honestly thought it would be all right after that. We'd sent Ella towards the light and there would be no more deaths. Mum continued to seem stressed though. On the day after the summoning, she disappeared all morning and came back behaving very oddly. Ty and I cooked her Sunday lunch and she didn't seem all that grateful. Afterwards she was really weird, saying that Ella's killer might be 'interested' in her too and that we had to be very careful. I wanted to tell her that there was nothing to fear but fear itself but I just ended up saying that I was sure everything was going to be OK. She agreed, but without much conviction. She was distracted anyway because it was fireworks night and Herbert was having fifty fits.

I promised Mum that I wouldn't come home on my own, etc., etc. I had to miss the creative writing class that week but I gave Patrick one of my short stories to show to Miss Hughes. Patrick walked me to the library to meet Mum and I could see that she wasn't best pleased to see us together. It was a claustrophobic week all round and I was glad when Dad came to collect me for the weekend. Even then, he had to take Friday afternoon off and drive to the school to collect me. Mum wasn't going to risk me going on the train as usual. What harm could possibly come to me on a train?

I had a fairly good weekend with Dad. He's a bit twitchy about Miss Elphick's death; I don't know how much Mum has told him. He's putting a bit of pressure on me to live with them but I'm not sure that Fleur is all that keen on this plan. Still, she was very nice to me. We took the kids to the swimming pool on Saturday. Ocean, despite her name (ha!), was scared of the water but Tiger is like a little fish. I do love him. He's so sweet and he adores me, following me everywhere. Fleur got a babysitter on Saturday night and we (me, Dad and F) went out for a meal in China Town.

It was great. There were just two big tables and everyone sat together. There were no knives and forks, only chopsticks, and there wasn't even a proper menu — dishes kept appearing as if by magic, steamy and fragrant. Dad was happy because there were lots of Chinese people eating there — he's keen on things being 'authentic' — and I think that Fleur was just glad to be away from the kids. We only drank jasmine tea but it seemed to affect Fleur as if each cupful was a double vodka.

'How's your love life, Georgie?' she asked, crunching a piece of prawn toast.

'OK,' I said carefully. 'Still going out with Ty.'

'Have you got a picture?' I showed her one on my phone. Ty on the beach holding a lucky stone — the sort with a hole in the middle, witch stones Miss Hughes says they're called — up to the light.

'Wow, he's gorgeous,' said Fleur.

'He's too old for you,' said Dad, somewhat predictably.

'Mum doesn't think so. She's started to really like him.' This was stretching things a bit but Mum *had* said that she preferred Ty to Patrick.

'How is Mum?' said Dad, in a really heavy voice. I hate it when he calls her that, without the pronoun. It's disrespectful somehow.

'Fine,' I said, manoeuvring rice and prawns into my bowl and hoping he would pick up on the signal.

Fat chance. 'She must be under a lot of strain.'

'She's OK.'

'What with her friend dying and everything. And she seems to think that someone's watching her.'

He made it sound as if Mum was seriously cracking up.

'Is she seeing anyone?'

'A psychiatrist, you mean?'

'No.' He sounded quite shocked. 'Counsellor, therapist. Someone like that.'

'No, she isn't,' I said.

It was only later that I wondered if Dad was actually asking if Mum was *seeing* someone, as in 'having a relationship with'. Now that would be seriously weird.

The rest of the weekend was fine, though. On Sunday morning Fleur and I took the kids to the park and F cooked a delicious lunch. I did some homework in the afternoon, then Dad drove me home at about four.

When we got in, we were met by Mum, who seemed determined to confirm all Dad's worst fears about her.

'Something awful has happened,' she said, at the door.

'Hi, Mum,' I said. 'I had a great weekend. Thanks for asking.'

'What is it?' said Dad, the 'now' unspoken.

'Rick. He's been killed.'

I stopped, halfway through greeting Herbert. 'Mr Lewis?'

'Yes. He's been killed. Just like Ella.'

'Jesus,' said Dad. 'What's going on at that school?'

I thought this was a bit unfair considering Ella had been killed at home but it turned out that Mr Lewis' body *had* been found at the school, actually in R.M. Holland's study. Mum tried to stop me hearing this bit but, of course, I wasn't about to be shut out of the conversation. I noticed that Mum was a bit cagey about who found Mr Lewis' body. Could it have been her? And, if so, what was she doing wandering around the school at the weekend?

When Dad eventually left, he whispered as he hugged me, 'If you need me, I'll come and get you, any time of the day or night.' Mum poured herself a huge glass of wine and sat on the sofa to have a nervous breakdown. I raced upstairs to message the group. Mum had said that it was confidential but I knew it would get out soon. Sure enough, while we were WhatsApping, I got a text from school saying that it was closed tomorrow 'due to unforeseen circumstances.'

'OMG cant believe Mr L is dead.' That was Tash.

'Must be a cereal killer.' That was Venetia. She can't spell.

Patrick was so quiet that I thought he'd gone but, about ten messages later, he came up with *'this is some serious shit'.*

'whos next.' Venetia. *'omg tell yr mum to be careful G.'*

'dont be stupid,' Patrick came back.

'I just mean sone's killin all the english teachers.' You could tell that Venetia was offended.

'We have to tell Miss Hughes,' I typed. *'She'll know what to do.'*

After the chat had stopped, I got a private text from Patrick.

'we need to talk.'

I didn't get to talk to Patrick until Tuesday. On Monday we had a huge panic because Herbert went missing. I took him out for a walk in the morning. We got to the field so I let him off the lead and he was off, sniffing and racing round in circles. I got a text from Patrick, stopped to answer it and, when I looked up, Herbert had disappeared. It was awful. I called him and called him. I thought that he must have gone home. But, when I got back, no Herbert. Mum and I went back to the field but he wouldn't come, not even for his special whistle. We were panicking now. Mum told our two nice police 'minders' and they went off in the car, looking for him. I kept thinking that it was all my fault. If only I hadn't looked down at my phone. But Patrick seemed in such a state, saying that the police were after him, that they were waiting outside his door. I wondered if he was making it up but it turns out that it was true. The police really had come round to his house.

When Herbert still didn't come back, Mum called scary DS Kaur and she actually came. I couldn't believe it. And she was brilliant. She made us calm down and think logically. We went into the garden to check the shed and DS Kaur (Harbinder to us now) heard a dog barking. The sound turned out to be coming from the old factory. I was scared to go inside but Harbinder was fearless. She found an open door and in we went.

I've long suspected that there are unquiet spirits in the factory. There's a story that a little girl was drowned there, in the cement, and that you can hear her crying at night. I don't know if this is true but there's definitely a poltergeist at work. I've seen lights at night, heard strange noises and there's a sadness about the place, as there is in the Old Building at school. When we got inside, the supernatural activity was like a miasma. Mum and Harbinder didn't notice. They were on the trail of Herbert, regardless of anything else. It was funny, they suddenly seemed quite alike, both single-minded and brave. I felt like a child tagging along behind them but sometimes, as Miss Hughes says, we have to listen to our inner child.

Eventually we found him, locked in a tiny room where someone had clearly been sleeping. Harbinder was obviously very excited about the rough sleeper. The police are probably going to try to pin the murder on him/her. Mum was just thrilled to have Herbert back. I was too. We took him to the vet because he'd hurt his paw and, when we got him home, we put him on a cushion in the sitting room and gave him all his favourite treats: bonios, squeaky toy, sweetened tea.

I went upstairs to write and to message Patrick. I heard Harbinder come round at about six-thirty and the familiar gurgle as Mum poured them both wine. Is DS Kaur a family friend now? I like her and admire her but somehow I don't want her too close. Her aura is blue like an old-fashioned police light. I think she'd stop at nothing to get to the truth.

We were back at school the next day. The Old Building was closed and there was actual police tape over the main doors. Everyone was very over-excited and, what with us all being crammed together in the crappy New Building, the atmosphere was febrile in the extreme. Patrick and I just managed a few words before I went into registration.

'Everyone thinks I'm a murderer.' He looked wilder than ever, his eyes shadowed, his hair unwashed. I noticed that he was getting stubble too.

'They don't,' I said.

'Everyone's looking at me.'

'They're probably wondering why we're whispering together. They probably think we're going out.'

He laughed then. 'I'm going to finish with Rosie. It's not fair on her.'

'Don't be so melodramatic.'

'I mean it, Georgie. Perhaps you and I should be together. Ty's too old for you.'

'You sound like my dad.'

'I mean it. He doesn't understand you. I do. We're the same, you and me.'

'See you later,' I said. 'I've got to go into class now.'

Some things are best left unsaid.

• • •

Mr Sweetman did another one of his special assemblies. He said that we mustn't dwell on how Mr Lewis died but remember how he had lived. Fat chance of that. Everyone was obsessed with the murder. One person actually asked me if I thought my mum had done it.

'Yeah, right,' I said. 'Because she *really* wanted to be head of English.'

Most people, though, believed in the crazed serial killer scenario.

'What if it's an ex-student?' said Paige. 'Ronnie Bellows really hated Mr Lewis and he was dead creepy. He always wore black and he listened to heavy metal.'

'Great,' I said. 'Case solved. Are you going to ring the police or shall I?'

It struck me that I could actually ring the police. I had Harbinder's special 'panic number' on my phone.

Patrick and I met up at lunchtime. We wanted to go to the graveyard but the teachers were being really strict about not letting us go out-of-bounds. It was like that bit in Harry Potter when they think that the basilisk is loose in Hogwarts; teachers patrolling the corridors in twos, the caretakers manning the gates, everyone talking about who the culprit might be. We ended up in the art room. Patrick said that he had to work on his GCSE art coursework and I claimed to be working on a history project.

We sat there surrounded by terrible self-portraits painted by the Year 7s. The room smelled of oil paint and pencils, which was curiously comforting. Patrick's coursework was really very good. It was a seascape with a huge figure rising up out of the water, all greys and blues and baleful sky. It reminded me of a book I had read as a child, *The Iron Man*.

'It's Shoreham beach on a good day,' he said. I saw that he'd signed the picture 'Puma', his science fiction alter ego.

'I wish I lived nearer to the sea,' I said.

'You wouldn't like it where I am,' he said. 'Most of the houses are chalets and holiday homes. No one really lives there. It's too quiet in the daytime and the fog horns are on all night.'

'What happened yesterday?' I said. 'You said that the police came round.'

'Yeah,' he said. 'They'd caught me on CCTV outside Miss Elphick's house.'

'Oh my God,' I said. 'Do they think you killed her?'

'I'm not sure. I told them about seeing Mr Lewis and they seemed interested in that. He could have murdered Miss Elphick but now he's dead too.
The police probably think I killed both of them.'

'Do you have an alibi for Saturday night?'

I couldn't believe I was asking this. I was actually asking my friend if he
had an alibi for a murder. Patrick turned away so that I couldn't see his face.

'Yes. This is why I wanted to talk on Sunday. Vee came round.'

'What?'

'There's nothing going on between us,' he said, but I thought he sounded
very defensive. 'I was on my own and I was lonely. Rosie's parents wouldn't
let her go out. You were in London with your dad. I texted Vee and she came
round.'

'How long did she stay?'

'She slept over.'

I said nothing. On the one hand, I was shocked and not all that pleased.
I didn't believe for a second that nothing was going on between Patrick and
Venetia. They might not be 'going out' but they were definitely sleeping together. I was furious that Venetia had lost her virginity before me *and* kept
it a secret. Neither of them had breathed a word on MySecretDiary. On the
other, I was glad Patrick had a good alibi.

'I should go,' I said.

Patrick caught hold of my hand. 'Don't be angry, Georgie. It's you I love.'

'Stop saying that,' I said. 'You don't love me. We're like brother and sister.'

'Vee says that she was my twin sister in a former life. She says we have the
same soul.'

'I think you'll find that twins have their own souls.'

Patrick was still holding my hand. 'I'm so messed up, Georgie. I don't
know what to think.'

'Why don't you ask your twin sister Venetia?'

'Don't be angry,' he said again. 'Vee said you'd be angry if I told you.'

'I'm not angry.'

I was *furious*.

· · ·

Mum was still driving me home every day. She seemed very distracted, which was only to be expected, I suppose. We collected Herbert from Doggy Day Care and, as soon as we got in, I escaped upstairs. I was typing my diary entry when I heard Herbert barking and voices downstairs. DS Kaur. Auntie Harbinder. Our new best friend.

I crept out and sat on the stairs, listening. Harbinder was talking about 'forensics found at the scene'. She had a list of what she called 'significant objects' that had been found in R.M. Holland's study the night when Mr Lewis was killed. She wanted Mum to tell her if she'd seen any of them. So Mum *had* been the one to find the body. I knew it.

'There were three candles on the desk and some leaves and petals from a potpourri.'

'I don't remember seeing . . .' Mum's voice was indistinct.

'And CSI found this. Here's a photo from the scene.'

God, I wished that I could see what it was. Luckily Mum asked the question.

'I looked it up. Apparently it's a stone called black obsidian.'

CHAPTER 36

I knew what I had to do. I had to see Miss Hughes. Unfortunately that was easier said than done. Mum was still watching me like a hawk and collecting me from school every day. Eventually I had to take Tash partly into my confidence. I just told her that I needed to see Miss Hughes privately and urgently. I think she assumed it was about creative writing. Tash asked her mother if I could come home with her after school on Thursday. The mothers conferred and said yes. It was agony waiting two days. I went out with Ty on Wednesday night, just for a drink in Steyning. We had a good time but I kept thinking about what Patrick had said, that I should be with him and not Ty. Is this true? I do feel a connection with Patrick that I don't feel with Ty but, on the other hand, I feel safe with Ty and I don't always with Patrick. Ty brought me home on the dot of ten and Mum was really nice to him, inviting him in for hot chocolate and asking him about his work and his grandparents. It was a bit cringy but I could see she meant well.

On Thursday Tash and I left school together and waited at the Chichester bus stop. Tash got off at her stop but I stayed on the bus until it got to the sixth-form college. West Sussex sixth-form is like the New Building at Talgarth, modern and featureless with lots of glass and plastic everywhere. Mum approves of it because it gets good exam results but I'm rather dreading going there. At Talgarth I might be 'Miss Cassidy's daughter' but at least I'm someone. At sixth-form college I think I could disappear altogether. In the prospectus they say they 'treat their students like adults', but that's overrated, in my opinion. The only bright point would be being taught by Miss Hughes.

I'd told her that I was coming and she was waiting in one of the classrooms. They're all the same. This one was called something like B2 11-C. Goodness knows why.

Miss Hughes was marking papers but she got up when I came in. I was so pleased to see her. Unlike other people, she never changes. Her hair was in its neat grey bun and she was wearing a pinkish jumper with a frilly collar. Mum would have said that she looked 'frumpy' but, to me, she was just right. Safe and ageless.

'Georgia.' She never shortens my name. 'How are you, my dear?'

'I'm OK.' I sat down opposite her. 'Well . . . not really.'

'Relax, Georgia. Breathe.'

I closed my eyes. The classroom smelled like classrooms everywhere but Miss Hughes' presence made it a safe place. I tried to breathe more slowly. Her voice was very soft and gentle.

'What is it, Georgia?'

I opened my eyes. 'It's about Patrick,' I said.

'Ah, you have discovered his true feelings for you.'

'No. Yes.' I was a bit thrown, to be honest. I had never thought of Miss Hughes caring who fancied whom. And, until that bizarre moment before class when he suggested we should be together, followed by his weird declaration in the art room, I had never thought of Patrick fancying me.

'It's about Mr Lewis' murder. You know about that?'

'Yes. A policewoman even came to visit me here.'

'DS Kaur?'

'A bright young woman but an angry one.'

That sounded like Harbinder.

'Well,' I said, 'Patrick told me something . . .' I told her about Patrick and Miss Elphick. About him seeing Mr Lewis outside her house that night. About Patrick spending the night with Vee and about the black obsidian being found in the study.

'It was one of the stones you gave us for protection,' I said. 'It has to be.'

She looked at me for a long time, really looked, her blue eyes both mild and terrifying. Then she said, 'Have you mentioned this to anyone else?'

'No.'

'And you heard the detective say that the stone had been found at the crime scene?'

'Yes.'

'Do you suspect Patrick?'

I was dreading this question but Miss Hughes asked it so calmly that I was able to answer.

'A little. He liked Miss Elphick and he hated Mr Lewis for taking him out of her class. And Patrick . . . well, he has got a temper.'

'Yes,' said Miss Hughes. 'Patrick has a dark aura sometimes. He's a fire-starter, a thrill-seeker. He can be dangerous. You can see that in his writing.'

'But he can be so sweet,' I said, thinking of the time when he bought me asparagus for my birthday because it's my favourite veg, or when he recorded a programme about a dog because it reminded him of Herbert. All the Dodo clips he's sent of people saving animals, all the times when we've laughed together in the creative writing group.

'Yes, you are his good angel,' said Miss Hughes. 'You open his eyes to the light. Venetia . . . she's not such a wholesome influence.'

'What shall I do?' I asked. 'I know I should tell Harbinder—DS Kaur—or Mum. But I don't want to get him into trouble.'

Miss Hughes was silent for what seemed like a long time. She's one of the only people I know who can sit completely still.

Then she said, 'I understand you conjured Ella's spirit.'

I stared at her. 'How do you know?'

I thought she would say that she sensed it in some mysterious wiccan way but instead she said, 'I read it on MySecretDiary.'

I had never thought of her looking on the site. We've talked about it in class but I always think of Miss Hughes as somehow being above social media. She barely even uses email. I have hundreds of handwritten notes from her. It occurred to me that if she was a member, she must be using an alias.

'Very well-written it was too,' she said, smiling at me kindly. 'Excellent use of varying sentence structures.'

'Thank you.' I couldn't help feeling pleased. 'How did you know it was Ella? I didn't mention her name.'

'Who else could it have been?' she said. 'And I have felt a release. As if she's at last free to the elements.'

'Do you think we should do the same for Mr Lewis?'

'I'm afraid Richard is still earthbound,' said Miss Hughes. 'He's a much less advanced soul than Ella.'

'And should I tell anyone about the stone?' I said.

'Sometimes silence is best,' she said. 'The universe has a way of working things out for itself.'

I breathed a sigh of relief. Everything was going to be all right.

The bus dropped me off at the crossroads. It was a short walk home. I could see the factory walls very clearly, with the chalk cliffs behind them, gleaming in the darkness. If Mum asked, I would say that Tash's mum dropped me off but couldn't wait because she was picking up Fergus, T's annoying little brother, from football. I walked along the edge of the fields because there was a verge there and cars were speeding along the road. It was six o'clock, still rush hour and stressed commuters were whizzing past in their BMWs and Audis. When I was a child, seven o'clock was my bedtime and I always think of the hours afterwards as adult time. I used to hear Mum and Dad talking downstairs, drinking wine and watching sophisticated things on the television. Of course, pretty soon they stopped chatting and starting hissing at each other, then shouting and, by the time I was ten, it was just me and Mum. But the *University Challenge* theme tune still makes me feel nostalgic.

So I wasn't scared at all. It wasn't a frightening time of day.

Then the breathing started.

I had my earphones in so, at first, I thought it was coming from the podcast I was listening to. But then I stopped and took them out. The breathing continued, right behind me, coming from the hedgerows and the dark fields. A soft, animalistic sound but, all the same, I knew it wasn't an animal. I thought of "The Monkey's Paw" and the Thing that comes back from the dead, dragging itself up to the old couple's front door. I thought of Patrick's picture and the creature rising from the sea. I thought of Miss Hughes saying that Mr Lewis' spirit was still 'earthbound'. I started to walk faster and faster but the breathing followed, always just a few paces behind. I could see our house, the lighted window that meant Mum was home, her car parked outside. I began to run and then the breathing got faster, as if my pursuer was running too.

I zigzagged across the road, narrowly avoiding the Audis, and sprinted down our little side street. The breathing had stopped and from the safety of our porch I looked back towards the fields. Was that a shape I saw, moving through the trees? But the night was dark and gave nothing away.

I broke off my engagement to Ada. I wasn't fit company for any decent person. I kept to my room, ostensibly working on my thesis but, in fact, writing the story with which I am now regaling you, my dear young friend. About the Hell Club and Halloween at the ruined house. About the dead bodies and our vow, made in the blood of our comrade. About Ebrahimi and Collins. About the nemesis that seemed to be following me. Again and again, I wrote the words:

Hell is empty.

When 31st October came round again, I was a mere shell. I knew people were worried about me. My tutor had tried to talk to me (even though he hated me now because of the way I had treated Ada), and the Junior Dean had gone as far as to request an interview, during which he impressed upon me the necessity of eating well and performing regular exercises. Mens sana in corpore sano. If only he knew the true state of my mind.

All day I waited. I didn't leave my room because I knew the nemesis would come, locked door or not. I didn't hear the news until the next day, All Saints' Day. I went for a stroll through the town, late at night. I often liked to do this, prowling the silent streets, alone with my thoughts. But, outside St John's, I saw a fellow called Egremont standing in the shadow of the lodge, smoking his pipe. I recognised him as a member of the Hell Club but I hurried past, not wanting to get into conversation.

'Hallo there.' He called after me. 'You were a friend of Bastian's, weren't you?'

'I knew him,' I said cautiously, although my heart was pounding.

'Have you heard what happened to him? Awful news.'

'No,' I said. 'What has happened to him?'

'I heard it from one of the bedders just now. Bastian was in a train. One of the new sorts with connecting carriages. He was moving from one carriage to another when the train suddenly divided. He was crushed under the wheels. Poor fellow. What a terrible death.'

I looked at Egremont, saw his pale face and the skull's head badge on his lapel.

'When did this happen?' I asked.

'Only yesterday,' he replied. 'I'm sure it'll be in tomorrow's Times.'

It was a week before the newspaper cutting reached me, with the now familiar addendum.

Hell is empty.

PART THE SEVENTH

Clare

Clare's Diary

Thursday 16th November 2017

I've really had it with Simon now. What right does he have to be so patron-
ising, so condescending? 'I can't stand by and see my daughter in danger.'
That's what he said on the phone just now. *His* daughter. As if I would let
anything happen to her. Just because I said that she was with Tash tonight.
'I thought we agreed that she'd come home with you after school every day.'
'She's with Tash,' I said, 'Tash's mother is driving her home.' 'What do we
know about this woman anyway?' he asked. 'You should have cleared it
with me.'

Cleared it with him! The man who ran off and left me, set up with a
woman half his age and proceeded to have a brand new family. OK, we'd separated before he met Fleur and she's technically only ten years younger. But
the fact is, he's become a pompous arse since he married her. That's the trouble with lawyers. If people are paying you God-knows-how-much per hour,
you start to think that your words are worth something.

I'm the one who's in danger and Simon doesn't know the half of it — about
the diaries, about the rough sleeper in the factory, about the fact that I was
the one who found Rick with a knife sticking into him. Simon wants Georgie to go and live with him but that's never going to happen. Oh, she likes it
well enough for a weekend, but I think Fleur treats her like an au pair, using
her to help take the kids swimming, etc. Georgie does like her half-siblings
and I think she enjoys being in London, going for meals in China Town
and all that. But she doesn't want to live there full-time. She wants to stay
with me.

I didn't tell Georgie about my argument with Simon. She came in a bit
hot and bothered from Tash's. She said she was worried about homework
but, when I offered to help, she said no immediately. After all, what would
a teacher know about homework? Work is a nightmare too at the moment.
Thank God that our new supply teacher, Susan, brought in to cover for
Rick, seems quite competent. Don is worse than useless and can't control his

classes at all. I have all the timetabling and the exam predictions on top of everything else to do. I don't see how that school can keep going but it has to, of course, and, in a way, that's all that's keeping *me* going. The only way to get through it is to get through it. Who said that to me recently?

My only other solace — apart from Herbert — is Henry. He FaceTimed again tonight. I love seeing him in his Cambridge room, the leaded light of his window, the monkish simplicity of it all. And he wasn't put off by a little thing like finding a dead body on our first date. He wants to see me again. I must admit, I do find some comfort in that.

Simon, though. I will never, *ever* let Simon take my daughter away from me. I can't believe that I ever loved him. Sometimes it feels as if my life started to go wrong the day I met him.

CHAPTER 37

Life staggers on for a bit. Herbert soon recovered from his injury but still holds his paw in the air if Georgie says 'poor little fellow' or 'hero dog' in a certain tone of voice. Georgie didn't want to go to Simon's for the weekend (ha!) and we had a quiet time at home. She went to the cinema with Ty on Saturday night but was home by eleven. We went to Debra's for Sunday lunch and Georgie enjoyed playing football with the boys and talking about books with Debra and Leo. Sometimes she sounds so sparky and intelligent. At those times I feel that I have done right by her and her education, whatever Simon says.

School continues to be a trial. There's so much work to do and all the students are hysterical, full of theories about Rick's murder, liable to tears or outbreaks of minor violence. Rick's funeral is on Thursday, at the church he and Daisy attended in Brighton. At least it won't be in the chapel. I don't think I could stand seeing another coffin being brought into the school. Tony is going to the funeral and he thinks I should too. 'After all, you were . . . involved.' He means I was the one who found him. To be fair, he hasn't said a word about me being in school that night, despite how it must look. I think I probably *should* go to Rick's funeral but I don't know if I can bear it. Perhaps I'll say that I can't be spared from the timetable; that will almost certainly be true. We're fully stretched, even with two supply teachers. But everyone is doing their bit and, in a funny way, it feels as if we are more of a team than when Ella and Rick were here. When they were *alive*. Anoushka and I are still plodding on with the play although it seems as if it will never be ready. Pippa is very good as Audrey but Bill doesn't know his lines and the Plant has missed half the rehearsals.

I hadn't heard from Harbinder since she called round to tell me about the objects found 'at the scene'. The night before we had drunk wine together and it seemed like we were almost friends. But, on Wednesday, when I get home from another hellish day, her car is outside the house.

'What does *she* want?' says Georgie. She doesn't say much to me during our drives, just stays plugged into her phone. The only time she perks up is when we collect Herbert from Doggy Day Care.

'With any luck, she's come to tell us that they've caught the killer and everything's all right again,' I say.

'Dream on, Mum.'

It's pouring with rain. Harbinder gets out of her car with her hood up. She's on her own and I wonder if this means it isn't an official police visit.

'Come in,' I say, trying to stop my umbrella blowing inside-out. Georgie and Herbert have already shot inside. In the hall, Harbinder takes off her jacket. She looks as tired as I feel, shadows under her eyes, her hair scraped back in a ponytail.

'Let's go into the kitchen,' I say. 'Have some tea.'

We sit at the breakfast bar with the rain battering against the skylight.

'How's life at Talgarth High?' says Harbinder, helping herself to a biscuit.

'A bundle of laughs,' I say. 'Murdering the head of English does wonders for morale.'

'I thought you were head of English now.'

'Acting head,' I say. 'There's a world of difference.'

Georgie's upstairs so I feel I can say, 'Any news?'

'We've had some DNA reports back,' she says. 'That's why I'm here.'

I'm slightly disappointed that she hasn't come round just to drink tea with me.

Harbinder takes a file from her bag but doesn't open it. She says, very much in her 'professional' voice, 'We got quite a lot of DNA from the bedding found in the old factory. Lots of bodily fluids on the sleeping bag.'

'Spare me the details,' I say.

'OK. Well, that DNA was a match for DNA found at the crime scene.'

'Which crime scene?'

'R.M. Holland's study. We found nasal fluid on the victim's body and on the desk.'

'What does that mean?'

'It means that the killer probably sneezed,' she says, at her most deadpan. 'The point is, Clare, that the person sleeping in the old factory is the person who killed Rick Lewis.'

'Oh my God.'

'I have to tell you,' says Harbinder, her hand on the still-closed file. 'Our advice to you is to go to a place of safety, preferably far away from Sussex. What about your Scottish granny?'

I laugh. It's all too ridiculous. I can't leave Sussex, not when I'm the only person holding the English department together. But, at the same time, I get a vision of my grandparents' house in Ullapool, the light reflecting on the sea, the mountains in the distance.

'I can't leave work,' I say, 'we're really short-staffed. And Georgie can't miss school, either. This is an important year for her.'

'It might only be for a couple of weeks,' says Harbinder. 'And no one's irreplaceable.'

'I really think I might be at the moment.'

'And teachers always say that students can't miss school and it's never true. Georgia would probably get more out of some time alone with you than from weeks of boring lessons about probability.'

'What are you talking about?' I'm at the sink, refilling the kettle, so don't hear Georgie come in. She is standing there, in her hideous Talgarth uniform, suddenly looking incredibly beautiful, very pale with her hair streaming down her back.

'We're talking about you and your mum getting away for a bit,' says Harbinder, without missing a beat. 'Would you like that?'

'How could I miss school?'

'God, you've been brainwashed,' says Harbinder. 'I thought everyone wanted time off school.'

To my surprise Georgie laughs. 'Well, I do hate maths. Especially probability.'

'Me too,' says Harbinder. 'There's a lot of it in policing, unfortunately.'

'Why are you telling us to get away?' says Georgie. She sits opposite Harbinder. I feel marginalised, like the bartender in a Western. *What's eatin' you, Buck?*

'DNA found at the scene corresponds to samples taken from the bedding at the factory,' says Harbinder. This is *way* more than I would have told Georgie. I try to signal my distress from the sidelines.

'Have you found a match for the DNA?' says Georgie.

Harbinder laughs. 'That's the trouble with youngsters today. They know more about police procedures than I do. The DNA doesn't match any on file and we've cross-checked with known offenders in the area.'

'So it's a stranger?'

'In all probability, yes.'

I don't know why it should be a huge relief that there's an unknown killer on the loose but somehow it is. I can see my hands unclenching.

'Did you find anything else at the crime scene?' Georgie is asking.

'I've told you enough,' says Harbinder. 'I'll get thrown out of the magic circle.'

Georgie laughs and wanders off. Harbinder stays and eats more biscuits and we talk about Herbert. It's only afterwards that I wonder why she really called round.

CHAPTER 38

I do go to Rick's funeral in the end. I don't think I can really get out of it. I sit there between Tony and Liz Francis, the deputy head, and listen as people describe Rick as 'a man filled with God's light'. He was quite happy-clappy. I hadn't realised. The service is in a community centre and people raise up their hands when they sing the hymns. The music is actually quite good; the girl leading it has a wonderful gospel voice that reaches right up to the Halloween balloons still left in the rafters. The pastor makes rather a good speech. 'Without faith we have no hope of the resurrection and we are for ever reliving Easter Saturday without the dawn rising on the Sabbath.' I can see Daisy Lewis nodding vigorously in the front row.

I don't have any religious faith. My parents are atheists, in spite of the fact that my father — whose family was originally from Ireland — was brought up as a Catholic in a rather woolly 'aren't the saints nice, let's give up sweets for Lent' kind of way. At home we talked about religious people in the patron-ising way that anthropologists used to describe the so-called 'lost tribes'. My parents are both university lecturers and those sorts of conversations were meat and drink to them. Sometimes I used to long for them to be quiet so I could just read. Perhaps being a Catholic wouldn't be so bad, I used to think. At least people wouldn't talk through the service and you'd have a couple of hours' peace on a Sunday. Also, some religious education would have been useful for understanding T.S. Eliot, to say nothing of Milton and Chaucer. My brother Martin, the doctor who is always 'on call' at Christmas, has no patience with any such thinking. He has brought up his children on strictly rational lines. No tooth fairy, no Father Christmas, no Little Baby Jesus. They are bound to become Scientologists.

Simon and I were vaguer, more liberal. We told Georgie that some people believed in Father Christmas and LBJ and that they were lovely ideas that involved kindness and generosity. As far as I know Georgie has never hankered after Catholicism or any other supernatural philosophy. But looking at Daisy today I wonder if this is a good thing after all. At least she has *something,* something between her and the darkness.

I don't stay for the wake. I have to get back to teach in the afternoon and, besides, what could I say to Rick's friends and family? On the way out I stop to say hallo to Daisy and offer my condolences. In answer to my stilted sentences, she gives me a look of such disdain and hatred that I almost stagger backwards.

I'm driving Liz back to school (Tony has, of course, stayed to press hands and say how *very* sorry he is) and, as we stop for one of the countless red lights on Brighton's coast road, I say, 'Did you see the look that Daisy Lewis gave me?'

Liz is silent for a minute and then she says, 'It must be hard for her. Rick was all she had.'

I like Liz and I'm not about to let her get away with this.

'That doesn't explain why she hates me.'

'She doesn't hate you,' says Liz, looking out of the window towards the skeleton of the West Pier, 'she's jealous of you.'

'Jealous of me? Why?'

'She obviously knows that Rick was in love with you.'

'Rick wasn't in love with me.' The lights turn green and I stall the car. The bus behind me hoots. So much for everyone in Brighton being laid-back and green.

Liz says nothing so I say, 'It was Ella he had an affair with, you know.'

'I know,' says Liz. 'But it was you he liked first. I remember warning him about it. Poor Rick. I liked him but he was so weak.'

'That's how men get away with it, isn't it?' I said. 'Everyone makes excuses for them. Rick cheats on his wife and everyone says "poor Rick, he just couldn't resist Ella's wicked wiles".'

'That's not what I said,' says Liz.

'I didn't encourage Rick, you know. I told him that there could never be anything between us.'

'I didn't say you encouraged him,' says Liz. 'I just said that Daisy's obviously jealous of you. Rick was obsessed with you and you didn't even want his devotion.'

But this still sounds like a criticism. We don't talk much for the rest of the journey.

It's another long day. We have a rehearsal after school. The performance is less than two weeks away and I've had to replace the bloody Plant with a stand-in who's about two foot tall. Georgie comes to watch the rehearsal, partly because Tash is in the chorus. I'm less than pleased to see Patrick O'Leary slide into the seat beside Georgie and whisper to her throughout 'Somewhere That's Green'. Pippa, who plays Audrey, cries twice and keeps looking over at them. I hope she's not another misguided fool with a crush on the O'Leary boy.

When the rehearsal is finally over, Georgie, Tash and Patrick go into a huddle. Pippa is looking tearful.

'Are you OK?' I say. 'You're going to be really good, you know.' This is true. It's the others who are the problem.

'I'm OK, Miss Cassidy. Just time of the month. You know.'

Too much information. But I put on a caring teacher smile and say, 'Well, go home and get some rest. Full run-through on Monday. I need my Audrey firing on all cylinders.' I raise my voice. 'Come on, Georgie, time to go.'

'Keep your hair on, Mum.' This raises a laugh.

We drive home through another sea fret, landmarks appearing out of nowhere, eerie clouds drifting through the trees. Georgie is obviously carrying on an entertaining WhatsApp conversation on her phone. I switch on Radio 4. It's *The Archers* and an exhausted-sounding man is talking about artificial insemination.

'For God's sake.' Georgie unplugs herself. 'Do we have to listen to this?'

I turn off the radio. The mist is denser than ever, it's like driving through clouds. The factory has vanished completely. I can only just make out the orange light from the three lampposts on our pathetic strip of road. When I get out of the car, I can barely see my own front door.

It's a complete surprise, then, when Harbinder's voice speaks out of the fog.

'Clare. Something's happened.'

CHAPTER 39

'What?' I say. 'What's happened?'

'Let's go inside.' I can see Neil Winston looming behind Harbinder. An official visit, then.

'What's going on, Mum?' Georgie takes my arm. She's carrying Herbert, who has had a long session at Doggy Day Care.

'Have you got the house keys?' Harbinder's voice is almost disembodied. And, of course, I can't find the keys. My fingers are numb and eventually, Harbinder has to take my bag from me.

Once inside, Harbinder switches on the lights and ushers us into the sitting room. Neil is dispatched to make tea. Now I'm really worried.

'I don't want you to panic.' That's the first thing she says.

'Jesus,' I say. 'Now I'm really panicking.'

Harbinder glances at Georgie, who is sitting on the sofa with Herbert on her lap.

'It's your ex-husband, Simon.'

Whatever I was expecting, it wasn't this.

'What's happened to Simon?'

'He's been attacked.'

Georgie lets out a little scream. Harbinder says quickly, 'He's in hospital. He's going to be OK.'

I sit next to Georgie and put my arm round her. 'What do you mean "attacked"?'

'Someone waited for Simon outside his office and stabbed him. He must have managed to shout out because some passers-by came to help and the attacker ran off.'

'Stabbed.' I think of Rick and the knife in his chest. Of Harbinder telling me about Ella's murder. *'She was stabbed. Multiple times.'*

'It could be a random attack,' says Harbinder. 'Knife crime is a real problem in London. But we can't ignore the link to you.'

'Do you think it's the same person who killed Miss Elphick and Mr Lewis?' says Georgie.

Neil comes into the room with two mugs of tea which he places carefully in front of us. Harbinder says, 'Can I have a word in private, Clare?'

'No,' says Georgie, in a surprisingly strong voice. 'I've got a right to know what's going on.'

Harbinder and Neil exchange glances. 'Clare,' says Harbinder, 'can I look at your diary?'

'I gave them all to you,' I say.

'I'm sure you've started another one.'

I think of the Reporter's Pad, upstairs in my bedside table. She's right, of course.

'What's she talking about, Mum?' says Georgie. 'What diary?'

'It's nothing important,' I say.

'Can I see it please?' says Harbinder.

Herbert follows me upstairs as if we're going on a jaunt. The book is lying on the empty side of my bed. The side I don't sleep on. The side that was Simon's. I can't remember if that's where I left it.

I open it at my last entry.

Simon, though. I will never, ever *let Simon take my daughter away from me. I can't believe that I ever loved him. Sometimes it feels as if my life started to go wrong the day I met him.*

Underneath it, the italic hand has written, *'Leave it to me.'*

Clare's Diary

We're on the train to Inverness. The Caledonian Sleeper. It all seems so unreal. Yesterday I was taking a rehearsal of *LSOH,* looking forward to the weekend ahead. Now, Tony is having to find yet another supply teacher and Georgie and I are on our way to Ullapool. Harbinder organised it all, right down to this 'club room' with bunk beds and complimentary 'sleep pack'. It's a tiny space but surprisingly comfortable, with crisp white sheets and a table that folds up to become a sink. Georgie is lying on the top bunk listening to a podcast and I'm on the bottom bunk writing this on my phone. Herbert's with us too, taking up almost all of the floor space but behaving impeccably, as if hurtling through the night on an express train is an everyday occurrence. England is sliding past in the dark. When we wake up, we'll be in Scotland.

Spoke to Simon earlier. He's still in hospital but not critical. He sounded more irritated (*peeved* is probably the word) than anything. 'The police think that this is linked to those murders of yours.' Of mine! The police think that the killer was probably disturbed in the middle of attacking Simon, which is why he got away comparatively lightly with wounds to his chest and arm. I'm sure Simon doesn't think that he got away lightly at all. I'm sure he blames me for everything.

I can't wait to be with Gran again. I suppose she represents security to me, far more than my parents do. And, in Scotland, miles away from the school, from R.M. Holland, from the stranger who writes in my diaries, surely we will be safe.

Well, today's the anniversary of that day and I'm the only one left. What a strange thought that is, my dear young man. I am sure that your lively brain has long since recognised the pattern that is unfolding here and the inauspiciousness of the date. Why is he telling me this story? you must wonder. Have I been chosen to witness the demise of the narrator?

But do not fear. After all, I am not about to go up in a hot air balloon or attempt to drive a coach and pair across the fens. I can't plummet from the air or be dragged by footpads from my carriage.

I am in a train, it's true, but I'm not about to leave this carriage.

Harbinder

I didn't relax until I had seen Clare and Georgia onto the train. They stood there looking, despite Clare's designer red coat, like refugees or displaced persons. Georgia was in a parka and woolly hat, a backpack hunching her shoulders. Clare had Herbert, complete with his own little red coat, on a lead. I'd checked that dogs were allowed on the sleeper. It's really a very civilised journey. Leave Euston at nine, have dinner on the train, go to sleep in your room and wake up in Scotland. I felt quite envious, to be honest.

I had travelled up to London first thing in the morning for a conference with the Met. The SIO, DI Steve Hollings, said that Simon Newton had been attacked as he left his office near Holborn. It's in a mews and, of course, there's no CCTV. But Simon must have shouted and raised the alarm because the assailant ran off after only stabbing him a couple of times. Two commuters on their way to the tube heard the commotion and came to help. They found Simon scrabbling at the door of his office, trying to get back in. He was bleeding heavily but still conscious. No sign of the assailant. I think it's our man. The weapon is the same type, a sharpened kitchen knife, dropped at the scene and clean of prints. And the attack seems similar — the opportunism, the savagery, the speed of escape.

'You think it's your guy?' said Hollings.

'The modus looks the same and all the victims have links to the same woman.'

'I hope she's got a good alibi,' said Hollings, standing and stretching. He was the type that doesn't stay still for long. I was willing to bet that he wore a Fitbit.

'She has,' I said. And that was true. When Simon had been attacked, Clare had been overseeing a rehearsal at Talgarth, in the same feet-scented gym/theatre where we used to put on plays in my day. Not that I was ever in a play. I think Gary was, though.

I left Holborn Police Station and walked to University College Hospital to interview Simon. He wasn't looking his best — which was hardly surprising — but it's difficult to know what Clare ever saw in him. He was a colourless man, slightly built, with receding hair and a rather petulant expression. However, as I said, that could be something to do with his present predicament.

'I'm DS Harbinder Kaur,' I said. 'I'm investigating the murders of Ella Elphick and Rick Lewis.'

'Clare's talked about you,' said Simon. He had a Northern accent, which I hadn't expected.

'She's talked about you too,' I said.

'I bet she has.' He shifted awkwardly in the bed. His chest and one arm were wrapped in bandages and he had cuts and bruises on his face. He scratched his nose with his free hand.

'Do you really think it's connected?' he said. 'That the man who stabbed me was the person who killed the teachers at Clare's school?'

'We're investigating that possibility,' I said carefully. 'Can you tell us anything about the attacker?'

'Not really,' said Simon. 'It was dark and happened so suddenly. I'd just left the building and I was checking my phone and he leaped on me.'

'You're sure it was a man?'

He thought for a second. 'Yeah. He was big, heavily built. He knocked me flying.'

'How tall would you say?'

'Tall, taller than me. Not that that's hard.'

We'd obviously struck a nerve. Simon was not small. It was hard to tell with him lying down but I'd estimate five-nine. In heels, Clare would be taller.

'Did you see his face?'

'No.'

'Was he masked?'

'I'm not sure. That sounds stupid, doesn't it? But I'm sure I didn't see his face. He was either hooded or masked.'

'It's quite normal not to be able to recall your assailant's face,' I said. Normal but annoying. 'Maybe in a few days something will come back to you. Did you notice his shoes?'

'His shoes?'

'Yes. I always notice shoes.'

'I don't,' said Simon. 'I think he was wearing a dark coat, one of those waterproof ones with a shell.'

This would fit with the material found at Ella's house.

'Did he speak?' I asked.

'No.' Simon shuddered. 'That was what was so awful. He just leaped on me with no words. Like an animal.'

Like an animal. Like a ravening beast. I asked a few more questions but the nurses were hovering and Simon was obviously getting tired. As I stood up to leave, he said, 'What about Clare and Georgie? I mean, they must be in danger. Are you looking after them?'

'They're going to Clare's grandmother in Scotland,' I said. 'I've booked them on the sleeper train tonight.'

'Ah, the Scottish granny,' said Simon, lying back on his pillows. 'Clare loves it there. I'm surprised you got her to take time off work.'

'It wasn't easy,' I said. 'But we can't take any risks.'

'Look after them,' said Simon, closing his eyes.

'I will.'

On the way out, I saw a woman with two children getting out of the lift. She was mixed-race, extremely striking, with great hair in an afro. I felt sure that this was wife number two. What on earth had attracted two gorgeous women to this insignificant-looking man? Heterosexuals are a mystery sometimes.

I went back to Holborn to look at the scene of the crime. The mews was still cordoned off but there was nothing really to see. Plenty of places where the assailant could have hidden: behind the dustbins, in the shadow of the next building. The Good Samaritans hadn't seen him because they were, quite rightly, concentrating on Simon as he lay bleeding on the steps. There was still a bloodstain on the lowest one.

I was slightly at a loose end after that. Neil was driving Clare up to catch the train and I was going to meet them at Euston at eight. I really needed a place where I could sit down and gather my thoughts. We had so much: DNA, handwriting, murder weapon. Why weren't we any closer to finding this person? I walked down High Holborn and Chancery Lane onto the Strand. The shops were already full of Christmas stuff; Santas and reindeer and shiny baubles. It was only a month away. My parents celebrated Christmas as enthusiastically as any Christian and the house would be full of family eating, drinking and watching crap on the TV. I only hoped we had found our killer by then, otherwise I would be in a filthy mood.

Eventually, after drinking too much coffee in various Costas, I ended up in Charing Cross library. Libraries are wonderful places. You can just sit there with a book for hours and nobody bothers you. Charing Cross was full of Chinese students and elderly people reading the papers; one or two of them looked like they might be homeless. I settled down in a corner to go through my notes. I started one of my lists, much derided by Neil.

Possible suspects
 1. Clare Cassidy
    For: May have resented Ella (re: job and Rick). Disliked Rick for stalking her. Discovered R's body. Only person with any link to Simon Newton.
    Against: Alibis (though weak) for both. Alibi for Simon. The handwriting in her diary (if it isn't hers).
 2. Patrick O'Leary
    For: Had strong feelings for Ella and disliked Rick. Seen outside Ella's house on the night of her murder. Weak alibi for Rick.
    Against: No link to Simon and has an alibi. [Clare confirmed he was at the rehearsal.] Could he really have planned the murders and written in Clare's diary?

3. Tony Sweetman

   For: Twat. [I couldn't see this standing up in court, unfortunately.]

   Against: Alibi for Ella. Out of the country for Rick. No link to Simon.

4. Another member of the English department — Vera, Alan or Anoushka.

   For: May have resented both Ella and Rick. Knowledge of *The Tempest*.

   Against: All have alibis. We have handwriting samples and none of them match the notes found at the scenes. No links to Simon.

5. Bryony Hughes

   For: Knew Ella and Rick. Known to have quarrelled with Ella. Weird.

   Against: Doesn't seem to have known Rick well. Did not know Simon at all. No real motive. Not strong enough?

6. Stranger

   For: Unknown DNA at factory (but we don't have DNA samples from all suspects).

   Against: Motive? Also, how did they write in the diaries? And — who the hell is it?

That seemed to sum things up. I groaned out loud and one of the homeless people asked me if I was OK.

We saw Clare and Georgia onto the train. It was quite awkward, actually. We weren't on hugging terms but a handshake seemed too formal. I ended up patting Clare on the shoulder and just waving at Georgia. I was most effusive with Herbert, ruffling his fur and telling him to keep out of trouble. Neil, of course, hugged all three of them. Then he and I drove back to Sussex.

'At least they'll be safe in Scotland,' said Neil. 'I looked up Ullapool and it's miles from anywhere.'

'So did I,' I said. 'It looked like *Balamory*.'

'What's that?' This is what comes of having nieces and nephews. Lily is too young to have watched the CBBC classic.

It was Friday night and the M23 was busy. Where were all these people going, I wondered? They can't all be headed to Brighton for a dirty weekend. Do people even have dirty weekends anymore? As we passed the old Brighton gates, I said, 'I'm going to stay at Clare's.'

'What?' Neil was driving at exactly seventy-five miles per hour but, at this, he sped up slightly.

'I'm going to stay at Clare's tonight. If someone's getting into her house to write in her diary, I want to be there to meet them.' I'd brought pyjamas, toothbrush, toothpaste and a change of underwear with me to London. They were packed into my work bag.

'You can't do that,' said Neil.

'Clare gave me the keys,' I said, as if he hadn't spoken. 'You can drop me off. I don't want my car outside the house.'

'Harbinder,' said Neil, 'you can't do this. It's dangerous. Donna would never let you.'

'That's why I'm not going to tell her,' I said.

CHAPTER 41

I had my own way in the end, as I knew I would. Neil dropped me off outside Clare's house. It was nearly eleven and the street lamps were off. There was no moon. The factory and the chalk cliffs were just shapes in the darkness.

'I'll be round to collect you at eight a.m. sharp,' said Neil.

'Don't bother,' I said. 'I can get the bus into work.'

'I'm coming to collect you,' he said firmly. 'Ring me if anything happens tonight. I'll have my phone by the bed.'

I let myself into the house. It felt odd being there without Clare. I sat in her blue-grey sitting room in the dark and tried to imagine what it was like to be her, sitting there with my scented candles and my classic nineteenth-century novel, tucking my long legs under me on the sofa, repairing my nail varnish, wondering whether to sleep with my Cambridge professor lover. I looked at my phone. Two messages from my mother. I'd told my parents that I was staying in London for the night. 'At a hotel?' said Mum. 'I love hotels.' She has probably stayed in a hotel twice in her life, once on her honeymoon. The first text was asking me to bring back 'some of those little bottles of shampoo.' The second told me not to because Dad says it's petty theft. Because he's kept a shop all his life, Dad is obsessed with stealing. Maybe that's why I joined the police. I texted back that the toiletries are not that nice anyway.

I played a few games of Panda Pop then went into the kitchen. The fridge whirred gently and the skylight was navy blue. I didn't want to turn on the tasteful spotlights — if someone was watching the house, I wanted them to think that it was unoccupied — but there was enough light for me to make myself a cup of tea. Orange and bergamot. It tasted like perfume.

I went upstairs in the dark. In Clare's bedroom I turned on the bedside light, which was dim enough not to show much. The room was everything I would have expected: French colonial bed, white-painted wooden furniture, chair patterned in blue and white fabric, a modern print in blues and browns, a bookcase with paperbacks — including titles she wouldn't want on display downstairs (Georgette Heyer and Jilly Cooper) — and a white fluffy rug that looked rather like Herbert. I snooped about a bit. There was ibuprofen and Gaviscon in her bedside cabinet. No birth control pills. Maybe she was through the menopause. No sleeping pills or anti-depressants either. A silver frame on the bookcase showed a diptych of Georgia and Herbert. Clothes were neatly arranged in the wardrobe. Not that many of them. I could already tell that Clare was the sort who prized quality over quantity. Black, grey and white with the occasional red or pink jacket. Jumpers and tops folded into drawers that smelled of lavender. Some surprisingly sexy underwear. Some letters signed 'Your loving Granny', saved with a conch shell and some dried flowers. Nothing from her parents. The whole room smelled of her. Jo Malone English Pear and Freesia.

There were only two rooms and a bathroom upstairs. I went into Georgia's room next, which was actually the biggest, with a window looking out onto the road. I used my phone torch rather than turning on the light. Black-and-white Harry Potter duvet, a pink 'accent' wall, lots of photos of G and her friends, a bookcase (I was willing to bet that there was a bookcase in every room, including the bathroom), a collection of miniature animals, nail varnish, make-up, some candles and potpourri. This last made me stop. What sort of schoolgirl has potpourri in her bedroom? I sniffed some; it had lost most of its fragrance. Was it the same sort that had been found in R.M. Holland's study? I sat at Georgia's desk. There would be no excuse not to do your homework with a set-up like this: pens in a special metal container, anglepoise lamp, highlighters and Post-its in every shade. There was also a pinboard with a school timetable and a jumble of postcards, photos and inspiring pictures of poodles. Two books were on the desk. One was *York's Notes on the Tempest,* the other was a collection of ghost stories. A page in this last had been marked with a leaf. I opened it. *The Stranger* by R.M. Holland.

> *'If you'll permit me,' said the Stranger, 'I'd like to tell you a story . . .'*

Georgia had taken her laptop with her (I'd seen her put it in her back-pack) but I rifled through some of the loose papers in the painted box she used as an in-tray. Photocopied worksheets from school ('The History of Medicine', 'The Respiration Equation'), some study notes with words high-lighted and . . . what was this?

> *. . . my first murder was the easiest. Just a chance encounter, a knife sliding through butter, two bodies moving in the dark. How quickly they fell, how easy it was. The second required planning. I could no longer rely on random victims. This time I would kill closer to home, I would fall on the unwary like a ravening beast. I would wait, I would bide my time. No one seeing my innocent outward façade would ever guess what lay beneath. And then the victim presented herself to me. She was just a girl, someone at school. A friend, I suppose. Her name was Eva Smith. Did Eva mark herself out in some way? Did she have an unwitting sign on her forehead saying 'victim'? No, she was ordinary in every way. I sat next to her in maths and watched her doodling little hearts on her graph paper. Hearts and flowers, sometimes merging together. Hearts, clubs, dia-monds, spades. What were the odds, I wanted to ask her, that the girl sitting next to you, sometimes lending you a protractor or offering a cheery word over the difficulty of the equations, would one day plunge a knife into your carotid artery, killing you instantly?*

Jesus. There were a couple of pages like this. No author or note but they were clearly printed from a website. Its address was at the bottom of the page. MySecretDiary.com. I got out my phone and found the site. You had to log in but that only took seconds. I gave the false name I always use, Jenna Barclay. Password: Jennbar17. I don't know why but this always strikes me as the perfect white, Anglo-Saxon name. Jenna would have been one of the popular girls at school, the ones who ignored me but went out with Kush: blonde hair, fluffy pencil case, always wearing her boyfriend's football top with the sleeves pulled down over her hands. Not a girl who would have a victim sign on her forehead. And now Jenna was on the secret diary website. Turns out it wasn't all that secret, after all.

It was like reading a hundred teenage diaries at once. The outpourings scrolled down the side of the screen. *Doesn't understand me . . . hate myself in the mirror . . . his fingers turn me to jelly . . . why am I so . . . why can't I . . . why is everyone . . .* I typed in an entry for 'Jenna'.

I'm so cute and blonde. Everyone loves me. I'm a Barbie girl in a Barbie world. I'm so perfect, I've never had a day's self-doubt in my life. Why should I? All the girls in the magazines look just *like me. Hey, hey, hey.* I didn't think my offering was about to win the Booker Prize in a hurry. It looked like I could keep it private or share it with everyone. I searched the shared entries for the word 'butter' and after skimming through much anorexic soul-searching, I found it: *Just a chance encounter, a knife sliding through butter . . .* It was a long short story — or short novel — posted by someone called Mariana. Was Mariana Georgia? If so, she knew how to write one hell of a horrible story. A sick fantasy about killing someone in her maths class. But Georgia, I remembered, didn't like maths. She didn't like probability. What was the probability of a normal, well-balanced girl writing something like this? The detail about the carotid artery, for instance. Ella Elphick had been killed by stab wounds to the neck. The maths girl was called Eva. That wasn't a million miles away from Ella. And 'the ravening beast', the so-called unknown, unpublished novel by R.M. Holland. Had Georgia somehow known about that?

I looked in Georgia's desk drawers and, underneath the worksheets and the letters about school trips that she had forgotten to give Clare, I found some more pages of the novel or journal, or whatever it was. I put them in one of Georgia's many colour-coded plastic files. And, right at the bottom of the pile, I found something else. A picture of Ella Elphick. I recognised it as a print-out from her Facebook page. But that wasn't the most significant thing about the picture.

The most significant thing was that it was stained with blood.

There was no point ringing Neil. In the morning I'd take the photograph into the lab to be analysed. I remembered what Georgia had said, when I told her about the DNA on the bedding at the factory. 'Have you found a match?' I didn't have Georgia's DNA but I had her fingerprints. I could cross-check them with the fingerprints found at the scene of Rick Lewis' murder, on the candles and on the black stone. I went downstairs and found some freezer bags. I put the blood-stained photo in one and some of the pot-pourri in the other.

Did I really think Georgia could have murdered Ella or Rick? I didn't know but I wasn't ruling anything out. She had alibis for both of them. She was at home with her mother when Ella was killed and in London with Simon when Rick was murdered. And, even if I did think her capable of attacking her dad in the dark, she had been at school watching a rehearsal when Simon was stabbed.

But Georgia could have written in Clare's diary. She could have added the quotation from *The Woman in White,* a book she must often have seen around the house. I thought of the girl, tall and already beautiful, the way she'd looked in the chapel on the day of Ella's funeral: cool and collected, not at all hysterical like the other pupils. I remembered that Georgia had not wanted to go into the factory on the day that we'd found Herbert there. Why not? And why was she writing about killing people, about stabbing them, *a knife sliding through butter?*

I went back into Clare's room and put the freezer bags into my briefcase. I didn't feel like getting undressed but I did my teeth and got into bed fully clothed. I plugged my phone into the charger and put it under my pillow, despite my mum saying this will give me a brain tumour. I hadn't pulled the curtains and, dark though it was, I could see the factory, its sinister bulk against the night sky. I thought of the night when Gary and I had seen the white lady and the scream that had echoed through Holland House. I half-expected to be woken by some similar horror but the house was silent and, after a while, I fell into a dreamless sleep.

CHAPTER 42

When Neil came to collect me I was waiting by the door. I had already rung the lab and asked them to cross-reference the fingerprints found in the study with Georgia's on file.

In the car I explained my findings to Neil. He'd thoughtfully provided coffee and croissants but I ate carefully because he's obsessive about keeping his car tidy.

'I don't buy it,' he said. 'Georgia's just a kid.'

'She's fifteen,' I said. 'And she's highly intelligent.' She's Clare's daughter, I added in my head.

'But do you really think she was mixed up with the murders?' Neil's voice started to rise and he almost, but not quite, exceeded the speed limit on the Chichester road.

'She's written a graphic account of a murder,' I said. 'A stabbing. She had a picture of Ella that was stained with blood. And she's friends with Patrick O'Leary. I saw them together at Ella's funeral. It could be some teen black magic thing.'

'Black magic?' The speedometer hovered at fifty-five.

'There were the candles and the herbs,' I said. 'Ella's sitting room had candles, too, but I just thought that she was that type of woman. Clare's house is full of them. It's like a bloody Catholic church.'

'But like you said, those sort of women always have candles. Kelly's the same. Tealights and little bowls of scented crap everywhere.'

'Sounds delightful.'

'It's a woman thing.'

'I don't have candles everywhere.'

'Yeah, but you're different.' He didn't have to explain further. I lived at home, I was Indian and I was gay. A triple whammy.

'I think we should see Bryony Hughes again,' I said. 'She knows Georgia and Patrick. They go to her creative writing class. And there was a Bryony in Georgia's story. A "wise woman", apparently. Plus, Clare said that she was a white witch.'

'A white witch? Surely you don't believe in that crap?'

'I don't believe in it,' I said patiently. 'The question is whether other people do.'

Donna was also not convinced by the story but she agreed to us interviewing Bryony. I left the photo and the potpourri with the lab and we drove to the sixth-form college. It was Saturday so the college was officially closed but I'd checked and was told that Miss Hughes was in. There were actually quite a few people wandering around; there was a football match going on and musical rehearsals of some kind, judging from the discords coming from the ground floor. Miss Hughes met us in the English office. She said that she had been catching up on her marking, and, once again, there was a pile of essays on her desk. A dedicated teacher and one who obviously had a great influence over her pupils. Was it possible that she might also incite them to murder?

Nothing could have been more gracious than the way she received us.

'Sergeant Kaur. How delightful to see you again. And . . .'

'Detective Sergeant Neil Winston.' Neil was almost standing to attention. Women like Bryony Hughes unnerved him.

'We'd like to ask you a few questions about Georgia Newton,' I said. 'She's one of your creative writing group, isn't she? Your small, select group. With . . .' I looked at my notes. 'Patrick O'Leary, Natasha White and Venetia Sherbourne. Are they all pupils at Talgarth High?'

'Venetia goes to St Faith's, I believe.'

'Have you heard of a website called MySecretDiary?'

'Yes, it's a creative writing forum.'

'Have you seen these stories before?' I pushed the print-outs across the table. Bryony read them with a slight smile. The Shakespeare quotes shouted at us from the walls. *It will have blood they say; blood will have blood. Nothing will come of nothing. Hell is empty.*

Bryony put the pages neatly in line before answering us. 'Yes,' she said. 'It's Georgia's work. Quite remarkable writing, some of it.'

'Remarkable writing?' I said. 'It's about killing someone.'

'So is *Macbeth*,' she said, 'and I'm sure you wouldn't deny that is remarkable writing, Sergeant.'

'It's Detective Sergeant,' I said. 'And I'm investigating a double murder. So, if a schoolgirl who knew both of the victims is writing about violent death, I'm interested. I'm surprised you didn't make the link yourself. Do you know the name Eva Smith?'

'Yes,' said Bryony Hughes.

'Yes?'

'She is a character in the play *An Inspector Calls* by J.B. Priestly. However, strictly speaking, Eva doesn't appear in the play. It is one of Georgia's set texts for GCSE.'

'So you are pretty sure that Georgia wrote this?'

'Yes. It has many of her stylistic tics. And the medical detail. Georgia is a fan of *Grey's Anatomy,* if I remember. It's an American television series,' she added kindly, seeing our faces.

Stylistic tics. Heaven help us.

'When did your creative writing group last meet?' asked Neil.

'On Monday. Georgia was unable to come. I think her mother is keeping her on a tight rein at the moment.'

Not tight enough, I thought. There was definite antagonism in the way she said 'her mother'. I remembered that Clare had not been one of Bryony's dear friends.

'So when did you last see Georgia?' I asked.

Bryony hesitated and patted her hair before replying. A tell, if I ever saw one.

'Last Thursday,' she said. 'She came to see me after school.'

'Why did she do that?'

'She wanted to show me some short stories. She's very serious about her writing.'

'Can we see them?'

'They're at home.' I wondered if she was lying.

'When did you last see Patrick?' asked Neil.

'At the creative writing class on Monday.'

'Is he a good writer too?' I asked.

'Quite promising,' said Bryony. 'Very visceral.'

I wasn't entirely sure what this meant but wasn't about to give her the satisfaction of asking.

'Does Patrick ever post on MySecretDiary?' I said.

'Yes. I think his *nom de plume* is Puma.'

My phone buzzed but I ignored it. Seconds later, Neil's went off and he left the room to answer it.

Bryony Hughes smiled at me. 'Have you remembered meeting me when you were here, Harbinder?'

'Yes,' I said. 'You read a short story that I had written. You sent me a note saying that it was good.'

Goodness knows why I wrote a short story for the school magazine. I had never done such a thing before. I didn't think anyone actually read the damn thing but Miss Hughes evidently did. She had sent me a card, a picture of Muriel Spark at her desk. Of course. Miss Jean Brodie.

'It was about the Holland House ghost,' she said. 'I'm very interested in ghosts.'

Before I could answer, Neil came back into the room. 'Harbinder. We need to go.'

I gave Bryony my card and said that I'd be in touch. She said that she'd look forward to it. As we clattered down the stairs, Neil told me what the call had been about.

'That was Olivia. A Mrs Sherbourne has been into the station. Apparently Venetia and Patrick are missing.'

'Venetia's a good girl,' said Alicia Sherbourne. 'She would never run away like this.'

Alicia — ash-blonde hair, cashmere jumper, tight jeans and flat pumps — was a typical Haslemere mother. I remembered that Venetia attended St Faith's, the private school, and was, presumably, several social notches above Patrick O'Leary.

'When did you last see Venetia?' asked Neil.

'On Friday morning when she left for school,' said Alicia, taking out a tiny, lace handkerchief. 'She said that she was going to spend the night with a friend, Natasha. She was meant to be going straight to her clarinet lesson at nine this morning but her teacher rang to say that she hadn't turned up. Then I rang Natasha and her mother said that Venetia had never been there.'

'What did you do next?' I asked. It was now nearly eleven so we obviously hadn't been her next port of call.

'I rang round her friends, but no one had seen her and apparently Georgie's on her way to Scotland. Then I rang the O'Learys.'

'Is Patrick Venetia's boyfriend?' I said.

'No!' This was said with some vehemence. 'Venetia doesn't have a boyfriend. She's not that sort of girl.'

I didn't look at Neil. 'Why did you ring the O'Learys then?'

A silence and some handkerchief twisting. 'Venetia knew Patrick through Natasha and some of the Talgarth girls.'

There was quite a lot of contempt in that phrase. It made me rather proud to be a Talgarth girl myself.

'And Patrick is missing too?' said Neil.

'Yes. He didn't come home last night. Not that his mother seemed at all concerned. "He's probably with a mate". She made a delicate attempt at an Irish accent.

'And you've tried ringing Venetia?'

'Yes. Her phone's turned off. Her phone's never off.' Alicia started to cry in earnest. I'm not good with tears so I went to find Olivia. Donna was waiting outside the interview room.

'The results are back from the lab,' she said.

'That was quick.'

'It's a match,' she said. 'Georgia's prints were on the stone. The one found in Holland's study. The black obsidian.'

Georgia

It's so strange being on this train. It's as if we're in a capsule hurtling through space. We're in this tiny room, Mum on the bunk below me and Herbert on the floor, and it's like there's only the three of us in the world. We had supper in the 'lounge car' and it even included haggis. Mum ate a bit and said it was quite nice but I'm training to be a vegetarian so I said no thanks. The steward had such a strong Scottish accent that I hardly understood him. But he did say I was 'bonny'. I understood that. I think it's a compliment despite sounding rather fat.

Now, we're in our berth and the train is rattling through the night. I haven't got a phone signal and the Wi-Fi connection keeps going off but I'm listening to a podcast that I downloaded earlier so that's OK.

We must pass a mobile phone mast because messages suddenly appear. One from Ty and two from Vee. Ty's says, *'Hope u r ok xx.'* Vee's say: *'Where r u?'* and *'Need talk.'*

'On a train,' I text back. *'On way to Scotland.'* A little blue and white flag appears helpfully next to the words.

Vee's answer comes back immediately. *'Pls call. Need talk.'*

But the signal goes off again before I can reply.

'Georgie?' Mum's voice from the bottom bunk. 'Have you got a phone signal?'

'No,' I say. 'It's just disappeared.'

'Mine too. I wanted to ring Fleur to see how Simon is.'

Something makes me wonder if she is telling the truth. I'd looked at her phone earlier and seen two messages from Henry Hamilton.

'Dad's not in any danger,' I say. 'That's what Fleur told me.'

'No,' she says quickly. 'He's not in any danger.'

'Who do you think attacked him?' Somehow it's easier to ask her this without seeing her face.

'I don't know,' she says. 'Maybe it was just a mugging.'

'Do you think it's the person who killed Miss Elphick — Ella — and Mr Lewis?'

'I don't know,' she says again. 'I just hope the police catch them soon.'

'Harbinder said they would,' I say. 'She said they were close on the trail.'

'Yes,' she says. But I can tell she doesn't believe it. Herbert whines softly.

'He's getting bored,' says Mum. 'I should take him for a walk down the corridor.'

'I'll take him,' I say.

Suddenly I want to escape from this room, where I can touch both walls at the same time. I swing myself down and put Herbert's lead on. 'Come on, animal.'

'Be careful,' says Mum.

The corridor is empty. The train judders as it flies through the night. How fast is it going? A hundred miles an hour? Two hundred? Herbert doesn't like it. He whimpers as we cross between carriages; I never like that bit myself. It doesn't seem right, like walking into no-man's land, one wrong step and you could be lost forever.

I walk down to the lounge car. There's only one man there, sitting reading a book. It seems so odd to see someone without a phone that I stop. He looks up.

'Hallo.'

'Hi,' I say. He's old, about fifty, with longish grey hair and a beard.

'I like your dog.' He has an old-fashioned voice, posh and somehow papery.

'He's called Herbert.'

'A fine name.'

'Thank you.' I want to go back to our berth but I make myself walk the length of the carriage and then turn back.

I know that the man is watching me all the way.

Harbinder

CHAPTER 44

'We need to talk to Georgia,' I said. 'They should have arrived by now. The train gets into Inverness at eight-thirty.'

'Then they've got another train to Ullawhatsit,' said Neil.

'Ullapool.' I tried Clare's mobile but there was no answer. It was half-past eleven. She should have arrived at her grandmother's house by now.

'Do you think that the missing kids have any connection to the case?' asked Donna. 'Venetia and Patrick?'

'It's possible,' I said. 'We know that Patrick had a crush on Ella and he's admitted to visiting her house on the night that she died. We also know that he didn't like Rick much.'

We'd put out a Missing Persons alert for Venetia and Patrick. Neil kept saying that they'd run off together but, even if they were in a relationship, what modern teenagers would run away together like some Abba song? There was nothing really — barring a bit of parental snobbery — to stop Venetia and Patrick being together. They were both sixteen, after all, a little older than Georgia.

'There's nothing to link Georgia to the murders,' said Donna. She was worried. I could tell because she hadn't eaten her mid-morning doughnut. It sat, sweating jam gently, on her desk.

'Except her fingerprints were found at the scene,' I said.

'She was in London when Rick was killed,' said Neil.

'London's not that far away,' I said, more for form's sake than anything.

'We need to find out about the bloodstain on the photo. Hopefully the lab will have those results soon,' said Donna. 'If it's Ella's, then Georgia has some explaining to do. She may have been present at the murder even if she didn't commit the crime.'

'She knows something,' I said. 'Did you read the story she wrote?'

'Yes,' said Donna. 'It was very bloodthirsty. But teenagers like horror.'

'I was a James Herbert fan myself,' I said. 'But I never wrote stuff like that. And there's something odd about Bryony Hughes and that whole creative writing group.'

'Go and see the other girl,' said Donna. 'What's her name? Natasha White. We just have to hope that Patrick and Venetia turn up. We're going to increase the priority soon.'

'Venetia's mum looks the sort who won't let it rest,' said Neil.

'We won't let it rest,' I said. 'We're close. I'm sure of it.'

Natasha White lived in Steyning, in a pretty Victorian house just outside the main village. She was a pretty girl too, with freckles and the kind of bouncy, curly hair that I always wanted. Her mother Anna, who opened the door, was very similar, although the curls and the freckles were fading a little. Someone was thumping out a piano scale in the background.

'I'm sorry,' said Anna. 'I teach private pupils at weekends.'

What was it with everyone and their music lessons?

'It's OK,' I said. 'We'd just like a word with Natasha.'

'Is it about Venetia?' said Anna. 'I was so shocked when Alicia phoned me.'

'Do you have any idea where she could be?' I asked. Anna had led us into a comfortably messy kitchen where Natasha joined us. Presumably the sitting room was taken up with piano lessons.

'No,' said Anna. 'But she's with Patrick, isn't she? They're all sweet on Patrick.'

'Mum!' said Natasha furiously.

'Well, he's a very good-looking boy.'

'Mum . . .'

We sat at the table and Anna pushed breakfast things aside. 'Sorry. It's a bit chaotic. Do you need me to stay? It's just my husband's taken Fergus, our ten-year-old, to football and I'm halfway through my lesson. Danny can't keep murdering C flat for ever.'

'It's not a formal interview,' I said. 'You don't have to stay.' Was it my imagination or did Natasha look rather relieved?

When Anna had gone, I said, 'Do you have any idea where Venetia and Patrick could be, Natasha?'

'No.' But she averted her eyes. She was casually dressed in tracksuit bottoms and a hoodie but she'd put on her mascara and eye-liner.

'Is it true that she's sweet on Patrick O'Leary?' asked Neil.

'Yes,' said Natasha. 'But it's not true that we all are. He's like a brother to me and Georgie. Anyway, Georgie's got Ty.'

Did Natasha have anyone, I wondered. Even I'd had a boyfriend at fifteen.

'When did you last see Venetia?'

'At the creative writing class on Monday.'

'Did you know that she said she was staying with you last night?'

A silence.

'You can tell us,' said Neil, absent-mindedly wiping crumbs off the table. 'We won't get you into trouble.'

'Yes, I did,' said Natasha. 'But I just thought she was going to spend the night with Patrick. Like she did a couple weekends ago. When Mr Lewis was killed.'

We looked at each other. Did Natasha really not see what she was doing in giving us this piece of information? Either Venetia and Patrick could give each other alibis or they were both involved.

'When's the last you've heard from either of them?'

'I got a text from Patrick last night.'

'What did it say?'

Natasha looked at us with her kohl-ringed eyes. 'It said, "Hell is empty".'

'I need to go back to Clare's house.'

'Why?' Neil was driving us back to the station, frowning with concentration as he negotiated the weekend traffic. Things were getting serious now.

We'd had a call from Donna saying that Patrick's parents, worried at last, had found searches for flights to Scotland on his computer.

'I've just remembered something that I saw in Georgie's room.'

Neil didn't make any further objections; he took the country road to the old factory and the town houses in the middle of the field. I still had Clare's keys so let myself in while Neil waited in the car. In Georgia's bedroom I went straight to the pinboard. There was a postcard with two cartoon rabbits holding a pink heart-shaped balloon. I turned it over.

Just a note to say I love you.

It was the same writing as the 'Hell is empty' notes. The writing from Clare's diaries.

Georgia

CHAPTER 45

When I wake up we're in Scotland. I lean out from my bunk to pull the blind back and I can't believe how beautiful it is, like something out of a fairy tale: mountains, forests, the occasional sparkle of sea, castles high on cliffs, villages in the lowlands. Once or twice I see deer, grazing amongst purple heather, and when we pass a cove, there are seals sunning themselves on shiny, black rocks. There's snow on the hills but the sky is the very bluest of blues.

I must have got some signal in the night because I have about ten messages from Vee, one from Ty and one from Patrick. Vee's are all variations on *'where r u. we need 2 talk'.* Ty's says, *'Night xxx.'* Patrick's says, *'Hell is empty.'* I try to call him but the signal has vanished again.

'Georgie,' says Mum from below. 'Are you awake?' Herbert, who is sitting on her bunk, starts to bark.

'Shh,' says Mum to him. 'Are we in Scotland?'

'Yes,' I pull back the blind again. 'It's gorgeous. Why didn't I remember that?'

'We've always come on the plane before,' says Mum. 'You don't see all this. Have you got a phone signal?'

'No.'

'Me neither.'

'Who are you trying to text, Mum?'

I bet it's Henry but she just laughs and says, 'Let's go and have some breakfast.'

We have breakfast in the dining car: scrambled eggs, bacon and baked beans. Mum drinks coffee and I have two cartons of orange juice. I look round for the man from last night but don't see him. Did I imagine him? Was he The Stranger on the Train? R.M. Holland's ghost? I tell myself not to be ridiculous. It's one thing to develop your imagination, Miss Hughes says, and another to let it consume you. I remember the night when I heard breathing coming from the empty fields, that terrifying sensation of being followed. Am I going mad? But if I'm not, then maybe there is someone there, someone just out of sight but following our every step. What's that bit in *The Rime of the Ancient Mariner*? *Like one that on a lonesome road, Doth walk in fear and dread . . . Because he knows a frightful fiend, Doth close behind him tread.*

The nice steward lets Mum get out at Aviemore so Herbert can have a wee. I'm more scared than ever. What if the train leaves without them? What if the man appears again, smiling his strange carnivorous smile? 'I like your dog,' he'd said, almost as if he wanted to eat Herbie whole. But all is well. Mum gets back in carrying Herbert who is squirming with excitement. The steward slams the door and we're off again. We reach Inverness just before nine and have to move quickly to get our connection for Garve, the nearest station to Ullapool. I start to relax slightly. Scotland scrolls past, moors on one side, the sea on the other. Even Herbert watches, entranced. But, when we get to Garve, it doesn't seem possible that this is where we get off. This isn't a station, like Victoria — or even Chichester — it's just a yellow house and a footbridge in the middle of nowhere. But Mum tells me to get out and she passes Herbert down to me. Then she gets her case down. She seems energised and efficient, entirely unlike her English self. Maybe it's the air. It's bloody freezing.

In the car park there's an ancient Range Rover and a woman I don't even recognise as Great-Grandma. Last time I saw her, it was at my grandma's house in London and she seemed really old then — I mean, she must be nearly ninety — but here she is wearing jeans and a Barbour and giving me a fierce hug.

'Georgie! Ah, you've grown so bonny. Just like your ma.'

'Hallo,' I say, feeling shy for some reason. But Mum, who never chats, is chatting away like mad so it doesn't matter if I'm quiet. I get into the back of the car with Herbert. Mum is talking to Great-Grandma about The Situation.

'We just had to get away.'

'You'll be safe here,' says Great-Grandma, swerving to avoid a Highland cow.

I try to block it out. 'Ella . . . diaries . . . Simon . . . school . . . Rick . . . stalking . . . scared . . .' I'm watching for the first sight of Ullapool, the harbour with the white houses on the edge of the sea, the mountains behind. It's like that TV series I used to watch as a child. I start to hum the theme tune.

'*Balamory*,' says Mum. 'Are you happy to be here, Georgie?'

'Yes,' I say. Last night's train journey seemed so strange and surreal: Vee's texts, the man with the smile, Patrick saying 'Hell is empty'. Now, it's as if we've come back to life. The sun is sparkling on the water and even the cows seem to be benevolent, smiling underneath their hennaed fringes. Great-Grandma is talking about snow; the highest hills are completely white.

'It's so warm today,' she's saying. 'Like the Bahamas.'

The temperature dial on the car says minus one.

I remember Great-Grandma's house quite well. It's a little away from the others, on a spit of land with water on both sides. I don't remember Great-Granddad but apparently he used to have a boat and would row across the harbour every morning to get the paper. Herbert is very excited and starts barking at the seagulls. In the distance the ferry is making its way slowly towards the open sea.

GG shows me to my room, which is in the attic. The bed has a patchwork quilt and the white walls reflect the water. There's a desk, a bookcase and even a little rocking chair. I want to stay there for ever but there's lunch downstairs, bread and soup and a funny cheese that comes wrapped in a cloth. If it does snow, maybe we'll be cut off from everything. Maybe we'll be here for Christmas.

Mum and GG start another long conversation. Once again I'm amazed how chatty Mum is with her grandmother. She's always very clipped and reserved with her mother, my grandmother. But now she's talking about Henry, the man from Cambridge. It's quite interesting—I had no idea Henry was with her on the weekend when Mr Lewis was killed — but after a while my eyes start to close.

'Och, she's tired out,' says Great-Grandma. 'Why don't you go upstairs and have a snooze, Georgie?'

I'm only too happy to go back to my little room in the rafters. Herbert comes with me and I pull the patchwork quilt over us both. I dream about trains, old-fashioned trains like in *The Stranger*. I'm trying to escape, running through the tilting carriages, ricocheting off the walls, jumping the nightmare chasm between the cars. But he's there — out-of-sight but always the same distance behind me — moving smoothly and relentlessly, unknown but somehow also hideously familiar.

When I wake, it's dark outside. Herbert is sitting up, listening.

There are voices downstairs. Someone must have knocked on the door.

'Oh, it's you,' I hear Mum say. 'What on earth are you doing here?'

Herbert starts to growl, a noise I've never heard him make before, right in the back of his throat, like a much bigger dog. His teeth are bared and, for a second, I'm almost scared of him. I move towards the door and then there's a terrible scream from Mum. 'Georgie!' she cries. A downstairs door slams and there are footsteps on the stairs, steady, determined footsteps. I back to the very farthest corner of the attic room. I try to make Herbert come with me but he's still standing by the door. He has stopped growling; it's as if he's waiting.

The door is flung open. I see a dark figure, a raised knife and Herbert, like a tiny white bullet, flying into action.

Then he's lying in a bloodstained heap on the floor and the knife is moving towards me.

PART THE TWELFTH

Harbinder

CHAPTER 46

We left Clare's house at midday and I was on the plane to Inverness at one-forty. We rang the local police and asked them to check on Clare and Georgia in Ullapool. But I wanted to get there myself and Donna agreed. I had never travelled on a domestic flight before. In fact, I've only been on a plane twice, once to India when I was ten and once on a so-called romantic mini-break to Barcelona. I was amazed at how easy it was. I had no luggage and I just whisked through security, waving my warrant cards at the officials.

Sitting on the plane was sheer torture though. I wanted to get there immediately. It was a nightmare not being able to use my phone. I'd read somewhere that all that stuff about not using your phone on aeroplanes is made up but I didn't like to risk it. What if it interfered with the radar or something? So I sat with my phone in 'flight mode' on my lap, trying to read an article about 'The ten best beaches in the world'. Ironically, Ullapool was one of them. The businessman next to me was tapping importantly at his laptop, as if the world would end if he stopped working for a second.

We landed at three-twenty and I was at the taxi rank at half-past, having elbowed all my fellow passengers out of the way. A police car was waiting for me.

'DS Kaur?' He added about a dozen extra Rs.

'That's me.'

'I'm Sergeant Jim Harris.' He was tall, about thirty with dark-red hair and a rather wolfish expression. I was pleased. He looked like someone who would drive fast and not ask too many questions.

'How long will it take to get to Ullapool?' I asked as we left the airport.

'About an hour forty,' said Jim Harris. 'It's one of the bonniest drives in the world.'

He may well have been right. We certainly passed greenery and mountains and lakes (lochs?). But I could only think about getting to Clare and Georgia in time. Jim said that the local 'polis' had checked on Mrs Cassidy's house and there was nothing amiss but I still had a cold feeling in the pit of my stomach. I tried to ring them both but there was no answer. 'Och, the signal is bad up here,' said Jim. He actually said, 'Och'.

It was dark by the time we arrived in Ullapool, the harbour lights glittering. To be fair, Jim hadn't spoken much on the journey and now he drove efficiently through the narrow streets and out onto a spit of land with water on both sides. The Cassidy house was on the end. Light shone from a room in the roof. I thought of *The Stranger* and the lights in the ruined house, of the lights I'd seen in the old factory, of will-o'-the-wisps and the ghosts of dead children calling from the sea.

I was out of the car almost before it stopped. There were two cars parked outside the house, a battered Range Rover and a red Toyota Aygo. The front door was swinging open — not a good sign in Scotland on a winter night. I sprinted up the path, calling, 'Clare! Georgie!'

There were shouts from downstairs where a heavy chair had been pushed against a door but I knew that I had to go up. Two flights up I reached the door of an attic bedroom where a tall young man was standing over a terrified Georgia, knife raised. Herbert lay, covered in blood, at her feet.

I threw myself on the man but he was so big that I merely knocked him off balance. I grabbed at the arm with the knife but he threw me backwards, so hard that I hit my head on the floor. I scrambled upright and launched myself at him again. There was screaming coming from downstairs and — thank God — heavy policeman's footsteps on the stairs. Jim Harris took the man down with a neat rugby tackle and I knelt on his chest to read him his rights.

'Ty Greenall, I'm arresting you for the murder of Ella Elphick and Rick Lewis and the attempted murders of Simon Newton and Georgia Newton.'

Harbinder and Clare

CHAPTER 47

Harbinder

It was Natasha's mention of Ty that made me think of the postcard. Georgie had a boyfriend who sent her pictures of cuddly rabbits and hearts. When I saw the writing, I knew. We drove straight to the pub where Ty worked and were told that he had a few days off. 'Do you have an address for him?' I asked. 'No,' said the manager, looking worried, 'but he was very reliable. Never late for his shift.' That was because Ty had been living just down the road, squatting in the old cement factory. He admitted as much when I interviewed him at the police station in Garve.

'I was living in the factory,' he said. 'I was watching Clare. I used to light candles at night and watch her. I love her.'

'When did this start?' I asked. I didn't want to do an in-depth interview until I got Ty back to Sussex — I reckoned that Neil and Donna deserved to be involved — but I had to know a few things first.

'I was working as a barman in Hythe,' he said. 'Clare came to the hotel for a training course. I fell in love with her at first sight. I used the pass key to get into her room and read her diary. I decided there and then. She needed protecting. I followed her to Sussex and got a job at the pub. I met Georgia in town. She was drunk — she's too wild for my liking, it must be a terrible worry for Clare — so I decided to become her boyfriend and look after her.

And, of course, it brought me closer to Clare.' He smiled as if this was all perfectly logical, commendable even. He was a big man, good-looking even with
the bruises from Jim Harris's rough handling all over his face. But, as soon as
I looked into his eyes, I knew that the defence would be pleading insanity.

'Why did you kill Ella?' I asked.

'She was upsetting Clare,' said Ty immediately. 'Going on about sleeping
with a married man, making Clare do all the work at school. Ella was nothing better than a whore. Rick wasn't any better. Clare said that she hated him
in her diary. So I killed him too. I rang him and told him I knew something
about Ella. He was shitting himself. Thought I was going to tell his wife
about him playing away. I told him to sit in the chair and then I went behind
him and strangled him with the wire. I tried to make the murders like *The
Stranger*. I found the book in Georgie's room and I knew it was one of Clare's
favourites. Along with *The Woman in White* of course.'

That smile again.

'What about Simon Newton? What about Georgia? You can't have
thought Clare wanted them dead. Clare adores Georgie.'

'She said she was happier before she met Simon, before Georgia was
born,' said Ty. 'Simon was always upsetting her, calling her a bad mother,
going on about his new wife and children. Anyway, I needed to get rid of
them both so Clare and I could start again.'

I was getting worried now. More of this stuff and he'd definitely serve
time in a mental institution rather than the top-security prison he deserved.
But, when I spoke to the police in Kent, where Ty had lived with his grandparents, I found that he already had a police warning for stalking a woman,
his ex-English teacher, as it happens. Even if we couldn't use this in court, the
incident strengthened the case for Ty Greenall being the sort of killer who
watched and waited and then pounced.

I left Ty in the tender care of the Highland Police and went back to the
hotel where I'd booked a room. Clare had said that I could stay with her
grandmother but I thought that the Cassidy women probably had enough to
cope with without putting up with me. Besides I was terribly tired. The hotel
was modern and featureless, just what I wanted. I bought chips on the way
back and chased them down with a can of Irn Bru, which, as Jim had prom-

ised me, really did taste like iron filings. At The Caledonian Thistle I show-
ered and put on the scratchy white bathrobe hanging in the wardrobe. Then
I lay on the bed and rang Neil.

'I always thought the killer was someone close to home,' he said.

'Yeah, right. You thought it was Patrick O'Leary right up to the end.'

'Did you hear about Patrick and Venetia?' he said.

'No.'

'They ran away to get married. They were trying to get to Gretna Green.
The Scottish police picked them up at a Travelodge in Edinburgh.'

'Isn't Gretna Green in Dumfriesshire?'

'Yes. They hadn't quite worked out how to get there. And it was quite
easy to find them because they'd checked in their location on Facebook.'

'Idiots,' I said.

'Oh well,' said Neil. 'Young love and all that.'

I was almost asleep by now but I had just enough energy to ring Mum
and tell her where I was. She asked if I'd seen the Loch Ness Monster. I told
her that he was on holiday.

Clare

Harbinder and I walk across the white sand of the bay. It's a beautiful morning, the sea sparkling like a picture postcard, the mountains dark in the background.

'I feel so guilty,' I say. 'I didn't even recognise Ty from Hythe, though now
I remember Ella saying something, when we had that row, about the barman
giving me the eye.'

'Don't beat yourself up,' says Harbinder. 'You couldn't have known.'

'I didn't like Georgie going out with Ty,' I say, 'but only because he was so
much older. I actually thought she was safe with him. Jesus.'

'On a more important subject,' says Harbinder, 'is Herbert going to be
all right?'

'The vet says he'll be fine. Luckily the knife didn't pierce any vital organs.
He's got nine lives like a cat.'

'He was pretty brave to go for Ty like that.'

'Yes. He adores Georgie. He'd defend her with his life. Both of us.' I have to stop to wipe my eyes.

'Ty had some pretty deep bites on his arms when we took him into custody,' says Harbinder.

'Good,' I say.

'How's Georgie feeling about Ty?' says Harbinder.

'She's terribly shocked,' I say, 'but this morning she was going on about the need to forgive him. I can't say that I'm ready for that yet.' Georgie had been taken to hospital last night but she had no physical wounds and had been discharged after a few hours. This morning she was talking about forgiveness and redemption, 'otherwise he wins, don't you see?' Grandma, who had been locked in the sitting room with me and listened to me screaming when I thought my daughter was being murdered upstairs, was similarly serene, cooking us all a huge breakfast. 'You'll need the energy.' It's funny, Grandma and Georgie are alike. I'd never noticed it before.

'Of course,' I say, 'it was Ty who looked after Herbert when he hurt his paw that time, wasn't it?'

'Yes,' says Harbinder. 'Remember, deep down, Ty persuaded himself that he was doing what you wanted. He knew how much you loved Herbert. I'm sure you never criticised *him* in your diary.'

'No, I didn't,' I say. 'It was all about how much I loved him, how precious he was to me. God, I feel awful. Like I was writing a hit list.'

'Well, you shouldn't,' says Harbinder. 'You didn't ask Ty to go on some killing spree on your behalf. And you never meant anyone to read your diaries.'

'What about *The Stranger*?' I say. 'Ty must have read that. It's where he got the quote and . . . and the way he killed Ella and Rick.' Harbinder told me last night about the way Rick had died.

'He got that from Georgie. She's obsessed with the story and Ty apparently found a copy of it in her room. We found lots of books in the factory, including *The Woman in White*, Georgie's copy of *The Tempest* and several editions of *The Stranger*. It can be a dangerous thing, reading too much.'

I don't know if she's joking or not.

'We think he got the candle and the potpourri idea from Georgie and her friends. He took Georgie's black obsidian stone too. We don't know why. Apparently Bryony Hughes gave the stones to all the members of the creative writing group. For protection. I saw one in her office when I interviewed her.'

Last night Georgie had finally opened up about Bryony Hughes, babbling away about how she was a white witch, about how she taught Georgie to exorcise spirits. I make a mental note to find out more and to stop her attending the meetings at the sixth-form college. But it also makes me sad to think that, all this time, she has been reading and writing fiction and I never knew about it.

'Georgie's fingerprints were on the stone,' says Harbinder casually. 'That made us interested in her for a while.'

'My God. Did you suspect her?'

'Not really. But I found a blood-stained photo of Ella in her room. Turns out it was animal blood, we got the results back this morning. I think it must have been in Georgia's pocket when we found Herbert and he'd cut his paw.'

I remember Georgie holding Herbert in her arms as we sat at the vet's. Our little hero dog.

'I did suspect you for a while,' says Harbinder. 'You seemed more the type.'

'Thanks very much.'

'But then we concentrated on Patrick O'Leary. He'd had a crush on Ella and had reason to resent Rick. We knew he'd been at Ella's house on the night that she died. And then he disappeared, which is usually a sure sign of guilt. He'd sent a message to Natasha saying "Hell is empty". His idea of a joke, apparently.'

'He sent the same message to Georgie,' I say. 'Did you find Patrick and Venetia?'

Harbinder rolls her eyes. 'Yes. They were staying in an Edinburgh Travelodge trying to work out how to get to Dumfries and Galloway. Their parents are coming to collect them today. Fancy thinking that they could go to Gretna Green and get married. What's wrong with the kids today?'

'Georgie says that Venetia's a big Georgette Heyer fan,' I say. 'Her characters are always having runaway marriages.'

'As a matter of fact, Georgette Heyer is very practical about marriage,' says Harbinder, surprising me, not for the first time. 'She never forgets that you need money too. I always think she's a bit like an Indian mother.'

'I wouldn't have had you down as a romance fan.'

'I'm more of a horror girl,' says Harbinder, kicking a stone into the shallows, 'but I've had my moments.'

'Has Ty confessed everything?' I ask. I'm hoping that, if he does, Georgie and I won't have to go to court.

'Singing to the rooftops,' says Harbinder. 'In fact, my problem was stopping him telling everything to the Scottish police. I want him to save it for me and Neil. I'm flying back with him tonight. That should be a jolly flight, handcuffed to a murderer. Mind you, could be worse. Could be a hen party.'

'Will I see you when I'm back in Sussex?' I say. I don't want to leave Ullapool but there are still three weeks of term left. I should go back on Monday.

'You won't be able to get rid of me,' says Harbinder. 'There's always a lot of mopping up to do with cases like this.'

'It seems impossible that life will just go on as normal,' I say, 'but I suppose it will.'

'Normal's overrated in my opinion,' says Harbinder. 'But yes, life will go on. It always does.'

We've reached the end of the beach and look back over the bay. The tide is coming in. Our footprints have made little impact on the firm sand and, in a few minutes, they will be washed away altogether.

Nothing in the world is hidden forever.

The Third Time

We climb the spiral stairs in silence. It's the Christmas holidays and the school is closed but, far below, I can hear a clock ticking and the floorboards sighing as they expand.

'It looks different without a dead body,' says Harbinder. Always adept at destroying atmosphere.

Tony has gone to head up an academy chain in the north-east. Liz Francis is the new head teacher and she has asked me to apply for the deputy's post. Liz wants to get rid of this room and turn it into an IT suite. She's probably right, but the school won't be the same without the ghost of R.M. Holland.

Georgie moves into the room and goes up to the desk. She pauses for a moment looking at the framed photographs and then she does what I would never dare to do: she sits in R.M. Holland's chair.

'Georgie,' I say. 'Don't sit there.' I can't forget my last two visits to this room. The last occupants of that chair were the dummy (thank you, Patrick O'Leary) and Rick's dead body.

'Why not?' says Georgie. 'It's a good place. Good energy. I feel as if I could write something powerful, sitting here.'

That's been one of the biggest shocks of the last few weeks. The fact that my daughter is a writer. She's shown me some of her story and, while I find the subject matter somewhat disturbing, there's no doubt that she has talent. I suppose I should thank Bryony Hughes for nurturing this gift but I still don't want Georgie going back to her after-school classes.

'Perhaps I should sit there then,' I say. 'Sometimes I think I'm never going to finish my book about Holland.'

'Henry Hamilton thinks you will,' says Georgie with a sly smile.

I saw Henry last week and he's still enthusiastic about the book. To my surprise, he's also still enthusiastic about me.

I say, hoping that I'm not blushing, 'Henry thinks that there might be more papers at St Jude's. If I can solve the mystery of Holland's wife and daughter, I think there's a story there.'

'It's not that easy to solve a mystery,' warns Harbinder. 'Ask any police officer.'

'You solved this one,' says Georgia. She is still sitting at the desk, her hands flat on the blotter. Her dark hair, lit by the low winter sun behind her, shines like an aureole. She looks beautiful, like a Pre-Raphaelite painting, and suddenly very grown-up. In a few years, I think, she'll be leaving home.

'Well, Ty did rather help by trying to kill you,' says Harbinder, moving to examine the photographs on the red walls.

Ty's case is due to come to trial in the spring. Because he's pleading guilty and has made a full confession, Harbinder thinks that Georgie and I won't have to give evidence. Georgie still says she forgives him but I'm not there yet. I keep thinking about Ella and her parents, about Daisy Lewis, about Simon, who is apparently still having flashbacks about the attack. Only Herbert seems — thank God — to have escaped without trauma. He's back to his old self. Georgie has bought him a reindeer outfit for Christmas.

'So what's the mystery with the wife and child?' says Harbinder. 'Perhaps I can solve it for you.' She speaks with the confidence of someone who has just applied to take her Detective Inspector's exam.

'Holland's wife, Alice, probably killed herself,' I say. 'And we don't know anything about the daughter. He mentions a Mariana in his letters and there's a poem, "For M. RIP", but there's no record of the girl's birth or death and no one's ever found her grave. In one of the letters Henry found, Holland talks about Mariana inheriting "her mother's taint". Maybe this means depression or mental illness. We don't know.'

'I saw Alice's ghost once,' says Harbinder. 'Did I tell you?'

Georgie and I stare at her. 'No,' I say. 'You didn't tell us.'

'It was the Christmas term when I was fifteen,' says Harbinder. 'I was snogging my boyfriend Gary Carter in one of the old classrooms. Mr Carter, the geography teacher,' she adds for Georgia's benefit.

'Oh God.' Georgia covers her eyes. 'Gross.'

'Anyway, there we were, snogging away, and suddenly the room went cold. We went into the corridor outside and we saw this white shape rushing past us. It threw itself over the balustrade and there was this terrible scream. That's all.'

'Did anyone die after you'd seen the ghost?' I say, somewhat sarcastically, remembering the school legend.

'Oh yes,' says Harbinder. 'Someone died all right.'

'It was her,' says Georgia, her face alight. 'It was Alice Holland. We should try to contact her. She's not happy here, she wants to move on.'

'No!' I say, louder than I intended. I've now heard all about the so-called exorcism of Ella's spirit. Four teenagers dabbling with the undead when they should have been eating pizza and watching *Friends*. Once again, I blame Bryony Hughes.

'All right,' says Georgia. 'Take a chill pill, Mum. After all, you're the one planning to write about her. That's not leaving her in peace, is it?'

'It's not the same,' I say. 'But if I can solve the mystery of Mariana, maybe that will be an exorcism of sorts.'

'Oh that,' says Georgia. 'I've solved that.'

She gets up and walks to the wall of photographs. She points to a small black-and-white picture at eye level. Harbinder looks at me and we both move closer.

'With Mariana,' Georgia reads out the caption.

'But there's no one else in the photograph,' says Harbinder.

'Look closer, ace detective.'

We lean in and it's Harbinder who sees it first.

'The dog,' she says.

There, in the middle ground of the picture, is a white blob, almost lost in the grey grass. But it's definitely a dog, of indefinite breed, one ear up and one ear down, tail curled tightly over its back.

'Her mother's taint,' says Georgia. 'I bet that was the curly tail.'

'Breeders sometimes call it a gay tail,' I say.

'I like that,' says Harbinder. 'I think it could catch on as an accessory.'

'Mariana,' I say. 'Holland writes that she was a constant solace, an angel, sweet-natured and kind.'

'Sounds just like Herbert,' says Georgia, in the voice she puts on for him.

'He also said that Mariana enjoyed his novel, *The Ravening Beast*.'

'I can understand that,' says Georgia. 'I often read my stuff to Herbie. He thinks I'm a genius.'

'Who took the photograph?' says Harbinder.

But that's something we will never know. We all look back at the photograph, at the man and his dog sitting on the lawn, a snapshot in time captured by an unknown, ghostly hand.

The Stranger, by R.M. Holland

'If you'll permit me,' said the Stranger, 'I'd like to tell you a story. After all, it's a long journey and, by the look of those skies, we're not going to be leaving this carriage for some time. So, why not pass the hours with some story-telling? The perfect thing for a late October evening.

Are you quite comfortable there? Don't worry about Herbert. He won't hurt you. It's just this weather that makes him nervous. Now, where was I? What about some brandy to keep the chill out? You don't mind a hip flask, do you?

Well, this is a story that actually happened. Those are the best kind, don't you think? Better still, it happened to me when I was a young man. About your age.

I was a student at Cambridge. Studying Divinity, of course. There's no other subject, in my opinion, except possibly English Literature. We are such stuff as dreams are made on. I'd been there for almost a term. I was a shy boy from the country and I suppose I was lonely. I wasn't one of the swells, those young men in white bow ties who sauntered across the court as if they had letters patent from God. I kept myself to myself, went to lectures, wrote my essays and started up a friendship with another scholarship boy in my year, a timid soul called Gudgeon, of all things. I wrote home to my mother every week. I went to chapel. Yes, I believed in those days. I was even rather pious — 'pi,' we used to say. That was why I was surprised to be invited to join the Hell Club. Surprised and pleased. I'd heard about it, of course. Stories of midnight orgies, of bedders coming in to clean rooms and fainting dead away at what they discovered there, of arcane chants from the Book of the Dead, of buried bones and gaping graves. But there *were other stories too. Many successful men had their start at the Hell Club: pol-iticians — even a cabinet member or two — writers, lawyers, scientists, business tycoons. You always knew them because of the badge, a discreet skull worn on the left lapel. Yes, like this one here.*

So I was happy to be invited to the initiation ceremony. It was held on Oc-tober 31st. Halloween, of course. All Hallows' Eve. Yes, of course. It's Halloween today. If one believed in coincidence one might think that was slightly sinister.

To return to my story. The ceremony was simple and took place at midnight. Naturally. The three initiates were required to go to a ruined house just outside the college grounds. In turn, we would be blindfolded and given a candle. We had to walk to the house, climb the stairs and light our candle in the window on the first floor landing. Then we had to shout, as loudly as we could, 'Hell is empty!' After all three had completed the task, we could take off our blindfolds and re-join our fellows. Feasting and revelry would follow. Gudgeon . . . did I tell you that poor Gudgeon was one of the three? Gudgeon was worried because, without his glasses, he was almost blind. But, as I told him, we were all blind-folded anyway. A man may see how the world goes with no eyes.

Are you cold? The wind is getting up, isn't it? See how the snow hammers a fusillade against the windows. Ah, the train has stopped again. I very much doubt if we'll get farther tonight.

Some brandy? Do share my travelling rug. I always prepare myself for the worst on these journeys. A good maxim for life, young man. Always prepare yourself for the worst.

So, where was I? Ah yes. So Gudgeon and I, together with a third fel-low — let's call him Wilberforce — approached the house. Three established members of the Hell Club provided us with blindfolds. They were masked, of course, but we knew some of them by their voices. There was Lord Bastian and his henchman, Collins. The third had a foreign accent, possibly Arabian.

Wilberforce was the first to don his blindfold. He set off, holding his candle and a box of matches, stumbling like a blind man towards the ruined house. We waited and we waited. The winter wind roared around us. Like this one, yes. We waited and, after what seemed a lifetime, we saw a candle flickering in the window embrasure. Very faintly, on the night air, we heard, 'Hell is empty!'

We cheered and our voices echoed against stone and silence. Bastian handed a candle to Gudgeon, together with a box of matches. Slowly Gudgeon removed his glasses and pulled the blindfold over his eyes.

'Good luck,' I said.

He smiled. Funny, I remember it now. He smiled and made a strange gesture with his hands, splaying them out like a shopkeeper advertising his wares. I can see it as clearly as if he were standing in front of me. Lord Bastian gave him a push and Gudgeon too staggered off over the frosty grass.

We waited and we waited and we waited. A night bird called. I heard somebody cough and someone else smother a laugh. I was breathing hard though I scarcely knew why.

We waited and, eventually, a candle shone in the window. 'Hell is empty!' Our answering cheers rang out.

Now it was my turn. I was handed the candle and matches. Then I pulled on the blindfold. Immediately the night seemed not just darker, but colder, more hostile. I didn't need Bastian's push to start me on my journey. I was anxious for it to be over. Yet, how long that walk seemed when you couldn't see. I became convinced that I was heading in the wrong direction, that I had missed the ruined house altogether, but then I heard Bastian's voice behind me, 'Straight ahead, you fool!' Stretching my hands out in front of me, I stumbled forwards.

My hands hit stone. I was at the house. Feeling my way along the façade I eventually reached a void. The doorway. I tripped over the doorstep, landing heavily on flagstones, but at least I was in the building. Inside, the wind was less, but the cold, if anything, more. And the silence! It echoed and re-echoed around me, seeming to weigh down on me, to press me close to the earth. I knew that I was bending almost double, like a beggar under his sack. I could hear my breathing, jagged and stertorous. It was my only companion as I inched towards the staircase.

How many steps? I had been told it was twenty but lost count after fifteen. Only when I stepped on a phantom stair did I realise that I was on the landing. I had thought that Gudgeon or Wilberforce might whisper a greeting but they were silent. Waiting. I edged forwards. I had to find the window and bring this pantomime to an end. My hands swept the plaster of the wall in front of me *until . . . there! I found the wooden sill. I pulled off my blindfold and my cold fingers fumbled with a match to light the candle. Then I dripped some wax onto the sill and stood it upright.*

'Hell is empty!' My voice sounded puny in my own ears. It was only then that I turned around and saw the dead bodies at my feet.

I heard a scream echoing through the corridors of the deserted house and I realised that it was mine. My friend, Gudgeon, lay dead at my feet. Wilberforce was a few yards away. I felt both their necks for a heartbeat but I knew that there was nothing to be done. Someone, or something, had fallen on these men like a beast from hell and slaughtered them. Gudgeon's chest was red with blood where he had been stabbed again and again. His arms were spread wide and I could see on his palms — oh horrible sacrilege! — gashes which resembled the stigmata of Our Blessed Lord. I thought at first that Wilberforce had been stabbed to death too, but, looking closer in the flickering light from my candle, I saw that he had been garrotted, a white cloth pulled tight around his neck, making his appearance ghastly in the extreme. However, the assassin's knife had not escaped him. The handle of a dagger was embedded in his chest.

I was shaking, my candle making wild shapes on the wall, and, for several minutes, was frozen with fear. Because the fiend that had killed my companions was surely close at hand. Would he now descend on me, knife and hands incarnadine?

But the ruined house was still. I could hear nothing except the rats scuttling on the floor above. Then, from outside, I heard a cry. 'What's happening in there?' Then Collins, Bastian and the third man came running up the stairs. I still held the candle and their first sight must have been my ashen face, illuminated by the spectral light, before the true horror of the scene unfolded itself.

I will draw a veil — no, not a veil, a heavy curtain — over what happened next. I wanted to inform the college authorities but Lord Bastian pointed out that we would get in trouble, perhaps even be sent down. Besides, he said, the Hell Club would not be happy if the news got out. This opinion seemed to carry great weight with the other two, and they were all senior men, you must remember. To cut a long story short, I was persuaded that the best course of action would be to leave the dread house and return to college as if nothing had happened. The bodies would be found, of course, and there would be an enquiry, but we would deny any knowledge of the events. We would never speak of this night again.

'*We must swear,*' *said Bastian and, to my horror, he knelt down and, in a horrible echo of Doubting Thomas testing Our Lord, put his fingers into the wound on Gudgeon's hand.*

'*Swear,*' *he said.* '*Swear on his blood.*'

Can you imagine the scene? The candlelight, the wind outside now rising to a crescendo, Bastian standing there with Gudgeon's blood on his hands. We were all half-mad, that's the only way I can explain it. Bastian pressed his bloody thumbprint to our foreheads as if he were a priest administering the ashes. Remember, man, that thou art dust and to dust thou shalt return.

'*I swear,*' *we said, one after another.* '*I swear.*'

What happened next? Ah, my dear young man, there's no need to look so alarmed. Time passed, as it must always do. The bodies were discovered. There was a police enquiry but no murderer was ever found. No one ever asked me about my movements that night. The Junior Dean made a point of consoling me over my friend's death and I said, truthfully, that I was grief-stricken. He sympathised but quoted a chilling little epithet from Homer, doubtless intended to foster a stoical spirit. Be strong, saith my heart; I am a soldier; I have seen worse sights than this. *And it was over.* Consummatum est.

Or so I thought.

Listen to the wind howling. It seems to rock the train, does it not? We're quite safe here, though. After all, there's no connecting door between the carriages. No one can come in or out. More brandy?

What happened next? Well, the prosaic truth is: nothing much to speak of. Gudgeon's parents took his body away and he was buried at his home in Gloucestershire. I didn't attend. I don't know what happened to Wilberforce. As I said before, the police never found their killer. A year later, the ruined house was demolished. I continued my studies. I think I became quite solitary and strange. Other students would look at me oddly as I crossed the court or sat in the dining hall. 'That's him,' *I heard someone whisper once.* 'The other one.' *I suppose I became* 'the other one' *to most men in Peterhouse, possibly even to myself.*

I didn't see much of Bastian or Collins. I was now officially a member of the Hell Club but I didn't attend their meetings or the infamous Blood Ball, which was held every year. I spent most of my time in my rooms or in the library. My only contact with my fellow students was with members of the shooting club. With them, at least, I managed some uncomplicated, comradely hours.

I graduated with a first, which was gratifying. I had heard that Lord Bastian had been sent down and that Collins did not complete his degree. But they were at different colleges and our paths had long since diverged. I began to read for a doctorate, continuing with the solitary, bachelor existence that I had established in my undergraduate days.

Then, in my first term as a postgraduate student, I received some rather strange correspondence. It was November, a bitterly cold day, and I remember the frost crunching under my feet as I walked to the porters' lodge to collect my post. Not that I ever received many letters. My mother wrote occasionally and I subscribed to a couple of scholarly theological journals. That was it. But on this day there was something else. A letter with a foreign postmark, inscribed in a strange, slanting hand. I opened it with some curiosity. Inside was a cutting from a Persian newspaper. I did not, of course, understand the Perso-Arabic script but there was a translation, written with the same italic pen. It said that a man called Amir Ebrahimi had been killed in a freak accident involving a hot air balloon. The ascent had gone perfectly but, at some point during the flight, Ebrahimi had fallen from the basket underneath the balloon and had plummeted to his death. I turned the letter over in my hands, wondering why someone would have thought that I would be interested in this gruesome event. It was then that I saw the words written on the reverse of the paper. Hell is empty. *And I remembered that Ebrahimi had been the name of the third man, the companion of Bastian and Collins.*

The other one.

Of course Ebrahimi's death was a terrible shock. I remember standing there with the newspaper cutting in my hand, then going back to my rooms, lying down on my bed and shaking. Who had sent me the fateful papers? Who had written the translation with that slender, slanting pen? And who had written the words 'Hell is empty' on the reverse? Could it be Bastian? Or Collins? It seemed impossible but who else could possibly have known about the Hell Club and that terrible night?

I pondered these questions over the next few days. Indeed, I thought of little else. But in the end, I pushed my fears away and carried on with my life. After all, what else could I do? And I was young, I had my health and my strength. You understand, my dear young friend? Yes, I see that you do. Youth is arrogant, which is as it should be. I was sorry that Ebrahimi was dead — and I sincerely mourned my friend Gudgeon — but there was nothing that I could do to bring them back to life. So I continued with my studies and even began to court a young lady, the daughter of my tutor. Life was sweet that spring, perhaps all the sweeter for the thought that I had escaped from the pall of death. For, at that time, I believed that I had escaped.

How the wind howls.

'What happened next?' Ah, the perennial, unanswered question. That is the very essence of narrative, is it not? 'Please read another page', begs the child at bedtime. Anything to ward off the horrors of the dark. And you have not long left childhood behind yourself, my dear young friend. It is only natural that you should want to know what happens in the next chapter.

Another year passed. I became engaged to Ada, the daughter of my tutor. I started work on my thesis, which dealt with the Albigensian heresy. I also taught undergraduates, though, in truth, I was a solid and uninspiring lecturer. I heard them whispering about me sometimes, caught the words 'Hell Club' and 'murder'. But I chose to dwell in the light that year. And I acquired a companion. Yes, the very animal that you see before you in this train carriage. What a friend dear Herbert has been to me in my trials. Truer and more steadfast than any human acolyte.

Autumn passed and with it Halloween. I confess I breathed a sigh of relief when the dread day passed without incident. But then, several weeks later, I heard the bedders talking in the corridor and caught the name 'Collins' and the word 'killed'.

I burst out of my room and demanded, with a passion that surprised them, 'What are you talking about?'

'Mr Collins, from King's, as was, sir,' came the reply. 'We were talking about the way he died. So unnatural.'

'What happened?' I said, aware that a coldness had swept over me. Collins, the companion of Lord Bastian, had been a student at King's.

'He was killed, sir. He was driving his own carriage across the fens. He set

*off from Ely, as right as rain, heading for Cambridge. No one knows what hap-
pened but his horse was found a day later, running wild, still harnessed to the
carriage. A search party was sent out and Mr Collins was found in a ditch. His
throat had been cut, sir.'*

'When was this?'

*The older of the two bedders answered me. 'It was on Halloween night, sir.
I remember because Bert, who was one of the searchers, said it fair chilled the
blood to see the horse galloping on his own as if the hounds of hell were after him.'*

*It was another week before the newspaper cutting reached me. 'Cambridge
man found murdered on the fens.' And scrawled across the headline the hand-
written words, 'Hell is empty.'*

*I broke off my engagement to Ada. I wasn't fit company for any decent per-
son. I kept to my room, ostensibly working on my thesis but, in fact, writing the
story with which I am now regaling you, my dear young friend. About the Hell
Club and Halloween at the ruined house. About the dead bodies and our vow,
made in the blood of our comrade. About Ebrahimi and Collins. About the
nemesis that seemed to be following me. Again and again, I wrote the words:*

Hell is empty.

*When 31st October came around again, I was a mere shell. I knew people
were worried about me. My tutor had tried to talk to me (even though he hated
me now because of the way I had treated Ada), and the Junior Dean had gone
as far as to request an interview, during which he impressed upon me the necessity of eating well and performing regular exercises.* Mens sana in corpore sano.
If only he knew the true state of my mind.

*All day I waited. I didn't leave my room because I knew the nemesis would
come, locked door or not. I didn't hear the news until the next day, All Saints'
Day. I went for a stroll through the town, late at night. I often liked to do this,
prowling the silent streets, alone with my thoughts. But, outside St John's, I saw
a fellow called Egremont standing in the shadow of the lodge, smoking his pipe.
I recognised him as a member of the Hell Club but I hurried past, not wanting
to get into conversation.*

'Hallo there.' *He called after me.* 'You were a friend of Bastian's, weren't you?'

'I knew him,' *I said cautiously, although my heart was pounding.*

'Have you heard what happened to him? Awful news.'

'No,' I said. 'What has happened to him?'

'I heard it from one of the scouts just now. Bastian was in a train. One of the new sorts with connecting carriages. He was moving from one carriage to another when the train suddenly divided. He was crushed under the wheels. Poor fellow. What a terrible death.'

I looked at Egremont, saw his pale face and the skull's head badge on his lapel.

'When did this happen?' I asked.

'Only yesterday,' he replied. 'I'm sure it'll be in tomorrow's Times.'

It was a week before the newspaper cutting reached me, with the now familiar addendum.

Hell is empty.

Well, today's the anniversary of that day and I'm the only one left. What a strange thought that is, my dear young man. I am sure that your lively brain has long since recognised the pattern that is unfolding here and the inauspiciousness of the date. Why is he telling me this story? you must wonder. Have I been chosen to witness the demise of the narrator?

But do not fear. After all, I am not about to go up in a hot air balloon or attempt to drive a coach and pair across the fens. I can't plummet from the air or be dragged by footpads from my carriage.

I am in a train, it's true, but I'm not about to leave this carriage.

Ah, my dear young man. How still you are. That was the brandy, of course. Atropa belladonna *or Deadly Nightshade. It will give you strange visions, I fear, and your sight will be impaired. I am sure that, even now, I am metamorphosing before your eyes, becoming watery and indistinct. Perhaps I have disappeared altogether. Though who is to say what is real and what is not? As I quoted earlier, a man may see how the world goes with no eyes. How wildly you look at me, your orbs completely black now. But, of course, you cannot move. I am sorry, you know. I wish it didn't have to be this way. But whatever demonic entity it is that demands my blood — the same that has already taken the lives of Gudgeon, Wilberforce, Ebrahimi, Collins and Bastian, so many, alas, so much blood — this creature will not be satisfied until it has garnered another soul. Oh, it wants me, of course. This day, this Halloween night, was meant to be the *day of my death. The day of reckoning. Hell is empty and all the devils are here. The ghoul awaits. He is hungry, I hear him in the howling of the wind and the anger of the storm. But I think it will be satisfied with you, innocent soul that you are.*

Do not fear. The end will be painless. And who knows what will await us on the other side? Perhaps I am simply hastening your journey towards perfect felicity. I hope so. I really do.

Farewell, my dear travelling companion.

DISCUSSION GUIDE

Questions for Discussion

1. Discuss how having three different points of view contributed to the story. Was Clare a reliable narrator? How did Harbinder's feelings about Clare affect the investigation? How does it serve the story to incorporate Georgia's young perspective to the narration? And how does the experience of having all three in tandem change the way you engage with each one individually?

2. What does Clare teach about the role of animals in literature? What role does her dog play in *The Stranger Diaries*?

3. Elly Griffiths has noted influences in writing *The Stranger Diaries,* including Wilkie Collins's *The Woman in White* and Edgar Allan Poe. Where do you see these references, and if you've read Collins or Poe, how do they enhance your reading of the book?

4. *The Stranger Diaries* has been described as a "modern gothic thriller." Do you agree with this description? What is gothic literature and how does *The Stranger Diaries* fit into this category?

5. Interwoven into the narration of *The Stranger Diaries* we see Clare's diary entries. What texture do they bring to the text? What insight into her character do they offer that you might not find in the third-person narration? How, if at all, does Clare's diary differ from Georgia's online journal?

6. In investigating this case, Harbinder is returning to her former school. How does her past relationship with the place change the way she engages with the suspects and persons of interest in this investigation? What does that tell us about the bias that she, or another officer, might bring to the case?

7. Griffiths notes throughout the book the different ways in which the media and the police engage with the murder of a woman versus the murder of a man. What observations does she make here? Do you feel that this is reflected in real-life news coverage?

Recommended Reading

Magpie Murders by Anthony Horowitz
The Lake House by Kate Morton
The Woman in White by Wilkie Collins
The Thirteenth Tale by Diane Setterfield
Jane Eyre by Charlotte Brontë
The Lost History of Dreams by Kris Waldherr
The Mysteries of Udolpho by Ann Radcliffe
Great Tales and Poems by Edgar Allan Poe

ABANDONED ESTATES, EMPTY HOTELS, AND ISOLATED SCHOOLS: EXPLORING THE CIVIC LANDSCAPES OF GOTHIC FICTION THROUGH THE AGES

by Elly Griffiths
Originally published in *CrimeReads*

Think of gothic and what comes to mind? Ruined towers, brooding castles, women in crinolines fleeing from an unknown horror? The title quotation comes from Mary Shelley's *Frankenstein* which, for many, remains the classic gothic horror story, but is the archaic setting really necessary or can evil rise just as easily from a modern-day factory, hotel, or school? In fact, *Frankenstein* starts with a polar exploration and much of its action takes place in a university laboratory. The late Brian Aldiss called *Frankenstein* the first science fiction story because the central character turns to modern experimentation to achieve the novel's fantastical results.

The first truly gothic text is thought to be Horace Walpole's novel of 1764, *The Castle of Otranto,* and the book contains many of the tropes that have come to be associated with the genre: foreign setting, evil villain, woman in peril, and of course, the eponymous castle. In the second edition, Walpole himself added the subtitle "A Gothic Story." The European setting is significant; a fear of foreigners—and especially Catholics—is evident in many Victorian gothic novels, including Matthew Lewis's *The Monk* and Ann Radcliffe's *The Italian*. However, some gothic revivalists, such as the architect Augustus Pugin (who designed the Palace of Westminster in London) looked back to medieval times as a halcyon period of Catholic faith, before the coming of the Reformation.

Looking back does seem to be a feature of gothic literature and yet the books often look forward too, fearing a future where industry dominates nature. William Blake wrote about "dark satanic mills" in his poem "Jerusalem" (1804), and there is both a fascination with and a dread of industrialisation that runs through Victorian fiction. The duality is important here. Edmund Burke's seminal essay "A Philosophical Enquiry into the Origin of our Ideas of the Sublime and the Beautiful" (1757) divides aesthetics into two categories: beautiful, small, symmetrical, pleasing; and sublime, vast, fearful, and awe-inspiring. According to this definition, the factories that came to tower over the British Midlands were sublime indeed. Two hundred years earlier, it's significant that Milton's vision of hell in *Paradise Lost* was one of *building,* as the demons labour to build Pandemonium "the high capital of Satan and his peers," a feat supposedly achieved in an hour. Milton dwells on the work of construction and of mining, smelting and extracting metals from the earth. The Victorian painter John Martin was obsessed with the hellish capital and depicted it in works like *Pandemonium* and *Satan Presiding at the Infernal Council.* In this last Satan sits in what looks like a huge amphitheatre lit by the new technology of gaslight. It certainly fits Burke's definition of the sublime.

The industrial and civic landscape still exerts a fascination today, especially where places that were once full of activity are now deserted. Photographers like Christian Richter specialise in images of empty hotels, hospitals and power stations. Abandoned theme parks are another popular subject: Ferris wheels choked by ivy, grinning clown faces rotting into the ground, roller coasters like nightmare highways to nowhere. These images recall the narrator's dream of a desolate and overgrown Manderley in that most gothic of modern novels, Daphne du Maurier's *Rebecca.*

Hotels, grand, luxurious and also somehow soulless, feature in many horror stories, from Stephen King's *The Shining* to Hanna Jameson's 2019 novel *The Last.* The motel in *Psycho,* its ominous light shining through the rainstorm, is as much a character as Norman Bates or Marion Crane. *American*

Horror Story, the TV series created by Ryan Murphy and Brad Falchuk, has a hotel as one of its series settings. These narratives replace the gothic castle with a modern-day edifice built to house multitudes. If the hotel has started to decay, or has even fallen into ruin, then so much the better. A traveller arriving at an unknown location is a classic beginning for a gothic novel, where the central character must quickly be made to seem vulnerable and alone. When Jonathan Harker first visits the famous castle in Bram Stoker's *Dracula,* it is as if he is staying in a hotel, albeit one where the manager climbs the walls at night. Dracula is, at first, every inch the gracious host, as is the proprietor of the Bates Motel.

Schools are also popular with modern gothic authors. A high school is the setting for the *Coven* series of *American Horror Story* and for films like *Carrie* and *The Craft.* Hampden College, isolated and beautiful with its own resident shaman, is the perfect background for madness and murder in Donna Tartt's *The Secret History.* When Richard first visits tutor Julian Morrow's office, he is even given the traditional warning to steer clear for his own good, yet, like so many protagonists before him, Richard ignores this and is soon drawn into a truly gothic web of violence, incest, and hallucinogenic drug-taking.

When I set out to write my own modern gothic novel, *The Stranger Diaries,* I wanted to create the feeling of a Victorian ghost story yet remain in the twenty-first century. My solution was to set the book in a modern school that included an "Old Building," a house that had once been home to a writer called R. M. Holland, famous for a chilling little tale called *The Stranger.* I was inspired by West Dean College, where I teach creative writing, and by my own comprehensive (non-fee-paying) school, which included an old wing, mostly out of bounds to students and (of course) possessing its own resident ghost. I wanted to combine the world of iPhones, Saturday night TV and computer gaming with ancient buildings, half-glimpsed figures, and sudden screams in the night. My protagonist, Clare, even lives beside an abandoned factory. This setting is also drawn from life. I often drive past an old cement works near Steyning in West Sussex and am always intrigued by the neat row of cottages in front of it. What would it be like to live there, with that nightmare edifice behind you, its sightless windows sometimes glowing with strange lights? I was sure that Mary Shelley would have felt right at home.

—Elly Griffiths, 2019